CHILD OF THE HEART

Child of the Heart

Bernice

Willms

This book is a work of fiction. Names, characters, places and incidents are products of the author's imagination or they are used fictitiously. Any resemblance to actual persons, living or dead, or to actual events or locales is entirely coincidental.

Cover design by Jacqueline Roland

Copyright   © 2013

Eirene Publishing

ISBN-13: 978-0-9910645-1-9

Bernice

Peace + Love

CHILD OF THE HEART

The best and most beautiful things in the world cannot be seen or touched. They must be felt with the heart."

---Helen Keller.

"It is only with the heart that one can see rightly, what is essential is invisible to the eye"

---from *The Little Prince*

By Antoine de Saint-Exupery

ACKNOWLEDGMENTS

I would like to thank all those who helped me get this book published, especially Terry and Betsy, who have helped me to understand that being blind is only a pebble and not a rock to crush my caring, productive and creative spirit.

I was working on my first novel when I woke up one morning and could no longer see the print. At first I panicked, then I cried. Actually I cried a lot. Then one morning while lying in bed I decided crying sure didn't help. I got up, turned my computer on and started writing again. Losing my eyesight did not dim my creative talent. I kept on writing one book, then another book, and then went back to the original one I started before losing my eyesight. That book has now become a series because I fell in love with the characters and saw the potential for more. So far I have written twelve novels in all, and intend to write more, but first I have to get these published. After all, good should be shared.

CHAPTER ONE

It was a time of innocence for me, those first years of growing up. A time of naiveté when I thought that "being different" simply meant the differences between being a boy or a girl. A wonderful time, when I still believed in happy endings and dared to dream. It was a childhood of joyful days spent with my Uncle Joey, or to be more specific, Joseph Lawrence Harrison. An impressive name for someone like Joey, who, totally unbeknownst to his parents when they chose his name, would forever remain a child in many ways. There were none of the outward signs usually attributed to a child like Joey. Labeled a slow learner by people who have been taught to be kind, and a retard by the not-so-kind. My parents have another label for him. To my father he's an obligation, and to my mother he's an embarrassment, but to me he's Joey, my friend.

I guess those labels never meant anything to me then. I just thought Joey was the smartest person in the world. After all, it was Joey who taught me the difference between a flower and a weed. He showed me how soft the fuzzy fur on a caterpillar feels, when one day he gently picked it up and let it crawl

11

on my arm. It was Joey who held a frog carefully in his hands and let me feel its smooth white belly. Every creature Joey touches, he touches with loving tenderness. That's how I describe him if anyone asks: gentle, kind, and ever protective of the helpless.

"Be careful" he'd always say whenever I picked up a small animal to examine or pet. "You don't want to hurt it." Growing up with Uncle Joey I learned not to hurt or hate.

It's only later, when I got older that I learned of those things, of the darker side of human nature; when people started looking at the child in a man's body with suspicion. When the foreshadowing of Joey's future scared me. I worry that people might think my uncle is even capable of hurting another living thing, this man who wept openly when my kitten died.

Now I've grown, and still live in the big old white house along with my parents, a brother and sister, and Joey. Mom always said that when she had me, she got two kids, since Joey came to live with us the same year I was born. I was a baby and Joey was seven, but the both of us were viewed as an embarrassment, especially to my mother.

I think my mother expected me to be like my sister, Angela Lorraine. Mom is into impressive names, just like my grandmother was. The problem with that is the impressiveness never stuck. With much disappointment on the part of the givers of the names, the implied greatness of such an impressive name was always reduced, inevitably watered down to be less of a mouthful. For instance, my sister ended up being called "Angie," while my brother, Harold Leopold, became "Harry." Even my dad's name, James Henry, is shortened to "Jim". Only my mother's name, Margaret Ann, remains Margaret, at least when we talk directly to her. But behind her back, it's always "Maggie".

When I was born, my mother was determined to defy the tendency of those who love to shorten names, naming me Felicia Francine. However she didn't take into account how difficult it is for a five-year-old to pronounce "Felicia," and one day my sister discovered that it's easier to simply say "Freddy." From that day on, "Felicia" became "Freddy." Only with my mother do I maintain the name originally given to me. Even so, to this day when she says that name I have to take a glance around the room to see if there is a Felicia present as my birth-name has become so alien to me.

My nickname was the first of many embarrassments to my mother, but by no means the last. The truth is, I looked more like a "Freddy" than a "Felicia." I was born with wild red hair and the accompanying freckles, and from the very get-go, I was a tomboy. In both appearance and behavior I am the exact opposite of my sister, who inherited her natural dark beauty from my mother's side of the family. My mother is beautiful, graceful, and can cause people to cease their chatter simply by walking into a room.

My sister and I were never what one would call close. While she went to ballet and music lessons I went out in the garden and dug up worms for fishing or plants for re-planting. Sometimes I just dug in the dirt for the simple pleasure I got out of it. My fingernails were always caked underneath with the black stuff, the white half-moons of my cuticles turned dark by the soil. It didn't bother me, but it sure did bother my mother. In vain I attempted to play the part of the textbook "Little Lady." I strove to be the over-achiever that mom always wanted, but whenever I tried it inevitably resulted in an even worse embarrassment to my mother than before.

Take the time when I was about eight, and the community playhouse was putting on the popular production of the Broadway play Annie, and I auditioned for the lead role. I figured, heck, if landing the part depended anything on looks, I was a shoo-in, for sure! My mother even cut my red curly hair short, so it looked just like Annie's. Except for the whole not-actually-being-an-orphan thing, I was Annie--at least, until I was told to sing. All the notes of the song followed this neat little pattern. That's how the director explained it, and all I had to do is follow one note after the other, kind of like cars following the lead car. It sounded easy enough; though I tried my best, when I opened my mouth, all my metaphorical 'cars' went in the opposite direction, bumping into each other, squeaking and squealing, clashing and colliding, creating a horrible mess of the song. Even though I botched the entire thing, I will admit that my volume and projection were good. After my pitiful attempt at singing I wasn't allowed to remain long enough to demonstrate my acting abilities, and so I never found out how good of an actress I might have been. That didn't happen until years later, when the day came that I had to tell Joey that what people say doesn't matter-when in my heart I knew it did. But that was after I grew up, leaving Uncle Joey behind and locked in a state of permanent childhood.

Joey was born late in life to my grandparents. After having my dad they tried for more children, but they were perpetually unable to reap the fruits of their love. Grandma would always have a miscarriage, until finally her womb couldn't even produce another stillborn. It was at the age of forty-three and in the midst of her final change in womanhood, just before menopause, that she got pregnant again. It came as quite a surprise to everyone involved that this time she stayed that way, and carried the child to term. My dad was already twenty-two and married to my mother, and they were expecting their first child. This served as yet another item to add on the long grocery list of embarrassments for my mother. Imagine going to your ob-gyn, eight months pregnant, and meeting your mother-in-law there, every bit as pregnant as you are!

Grandma didn't get to enjoy Joey for very long,

though. She died of cancer when he was six, leaving my grandfather, already in his fifties, to raise Joey. My grandfather tried his best with the boy, but his arthritis was getting worse, and staying in the Midwest climate only aggravated it further. That's how Joey came to live with us. Grandfather went to Florida one winter, in the hopes that the warmer climate would improve his deteriorating health, and he never came back. He met a widow there; she wanted Grandpa but not Joey. So Grandpa signed over the garden store, the landscape business, and even the house to my father, in exchange for my parents' taking over the responsibility of caring for Joey. My mother agreed, mainly because I think she was afraid that if she didn't accept the opportunity when it was offered, that would be that, and they would end up regretting it later. She knew that, should anything happen to Grandpa, the widow would end up with the business and the house, but she and my father would be stuck with Joey.

It would certainly appear this way, and there was even gossip which suggested that the only reason mom took in Joey was for the money, but that's just not so. My mother loves Joey; it's just some of the things he does that she doesn't like.

For example, take the time when Joey urinated all over the church steps. I was just a baby then, but that story will live on in the annals of our quiet, conservative Midwest church's history forever. It inevitably gets elaborated on with each telling.

Anyway, this particular incident happened after church. As usual on a beautiful Sunday morning, much of the congregation stood outside and chatted. My mom and dad were standing and talking to the minister, where a small crowd had gathered around, when Joey announced to anyone who would listen that he had to go to the bathroom. Involved in conversation with the minister, Joey was ignored by my parents, not just once, but a couple of times, until finally he became weary of asking. His full bladder became too large a burden for a small boy, and so Joey just whipped it out and peed, looking every inch a statue of the little boy "peeing" water into that fountain in Brussels.

Joey just kept going, yellow liquid trickling down the steps like a miniature waterfall. Totally unaware of the terrible breech in etiquette, he ended up splashing on anybody within range, including the minister. By the time my father could pick Joey up and carry him over his shoulder to the car, the boy's zipper still undone, there was a little puddle pooled at the bottom of the previously immaculate steps, and a severe red shame spreading rapidly across the whole of Dad's face and neck.

The last words heard that bright Sunday morning as we drove off were my mother yelling at the confused little boy in the back seat, "Then pee in your pants next time if you have to! Just don't ever do that again!"

Joey never did do that again, at least not at church; there are times when I'm working with Joey, digging in the dirt, or helping him get a yard ready for planting, that Joey "waters" it, first. I never say anything; I just turn my head politely away. I don't share the same opinion as my mother. It isn't better to "pee in your pants." Hell, there were times there wasn't a bathroom around and I had to go where I simply squatted down and did what I had to do. I was more discrete about it than Joey, always taking care to go behind a bush or tree before I dropped my pants. That was when I was still just a kid. It was all so innocent, so natural, but when you're a kid, you have no idea how innocence and childlike ignorance can be misconstrued as 'bad' things by adults. My problem now, is that if Joey gets in trouble, I might not yet be wise or old enough to comprehend this aspect of what I am still learning to be 'harsh reality.'

CHAPTER 2

I am sixteen now, and as sometimes happens moving from childhood to young womanhood my life has taken some twists and turns. My hair isn't quite so wild anymore, but it is still red and curly-- really red and really curly. I still have the freckles, and they're real, too. My idea of appropriate dress is different from my mother's, and even though I'm still an embarrassment, it's a different kind of embarrassment. Arguing with my mother about almost everything is one of the twists and turns I've taken since those wonderful days of growing up with Joey. When I thought digging in the dirt was fun, and Joey was the smartest person in the whole world. I still dig in the dirt with Joey, but now I do it working for my dad, who has taken over the garden store. It was part of the deal for us taking Joey. I believe my mother was right when she said that if we didn't take when the taking was good, we'd be left out in the cold.

My grandfather died shortly after my birthday, leaving the widow woman his whole inheritance, with the exception of one condominium in Florida, and money sufficient for them to care for Joey for the rest of his life, provided that wouldn't be too long. Luckily, Joey's needs are simple, and Dad decided to build a little house on our property especially for Joey so he can have some semblance of independence. At this point Joey is twenty-three years old, but mentally he remains a child. It is a big step for Joey to be on his own, so I do my best to help him adjust.

Every morning before school I go to his little house and have breakfast with him, and every evening I carry dinner over for him. I always eat something with him, even if I've already eaten at home with my other family members. It's a wonder I don't get fat from eating all those extra meals, but thankfully, all the fetching and carrying I do back and forth helps me to work off any excess calories. Recently my dad's opened another store, so it isn't just the fussing over Joey and going to school that keeps me running, but also working for Dad in his new store on weekends and in the summer. The summers are easy for Joey when I'm around, the two of us digging in the dirt, planting something or other. And now that I have my driver's license, I can take Joey with me when I make deliveries for my dad. It's the time when I go to school that's hard on Joey. I convinced Dad to add a little greenhouse onto the back of Joey's place, so he can putter with the plants when he gets lonely. They're his only friends in my absence. And as things sometimes happen, unforeseen benefits emerge. My idea for the addition of the greenhouse turned out to be a good investment. Joey is second-to-none in his careful nurture of plants and we are able to harvest and sell those flowers and vegetables that Joey so lovingly looks after, actually making a small profit.

Life has always been pretty predictable for Joey, working with me for my dad. And except for the days it rains we're usually outside working in somebody's yard. Today is no exception. It's summer, it's not raining, and Joey's arguing is predictable when I drop him off to start work, while I make a delivery.

"I don't want to stay, I want to go with you," Joey argues, and I force myself to be firm when I tell him, "You have to get started, Joey. It's going to take all day to get everything that's come in planted. If we let those plants sit around any longer, they'll die. You don't want those plants to *die*--do you, Joey?" I say, putting emphasis on the word *die*.

Noooo--" Joey says slowly, like I just said a dirty word. "But we can work real hard, Freddy, even if I go with you. It won't take long."

"But if you get everything ready, by the time I deliver the rest of this stuff, I'll be back to help finish up. I'm going somewhere tonight, Joey, so we've gotta finish early."

"Ooookay," Joey agrees, reluctantly opening the door and stepping out to help me take the flats of plants off the back of the truck. "But you're no fun anymore--not since you started having to go places early," he says with pout in his voice.

I feel a twinge of guilt as I begin the task at hand.

I've been going places early, ever since I started

going out with Erik. But I'm sixteen, for crying out loud; why shouldn't I be hanging out with kids my own age? Mom says that I should. Dad says I should. So why, I wonder, can't Joey share their opinion? But then I remember that Joey just doesn't understand about dating. Joey doesn't understand anything about this boy/girl stuff, and so, once again trying to find some compromise, I say, "Look, Joey, tomorrow night we can go to the movies--okay?" But no sooner have the words left my mouth than it occurs to me I might run into some kids I know, so I change my proposition a little.

"Better yet, I'll rent a movie and we can watch it on your new VCR. Would you like that, Joey?"

"Well, what kind of movie?" he asks, absently picking the dirt from under his nails.

"I don't know, what do you want to watch?" I ask, picking up a box of plants off the back of the truck.

"*The Three Stooges*. I want *The Three Stooges*," he answers, taking the box I hand him.

"But you watch them all the time. Don't you want something different?"

"But I don't watch them with *you*. It'd be more fun with you," he says with a smile, and I can't help but give in. It's always hard to say no to Joey, especially when he flashes me that sweet, genuine Joey-smile, his secret weapon that almost never fails.

By the time we get the whole movie issue settled, we're finished with taking the plants off the truck, and I help Joey set the flats by the flower beds, making sure he knows what goes where.

"Are you going someplace early with Erik?" Joey asks with obvious hurt in his eyes. Ever since Erik started working for Dad, Joey has that hurt look in his eyes.

"Erik thinks I'm beautiful I say, avoiding a direct yes to his question. "He says he doesn't mind my freckles at all. He thinks they're cute. No boy ever told me I was beautiful before, Joey," I explain, but despite my best efforts to avoid hurting him further, Joey knows my feelings for Erik are more than friendly. It's a common misconception that, just because Joey is a little slow he is also stupid, but I'm one of the few who knows better.

"You *are* beautiful, Freddy," he says, real serious. "Yeah, sure--and maybe cows fly, but *I* haven't seen any flying--have you?"

"Cows can't fly, Freddy," Joey says, still serious. Then, doubt creeping in, he asks, "Can they, Freddy?"

"Of course not, you silly goose!" I reply, laughing, a kind of laugh *with* him, not *at* him laugh. I give his shoulder a loving pat just to make sure he understands the laugh. "It's just an expression, a figure of speech. You know, like when Mom says, 'it's raining cats and dogs,' but it's not *really* raining cats and dogs, just really hard." He's silent for a moment, eyes downcast, seemingly studying the flowers he's going to plant, like he's through with talk, but then, yet another question.

"Then--why does she say it?"

I take a deep breath, wishing he didn't take

23

everything so darn literally. I wonder how I get myself into these conversations anyway. I've explained this all before to Joey, all of it! Maybe not the cats and dogs thing, specifically, but definitely similar stuff.

"Sometimes people just say dumb things, Joey," I say, hoping he catches on to the note of finality in my voice. But, of course, Joey doesn't let it go, not yet.

"You're not dumb, Freddy," he protests.

"I said people sometimes *say* dumb things, Joey, not that *I'm* dumb. And anyway, the issue here isn't how smart I am. What I said was that I wasn't beautiful; that when I look in the mirror, I don't see beautiful. Take this hair, for instance," I say, removing the baseball cap from my head and fanning myself with it. "Why do you think I always wear this baseball cap?"

"Why?" Joey asks innocently, and I take another impatient breath before answering.

"Because, Joey, I *hate* my hair. Because Angie has beautiful black hair and I have this crappy red hair," I say, tugging on an unruly lock for emphasis. "Because Angie has beautiful *everything*, and I have beautiful *nothing*," I finish, and I hope Joey is finished with his questions because these negative thoughts are starting to piss me off.

"Your heart is beautiful," Joey says softly, in earnest, and now I really feel guilty, not just for losing my patience, but for everything in general. Before I do something I know I'll regret later, like say I'll break my date with Erik and take Joey to a movie instead, I head for the truck.

"Boys aren't interested in the heart, Joey, it's the *body* they're after," I say just before I step up into the truck and drive off. With mixed emotions, I watch Joey in the rear-view mirror as he starts digging in the dirt: a lonely figure against the backdrop of blue sky.

I rush through deliveries, feeling the usual guilt of abandoning him whenever I leave Joey, but when I get back to the Claytons' I discover he's not alone. He has most of the flowers planted, but at some point while I was gone Joey acquired some help. A little girl is digging along with him, and I feel a little jealous thinking of how familiar it all looks. Wasn't that me not so long ago? Why did I have to grow up and leave Joey behind?

When I go to help Joey finish up, throwing the empty flats into the truck bed, Joey tells me that his new friend's name is Karen, and that she lives in the house where we are working.

"Hello, Karen," I say, doing my best to forget my jealousy in order to be kind to the little girl, who can't be much older than six or seven. "You're very good at planting flowers. I bet Joey told you the names of everything the two of you planted." I smile at her, but it doesn't quite reach my eyes.

"I even told her that some plants have to have sun and some need shade. That she will have to water the flowers or they will die. I told you all that, didn't I, Karen?" Joey says, real proud- like.

25

"Yes," Karen says with a nod. "He knows lots about flowers. He's real smart."

"Yes, he is," I say, thinking that Karen is a lot like me ten years ago, except for the hair and freckles, that is.

Karen looks pleased, Joey looks pleased, and maybe I don't look it, but really, I'm pleased, too. I'm sixteen years old, and I still like to think Joey is the smartest person in the world. Not only that, but he has a beautiful heart, too.

CHAPTER 3

At the supper table, Dad tells me that Joey and I have to go back to the store and get the plants ready to take over to the Davis's for planting the next day.

"But I thought we were going to wait with that until next week. Why the big rush now?"

"Because Mrs. Davis decided she wants a garden party instead of just a dinner party this weekend, and the garden isn't ready."

"Tell old lady Davis to have her garden party the next weekend, and by then her garden will be ready."

"You know I can't do that. Mrs. Davis is one of our biggest accounts."

"But I have a date with Erik tonight."

"Go out with Erik tomorrow."

"Dammit, Dad, you just don't break a date with a guy like Erik and expect him to be there the next night. Guys don't like it when you break a date."

Now my mother gets into the conversation and says "Ladies don't swear, Felicia. Boys don't like girls who swear either."

"The hell they don't, Mom. Girls at school swear all the time."

"Well--you don't swear in this house," Mom says, real loud.

I can see this is getting me nowhere, but still I have to argue. Mothers with daughters my age always argue. I'm not about to change the course of things.

"You know, Mom, you really kill me, you know that. You keep harping about how I should be more of a lady. That I should be more like Angie."

I see my mother cringe when I say Angie, instead of Angela, and I glow inside with the satisfaction of it.

"So go tell Angie to get things ready for old lady Davis. I've got a date."

"That's impossible. You know Angela is out East for the summer."

"And Harry's in Texas working on his precious computer stuff," the glow getting even brighter after I say 'Harry.'

"But hell," another cringe. "Even if they were here, they wouldn't want to get their hands dirty working in all that dirt. Would they, Maggie?"

I think I just crossed the line when I called my mother Maggie, because now my Dad gets into the conversation again.

"Look, I'll go. Anything's better than listening to you two fight."

I look at my Dad. He looks so tired lately. Between the obligation of Joey and my mother harping on how Grandpa screwed him out of a fortune, not to mention my mother and me at each other all the time. It's taking its toll, so I say, "No Dad. Joey and I'll go. I'll stop at a McDonald's on the way and pick something up for Joey. He can eat on the way."

"You don't have to, Freddy. I just thought you liked working in the store," Dad says, hurt in his voice.

I see Mom cringe again when Dad says Freddy, and I say, "I do like working for you, Dad, and it's OK, I'll go."

"You don't have to," Dad says again.

"Yeah, I have to," I say and get up to go to my room to call Erik and break our date. I'm going to miss Erik. God, I'm going to miss him. I'm not the only beautiful girl he knows.

There's a whole line out there waiting to go out with the best-looking guy in school who is also the football team's star quarterback. He even got a football scholarship, and someday he is going to be a doctor. No, Erik doesn't have to take shit like this, and before calling him I change into my jeans and the T-shirt with the words "Harrison's Landscaping" written on it. I flop down on the bed, leaving my shoes on in defiance of my mother, and dial Erik's number. I have to wait for his mother to get him, and while I wait I think I'll hang up, but before I can chicken out Erik comes on line.

"What's up?" he asks, and I wish I had hung up when I had the chance. Maybe Dad and Joey could go. When I think of how tired Dad looks lately, I say, "I'm afraid I can't go out tonight. Something came up at the store."

"Like what?"

"Like I have to go and get the stuff ready for the

Davis's."

"I thought that was scheduled for next week."

"It was, but old lady Davis decided she wants it this week. She's one of our best customers so I guess I have to go. I'll take Joey with me, but it will still take a long time. It'll be too late for us to go out when I finish. But maybe we can do something tomorrow," I say, with hope in my voice.

"I can't tomorrow," Erik says, and I think that this is it.

I should just hang up and make it easy for both of us. But it sure is going to be hard facing him at work from now on.

"My aunt from California is coming to visit tomorrow, and my parents insist I have to be here," Erik explains, and I'm not sure if I should believe him, then he says, "But I'll go with you tonight instead of Joey." Now I believe him.

"Are you sure? I mean it's not a date. It's work."

"I'm sure, and you won't even have to pay me," Erik says with a laugh, and I laugh, too. God I really like him, and I think he really likes me, too. He must if he's willing to work for nothing just to be with me.

On my way to the store I drive around and pick up Erik. We listen to music from the stack of CD's I have stashed in the van, and if I feel a twinge of guilt for not taking Joey his supper tonight, I drown it out by turning the music up, making the van vibrate with loud thumps as we move our bodies back and forth to the beat.

When we get to the store, we go directly to the greenhouses and start sorting out bushes and flowers.

Finally, after hours of sorting and figuring, "old lady Davis is sure going to have a beautiful garden for her party but it's going to cost her." I lie down on one of the low plant tables and stretch out. Erik goes to the soda machine that we keep stocked for the employees, and carrying one in each hand, comes and sits next to me.

"Want a Coke?" he asks.

I'm ready to sit up and take the can of soda that he's holding out to me, when Erik puts both cans down and gently pushes me back. Our lips make contact, and when he puts his tongue in my mouth I taste Coke. He puts his hand under my T-shirt and reaching behind, unhooks my bra. Without a word from either of us, he moves his face down to kiss my exposed breasts, and I think that I should make him stop, but his mouth is doing things that makes the words fly out of my head. I think he's really getting hard between his legs, and when he takes my hand to touch him there, I know he is.

"Erik, I can't do this," I say, but Erik has his pants unzipped and after he unzips my jeans, slips both panties and jeans down, kind of pushing the rest of the way with his feet, all in one motion, I feel between my legs what I felt in my hand only a little while ago.

"I've never let a boy do this before," I say, my voice quivering with the sensation of him pushing against me, the sudden pain of penetration.

31

"I'm not just anybody. We love each other. You do love me, don't you, Freddy?"

"Yes," I say, and before I know it, on a table where only a little while ago boxes of plants grew, I let Erik take my virginity.

On the way home, just before I drop Erik off, he turns to me and says, "I'll say I'm going to bed early tomorrow night. That I have to go to work early in the morning, and I'll sneak out to see you. Can I come to see you tomorrow night, Freddy? I don't think I can stand being away from you."

"You'll see me at work tomorrow," I say.

"But not the way I want to see you. It was great, wasn't it? Did you like it, too?"

"Yes," I say, and Erik kisses me again with his tongue, and before we get to the point of no return, I give him a little shove away.

"I'll see you tomorrow night," I say.

"Where?" Erik asks.

"Behind the greenhouse by Joey's place," I say, then watch while Erik gets out of the van and goes into his house. I sit in front of his house a long time. I watch the light go on in Erik's bedroom and then off again. And I wonder what my mother would say if she knew what happened tonight. What is going to happen again tomorrow night--boy, would there be a fight!

CHAPTER 4

Erik and I see each other every night. We either
go out to a movie, or else sit with Joey and watch
television for a while, but we always end up behind
the greenhouse at Joey's place and make love. Our
bodies are familiar to each other now. I no longer
hesitate when I reach down and touch him, and we
even experiment with different positions. Erik tells
me that he loves me and gives me his class ring, and
I take birth control pills.

Just after Angela left for out East I discovered the
pills in her room that she forgot to take with her.
Then they didn't interest me, except for the
satisfaction it gave me knowing my sister wasn't
always the lady my mother made her out to be. Now
I know just where to look for them, and every day I
make sure, even before breakfast, that I take the pill.
What could my sister say if she came home and
found out they were gone. She sure can't complain
to our mother.

Sometimes when we're working together, I see
Erik watching me and I know what he's thinking.
What he wants. It's getting harder and harder to hide
how we feel in front of the other employees. It's
even harder to keep meeting behind the greenhouse,

and then sneak home after. I'm sure if Mom were to see me when I come creeping up the steps, she'd guess what I just did.

One night, after we are through making love, reluctant to get up from the blanket we've spread on the ground, and go to our separate houses, Erik says, "I want to marry you, Freddy. I don't want to leave you like this. I want to wake up every morning next to you."

"We can't marry," I remind him. "Not yet. I have to finish school, and this fall you're going to college."

"Screw college," Erik says. "I love you, and you love me. We'll live on love."

I laugh and kiss him on the little cleft in his chin, pulling his blonde head against my heart, and before we part we make love one more time.

Erik and I see each other every day of the week. We spend the warm summer days, except for Sundays, working together, and the nights, including Sundays, making love. If it rains and we can't go behind Joey's greenhouse, then we go into the greenhouse. The only witnesses we have are the plants, and maybe we can talk to plants, but they haven't learned to talk to us.

The walls are built of cement block and the roof is all glass, and although it's warm inside, we compensate by taking off all our clothes.

A month of our secret meetings goes by, and I'm so wrapped up in the sweet agony of our love that I don't notice how quiet Joey is lately. How he only seems to come alive after working at the Claytons. And he finds lots of reasons why he has to go there. The yard needs raking after the windstorm blew branches off the trees. The grass needs cutting. If he doesn't take care of the flower beds the weeds will take over. When I drop Joey off he doesn't argue anymore about not staying alone, and when I pick him up, he always talks about the next time he has to go there. I think that Karen has something to do with it. She's always out there helping him when I pick him up. In a way I'm glad Joey has a new friend. I tell myself that it was bound to happen. That Joey and I would one day find new friends. Of course, Erik and I have long passed the just-friends stage and are talking seriously about getting married. Erik won't go to college after all, and just as soon as I finish school, we'll get married.

It's a beautiful dream, and I am in that dream world on my way to pick up Joey at the Claytons. I know something is wrong the minute I pull up and Mrs. Clayton, along with Mr. Clayton, are standing in the driveway waiting for me. Joey is standing out on the sidewalk, and there is no Karen around.

"What's wrong?" I ask Joey after I stop to pick him up, then pull into the driveway to turn around.

Joey doesn't get the chance to answer, and I don't get the chance to turn around, because Mr. Clayton comes running over to the van. When I roll down the window, he says, "We don't want you to work in our yard anymore. We don't want any of you people around here."

"Why?" I ask, all innocent-like.

"We don't want your kind around our daughter, that's why. A grown man like that shouldn't be exposing himself to a little girl. You're lucky I don't call the police and have him arrested."

I think I know what happened, and I apologize, saying, "I'll have my dad call you. It won't happen again, Mr. Clayton--I promise."

"You're damn right it won't happen again, because if I see that pervert anywhere around my daughter, I'm calling the cops."

By now a little crowd of neighbors has gathered in their yards to listen, and I get the hell out of there fast.

"You had to do it. Didn't you Joey? You peed right there in front of Karen. Didn't you, Joey?"

"I had to go."

"But you don't go in front of people Joey. I thought Mom explained that to you a long time ago."

"But you never minded when I did."

"I'm not other people, Joey. Jesus, can't you understand that? I'm not other people."

I'm repeating myself, my voice getting louder with every repetition--like Joey is hard of hearing.

Joey starts to cry and I think that maybe I'll cry, too. It's my fault; I should have known this would happen. I should have kept Joey with me and not left him alone so much. I love Erik, but I love Joey, too. God, sometimes love gets so complicated, and I wonder just how in the hell I'm going to explain this lost account to my dad. It's not the money that's going to break his heart. It's the reminder of a brother who's really not his brother, but his child.

When we get home, I tell Joey not to say anything to Dad, that I'll take care of it.

"It's going to be O.K., Joey," I say, even though I know it's not.

Joey wipes at his eyes and says, "Will I be able to see Karen again?"

"No, Joey, but I promise you, I'll spend more time with you from now on--Will you like that, Joey?"

"Maybe you and I and Karen can plant some flowers in somebody else's yard, if we can't plant them in her yard."

"No. You have to stay away from Karen. You heard Mr. Clayton; if he sees you with her, he'll call the cops."

"But why, Freddy? Is it against the law to pee?"

I want to laugh when he says that, but I dare not in front of Joey. This is serious.

"It's against the law to pee in front of little girls."

"Can I pee in front of little boys?"

Now this is really getting out of control.

"Not in front of anybody. Not on anybody's lawn, and especially not on Mr. Clayton's lawn."

"But Harry pees on lawns, and Dad does in front of boys too?"

I can't believe what I'm hearing, and I say, "Stop making things up, Joey. That's another thing; when you're caught doing something wrong, you make things up to explain why you did it."

"I'm not making things up, Freddy. You know Harry used to all the time when we were outside and playing."

"That was years ago, when we were kids. Harry's grown up now. He knows better."

"But grown-ups still do. When we went to the restaurant, Dad was standing there peeing and this little boy came in and stood right there next to him and peed, too. I swear, Freddy, I'm not making it up."

No wonder Joey is confused. I'm confused, and I have to think for a minute about what happened at the restaurant; then it dawns on me and I say, "If you have to pee in public, just make sure you're in one of those bathroom stalls by yourself with the door closed and locked." I figure that by telling him this, I've covered every situation that might come up in public, including urinals.

When I get home, I tell Dad what happened, and I see the lines around his mouth get deeper.

"Look Dad," I say, hoping to make those lines soften a little. "I think if you call the Claytons and explain to them that it will never happen again, it'll be O.K. That we'll send someone else to take care of their yard. Heck, I bet if you offer them a free fertilizer job on their lawn they'll come around." Then thinking of what I just said, I add, "On second thought, I think you better not say anything about fertilizer. Not after the way Joey watered it."

Dad laughs and the little lines around his mouth soften; then he heads for his study to call Mr. Clayton. I go to the kitchen to pick up the food Mom has all packed and ready for me to take to Joey. Now all I have to do is cheer him up.

Joey hardly touches anything, and when I try to entice him with the pie that Mom packed, he just shakes his head no.

"It's apple--your favorite," I say, but Joey just looks at it like he doesn't see.

"I always make people mad. Don't I, Freddy? I don't want to, but I do."

"They just don't understand you, that's all, Joey."

"But why, Freddy? You understand me. Why can't they?"

"Because most people don't understand different, Joey. It scares them."

"Do I scare you?"

"No."

"How come?"

"Because, in a way I'm different, too."

After supper, Erik comes over, and we watch *The Three Stooges* with Joey, then play Old Maid with him. It's been a long time since I've played Old Maid with Joey, but I think I owe him that. God knows, somebody owes him something. He asks for so little.

CHAPTER 5

The summer is almost over and the day that Erik will leave for college is fast approaching, but he still hasn't told his parents that he's not going. Mom buys me a whole closet full of clothes for my senior year that I'll never wear. She has no idea what kids wear to school these days. It's sure not plaid skirts and cardigans, but I don't have the heart to tell her that. Mom has her world and I have mine, and they're in totally different galaxies. I've run out of Angela's birth control pills, but Erik got me some more. His dad's a pharmacist, and if anybody can get them, it's him.

For my seventeenth birthday, Erik gives me a little locket with his picture in it. He also gives me an engagement ring. The diamond's not very big, but that's okay because I can't really wear it. Not on my finger, in plain view, anyway. As a compromise, until Erik tells his father about not going to college, I wear it on a silver chain around my neck, under my shirt, close to my heart. It's the symbol of our secret engagement. Every night before we make love, Erik undoes the clasp on the chain, removes my ring from the thin sparkling strip of silver that he then deposits into the pocket of his jeans, and slips it on my finger.

"We're going to be married, Freddy," he tells me, his smile making his boyish features light up and sending my heart all aflutter. "I just want you to remember that. This isn't like those other kids in school when they sleep with just anybody. I'm true to you, and I want you to be true to me."

"Of course I'm true to you. You're the only boy I've ever let do this to me, and there will never be another."

We always seal the promise with a kiss, before Erik undoes his fly and I slide my jeans and panties over my narrow hips and down my slim legs, shaking them the rest of the way off at my ankles.

Two weeks before Erik is supposed to leave we go through the ritual of promise, kiss, and sex, always in the same passionate and tender order. Erik is insatiable. It's like he can't get enough of me, until he finally collapses from exhaustion, lingers on top of me for a moment, breathing kisses onto my lips, face, and neck, and whispering "I love you" against my damp neck. It's such a wonderful feeling, his body covering mine, our sweat mingling, those sweet words poured into my ear like honey. Even though after a few moments, the dead weight of his fatigued body becomes a little too much for my slight frame and breathing becomes difficult, I always feel my heart sag within my chest just a little when he finally pulls out and away from me. Despite the fact that it gets a little difficult to breathe with him crushing me into the ground, I wish that we could stay like that for always. I want him inside me, all around me, his heartbeat pulsing throughout my entire body, his masculine form trembling with ragged breaths, forever.

He lies next to me on the blanket, his legs wrapped over mine, his hand stroking my belly softly. The moon is so full, so bright that I can see the outline of the greenhouse, the trees, even the little tool shed where we keep some of our garden tools that we don't keep at the store. If it weren't for the bushes surrounding us I'd worry that someone might spot our sweat-slick skin gleaming white in the moonlight.

After a few moments of silently basking in the afterglow that always follows our intimate encounters, Erik sighs, but it's not the usual sigh of contentment, and before I can ask what's the matter, he says, "I don't wanna leave you, Freddy."

My breath catches in my throat and there's a tightness in my chest. I prop myself up on one elbow and look at Erik, fear and confusion threatening to make my voice break.

"What do you mean? I thought it was all settled. As soon as I graduate next spring, we're going to get married. We *are* going to get married, aren't we?"

"Of course we're going to get married. I wouldn't have bought you a diamond for nothing," he says, nodding at the silver band around my finger, the stone set within it glittering in the blue-white light of the moon.

"I've just been thinking about it, and I guess I don't think it'd be the greatest idea to do it right when you graduate. I mean, what kind of a job can I get without a college degree? I've been looking for one, but there's nothing out there. Nothing that pays enough so I can support a wife."

"But my dad will hire you permanently. We can both work for my dad," I insist, feeling hot tears prickling the backs of my eyes.

Erik gets up quickly, shoving me backwards with his shoulder, and I land hard with my naked back flush with the ground, clods of soil and grass poking me uncomfortably. The night had started out so great, and now all of a sudden everything is falling apart. I close my eyes and think that when I open them this will all go away, and it will be like it was before Erik started talking about postponing our plans to marry.

"Is that what you really want? For your dad to take care of us for the rest of our lives?" he asks, pulling his shirt over his head and making a derisive noise in the back of his throat. "I've got more pride than that."

"Well maybe you should have thought of your damn pride before you started fucking me," I say coldly, sitting straight up and tugging hard at the ring on my finger, intending to throw it in his face if I can ever get the damned thing off. I've almost succeeded in removing it but I don't get the chance to carry out my plan, because Erik cups my small hands in his big, manly ones and brings them up to his face, pressing small kisses into my palm and against the back of the silver band. I feel the wetness on his cheeks before I see the tears.

"I love you, Freddy. I'll--I'll do anything you want."

He sounds so sad and defeated that I feel a pang of guilt at having sounded so spiteful. He was just trying to be responsible, after all, and I suddenly feel very ashamed for being so childish.

"I want you to get an education," I say gently, caressing his tear-streaked cheek with my thumb. "I'll wait for you, and we'll be true to each other."

We lay for a long time in each other's arms. We even fall asleep holding each other, and when I finally creep up the stairs into my bedroom, the eastern sky is already showing the first signs of dawn.

Our time together is precious now that we know how little of it is left. We don't want to share it with anybody. I forget about Joey, about my dad, and even about fighting with my mother. She buys me more clothes for school, and when she tells me to feel the material of a sweater she'd just purchased for me, how soft the wool is, I rub a patch of fabric between my thumb and forefinger and nod, but it's Erik I'm thinking about. I don't even notice the color of the shirt that I'm touching without really feeling it. When the week comes to a close he has to leave for college.

"I told my dad about us," Erik says the night before he leaves, and we meet for the last time behind the greenhouse. "He says that if we still feel the way we do now, that we won't have to wait until I get through medical school. We can get married after I finish college. He even offered to help out until I can take care of us on my own salary."

"I told my dad about us, too. I mean about the loving each other, not the rest of what we're doing. He said the same thing. I think I can wear your ring now, Erik, now that our parents know."

We promise to be true to each other, and then Erik slips the ring on my finger, never to be taken off until he puts a wedding ring there. I take the chain I'd been wearing around my neck and fasten the clasp around Erik's. I want him to keep it, now that I no longer need it to hide the symbol of our love. He smiles that gorgeous smile of his and we kiss.

We believe what we say to each other, what we promise each other, with everything that we are, and our lovemaking is so passionate that it leaves us both so completely exhausted that this time, we don't wake up until we hear Joey getting up and going outside. I sneak off to my house and Erik sneaks off to his, and that's the last I see of the boy who took my virginity and my heart and gave me a diamond in exchange.

I go back to school and work at the store nights and weekends. Joey and I rake leaves and get flower beds ready for winter, for just about everybody in town except the Claytons. Dad was able to keep the account, but he had to promise that whoever came to do their yard, it would not under any circumstances be Joey. It really hurts Joey to know this and I try to make it up to him by being extra nice. But Joey isn't fooled by my efforts to console him. He may have the mind of a child, but he still knows when people don't like him. He knows that he's different and the hurt caused by that knowledge shows in his eyes every time I look at him.

I write Erik every day and he writes me back at least once a week. I read his letters over and over. I devour them but they always leave me hungry for more. I fall asleep crying, and I cry in the girls' bathroom at school. Sometimes I even cry when I watch television with Joey, but I always tell him it's because the movie is sad. I don't think Joey believes me though because after I cry during *The Three Stooges*, Joey says, "It's because you miss Erik, isn't it, Freddy?"

"Yes," I say, wiping my eyes with my long sleeve, embarrassed by the tears that fill my eyes so easily these days.

"Me, too," Joey says, his eyes dropping down to his hands, which are folded in his lap. "I miss Karen, too."

Joey and I have a good cry together. We sit and watch *The Three Stooges* and cry our heads off. It's supposed to be funny, this movie that we've seen at least a hundred times. Most people would be laughing, but then, we're different, me and Joey. So I guess we can cry instead of laugh.

The next day after our crying session, I get a letter

from Erik and Joey gets to see Karen. We just happen to be going in to see the same movie that Karen is going into with her parents. Karen's mother won't let her talk to Joey, but Karen sneaks a little wave to us when her mother isn't looking. That little wave makes Joey happy for at least a week.

My letter from Erik makes me happy, too, but not right away. He starts out bragging about the game his football team won over the weekend. I get a blow-by-blow description of each touchdown they made--not exactly the most exciting thing in the world to me. He even boasts about how he threw the winning pass. He writes about the party they went to afterwards, and even though he doesn't mention anything about the girls at the party I read between the lines and know they were there. I remember how they use to throw themselves at him in high school after a big game. By the time I'm almost finished, I'm not just jealous, but mad, too. Then in the last paragraph—it's only a couple of lines—I know I have nothing to be jealous about.

"I love you, Freddy," he declares in writing, "and I hope you're being true to me, because I am true to you. I hope you're still wearing my ring, and I can't wait until Christmas so we can renew our promise to each other."

There's a whole bunch of x's after, like kids make to send kisses. They make me smile.

I sit down right away and write a letter back. I pour my heart out to Erik. I tell him that I don't even think of looking at another boy. I say so much in that letter of love. I talk about my ache for him.

47

My need to be touched by him--all the things I would've rather read from him than the football crap he wrote. But since he wrote it, it's precious to me, anyway.

Finally, after wiping away some of the tears that fall on the paper, blurring the words, I write: "My dad is going to hire a manager for the new store we opened, and I think if you talk to him at Christmas, he'll hire you. He even plans on retiring in a couple of years, and I think he'll give us a great deal if we want to buy the business, especially if I tell him that I'll keep Joey with us. Just think, Erik, we can own our own business and get married like we planned. I still want to marry you, Erik. More now than ever." I put a lot of x's after my name, too, along with some o's for hugs, and then send it.

Two weeks before Christmas, I'm still waiting for an answer to my letter, and I wonder, if in the Christmas rush, that maybe it got lost. I've already bought Erik his present, and even had my hair trimmed so it looks real soft and shiny now. Mom bought me a new blue velvet dress, but this time I went with her to the store and picked it out myself so I know I'll wear it. All I have to do now is pick up from the engraver's the watch I bought for Erik, and then I'm all set...except I still haven't gotten a letter back from him. So I think on my way to pick up the watch that I'll stop by the drugstore where his dad is a pharmacist and kind of subtle-like ask if he's heard from Erik.

At breakfast I tell my dad I'm going to be late for work, then after school I drop by the drugstore. Glad to see that his father is working, I walk up to the counter that says, "Drop off prescriptions here," and say, "Hi, Mr. Larson."

"What can I do for you, Freddy?" Erik's father asks in a pleasant voice. "I'm afraid there's about a half-hour wait for prescriptions. It's flu season, you know...everybody's sick with it."

"I'm not here for a prescription. I just thought I'd stop by and say hi. I'm on my way to pick up Erik's present from the jewelers. I bought him a watch and I'm having it engraved. I hope he doesn't have a good watch already, does he, Mr. Larson?"

Mr. Larson looks uncomfortable. He even fidgets with the papers in front of him, and I don't wait for an answer before asking another question.

"Have you gotten a letter from him lately? I wrote him two weeks ago, but he never wrote me back. I figure it's probably all this Christmas mail and it got lost. Heck, Erik will be home before his letter gets there! The mail's so slow lately."

There's this sudden silence...unspoken words that Mr. Larson is trying to say but can't quite get out. He shuffles his papers again and then says, "Erik's not coming home for Christmas this year. He's been invited to spend the holiday with a friend of his. His mother and I have been invited, too."

He doesn't have to say it, I can see it in his eyes...this 'friend' of Erik's is a girl. Erik and his parents are spending Christmas with a girl and her parents, and I wonder if there's a greenhouse there where Erik can take her and fuck her.

I run out of the store, the eerie strains of 'Silent Night' coming over a loudspeaker following me down the street. I don't go to the store, but go straight home to fling myself across my bed and cry. I cry so hard that I have to put a pillow over my face to muffle the noise. My head explodes with the bitter realization that Erik never meant to marry me. He just said it to get what he wanted. I hate him, but I still love him. I can't help myself.

When my dad asks me in the morning at breakfast why I didn't come to work, I tell him I suddenly got sick. It wasn't really all that far from the truth.

"Probably the flu," I say, but I don't think my dad is fooled one bit. When I take the glass of juice that he gives me, my hand is shaking. And I think that it's not the shaking that makes his eyes narrow with concern and the little lines tighten around his mouth. It's because I'm not wearing Erik's ring anymore.

CHAPTER 6

The seasons melt into each other and before I know it Joey and I are back to planting and weeding again. It's getting harder and harder to keep up with all the work and Dad has hired some extra help for the summer. After I graduated, Dad asked me if I were interested in taking the position as manager of the new store, but I turned it down. I'd rather be outside working with Joey than listening to the clerks gossip among themselves. Whispering behind my back that the reason Erik hasn't come home for the summer is because he went to work for some girl's father in some big law firm. That instead of being a doctor, he's going to be a lawyer, and when he graduates there'll be a cushy office job waiting for him. At least with Joey, I don't have to pretend I'm feeling something I'm not. I don't have to be bright and cheerful around Joey, because he understands hurt.

I've gone out with some boys at school. I'm quite popular with them now. My new hairstyle and the sexier clothes I wear did it. I think the reputation of being easy has helped in that department, too. I figured if Erik is screwing around, so would I.

Sometimes when I'm doing it, I close my eyes and pretend the boy on top of me is Erik. The problem is I always have to open my eyes when we're through.

But for the summer I've decided to give up boys. It gets tiring after a while, pretending to like somebody when I really don't. There isn't a single day that goes by that I don't think of Erik and love him with all my pathetic little heart. There isn't a single day that I don't think of Erik and hate him with all of that heart, which he broke into a thousand pieces without ever saying a word. Love and hate, it keeps me going, and I'm afraid Joey is the target of both emotions. One minute I'm hollering at him, and the next I'm on the verge of tears and apologizing for being so mean.

The summer has been hot and dry, but today the heat has relented a bit. It even rained a little last night; the dirt feels moist and warm as I make little holes in it. The air smells fresh and clean. We are working in the Davis yard, replanting some of the plants that died in the heat. Old lady Davis comes out to make some comments about how nice it looks, but shouldn't these petunias go here and those lilies go there? And then she totters back inside. I follow her retreating, aging figure with my eyes and for a brief moment I think of how good it is to be young. To look up at the sun and to know that even when it goes away at night, the next day it'll be there again. I breathe in the green smell of growing things, of dirt just turned over, and when I look down, I see a little green caterpillar crawling on a leaf. Carefully I reach down and put it on my arm. Inch by tickling inch it crawls, slowly making its way to my shoulder.

When it gets there, I'm suddenly aware that a part of me will always belong to Erik, but that there's still enough left for me.

"Are you okay, Freddy?" Joey asks, coming to stand over me.

"Yeah, I'm okay," I answer, and when I look up I see that Joey is smiling. The hurt in his eyes is gone, and I think that maybe he and I really are both going to be okay.

For two days we work in the Davis yard, making it perfect for Mrs. Davis's end-of-summer garden party. The yard is perfect, the party is perfect and so is the weather, but all that perfection doesn't last. It gets cold; the little rain we had dries up, and after the party Mrs. Davis lets the flowers and trees succumb to the effects of the fall weather.

That feeling of okay doesn't last either. Our quiet little Midwestern neighborhood is shocked to realize that it can happen in our town, what we always thought only happens in other towns. We become the center of national news when it's reported that a little girl is missing. The news on television describes it in detail, showing pictures of the search party being organized to look for her. My Dad and I join in the group that searches for Karen.

For three days, we search in every forest within the radius of Karen's house: places where she could have possibly wandered off, or the thought that any of us dare not say aloud but that's eating away in the backs of our brains, where a stranger in a car might have taken her and dumped her, once he was finished with her. It's horrible. Our search party is a line of concerned people that stretches a mile wide. Always close enough that we can see each other we walk through brush and check out caves. We even check to see if there are any abandoned wells in the area. With each day that passes our hopes of finding a live Karen decreases. I call her name so many times that my voice is hoarse. When it rains I put on high boots and a poncho to slosh with the rest of the group through mud and thick marsh grass.

The police bring in dogs, and when the scent they get from something that belongs to Karen takes us to the creek I stand with the small group of spectators to watch as they drag the muddy water. The church Karen and her parents attend holds a candlelight vigil, praying night and day for her safe return. I hardly see Joey. He's never around when I stop in to check on him, but I figure he's doing his own searching.

After one week of looking in every conceivable place a person can look, the group of searchers gets smaller every day, until finally the search is called off. By now, all hope of finding a safe Karen is gone.

I stop in to see Joey to break the news to him, and

I'm relieved when I find him home.

"They've decided to call off the search, Joey," I say softly, sitting across from him at the kitchen table. I'm trying like hell to keep the despair out of my voice for Joey's sake, but it isn't easy when you're cold and tired, when your feet ache from constantly walking on uneven terrain in sneakers unfit for the job, and you've got scratches on your arms from pushing through all the brambles. I'm surprised when the news doesn't seem to bother him.

"You don't understand, Joey," I try to explain in the gentlest way possible. "The police think that she's been abducted," and I start to cry, unable to hold my emotions in any longer.

"Karen's okay, Freddy. I won't let anything happen to Karen. I take care of my flowers, don't I? When people bring their flowers to me, they think they're dead, but I make them better, don't I?"

"Joey, Karen's not a flower" I say, wiping my eyes and taking a deep breath in an effort to stop crying. I don't think crying in front of Joey is the thing to do right now.

"Yes, she is. She's a little daisy. That's what I told her, that she's a little daisy."

"Even daisies die, Joey. When it gets cold, daisies die. It's been wet and cold at night, Joey."

"That's why I covered her with a blanket. She's nice and warm now, Freddy."

"Joey, why are you making this up? You don't know where Karen is and you know it."

"Yes I do, and I'm taking care of her, but she can't go home yet. Not until I make her better. If I tell

55

you where she is you have to promise me that I can keep her until she's better."

By now Joey is shifting from foot to foot, almost in a crazy kind of dance in front of me, and I look at him as if he's lost his marbles completely, and then thinking I'm just as crazy for finally asking, "Where's Karen?"

"She's okay, Freddy. Don't you believe me?"

"Take me to her," I demand, standing up quickly, ready to call Joey's bluff.

Joey takes me by the hand and leads me outside, all the while saying, "Promise me you won't tell anybody, Freddy. Promise me, Freddy."

"Yeah, yeah," I say dispassionately, as we walk toward his little greenhouse, not believing any of this even for a second. Joey's spun crazy tales before, but never anything as crazy as this, never about something so serious. He should know better, and the farther we walk, his big hand clenched tightly around my smaller one, the more I wish I'd never played along, and my curiosity be damned. The moonlight is bright around us. The trees look ghostlike as their branches sway in the breeze. I remember the summer when Erik and I laid under that same moon with swaying branches above us. When we both promised to be true.

I feel the part of me that still belongs to Erik tug at my heart and I say, "Come on, Joey, quit fooling around and let's go back inside."

"Don't you believe me, Freddy?" he asks, a note of hurt in his voice.

"Believe what, Joey? That you know where Karen is? For a week we've searched every possible place she could be and we still haven't found her. So I know you don't know where she is, because if you did, you would have told me. Wouldn't you, Joey?"

"I couldn't, Freddy, not until I made her better."

"Stop it, Joey!" I'm back to hollering at him, but I'm not about to apologize for it. I don't appreciate this joke at all. I start back for the house, but Joey is insistent. I know that if I want some peace I'm going to have to play, follow through, so reluctantly I let him lead me into the greenhouse.

The bright moonlight filters in smoky shards through the glass above, and I have to blink several times, thinking that what I just saw isn't real, couldn't be real. I open them again, and everything around me starts to spin wildly. When I finally get my vision under control, the eerie sight encased in bluish moonlight focuses in front of me. There's a whole garden of flowers circling one of the tables, and rising above the garden, like the little statue of an angel or a sleeping princess in a fairy tale, is Karen.

My chest feels like someone is sitting on it. It hurts so bad that I can't breathe, and when I finally catch my breath my stomach starts to heave. The sickly sweet smell of flowers and death fills my nostrils and I start to gag. I run outside gasping and choking, the taste of vomit in my mouth. I look up at the sky, but the stars are too-bright pinpricks in my eyes. They're flying around my head like a flock of birds, trying to draw me up into them. I close my eyes to stop the stars from pecking out my eyes, and when I open them again, Joey is standing in front of me, smiling.

CHAPTER 7

There's so much confusion. Not just in my head, but all around me.

Joey is screaming, "You promised, Freddy! You promised you wouldn't tell! I hate you, Freddy! I hate you...hate you!" And if not for my dad and the police stopping him I think he would have hit me for the first time in my whole life.

When I called Dad on my cell phone I must have sounded hysterical, because Mom came running over to Joey's with him in tow, both the very picture of parental concern. All this week, I've been carrying this cell phone strapped to my belt, just in case I found something to report. I never dreamed I would report something like this.

Finally the police take Joey away for questioning, and while my father stays to watch the ambulance take Karen away Mom takes me home. I don't want to go home--I want to go with Joey, but Mom looks like she will drag me if I don't obey, and for the first time, ever since I got too old to get a spanking, I don't argue.

"They don't understand him, Mom. He just thought he was making her well. He didn't know she was dead. Sometimes Joey doesn't understand the difference between people and flowers."

"Joey doesn't understand a lot of things, Freddy, and you can't always protect him," she says, putting a supportive arm around my shoulders as she guides me back to our house.

It suddenly registers that my mother just called me 'Freddy' instead of 'Felicia', and I stop to stare at her for the strangeness of it. But strange doesn't seem strange anymore, not after tonight. My mother takes me straight upstairs, almost carrying me like my legs don't work right, and I stand obediently as if I were five instead of eighteen while she undresses me and gets me ready for the tub.

"A hot bath is what you need to calm you down, Freddy," she says, and I stand naked and staring off into nothing, while my mother runs the water in the tub. I can't remember the last time my mother saw me naked. It was important to me, ever since my body started to develop, not to let my mother see me without my clothes on. I was afraid she would compare my body to Angela's and find me lacking. Now it's not important anymore, just like the impressiveness of my full name isn't important to my mother anymore. She helps me into the tub, bathes me, and then dresses me in my pajamas. I wonder how she can care so little about what has happened to Joey, how she can be so calm. Then I look down at her buttoning my pajamas and notice a slight tremor in her hands, and I know she cares.

"I love you, Mom," I say as she's helping me into bed.

"I love you, too, Freddy," Mom says, wiping at the tears in her eyes.

"Will Joey be okay?" I ask, the way I used to when Joey and I were kids and I'd first begun to realize that something was wrong with Joey.

"Dad is going to the station now, Freddy. Our lawyer is meeting him there. Joey's not your responsibility; he's ours."

My mother walks out, closing the door softly behind her, and in the dark I whisper, "It's too late, Mom--you and Dad let him be my responsibility for too long. I can't stop now."

It's late when my dad gets home. I listen to the sound of his footsteps ascending the stairs, then hesitating before coming closer to knock on my door.

"Are you awake, Freddy?" he asks, his voice barely above a whisper.

"Yeah, Dad," I answer softly.

"Can I come in?"

"Uh-huh."

His tall frame blocks the light in the doorway, and I flick on the lamp by my bed.

"Is Joey home now?" I ask as my father comes to sit on the edge of my bed. He doesn't answer at first. It's like he has to find the words from a confused jumble inside his head, and once he finds them he tells me.

"They had to take him to the hospital." The words come out tired, like it takes a massive amount of effort to say them. I sit straight up, horrified.

"To the hospital? He's not sick!" I exclaim. Then, after a thoughtful pause, "Is he?" I ask, my voice small and distant.

"Not that kind of sick, Freddy. They had to put him in the mental ward. He was so out of control, they had to take him where people know how to deal with this kind of a problem."

"Joey's not crazy, Dad. He's not very smart, but he's not crazy. He's just so mad at me for breaking my promise to him. I'll explain it all to him tomorrow. He'll understand and then he'll tell the police where he found Karen. That's what happened. He was looking for her too, and when he found her, he thought he could make her better, like he does the flowers. You know how we always say that a flower isn't dead, that it just needs Joey? Well, maybe *we* were joking, but Joey believed us. He just doesn't get it when people use a figure of speech. He believes everything people say. I'll explain everything to the police, when I go with Joey to talk to them."

"It's not that simple, Freddy. They think Joey killed Karen."

"How in the hell can they think that? Joey wouldn't kill a mosquito if it sat on him and drank his blood! He did that once, you know. He just let the mosquito sit there and when it was full, it just flew away."

"Karen's parents have already told the police about the time he exposed himself to Karen. They're not going to believe anything we say. We'll have to let our lawyer handle it."

"Well, our lawyer better know that there's no law that says you can't pee, because that's all Joey was doing in front of Karen--just peeing."

My father smiles a little, and I feel the usual connection between us, that feeling that I can always make him smile. No matter what I can always soften those hard little lines around his mouth, even if it's just a little bit.

"Joey's going to be okay, Dad," I say. "It's not the first time we've had to explain about Joey. This time we'll just have to explain a little harder...that's all." I say this to convince him as much to convince myself.

"I hope so, Freddy," Dad says, kissing me on the forehead and tucking the covers around me like he used to when I was a kid.

After my father leaves my room, I turn out the light by my bed and I whisper a prayer into the darkness. "Please God, help me know what to say tomorrow. There has to be a reason why you made somebody like Joey. Help me to explain why. Help me to understand why. Help Joey understand why."

I wake up in the morning with a bird singing outside my window, a cool morning breeze coming through the open crack, brushing the curtains against the sill. I lay quiet, trying to identify what kind of a bird it is, but it's different from any I've heard before. Maybe Joey will know, and I memorize the sound so I can mimic it later at breakfast; then I remember about last night, and I think the bird flew away because I don't hear it singing anymore.

I listen for the bird, but instead I hear a crow cawing in the distance. Just like I've been hearing for the last month of mornings. I pull the covers over my head, thinking that maybe last night didn't really happen. Maybe it was all part of the nightmare that I kept waking up from. The ghostly image of her still, blue face etched on the inside of my brain. I can't stop seeing it, even with my eyes wide open and the sunlight streaming warm through my window. She looked like a wax doll, and I can't believe I'd ever seen life in that limp little body.

I get out of bed with a shiver, rubbing the backs of my arms to get rid of the goose bumps, and pad downstairs in my bare feet.

When I come into the kitchen, Mom looks up from where she's sitting at the table with Dad and says, "Good morning, Felicia."

I was right, after all; last night was a nightmare. Mom would never call me Freddy. I sit down at the table and take the glass of orange juice that Dad pours for me like he does every morning. Everything is so normal. Except for the arguing between my mother and me about what I have on, or rather, the lack of it. Mom never likes anything I wear, but today she doesn't say anything. But that's just because I'm not dressed yet. I look down at my pajamas. I never wear pajamas to bed. Mom just thinks I do. The pajamas are part of the clothes Mom always buys and I never wear. I always wear an oversized T-shirt to bed.

I study my father's face for some clue to how bad

it is.

"Did you hear anything about Joey yet?" I ask.

"It's too early, Freddy," Dad answers. "But I'll be going to the hospital in a little while. I just have to wait until Mr. Garrett can meet me there."

"You mean you have to have a lawyer with you, just to talk to Joey?"

"That's his job, Freddy, to be there."

"Can I be there, too? I have to apologize to Joey for telling on him."

"Felicia, you have nothing to apologize for. You had no other choice," my mother says, putting a plate of pancakes in front of me. Mom has no idea what I like for breakfast either. Joey always pours me a bowl of cereal.

"Dad, I have to go with you," I plead.

My father puts down his cup with a clatter and says, "Honey, you have to open the stores. I'm not going to be there, so you have to."

My dad just called me *honey*. How can I argue with that? I get up from the table with an exasperated sigh, leaving my pancakes untouched, and go upstairs to get dressed. There will be a lot of gossip going on today, that's for sure. Next to this the gossip about Erik would be a picnic.

I'm ready to go, even though I don't want to-not at all. On my way past my parents' partly open bedroom door, I see that Dad has his arms around my mother, like she needs to be consoled. I take a couple of more steps so they can't see me and I listen. I'm not the kind to eavesdrop on my parents.

I'm not interested when my mother is talking directly to me; why should I care when she's talking to someone else? But now they might be saying something about Joey, and I'm suddenly very interested in every word coming out of her mouth.

"I'm worried about her, James," my mother says, and I think she's talking about Angela. Well, that sure as hell doesn't interest me. I take a couple of more steps, ready to complete my journey down the stairs, when I hear Dad say my name. I freeze in my tracks.

"Freddy is going to be all right, honey. She's a lot stronger than you think."

Gosh, Dad just called Mom *honey*, too. He's sure into sweet talk this morning. I only hope he can sweet talk those police people and get Joey home where he belongs.

"Do you know when I brought her home last night she was shaking so hard I had to put her in the tub myself? It was like she was two years old again. She couldn't do a thing on her own, not even walk. She was in shock, James. Just when she was starting to get over Erik, and now this has to happen. There are so many times I want to tell her I understand what she's going through, how hard a first love can be, but all we end up doing is fight over what she wears. I was just afraid the teachers at school would call and complain. You have to admit, James, there were days she left the house when there wasn't much covering her ass."

My God! My mother just said *ass*, and in the

house even, where it's absolutely forbidden to swear. But I guess *ass* isn't really swearing, because it's just slang for a part of the anatomy, or for a donkey.

"You mean another indecent exposure complaint?" my father says more than asks with a little sigh.

"What was I supposed to do, James? You know how people talk. I'm just getting so damn tired of these holier-than-thou people. What about the kids who are caught screwing in cars? Why isn't anybody complaining about those kids?"

Now Mom is swearing, but she sounds mad enough to swear. I wonder what she would say if she knew I was one of those kids screwing in cars. I just never got caught, that's all.

My mother's really on a roll and she continues. "It's my fault. I should have never let her feel so responsible for Joey. She's just so good with him. It's like she makes up for what is missing in Joey. It's so easy with Angela; all she's interested in is clothes and boys, but Felicia is so--complicated."

"You mean Angela's shallow, and Freddy cares."

"I wouldn't say that," Mom says with a little pause to punctuate the next words. "But you're right about our Felicia, that she cares. She just cares too much sometimes. I want her to have fun, James. I want her to find what we did in each other, but I'm afraid with her always feeling responsible for Joey, there won't be room in her life for anything or anybody else. Remember those nights when we would sneak out after bedtime and meet behind your father's barn? Before he tore it down?"

"I remember the sex, if that's what you mean."

Great, now my dad just said sex. I'm starting to think maybe listening in wasn't the greatest of ideas, no matter how curious I am.

"I sure hope that's not what you want for Freddy, at least not for a while yet," he adds, and he sounds like my dad again.

"I want her to find love like we did. That's what I mean."

It gets real quiet after that, and then I hear the bedroom door close, the turn of the lock, and I think Mom and Dad are doing in their bedroom what they used to do behind Grandpa's barn. But heck, if they never did that, I wouldn't be here.

I sneak down the steps quickly and quietly. The last thing I want is my parents to know I was listening in on their conversation, and I run to the company van as fast as my legs can carry me. As I back out of the driveway, I look up at my parents' bedroom window and I think.

"I want what you and Dad have, too, Mom. I just don't think I'll ever find it. I'll probably end up being an old maid. All alone, except for about a million cats."

CHAPTER 8

The papers print pictures along with the headlines that describe the finding of Karen in gory detail. I was right about the gossip at work; for two days I have had to listen as people talk behind my back, unable to do anything about it. After that, Dad comes back to the store and it's his turn to listen to the gossip while I go back to working in yards, but this time by myself. Joey doesn't get to come home, and it's a week before I even get to see him. But first, I have to see the police.

They come to our house and ask me to come to the station for questioning. "Just some questions about her relationship with Joey, that's all," the one detective says. He's short and fat and has a little bald spot on the top of his head. He's not how I visualized a detective would look, but I never visualized being taken in for questioning, either.

"What kind of questions?" my mother asks. Short and fat doesn't intimidate her, and I bet if she had to, she would swear him a blue streak. That's how mad Mom looks, right now, like she'd peck the guy's eyes out if she felt she had to. It's the mother hen thing and I'm still her little chick.

"We can't explain everything, ma'am, but you don't have to worry. It will only take an hour or two at the most. You can bring her down to the station yourself, if you want. We just have a few things to clear up."

"What things?" My mother sure knows how to argue, but she's had lots of practice. She can thank me for that, and I decide to get into the conversation. At least this time my mom and I are on the same side.

"I don't mind going, Mom. If they want to know about Joey, I'll tell them. I want to tell them, Mom."

"Felicia, I don't want you being dragged into this. You've been through enough already."

"It's too late, Mom--I'm already in this up to my neck. I have to have a chance to explain. I just have to."

"I'll call my husband and we'll both bring her to the station," Mom says, and then as if to herself, she adds, "I think I'll call our lawyer, too."

"That won't be necessary, ma'am. All we're going to do is ask some questions. She's not a suspect in anything."

Now the other detective gets into the act. I know him; he's the father of one of those boys who like to screw in the backseats of cars. I know this because I was with him in one once.

Dad meets Mom and me at the station, but our lawyer doesn't make it. He's tied up in court, and my dad has a few choice things to say about that. Since we're outside our house now, I guess swearing is okay. Unless they have a law against that, too. Maybe the same one that covers peeing.

"He will be here just as soon as he can," Mom says. Mom looks at me like she wouldn't dare let me out of her sight. She's become so protective of me lately. Kind of like I've always been for Joey. But I'm grown up, and I try to tell my mother this with my eyes.

"I just don't like this. He should be here to advise us. What the hell am I paying him for, anyway?"

"It's okay, Dad," I say, my voice sounding braver than I actually feel, and I glance back a couple of times at my parents as I follow Fat-and-Bald through a door.

They offer me a soda but I don't take it. Finally after the formality of introductions, I discover that Fat-and-Bald's real name is Lou Payne, and the other guy is Frank Markowitz. They say I can just call them Lou and Frank and I say they can call me Freddy. They ask me a lot of questions about school, and I wonder why Frank just doesn't ask his son those questions, they seem so general.

"You sure you don't want a soda, Freddy?" Frank asks, popping back the tab on the can in his hand with a loud hiss. "We got coffee here too, if you don't want soda. Maybe you would like a cup of coffee?"

"No thanks," I say, trying to keep the impatience out of my voice. I want to talk about Joey, like I came here to do. Not me, not school, and for the last time, I'm not thirsty.

After a long silence, Lou asks me to tell him about my relationship with Joey.

"Joey's older than me, and he's not real smart, but I guess you know that already. Joey's smart about some things, though," I say, automatically in his defense.

"Like what kinds of things?" Lou asks.

"About outside things. You know--flowers and stuff. That's all he was trying to do, when he worked with Karen in her parents' yard. He used to tell me stuff, too, when I was little. I think it makes Joey feel good that he knows so much about nature." I get ready to tell them that Joey would never hurt Karen or any kid. I'll even tell them the mosquito story to prove how harmless he is. When I pause for a minute to choose my words carefully, because I know how important it is that I use the right words, Lou interrupts me.

"Did part of that explaining about nature include a person's body?"

"No!" I say emphatically, and I wonder what the hell he's talking about.

"Did Joey ever expose himself to you, and tell you what he wanted to do?" Lou asks.

Now I know what he's talking about, and I don't like it one bit.

"Do you announce it every time you have to pee?" I ask, tongue in cheek, crossing my arms over my chest and squinting my eyes at him.

"But Joey *did* expose himself to you, right?"

72

"Joey sometimes goes when he's working in people's yards. I never watched. I know better."

"Look, Freddy, you don't have to worry about us judging you. We just want to know the truth, that's all," Frank says, real calm-like.

"The truth is," I say, real calm-like, too, "Joey isn't very smart, I'll admit, but he would never hurt anybody. He's a really nice, trusting person who doesn't understand about certain things."

"And you want to protect him?" Lou asks again.

"Of course. I love Joey," I say with conviction.

Suddenly, Lou gets up and leaves the room real fast like maybe after all this talk about peeing, he has to go to the bathroom.

"You used to go to the same school as my son, didn't you, Freddy?" Frank asks after Lou shuts the door.

"Yes sir," I answer. At least Frank hasn't made any accusations or nasty assumptions, so I figure he deserves a 'sir.'

"Were you popular in school?"

I wonder what he means by *popular*. If it is what I think it is, I'm not going to tell him.

"I worked at the store after school and weekends, I didn't have the chance to socialize much."

"But you still had time to go out, didn't you? With boys, I mean."

"No, I don't know what you mean. What has my going out with boys got to do with Joey? That's what I'm here for, isn't it? To talk about Joey, not my going out with boys, or anything to do with that part of my private life," I finish, beginning to feel a little flushed and put on the spot.

"Sometimes kids who are sexually abused at home are promiscuous. Like Lou said, we're not here to judge you, Freddy, we just want to know the truth. That's all."

I wish Lou would come back in and do the questioning, because Frank is making me mad. Mad and ashamed, though exactly why my cheeks are burning, I can't say. At least Lou doesn't intimidate me. I think I'm as mad as Mom was, but she didn't swear. I do.

"Just what in the hell are you accusing Joey of anyway? You want to know if I'm promiscuous? Go ask your son! Or maybe he was abused at home, too."

This time it's Frank who turns red, and I think I stepped over that line that Mom is always warning me about. In an attempt to make amends, I say, "It's just that after Erik left, I wanted to get back at him-- that's all."

Lou walks in again, this time carrying a cup of coffee, and asks, "Who's Erik?"

The last person I want to drag into this is Erik, and I say, "I think our lawyer should be here now. If you have any more questions to ask, I want him in here when you ask them."

Lou looks at Frank as if for an answer, but Frank just shakes his head like he gives up and says, "That won't be necessary. We're through."

We walk back out to my parents, and I think I want to cry. I never got to explain about Joey, to tell them about the mosquito, about the kitten, about a whole lot of things. Everything important, everything I had gone over in my head to say was never even brought up, or if it had, I missed my opportunity without even knowing it existed in the first place. I try not to be too upset about this because somehow, I don't think they would have believed me anyway. They already have their minds made up about Joey, I can tell. Feeling more helpless than I ever felt in my life, I cry all the way home.

CHAPTER 9

Joey has been formally charged now with the rape and murder of Karen, and when Dad goes to see Joey he takes me with him.

Mom has to go, too. Ever since I was questioned by the police my mother won't let me near a policeman without her there. And even though it's not exactly a prison where they have Joey locked up, there are still plenty of police.

I wish Mom would stop being so protective of me. It's making me nervous, and I long for the days when we used to pit our wills against each other. That was normal.

As Dad drives the two hours to the hospital where they incarcerate mental criminals, I think that nothing will ever be normal again.

"We can sell the condo in Florida," Mom says. "We never use it anyway. That should help."

"It won't be enough, Margaret. I'm going to have to mortgage the house."

I know Mom and Dad are talking about where the money is going to come from to pay the lawyer Dad hired. Mr. Garrett isn't a defense lawyer, and the one

Dad hired is expensive. I pretend not to listen, and make a big noise turning the page of the book I've got in the back seat, even though I haven't read a word of it. It's all part of the act I have to perform in front of my parents. That I'm okay when all the while I have this pain in my stomach that won't go away.

"It's not fair, James. There would be plenty of money to take care of Joey if your father hadn't left so much to that woman." Mom always calls Grandpa's second wife that woman, even once to my grandfather's face. Mom is back to harping about the widow woman that's now living it up in Florida, while we're starving. We're not really starving; Mom just makes it sound like we are, but my dad has his usual stock answer.

"That's all water under the bridge now, Margaret. It's no use crying over spilled milk."

That usually shuts Mom up but not today.

"It was you and your mother who built up the business in the first place. If it weren't for you two talking him into expanding your father would have still been working out of that old barn until he died."

Dad laughs a little, and says, "I had to if I wanted to marry you. With all those rich guys hanging around, I didn't stand a chance."

"Oh, James, you know that isn't true. I would have married you no matter what!"

"But your father wanted you to marry that guy whose dad owned that factory. What was his name anyway?"

"Marvin Lowenstein, and believe me, even rich,

he was no bargain," Mom laughs and Dad laughs. I want to laugh, too, but I'm not supposed to be listening.

"Your mother would be turning in her grave" Mom says, "if she knew that all her scrimping and scraping, denying things for herself, just so they could have money when they retired, ended up going to that woman."

In the rear-view mirror, I see those little lines harden around Dad's mouth and I say, "One thing for sure though, from everything I've been told about Grandma, Grandpa's going to spend eternity having to listen to her give him hell."

I just swore, but Mom doesn't seem to mind. Maybe it's because she sees those little lines around Dad's mouth soften, too. I go back to my book, and this time really reading. Things are bad, but they could be worse. Mom could have married Marvin Lowenstein.

When we pull up to the hospital, even though it's not a prison, it looks like one. There are bars on the windows, along with guards and fences everywhere. Poor Joey, I think as I notice there isn't even one flower anywhere. I remember that first day I met Karen. How excited she was about those flowers she and Joey planted. I want to cry thinking of Karen, but I can't now. I'll do it tonight, though. I've cried for her every night since this terrible atrocity happened. I pray, too, just before going to sleep, that the police get the killer before another terrible murder happens.

We're led into a room with some tables and chairs in it, like it is some kind of recreation room, but I wonder what they do for recreation. The tables and chairs are the only things in it except for the guard. Like part of the furniture, the guard is always standing over us with a somber look, but somber goes good in this room. Happy just doesn't fit the decor.

Joey is brought into the room, shuffling his feet like an old man, his gray pajama-like outfit hanging on his gaunt frame. I want to put my arms around him and hug him, but the guard might think the same thing Frank and Lou did when I went in for questioning, so I just shake his hand like Mom and Dad do. Joey looks so strange, hardly like himself at all. Maybe it's because I'm not around to remind him to comb his hair, or maybe it's what he's wearing. It's not the usual overalls I'm used to seeing him in. Joey's like me, kind of plain looking, different from the rest of the family. I have always wondered with parents like Mom and Dad, how I ended up looking the way I do. I'm not exactly an ugly duckling, but I'm no swan either.

We all sit down real awkward-like at first. I rehearsed all morning what I would say to Joey, going over and over my apology in front of the mirror. Now all I can do is sit real stiff in my chair, like Joey and I are strangers.

Finally Mom says, "Are you okay, Joey? Are you getting enough to eat?"

"I'm not hungry anyway," Joey says.

I can't believe Mom would ask such a dumb question. All I have to do is look and know Joey isn't eating, no matter how much they give him. I want to cry, but I can't in front of him. He's got enough to worry about without worrying about me, and Joey would worry. He's not smart but he makes up for it in compassion. I know how much he wanted to make Karen better. I have to let him know that I understand why he did what he did, but I also want him to understand why I did what I did, too.

"Joey, I'm sorry," I say. "God, I'm just so sorry." I can't get anymore out past the lump in my throat, and Joey puts his hand over my hand that's on the table.

"It's okay, Freddy. I forgive you."

Mom reaches over and squeezes both our hands, and I think I will start bawling like a baby, but Dad changes the subject.

"If there is anything you need, just tell Mr. Garrett or Mr. Baskins, and they will see if they can get it for you. Mr. Baskins is the attorney I've hired to defend you."

"I want to go home," Joey says, tears running down his cheeks. Tears are running down Mom's, too. I'm bawling like a baby.

Dad clears his throat and says, "In a little while, Joey. That's why I hired Mr. Baskins. He's real good, Joey, and I want you to tell him everything you know."

"I don't know nothing, Dad," Joey says, and I see

the same shock in my father's eyes that's there every time Joey calls him 'Dad.' But Joey's been calling his brother that ever since his own father abandoned him.

We're not allowed much time to talk, and when we get up to leave, I do hug Joey, and I don't care anymore what the guard thinks. If he knew Joey like I do, he'd know that Joey doesn't belong here.

"If I can't go home, can I have some flowers here?" Joey asks just before we walk out.

"I'll see what I can do," Dad says. But I don't think this is a place for flowers, even if my Dad can get Joey some. They would just die in here, and if we don't get Joey out of here pretty soon I'm afraid that Joey will die, too.

CHAPTER 10

The trial is set for after Christmas, and it's still only the beginning of October. But the lawyers need time to prepare their case, both the prosecution and the defense. These kinds of things always take lots of time I guess. Besides, this could be a long, drawn-out trial due to the nature of the case, and the judge doesn't want to keep the jurors tied up for the holidays.

I go every week with either Mom or Dad to see Joey. We even celebrate Joey's birthday in this awful place. We bring in a little cake, and we have to have it X-rayed like a million times first. As if I would bake drugs or sneak a gun or some crap into it. Joey wouldn't know what to do with that stuff anyway, even if I had done something so dumb. They said it was necessary to make sure we're not smuggling *contraband*, a word I'd never heard before and could have lived my entire life without knowing what it meant. It's amazing how fast I've adapted to this terrible situation. It kind of scares me, but hey, what can I do? Dad was able to get a little plant to Joey (after they practically killed it digging around in the dirt looking for contraband, no doubt). Dad chose an African violet, one of the more hardy varieties of flowers, which Mr. Baskins brought in with him when he came to talk to Joey. Each time I come to see Joey he looks thinner and paler, less and less like himself. I always end up crying all the way home.

The days drag by and I spend a large chunk of my time working alone in our customers' yards. I rake and haul and cover until I'm exhausted, then go to class in the evening, all sweaty with dirt still caked under my nails, having no time in between for a shower.

Instead of going out of state to college, I opted for classes at the community college.

"It's cheaper," I said one day when discussing it with Mom. "They're only basic classes, anyway. When I decide on a major I'll transfer over."

At first Mom made a big fuss and a lot of racket about it, but as soon as she realized our financial situation lately isn't the greatest she stopped arguing right quick. Dad doesn't come right out and say it but I can tell we're pretty broke. We've taken out a loan to pay for inventory for the holidays, something he wouldn't do unless he absolutely had to. We also lost some of our accounts because of the scandal, but not Mrs. Davis or Erik's parents.

Once a week I work for Mrs. Davis, pulling out the dead annuals and covering the perennials, and I don't think of her as old anymore. Sometimes, she comes out and keeps me company while I work, but most importantly, she agrees with me about Joey's innocence.

"Just circumstantial evidence, that's all they've got. I just wish my husband were still alive. He'd get Joey out of there in no time."

I wish Mr. Davis were still alive, too, and about forty years younger. In his day, he was one of the most prominent and respected defense attorneys around, and I think he was a lot better than Mr. Baskins. Maybe Mr. Baskins is expensive but I don't think he's earning his money. The best evidence of this is that we're slowly going broke and Joey's still not back home where he belongs.

"Mr. Baskins says it usually takes a long time for a crime like this to come to trial, but I don't think Joey would make it if it takes too long. He keeps getting thinner every time I see him." I say this with a sob in my voice, and Mrs. Davis must understand sob because she gives me a little hug.

"By now you'd have Joey home if Mr. Davis were the attorney. One way or another, Mr. Davis would make them move up that court date even more so Joey could be home for Christmas."

That's what Mrs. Davis tells me while I work, and I hang on every word she says.

I also work in the yard where Erik used to play when he was little, and one day while digging up some plants to take in for the winter, I run across a little car, one of those Matchbox kind. It's crusted with dirt and a wheel is missing, but I still pick it up and put it in my pocket, another part of Erik that's now a part of me. Working for the Larsons' is not like working for Mrs. Davis. I rarely see Mrs. Larson. She's sickly, and always has been, but I hear that this year she's even worse.

The nights that I don't go to school, I do my homework, or go out with Michael, a guy in my algebra class. Just before class one night, at the coffee machine, he asked me to go to a movie with him, and I said no. But Michael persisted, and finally after a few more failed attempts at asking me out, I accepted. Now he's the only other person besides Joey that I hug when we part.

That's all I do though, is hug him. Sometimes a little kiss passes between us, but no tongue-in-the-mouth kissing. Despite the lack of enthusiasm on my part when it comes to making out, Michael and I get along fine. Maybe he doesn't agree with me like Mrs. Davis, that Joey's innocent, but he doesn't think he's guilty, either. While I rant and rave about the injustice of it all, he just sits there and listens, sometimes nodding his head, always just looking at me like he wishes I'd be quiet and want to kiss instead. I think all that ranting and raving gets to him because right before Thanksgiving we break up.

About the same time that Michael and I call it quits, Mrs. Larson dies. I haven't seen Erik since he left me that night after promising me he'd be true to me forever. The day of the funeral I'm sitting at the breakfast table nibbling a piece of toast with jelly, and Mom asks me if I'm going to go to the funeral service.

"No, I've got too much to do today," I reply, trying to make my voice sound natural. I know that Erik will, of course, be there, and the idea of seeing him again is just too much for me to take. My chin wobbles a little at the thought and I try to hide it by taking a sip from my glass of orange juice.

"Really, Felicia, you can't be *that* busy at the store, that you can't take at least a couple of hours off. Is she, James?" Mom asks, looking to Dad for support. Dad knows better than to get in the middle of one of our arguments and just grunts in a noncommittal way.

"I promised Carl I'd help him set up the Christmas displays. He can't do it alone," I say, hoping my Dad will agree, or at least say something in my defense.

"Erik will be there. You'll get a chance to see him."

"I don't want to see him." My voice is cold as the earth they'll be putting Mrs. Larson into.

"Don't you think it's time you got over him, Felicia? I'm sure if you go today and see him, you'll realize that it was just puppy love you two felt for each other."

I look at Mom like I want to kill her or at least throw something at her. How dare she tell me that what I feel is just some stupid kid thing, while what she and Dad did behind the barn a thousand years ago was real.

"Tell me something, Mom--did you think it was

'just puppy love' with you and Dad? Well, the only difference between Erik and me and you and Dad, is that *you* did it behind Grandpa's barn, and *we* did it behind Joey's greenhouse. Don't tell me I'm going to get over Erik, because I never will. I want to, but I can't."

Before Mom can reprimand me for speaking so harshly to her, or ask how I knew about the barn, or say anything about how I'd just admitted in front of both parents that I was no longer a virgin, I jump up so fast my chair falls over backwards.

On my way out I hear Mom say, "I ache for her, James. She's hurting inside so badly and I ache for her."

I want to go back and tell my mother not to ache for me, but to ache for Joey. At least I have them while all Joey has is blank gray walls and a crummy plant. But I've argued enough with my mother for one day. Carl and that Christmas display are waiting for me.

For most of the day, Carl and I work on setting up trees, adjusting lights, and tripping over boxes. We have closed the store today, and when the doors open tomorrow, everything better be ready for the open house. I work like there is a fire raging around me, but the only fire is the one inside me. If I sit still too long I'll think about Erik. Mom didn't know it but a part of me really wanted to go to the funeral, the part of me that still belongs to Erik. In fact, up until yesterday I was planning on it, almost looking forward to it in a strange kind of way. But then I overheard Kathy, our centerpiece designer, tell one of the clerks that she saw Erik at the airport coming in for the funeral, and that he wasn't alone.

"She's gorgeous," were the last words I heard before I went out to one of the greenhouses and hid out for the rest of the day with the crew getting the poinsettias ready to sell.

By the time the funeral is over and Dad gets to the store in the afternoon, the store looks great but Carl and I look beat.

"It looks wonderful," Dad says, granting me a small smile that makes the lines at the corners of his eyes crinkle. "You know Carl, for a guy who runs a bulldozer, you're not half bad when it comes to being creative."

"It was all Freddy. She's the creative one. I just did what I was told. I'll take driving a bulldozer and tilling up yards any day before I work with your daughter on one of these projects again," Carl says, wiping his sleeve across his forehead like he's still sweating.

"You're just getting old, Carl. Admit it," Dad says, patting him on the back, and comes to stand by the ladder where I'm perched on the second rung from the top. "You did a good job, honey. What would I do without you?"

And I get another smile from my dad. I get down from the ladder and stand in front of him.

"Don't worry Dad," I say with a hint of bitterness in my voice. "I'm not going anywhere." Then go up on the ladder again.

Dad gets the message and says, "I saw Erik." The

smile is gone now, the tiny lines at the corner of his eyes disappearing as his expression turns serious.

"How does he look?" I ask in a small voice.

"Good."

"And his girlfriend? Dad, does she look good, too?"

"Freddy, looks aren't everything. It's what's inside that counts." He's been telling me this ever since I can remember, and right now I'm not in the mood for it.

"You mean like having a beautiful heart? Don't give me that crap, Dad." I pause and look down, biting my lower lip. "Joey has a beautiful heart, and look where *he* is."

Dad just walks away, shaking his head as if I'm hopeless. I want to tell my dad that there was a time when I had a beautiful heart too.

The next day we open the store again and stay open every day of the week from nine in the morning until nine at night. At least I don't have to worry about spreading the Christmas Spirit because after that there really isn't enough spirit left in me to even fill my own body let alone to spread.

Three days before Christmas, Angela and Harold come home. Angela isn't alone though; her fiancé, Byron Hennings is with her. I think Byron and Angela make a wonderful couple. She's beautiful and he is rich, a match made in heaven. Harold comes alone; he is in between girlfriends. While Mom flutters and fluffs up the nest, I fly the coop and don't come back except to sleep, until finally we close the store at noon on Christmas Eve.

We do the traditional opening of presents on Christmas Eve, with Angela making sure we all know how expensive the gifts are that she and Byron gave us, and how expensive the engagement ring is that Byron gave her. I couldn't care less. Around ten o'clock I'm sick to death of Angela's talk of wedding dresses, wedding flowers, and wedding receptions and just generally worn out. With one last "Merry Christmas, everybody" that sounds more like a yawn than anything, I trudge up the stairs and retire to my bedroom for the night. I open the top drawer of my dresser and take out the ring Erik once gave me. I think I might even slip it on, then quickly change my mind. I turn the watch over that I had planned on giving Erik last Christmas, and run my fingers across the words engraved '*Forever and always.*' I pick up the little car I found in his yard, some of the dirt still on it.

Finally I open the locket with Erik's picture for the first time in what seems like ages. All this stuff cost less than even one of the gifts Angela gave me, but if I had the guy whose picture is in this locket, I'd be the richest girl in the world.

On Christmas Day, right after dinner, Dad and I go to take Joey his presents. They consist of a picture book of flowers from me, along with a CD of Joey's favorite songs. Dad and Mom give him the CD player. The three of us look at the picture book together and listen to the songs on the new CD player. We eat some of the pie that Mom sent along. Before we leave, I go over one more time with Joey how to put the CD in and then push the play button, as well as how to control the volume. When I ask him if he gets it, he just nods, and that has to be enough for me. Even on Christmas, Joey isn't himself--not that I blame him.

"Thanks a lot for taking the time to go with me, Dad," I say in the car on our way home.

"He's my brother, honey. Family shouldn't be alone on Christmas, no matter where they are" Dad says, then adds with a little laugh, "Besides, it was an excuse to get away from Byron Hennings for a while. He reminds me too much of someone I once knew."

"I love you, Dad," I say, thinking about how glad I am that Mom never married Marvin Lowenstein.

CHAPTER 11

The day before Joey's trial, on a cold, snowy day in January, Mom and I drive to the next county. There's too much prejudice against Joey in our own county to give Joey a fair trial. At least, that's what Mr. Baskins was fighting for all this time, and he's exuberant in his interview with the press, as he explains the why and what for of the decision. I just hope that he's as exuberant about Joey's innocence as he is about being right.

The snow stops sometime early in the morning before Mom and I leave, and it strikes me how beautiful it is outside the car window as Mom makes tire tracks in the fresh snow pulling out of our driveway. All the tree branches are covered with a light dusting of glittering white. Dad leans on his shovel and waves good-bye to us, and before we round the corner he's back to concentrating on the task at hand.

After almost five hours of driving, with me acting as navigator even though I wish I could just fall asleep, Mom pulls into the driveway of a big red brick house that has a sign in the window saying,

'Rooms for rent by the day or by the week.' I have it rented for two weeks, with the option to stay longer if I have to. I hope I don't have to.

As soon as Mom gets me settled she'll go back home for a week or until after the jury is selected, whichever happens first. Dad will try to make it whenever he can. Someone has to stay and take care of the store; I'm just glad it's not me who is stuck with that dubious pleasure. Joey's going to need me now more than ever. I plan on sitting as close behind the defense table as I can, so even though he can't always see me, he'll know that I'm there.

While I check out the room, Mom looks through the window to check out the neighborhood.

"It looks safe enough," she says turning back to face me.

"It is, Mom, and I'm going to be okay. I'm a big girl now, remember?"

"You're still the baby of the family," she says, opening up my suitcase and starting to put my things in the drawers beside the bed.

"No, Joey's the baby of the family. That's why I'm here to make sure that he won't be too scared in front of all those people. You know how he hates crowds, Mom. They make him nervous."

This particular crowd will make me nervous, too. I never thought I'd have to sit in a courtroom, except maybe for jury duty.

"I know, I know," she says dismissively, scoping out the closet before hanging my two nice skirts and sweaters on the plastic hangers inside. Mom insisted I bring them with, but I'm not going to wear them. I don't think people wear plaid skirts and cardigans, at least not people my age. Not even in a courtroom.

Mom stays the night, and lying next to each other in the queen size bed, we talk. Mom tells me about the first time she met Dad. I talk about the first time I saw Erik in school...how popular he was, and how much I liked him from the very first day. We talk a lot about our feelings, but Mom never mentions grandpa's barn and I never mention Joey's greenhouse. There are some feelings my parents have that I just don't want to hear about. I think my mother has the same opinion when it comes to Erik and me. It's late when we finally stop talking and fall asleep. We end up oversleeping and have to rush our getting ready in the morning to go to court.

Despite our late start Mom and I are already in the courtroom when they bring Joey in, shackled hand and foot. God, he looks so thin, so scared, so sad. The last time I saw Joey in a starched white shirt and trousers was when he used to go to church with us. Joey hasn't been to church with us since he got too big for Dad to handle. He fidgets too much around crowds--even around church crowds, which are much nicer than the sort found in this somber room. I catch his eye and try to give him some of my courage with a small smile, but I don't think I have any to spare, and the smile doesn't make it to my eyes. Joey gives me a little wave of acknowledgement before he sits down at the defense table, and I give a little wave back. He doesn't smile. My heart feels as heavy as a boulder and I'm afraid that I'll burst into tears at any moment. Mom senses this and squeezes my hand in support, and for the rest of the morning while the lawyers interview prospective jurors, every time a new one is introduced Mom squeezes again. By break time, I've figured out the message Mom conveys with each squeeze. If it's someone she thinks is good, it's a hard squeeze, if not so good, the squeeze is not so hard.

After a quick lunch, of which I'm able to take maybe three bites, I take Mom to the bus station where she'll catch the bus back home, and then I go back to the courthouse alone to keep up the vigil.

For the rest of the week I watch, wait and pray, while the lawyers haggle. The defense wants jurors who believe that a man is innocent until proven guilty, while the prosecution wants jurors who believe a man is guilty because the prosecution says he is, and there's a lot of wild speculating, barely controlled arguing and finally a compromise before the jury is at long last selected.

By the weekend, I feel emotionally drained and figure I need some diversion from the stress of picking and choosing, even though I'm not the one who did the choosing. It's too far to go home. Besides, Mom and Dad are planning on coming here on Sunday night. By now I know the area around the courthouse and the rooming house well enough but no other part of town, so I decide to spend the two days exploring.

I get up Saturday morning feeling pretty adventurous, refreshed after a good night's sleep, and I start my little escapade by going to the nearby shopping mall. It looks like any other shopping mall I've ever been to. I buy myself some shampoo and conditioner as I've already gone through the small travel-sizes I'd packed. There's a really neat sweater that has all the right colors to go with my hair, and I buy that too. After lunch at the food court I head for the more trendy part of town, and find the kind of shops I like: a music store, a book store, video rental store, and even a neat little thrift shop. By late afternoon I'm all explored out, and decide to go to a movie.

Anything's better than going back to my room and sitting there alone with my thoughts. On my way out of the theatre I pass a little coffeehouse type place, and take a booth in a corner. While I'm waiting for my hamburger and fries and sipping my Coke, this guy comes over and introduces himself, but first he identifies me as, "that girl that's in court everyday" and asks me what paper I work for.

I have no idea what he's talking about and lift an eyebrow in confusion, figuring he's just one of those nuts that always seem to hang around trendy parts of town. I try to ignore him. It's kind of hard to ignore someone sitting down opposite you and staring, so I do the next best thing and try to beat him at his own game.

"What makes you think I work for a paper?"

"Why else would a beautiful girl like you be there

every day except to work? I can think of a lot of places that are better than a courtroom," he says laughing, but not a serious laugh, more of a smiling laugh. Silently I agree with him, but for some crazy reason this guy is getting to me, or maybe anything is better than going to that lonely empty room waiting for me at the boarding house.

For the sake of keeping the conversation going, I respond, cool as a cucumber, "Oh yeah? Like where?"

"Like out in the Caribbean, sailing my yacht, to name one."

Now I'm laughing again, but only with my eyes. "Well, I don't have a yacht, and I don't work for a paper."

"Just an interested spectator then."

"Interested, yes; spectator, no," I reply, now wishing he'd go away. Who in the hell does this guy think he is, sitting down at my table uninvited, calling me beautiful and assuming I'm just a spectator. I've suffered this past week and I'm sure the suffering isn't going to stop, not until it stops for Joey. How can he possibly understand? What a creep!

"Family, then. You know, I kind of figured that."

Sure you did, I want to say, but just sit and sip my soda in silence.

"What is he, your brother or what?"

"Frankly, it's none of your damn business. Are you always so nosy?"

The guy starts to laugh, and as irritated as I'm getting, I have to admit that he has a nice laugh, real

97

pleasant-like, friendly, and if it weren't for his presumptuously rude behavior I'd think the rest of him pleasant, too--maybe even good- looking.

"I'm afraid it's part of my job, being nosy. I'm Jerry, and a reporter for the local paper."

He starts to extend his hand for me to shake when I say, "I don't talk to reporters," and get up to leave. My hamburger hasn't come yet, but I've lost my appetite.

"No, wait--I'm not working, now. I never work on weekends. I just recognized you from in court, and thought you might want some company...that's all."

My hamburger comes. It looks and smells really good, and I feel my stomach respond with a rumble. Somewhat reluctantly, I slip back into the booth to eat, while Jerry from the local paper tells me all about the town and the paper.

"I've told you the whole town's history and you still haven't told me your name," he says, studying me, taking me in. Like wiping my mouth with a napkin is fascinating. The way I'm picking leisurely at my fries.

"So much for a history lesson about this town," I say, dangling a fry in front of me before putting it into my mouth. "But people history is what counts now. People who judge other people, and people who write about judging other people."

"My mother always told me not to tell strangers our secrets. I would hate to disobey my mother," Jerry says with a smile full of pearly white teeth.

Now that I'm done eating and ready to leave, I

say, "Felicia Francine, but everybody calls me
Freddy. And my mother always told me not to talk
to strangers--secrets or otherwise."

"In that case, I think we should get to know each
other better. How about lunch tomorrow? My treat,
of course. I'm on an expense account."

"I thought you said you don't work on weekends,"
I reply, a little smile tugging at the corners of my
mouth. I don't want to encourage him.

"I can always ask you a question to make it all on
the up and up." Another flash of perfect teeth.

"What kind of question?"

"Are you married?"

"No! Are you?"

"No! I thought I might once, but I was too
young," he says with a kind of sigh. I want to say, I
know exactly how that goes, but instead I ask him
how old he was when his almost-marriage had taken
place. He doesn't look to me like he's recovering
from a broken heart, so it must have been a while
ago.

"About five, but my mother wouldn't let me leave
home."

I smile, in spite of myself.

"Then you do have a mother. Funny, I thought
you were hatched from an egg."

Jerry laughs again. I'm beginning to like that
laugh. Actually, I'm beginning to like him.

"A father, too. Patrick O'Hara."

"So your name is Gerald O'Hara." I say,
thoughtfully looking up at the ceiling as if the answer
I'm searching for is written on it. "It sounds

familiar."

"My mother came from Down South. She was a real fan of *Gone with the Wind*."

"You're lucky your last name isn't Butler, or she would have named you Rhett."

"Or born a girl; she would have called me Scarlet."

I giggle a little and say, "My mother almost married a Marvin Lowenstein. Can you imagine being Felicia Francine Lowenstein?" I ask, wrinkling my nose in distaste.

"Lowenstein's not so bad."

"It's not the name, but the guy. My Dad says he was rich."

"What did your mother say?"

"That he was no bargain, even rich."

"So what is your last name?"

"Harrison."

"How did you end up being called Freddy?"

"My sister couldn't pronounce Felicia when she was little. Actually, there was this kid named Freddy in pre-school and she liked him. My sister was boy crazy from an early age."

"How early?"

"Five."

"That's a dangerous age, five. What was your dangerous age?"

"I haven't reached it yet," I say with a mischievous smile, getting up to go to the cash register to pay. Jerry is faster than me and beats me to the bill. I don't protest when he ends up paying for my food along with his.

On our way out we decide on the restaurant where we'll meet for lunch tomorrow, and later that night back in my room, I fall asleep wondering just what in the hell made me tell this Gerald O'Hara guy I'd go out on a date with him. No, it was never specified that's what it is, but when a guy asks a girl out to lunch, there's no need for specifics. If Mom knew I was making dates with strangers in a strange town, she'd be back here faster than I could say, "But I'm a big girl, now."

For my date with Jerry, I wear my new sweater along with my good pair of black slacks. My red hair is washed and shiny, not to mention that my freckles aren't so noticeable anymore, not with make-up covering them. I must look pretty good because when I sit down across the table from Jerry he says, "You look pretty this afternoon."

"So do you," I say, and we both burst into laughter. It feels good to laugh. We order quiche in little individual pie tins and drink flavored coffee out of thick ceramic mugs.

I like Jerry. He's easy to be with. He listens when I talk, but I make sure it's just casual conversation and not ranting and raving. Experience has taught me that the latter gets me nowhere with members of the opposite sex. Besides, he's a reporter, and I'd hate to see our family secrets in the local paper. It's better to be safe than sorry. After lunch, Jerry takes me to the older section of town where there are lots of antique stores, and we discover that we both like old poetry in old books, and we share a fondness for the way old things smell, especially books.

Sometime in the afternoon I tell him I have to go because my parents will be coming soon, and Jerry tells me that he's anxious to meet them.

"Not this time," I say, doubting there ever will be a time, but you never know. We don't hug or kiss or even shake hands when we part. We just say, "See you in the morning," and that's that.

CHAPTER 12

When we get to the courthouse Jerry is already sitting on one of the long benches, holding a place for us. I go in first and sit beside Jerry while Mom and Dad follow, sliding in next to me. There's a lot of whispering and shaking hands, introducing my parents to Jerry.

When things settle down Mom whispers in a voice loud enough for half the courtroom to hear, "He looks nice enough, Felicia. Where did you meet him?"

Before I can answer with more than a look they bring Joey in and I wonder just what in the hell they did to him over the weekend. He doesn't wave like he did all last week; he doesn't even look at us. He seems like he's in another world, and it's definitely not in the same one I'm in. I must look upset because Jerry takes my one hand and squeezes, while Mom takes my other. Dad just clenches his fists so hard his knuckles turn white.

The first witness the prosecution calls is the sheriff who was one of the first to respond after Dad's call. He describes what he saw when he got to Joey's greenhouse so vividly that the jurors lean

103

forward in their seats, making sure not to miss a single word, and making me see everything all over again: the eerie blue glow of the moon on Karen's lifeless face, the flowers arranged so carefully around the still little body on the table. I shiver and Jerry rubs the back of my hand with his thumb, bringing me back to the here and now. I'm glad he's here, and I turn to give him a look of appreciation.

Later, a collective shudder resonates throughout the courtroom as pictures from the supposed crime scene are passed around as evidence. Each time the prosecution asks another question and the sheriff answers I dig into Jerry's and Mom's hands. Dad just digs into his own, face blank, eyes glassy.

As soon as the prosecution has established the scene of the crime, Mr. Winters, the coroner, is sworn in to put in his professional two cents' worth on the rape and murder. *Alleged* rape and murder I find myself thinking, as my face grows hot with anger. I stare helplessly at the back of poor Joey's head and wish they would hurry up and call *me* up to the stand to testify on Joey's behalf. I'd set them straight.

"And what was the cause of the death of the victim?" the prosecuting lawyer asks in a voice so casual he could have been asking the time of day.

"Strangulation," Mr. Winters answers matter-of-factly, like he is answering with the time of day.

"Can you describe to the jury how you came to that conclusion?"

"Well, first of all, there weren't any marks on her body." the coroner says, shifting his weight in the witness's chair, taking a long pause, like he's taking pains to explain things in a nonscientific way so the jury will understand.

"Except the one around her neck, left by a rope of some kind. No other fatal wounds were in evidence."

"Are you saying there were no signs of struggle then?"

"I'm saying that whomever the deceased went with, it was someone she must have known, must have trusted, because there were no bruises on her body indicating that a struggle had taken place."

I hate how they always refer to Karen as *the victim* or, even worse, *the body*. She had a name, damn it, I want to say, but instead I just clench my teeth and try my best to maintain composure even though below my calm exterior my blood is boiling, my heart thudding so hard against my chest I'm surprised the entire room doesn't hear it.

At this, Mr. Baskins jumps up with an objection saying, "Your Honor, that's pure conjecture on his part. Just because there were no bruises present on the body doesn't necessarily imply the deceased knew her abductor."

The judge sustains the objection, telling the jury to disregard that remark, but I can see on their faces that the damage is done. I think the prosecutor sees that, too, and goes back to questioning with a self-satisfied look on his face.

I glare daggers at the smug son-of-a-bitch from

my seat, wishing I could get up there and punch his lights out, right here in front of God and everyone.

"Mr. Winters, you said that the victim was strangled by some sort of rope. Were you able to determine when examining the marks, what kind of a rope it may have been?"

"I sure could. In fact, there were still some fibers embedded in the flesh of her neck."

"And what did those fibers indicate?"

"That the deceased was strangled by kind of a rough twine, about an eighth of an inch in diameter. It wasn't thick, but it was strong, very durable; at least, strong enough to choke someone to death."

The prosecutor goes to his table and comes back with a piece of rope in a clear plastic bag labeled "Exhibit E" and holds it up for the coroner to inspect.

"Would you say the murder weapon could have been something like this?"

Mr. Winters looks at the rope and is allowed to take it from the bag so that he can get a feel for it. He holds it for a minute, rubbing it between his fingers while examining it, then says, "I would say it would be exactly like this."

"Have you ever seen a rope like this before? Now, take your time. I wouldn't want any conjecture on your part," this last with a mocking look in Mr. Baskins' direction. The defense lawyer's eyes narrow and his fists clench in anger, like he was just dealt a swift blow to the face, but the judge lets it pass.

"I sure have seen that type of rope before. I just

got through tying up all my plants with it this fall. I
bought it at the garden store. Works real good, too."

The prosecutor dismisses the coroner, but before
Mr. Winters steps down, he says one more thing. "I
forgot to mention something, and it's something
important. There were marks on her wrists identical
to the kind on her neck, with the same fibers
embedded in her flesh. I thought, maybe, whoever
assaulted and killed her tied her hands behind her
back, so that she wouldn't struggle while he raped
her."

The judge admonishes the coroner for talking
after being dismissed, and the prosecutor calls
another witness, though it's clear that he's glad Mr.
Winters decided to add that bit of information, even
after he'd been dismissed.

About the time I feel like I can't take anymore, the
court is adjourned for the day, and Dad leaves for
home looking more worn-out than ever. Jerry takes
Mom and me out to eat, but none of us is hungry.
It's real quiet in the car, except for Jerry, who tries to
make polite conversation. It's obvious Mom and I
don't want conversation, polite or otherwise, so
eventually he gets the message and shuts up, his face
as tired-looking as ours. He stops at one of those
places where you can buy groceries and gas, carrying
a jug of milk back out with him after paying for the
gas. When Jerry drops us off at the rooming house
we say a polite, "Good night," then, with hearts
heavy as lead Mom and I trudge up the two flights of
steps to my room.

In silence we get ready for bed, so different from the last time Mom was here when we talked long after we'd gotten into bed. This time it's not until we're in bed and tucked under the covers that I finally say something. Maybe it's the dark, or just the comfort of hearing Mom breathing so close to me, but the words tumble out of me like a flood after a dam bursts.

"I'm so scared for Joey. I've been watching the faces of the jury, especially when they looked at the pictures of Karen lying on that table surrounded by flowers."

I have to pause for a moment to get the image out of my mind before I continue into the darkness.

"Then the coroner, talking about the rope and everything. Joey and I use that kind of rope all the time in peoples' yards. We sell it at our store. Joey even has some in his greenhouse."

"I know--I know," Mom says, like she always does when she agrees but won't go into detail.

"But just because Joey has some of the rope in his greenhouse doesn't mean he used it to strangle Karen or tie her up or anything. *Anybody* can get that rope. We sell lots of it, and so do a lot of other places!" My voice becomes higher- pitched the more agitated I become.

"I know--I know," Mom repeats. She's beginning to sound like a broken record and for some reason that infuriates me even more. I just don't understand how she can sound so calm, so almost indifferent at a time like this.

"What are we going to do?" I practically screech out of sheer desperation. "How are we ever going to make them understand about Joey?"

I'm close to tears now.

"Right now, there is nothing we can do. We have to wait for our turn, until Mr. Baskins can do the questioning."

"I don't like Mr. Baskins, Mom. I think he's more interested in his image and making money than he is interested in proving Joey's innocence. Did you notice how Joey looked today, Mom? He looked like they had him doped up or something, and when I mentioned it to Mr. Baskins during the break, he said that Joey was agitated over the weekend and the doctors had to give him a little something. They gave him a lot more than a little, Mom--Joey looked like a zombie."

"I'll talk to Mr. Baskins tomorrow, Felicia. I'm not sure what I can do, but I'll talk to him. Now let's get some sleep."

It's quiet for a while, but my mind won't shut up, and I turn back toward Mom and say, "I'm worried about Dad, too. I think his ulcer is acting up. I saw him take his ulcer medicine at least twice today."

"Dad has a lot on his mind."

"That's why you should go home, Mom. I think you should take care of him. He doesn't eat right when you're not there."

"But I can't leave you here all alone."

"I won't be alone; Jerry will be here with me."

It's quiet again for a spell, then Mom says, her voice comforting like when I was a kid and afraid of the boogie man, "Do you like him, Felicia?"

I find myself saying yes, and I don't even have to think about the answer before I give it.

"I like him, too," she says. "But this time don't make the same mistake you did with Erik."

"Don't worry," I say. "There are no greenhouses here."

In the dark I hear my mother sigh, then the slow, even breathing of someone asleep.

The next day we go through the same ritual of sit and listen. Only now the prosecution calls to the stand a doctor to explain Joey's 'condition,' that is, the fact that Joey's not very smart, but, unlike us, the doctor gives it a name. There are a lot of doctors who explain Joey's 'condition,' like maybe the first one might be lying, but certainly not a dozen of them.

In the end, they're all asked the same question: "Does the defendant have the mental capacity to think like an adult?"

"No," is the answer.

"Does the defendant have the physical capacity of an adult such as sexual desire?"

"Yes," is the answer, and I'm sure that if it weren't for Jerry and Mom holding my hands tight, I'd jump up and kick those doctors in their "sexual capacity."

During break Mom talks to Mr. Baskins. I'm not sure what she says, but I think she told him that I would be a good alternative to whatever drugs they've been giving Joey to calm him down because by some miracle Mr. Baskins gets the go-ahead. We're informed that before we leave and Joey is taken back to be incarcerated we'll be allowed some time to talk with him. We're still in the courthouse in one of the rooms, and Mr. Baskins is standing looking out the window when Joey is brought in.

The moment he sees us, the first thing he says is, "I wanna go home," his voice quiet and sad.

First Mom hugs Joey, then I do, and I can feel the sharpness of his bones poking me as he hugs me back. Joey has lost a lot of weight, and I already know the answer when Mom asks, "Are you getting enough to eat, Joey?"

"I'll eat at home," Joey replies.

I say, "We can't take you home right now, but in a little while you can come home. We'll have a party then, Joey. Won't we, Mom?"

Mom nods, and I continue. "We'll throw a big party like it's your birthday. We'll even buy you presents. Would you like that, Joey?"

Joey's eyes light up for the first time in a long time, and Mom says, "Of course we'll have a party, and I'll make all your favorite foods, but until then you have to eat here."

"Can I have ice cream and a birthday cake at my party?"

"A chocolate birthday cake with all kinds of frosting flowers," I say with a smile. "But Mom's right. For now, you have to eat and behave where they take you. Do you understand me, Joey? You can't fidget or get mad or anything. You have to do what they say."

"But there's too many people, Freddy. I don't like all these people around me. Maybe if I can sit with you I'd feel better."

"You can't sit with me, Joey," I kind of scold, but only kind of. "You have to sit next to Mr. Baskins."

"But I don't like Mr. Baskins. He smells," Joey whispers in a loud Joey kind of whisper. I see Mr. Baskins turn red and I think I might laugh. Mr. Baskins sweats a lot, and when he sweats he smells, but only Joey has the innocent nerve to say it. I'm afraid Joey's comment isn't going to endear him to Mr. Baskins, so I change the subject, fast.

"Do you look at the picture book I brought you for Christmas, Joey?"

"Yes, but the plant died. I'm not there to keep it alive, so I think it died."

He fidgets nervously with a button on his shirt and looks down at the floor and I feel so bad for him. How can people even think him capable of hurting a human being when he feels this guilty about letting a plant die?

"I'll get you a new one when you get home. It's going to be okay, Joey, and in a little while you'll be home."

I want to believe the words that come almost automatically out of my mouth as much as I want Joey to.

When it's time to leave, Mom and I both hug Joey again, and when we go out into the hall, Jerry is waiting for us.

"I thought I'd make you ladies supper tonight

instead of going to a restaurant. You haven't lived until you've tasted my spaghetti," Jerry says with a wink, walking us to his car. I wonder what Joey is having for supper tonight. Not that it matters; he probably won't eat it, anyway.

Jerry and I work in his kitchen, or more accurately, Jerry works and I watch him, while Mom checks out the neighborhood.

"It's nice," Mom says turning back from the window. "A peaceful and quiet-looking neighborhood."

"It is, but when I was a kid I thought it was *too* quiet. This is the house I grew up in."

"Are your parents still alive?" Mom asks.

"My mother and father have both passed away and I inherited the house. It's small, I suppose, but it's big enough for me."

"It's lovely," Mom says, then goes into the living room to check out the bookcase. As far as Mom is concerned, you can tell a lot about a person by the books he reads.

The kitchen is small and I keep getting in Jerry's way when I help set the table. I don't think Jerry minds, though, because there is one time when we collide that it looks like Jerry might kiss me, and for a moment I think that he's actually going to do it. But, kissing in front of a girl's mother isn't exactly the right way to earn points with said mother, so we both just laugh, rubbing the parts of our bodies that we bumped, and Jerry announces that supper is ready.

Dinner is delicious and we all eat until we're

stuffed with salad, breadsticks, and spaghetti, with vanilla ice cream and hot fudge for dessert. Later Jerry and I do the dishes while Mom dozes by the fireplace. We play gin rummy until about nine o'clock, then Jerry takes us home, and again the thought occurs to me that if Mom weren't sitting in back, Jerry would lean over and kiss me goodnight.

Mom and I have our usual conversation in bed, the dark wrapped like a blanket around us as we talk. It's amazing the things you might say to someone in the dark that you wouldn't say in broad daylight. I guess it's because you feel safer with the dark hiding your expression from scrutiny.

"They're making him out to be an animal, Mom. Like he has no feelings, just urges. Like Joey doesn't care, but he does. Joey cares a lot."

"That's just strategy, Felicia. The prosecutor is just doing his job."

"Were those two detectives that questioned me just doing their job, too? Do you know that they were trying to get me to say that Joey tried to do things to me? That I was sexually abused by him?"

"Your dad was worried they might try something like that. That's why he didn't want you talking to them without our lawyer."

"Have you any idea how that makes me feel? How mad it makes me?"

"I know how mad it makes me, Felicia, but getting mad doesn't help Joey. We have to stay calm, like you told Joey to, remember?"

"It's just so hard, Mom. I never dreamed we'd be put through something like this. Not in a million years."

"We could have not gone to trial, Felicia. Our lawyer told us that Joey is incompetent to stand trial. Maybe we should have let them put Joey in the hospital and spared him from all this."

"From what, Mom? He's in the hospital now and he hates it. He's innocent, Mom, and we have to prove it, and only a jury trial can do it. We have to bring him home Mom."

And my voice breaks with the next words. "He'll die, even in a hospital. There are no flowers or dirt to dig in, mom. He can't be put in a place with bars on the windows. With no frogs or fish or any of that nature stuff."

"We have to pray, Felicia, that's all we can do now."

"You mean like when I prayed Erik would come home? Well, he came home all right, with his girlfriend, and she's beautiful, Mom. The people who went to the funeral said she is."

"There are, different kinds of beauty Felicia, and it's not all on the outside."

"You mean like a beautiful heart? Well, I used to have a beautiful heart, Mom. Joey taught me that and I used to think that if people would only let Joey show them how, they would have beautiful hearts, too. Do you know that Joey loves butterflies? He'd watch them for hours because he thought they were so beautiful, then one day he found one lying on the ground, and he picked it up and set it on a leaf on a bush and sat watching it so nothing would happen to it. I got tired of watching and went for a ride on my bike, and sure enough, when I came back, there was Joey, still watching it. All of a sudden, like Joey willed it to be O.K., it flew away and you know what his explanation was?"

"No, I don't, Felicia. Sometimes Joey says things I don't always understand."

"He said the butterfly was probably tired and had to rest."

"Maybe it was, Felicia, and I think we should get our rest now, too. It's going to be a long day tomorrow."

"Yeah, all those jackass lawyers arguing is tiring. They're so damn stupid."

"Felicia! You shouldn't swear like that. Not if you want God to hear your prayer."

"I don't think God hears my prayers anyway, because if He did He'd never let this happen to Joey."

I hear the usual sigh after I rant and rave, then Mom says, totally changing the subject, "That was nice of Jerry to ask us for supper. I notice he reads some of the classics, too. None of that trashy stuff."

"You mean like Harry reads."

"Harold doesn't read trash anymore, Felicia."

"No, he reads computer manuals. I think he's in love with his computer. That's why he can't keep a girlfriend." I say this with a little self-satisfied laugh.

Mom sighs again, and after a while with everything being quiet except for the sound of her breathing; I can tell she's fallen asleep, leaving me to my thoughts. I lie awake, thinking of Jerry and the kiss that almost happened. Would it be as nice as Erik's kiss? As long as my mother is here, I guess I'll never find out.

CHAPTER 13

In the morning Mom tells me she's decided to go back home right after court is adjourned, that she's worried about Dad.

"You'll be all right, won't you Felicia?"

"Of course, Mom. I'm a big girl, now. I can take care of myself. Besides, I have a friend here now. A guy who lives in a 'nice quiet neighborhood,'" I say with a little laugh, but Mom doesn't think it's funny.

"That's just it; he must be quite old to own a house and look at the job he has. I think he's too old for you, Felicia."

"Mom! He's just a friend. I am not planning on marrying him."

"But I don't want you to do anything foolish. It took you a long time to get over Erik. Maybe he's divorced; he's too good-looking to be that old and not married. He just hasn't told you."

"I'll ask him next time I see him. His age, his marital status, even his social security number, if it will make you feel better, okay?" I say, hurrying my mother out the door, not wanting to be late for court.

Joey expects me to be there to wave. I'm his anchor, his rock. Besides, this conversation with my mother is making me nervous. I haven't argued with Mom in a long time and I don't want to start again now.

There's a forecast of snow on the television. A really big storm is blowing in and the first signs of it hit us as we walk to the courthouse. I tug my collar up around my neck while I pull my wool cap down around my ears. Mom struggles with a wool scarf draped over her head that the sharp, icy wind is determined to blow away, taking us along with it. We stamp the snow off our boots and blow on our fingers the minute the warm air of the courthouse hits our faces.

Today is the day that Karen's parents are supposed to testify, but the prosecutor barely gets Mr. Clayton sworn in when the judge takes one look out the window and decides to call the whole thing off until tomorrow, or at least until the town can dig itself out.

After Mom and I talk to Joey, another tearful "I wanna go home," from him, and another promise of "soon, Joey," from me, Jerry and I take Mom to the bus station to go home before the weather gets any worse.

"Promise me you won't go out if it gets too bad, Felicia. You can eat at the rooming house. I've already talked with the landlady and she said you're welcome to eat with them."

"I promise, Mom. Besides, it'll give me a chance

to read that book I brought with me. I'll be able to get caught up with some of my letter writing, too."

"Well, just make sure you're bundled up if you do have to go out, but you shouldn't have to."

"I know, Mom, I know. I'll curl up with a good book until this all blows over. Call me on my cell phone when you get home," I say while the bus driver waits for my mother to take that step up into the bus.

"I love you! And tell Dad I love him!" I yell with a wave as the bus drives off, leaving a cloud of smelly exhaust in its wake. I wrinkle my nose in disgust behind the buttoned-up collar of my coat. It helps block the wind but it sure doesn't block the smell.

When we get back into the car, Jerry is laughing and I give him a "what's your problem" look.

"What's so funny? Haven't you ever heard a girl tell her mother she loves her?"

"I never heard a girl tell her mother she's going to curl up with a good book and mean it."

"And that's exactly what I'm gonna do. You heard me promise her."

"But I didn't hear you promise *where* you'd curl up. How about by a nice cozy fire, logs glowing in the hearth, wind blowing outside, and good company all around."

"Okay, I get the part about the wind blowing, but where am I going to find a fire and good company?" I ask, my voice sounding innocent, but not so innocent that it's unbelievable.

"I'll take you there," Jerry says with a little smile

playing across his lips, and takes off.

When we get to his house, the wind already blowing drifts of fluffy white all around us, I get out of the car and ask, "How many bedrooms do you have?"

"Three."

"Good," I say into the wind, hoping Jerry hears me. "Because I'd hate to see you sleeping on the couch just because you offered a poor lonely person your bed."

"Maybe we can share."

"In your dreams," I say, stepping up onto the porch, stomping the snow from my boots before going into the house. Jerry takes my coat and hangs it up in the closet, then starts a fire in the fireplace. By the time I have some water on for some instant hot chocolate there's a blazing fire crackling pleasantly in the fireplace. It gives the house a cozy, homey feeling. A little nest for waiting out a cold winter night or nights, depending on the storm that's starting to create some serious drama outside the window.

We are sitting on the floor with our feet propped up close to the fire and drinking hot chocolate when Jerry takes my cup out of my hand and kisses me. It's a nice kiss, not the tongue-in-the-mouth kind that guys, at least the guys I've been with, are so fond of, and when we move apart, he tells me, "I've been wanting to do that since the first day I saw you in court."

I stare into the fire, the wood hissing and

sputtering, thinking that Jerry's kiss was nice, but nothing like Erik's.

"Look Jerry, I've just gotten out of a relationship with someone, and I was hurt pretty bad." The wood in the fireplace falls toward the opening, making sparks fly. Jerry's up in a flash, poker in hand, pushing the logs back in place.

When he sits back down again I continue.

"I guess what I'm trying to say is, I don't want to get involved with anyone just yet."

Jerry sits quiet for a while then says, "I won't ask you to do anything you don't want to. I want you to trust me, Freddy. I won't ever hurt you. I promise."

"My mother will be happy to hear that. She thinks you're too old for me, and too good-looking not to have been married at least once," I say as I grab a pillow, first thumping it, then jamming it under my head. "How old are you, Jerry?"

"Twenty-five and never been married, not even once," he states with one of his signature grins.

"My mother thinks you're older because of your job."

"I worked summers for the paper while going to school. I just started full time. I can show you my driver's license if you don't believe me."

"It's not me, it's my mother. I believe you, even that part about almost getting married once."

Jerry lays his head on the pillow next to me, and together we listen to the wind howl in the chimney. Around seven o'clock, after my mother calls, Jerry warms up the spaghetti left over from the night before and we eat on little tray tables while watching television. We watch "The Late Show". And even "The Late, Late Show." Then, while Jerry goes to his bedroom muttering a brief "Good-night" as he disappears down the dark hallway, I go to my designated bedroom, two doors down from his.

The next day, while the rest of the world digs itself out of the snow, Jerry and I play in it like we are kids on a snow day. We build a snowman, slide down a nearby hill on a sled borrowed from one of the neighbor kids, and walk in the park. The world around us is so clean it's almost a shame to step on and mar such pristine white. It is a wedding cake of white frosting, with trees and bushes coated in sparkling sugar for decoration. Jerry and I struggle through the fluffy mounds, leaving our tracks behind. I walk under the branch of an evergreen heavy with snow and Jerry shakes it. The snow cascades down on top of me, knocking me off my feet. Jerry reaches out a hand to help me up, but his chivalry is too late; he needs to be punished. I pull him down and try to rub snow into his face but all I get out of it is snow in mine and him rolling on top of me. We wrestle with him still on top, then our eyes meet and everything changes.

It's a meeting of hearts first and then of physical attraction. Jerry kisses me again. I'm beginning to like his kisses more each time we kiss, just like I'm beginning to like Jerry more the longer I'm with him
. After the streets are cleared and Jerry has his driveway plowed out by one of his friends who has a

big plow on the front of his truck, we drive to the rooming house to pick up some clothes for me. I meet the landlady in the downstairs hall.

"I thought you were going to have your meals with us. I knocked on your door last night, but nobody answered," she says, looking confused.

"I'm sorry if I put you out, but court won't be convened again until Monday, and I've decided to spend the weekend with a friend."

Before she can say anything more, I take my suitcase and run out to Jerry who is waiting in the car. As we drive away I see the landlady is looking out the window. I can only imagine what my mother is going to say when she finds out about me not reading that book like I promised I would.

We start out the evening like we did the night before, except for the spaghetti--that we'd finished last night. Jerry makes us soup out of a can for dinner. There's a nice warm fire going, lighting the room with an orangish, welcoming glow. The pillow is under our heads when Jerry gets up on one elbow and, leaning over me, studies me for a while.

"You have beautiful eyes," he says, real romantic-like.

I try to joke the romantic out of the words and say, "You mean to go with my beautiful heart?"

Jerry doesn't take it as a joke. He doesn't have the background of arguments I've been having with myself lately and, still romantic, he says, "Your eyes are the window to your heart."

Then slowly, he lowers his head and kisses me,

but this time it's a tongue-in-the-mouth kind. I respond like I never dreamed I ever would again by doing what I promised my mother I wouldn't. Reaching down I touch what I know my hand will find. Technically, my promise only covered not doing it behind a greenhouse. A throaty moan escapes throughout my whole body, and Jerry takes that as a sign to go farther. Before I know it we're lying in one pile, and our clothes are heaped in another. Our bodies make shadows on the ceiling as we move together.

Then, just before he reaches climax, his voice hoarse with passion, Jerry says, "I love you, Freddy."

"I love you, too," I say, wrapping my legs around him tighter, feeling his warmth flow into me.

Later, when we're lying cozy together under the generous folds of a down comforter, our limbs all tangled around each other, Jerry traces a gentle finger along my mouth and asks, "Did you mean it when you said you loved me, or was it just the passion talking?"

"Did *you* mean it?" I ask.

"Every syllable."

"Me, too," I say with a smile in my voice, once again reaching down to touch what started this all in the first place, and wonder what my mother would say if she knew how I was spending my snowed-in weekend. I just hope she never asks me how the book was.

CHAPTER 14

The wind blows all weekend, howling in the chimney and rattling the windows. Huge drifts of snow pile up in the yard, burying the bushes as well as any cars unfortunate enough to be left out on the street. Just about the time everybody gets dug out from the first blast we're hit with another, only this time even worse. Jerry and I brave the storm once to go grocery shopping and to the drugstore. I'm back on the pill.

We hibernate inside like contented bears as the storm rages outside. Sometimes when I lay by the fireplace next to Jerry, I feel guilty that I'm here, all cozy and warm, while Joey is locked up. I ease my guilt in Jerry's arms.

"Do you love me?" I ask, looking into his bright eyes, made even brighter by the fire.

"I love you," he answers with certainty, then sets out to prove it. We make love a lot, and it's nothing like when I did it just to get even with Erik. There sure is a big difference between just fucking and making love.

Jerry talks about us getting married. He spins this fantastic tale about how he's going to become a

126

famous reporter at some big paper, and how Joey is going to be found innocent, and then he can come and visit us whenever he likes.

"He can even live with us, once we get a place where he can grow flowers."

I love Jerry when he talks like this, and I set out to prove it, too. When the storm blows over, leaving the town completely buried beneath a thick blanket of white, I'm torn between wanting to stay snowed in with Jerry and wanting to get on with proving Joey's innocence.

By Monday morning, the streets are all plowed. People have dug their vehicles out again, and it's back to business as usual.

Every day for the rest of the week I sit next to Jerry on a bench right behind the defense table, and I wave to Joey when they bring him in. Every day I sit there and listen to more damning testimony against Joey, feeling so helpless I could just scream. It's been arranged so that I'm always able to talk to Joey after court is adjourned, and like a broken record, I tell him that everything is going to be okay. Despite my best efforts to convince him I don't think he believes me, even though he always says, "I know, Freddy." I don't even believe myself, though I wish more than anything that I could.

Back at home, while Jerry writes his column about the trial and e-mails it to the paper, I give my report to Mom over my cell phone. I always end it with, "I love you guys. How's Dad doing?"

Then Mom always answers, saying, "The doctor

wants him to go to the hospital to get checked, but you know your father. He says he can't, that somebody has to take care of the store."

By now the guilt is piling up in me just like the snow did during the storm. If it isn't about Joey, it's about Mom, and now about Dad. I should be there to help. I feel like a bad person.

"In a couple of weeks everything will be fine, Mom," I say with as much conviction as I can muster, then quickly hang up before my conscience makes me do something I'd regret later, like move back to the rooming house.

The phone conversations with my mother all sound so fake and rehearsed, I really dislike myself for it. But if I sounded as upset as I really felt she would only worry more, and the last thing I want to do is to make things worse. I'm calm and in control until Friday, when finally I can't stand pretending anymore, and I'm back to my ranting and raving. Jerry handles it much better than the last guy I went out with. I think I needed an older guy like Jerry, someone with maturity who isn't intimidated by my venting, and who wants more from me than just sex. I wish I could explain this to my mother who isn't too keen on the age difference between Jerry and me. Not that she's aware of the extent of our relationship. Not yet.

On Friday, Mr. Baskins has his turn to defend Joey. He makes it sound like Joey did it, but that he's not to blame, society is, for not putting him someplace safe in the first place. I beg Dad to get another attorney. I beg Mr. Baskins to let me testify so I can tell the jury how harmless Joey really is. Dad says it's too late to get another lawyer, and Mr. Baskins says the prosecutor will tear me to pieces, but he's wrong. I'm already in pieces. Every day a little more of me is torn off, leaving Jerry to try and put me back together.

After calling my mother half a dozen times on Saturday complaining about Mr. Baskins, Mom and Dad come to see for themselves. While I stay at the rooming house, my parents stay with Jerry, and before they arrive, we rush around his house to erase any trace of me living there.

It's late Sunday evening when my parents finally pull their Cadillac into the driveway at Jerry's. Once they're settled in Jerry takes me back to the rooming house.

"I'll figure out some excuse just before we go to bed so I can leave and come to you," Jerry says, helping me carry into the room the stuff we stowed in the car before my parents came.

"Maybe you'll get into my room, but what if the landlady catches you sneaking out at a time when you shouldn't be sneaking out?"

"I'll climb out your window."

"Three stories up?" I look at him incredulously. "You'll kill yourself."

"But I'll die happy," he says with a smile.

"We'll just have to wait until they leave."

"Or we can get married--now."

"Spending my honeymoon in a courtroom isn't exactly how I dreamed I'd spend it. Besides, my mother will be heartbroken if she can't see her daughter walk down the aisle in a white dress."

"She'll be more heartbroken if you're pregnant and not married."

"I'm not pregnant."

"But you can say you are, and I don't think the dress will matter so much after that."

"Jeez, Jerry! Sometimes your logic doesn't make any sense."

"At least my logic is better than the prosecutors'," Jerry says with a little laugh, pulling me to him to give me a goodnight kiss.

"I love you," he says.

"I love you, too," I reply. Then, after a few false starts Jerry reluctantly pulls away and walks out. I watch out my window, and when he turns to look up, I wave. I'm going to have to tell Mom and Dad about Jerry, about our plans to get married, but all that can wait until tomorrow. Right now, it's time for bed.

I don't sleep very well and wake up more than once reaching for Jerry, but only touch space where he should be, leaving me empty and cold. I lay awake and worry about anything and everything. I'm glad when the sun finally shines through my window and I can get up and get ready to meet Mom and Dad and Jerry at the courthouse.

The day starts out like any other day in court. Joey

waves to me, a small but genuine smile on his face when he sees Mom and Dad. He keeps turning back all the time to wave until Mr. Baskins reminds him to stop. After that he just fidgets nervously in his seat.

Mrs. Davis is a character witness for Joey, along with some of our other customers. Mrs. Davis ends her testimony telling the jury, "Circumstantial evidence, that's all you've got, just circumstantial. Joey's a good boy. All you have to do is look at him to know it." I could kiss Mrs. Davis for that, even if the judge and prosecutor don't look too happy about this little outburst of extra testimony.

Dad is called to the witness stand, too. If I can't testify, I'm glad that at least my father can explain how harmless Joey is.

For almost half an hour, Mr. Baskins questions my father about routine stuff, like what Joey does when working and with whom.

"So what you're saying is that Joey was always with someone when he was working in people's yards. Is that correct?"

"My daughter was always with him, except for the few times she had to make a delivery. But most of the time she was with him. Yes."

"Did your daughter ever say anything to you that made you think that maybe Joey shouldn't be helping her anymore?"

Before Dad can answer, the prosecutor gets up and objects, saying that anything I might have said would be hearsay.

"Your Honor, I'm only asking the witness if his

daughter ever said anything that would prevent Joey from going with her. What she said doesn't matter. I just want to know if he took any action. Allow me to rephrase the question," Mr. Baskins explains, looking to the judge for permission. When he gives the nod to go ahead, Mr. Baskins asks Dad, "Was there any indication on your part leading you to believe that Joey shouldn't be working for you?"

"No," My father answers; his voice is weary at this point. His face has a gray cast to it, and I'm glad when Mr. Baskins finally is through. But the prosecutor isn't satisfied.

"Isn't it true that at least one time you did have to apologize to one of your customers for Joey's actions?"

"If you mean that time I apologized to Mr. Clayton, yes, but he remained a customer of mine."

"And isn't it true that the reason you apologized is because Joey exposed himself to the victim?"

"I wouldn't exactly say he exposed himself."

"Then what would you call it, when a man unzips his pants and relieves himself in front of a little girl?"

At this, my Dad's face turns red and Mr. Baskins jumps up to object.

"The prosecutor is harassing the witness. It's already been established what happened that day on the Claytons' lawn."

The judge sustains, and the prosecutor takes another approach.

"Are you close to your daughter?" he asks my father.

"Very close. She knows the business almost as well as I do."

"So, if something were wrong, you feel that she would confide in you, would she not?"

Mr. Baskins is up objecting again, but the prosecutor simply waves it off, saying, "Your Honor, he started this, now, I want to elaborate on it."

The judge overrules and the prosecutor continues. "Did your daughter ever tell you that she was almost suspended for her behavior in school? That not only did she dress provocatively, but that a teacher of hers also caught her in an illicit act?"

About the same time that Mr. Baskins jumps up to object, I do, too. I shout, "He's lying, Dad! He's lying!" I'm ejected from the courtroom, and for the rest of the day, while they say God only knows what about me, I have to sit in the hall and wait for my parents to come out so I can defend myself.

The minute I see my parents, I run to my father and say, "It's not what you think, Dad. Let me explain."

"There's nothing to explain, Freddy. I know what they're trying to do. Mom told me what happened when you were questioned by those detectives. I blame myself for letting you go in there without our lawyer."

It is suppertime but I'm not hungry, and before my parents and Jerry go out to eat Jerry drops me off at the rooming house.

"I love you, Mom, Dad," I say as I get out of the car.

Jerry doesn't offer to walk me to my room, to kiss me, nothing. But then what can I expect? He couldn't even look at me when he came out of the courtroom.

After Jerry drives away I stare after the car, emotions swirling inside of me. When they've rounded a corner and the taillights are no longer in view, I go up to my room, swearing, "Damn you, Jerry." I toss my purse down in the general direction of my bed and think I'll take a hot bath. That's Mom's remedy to calm someone in shock, but I'm not in shock. I'm pissed. Jerry's not the man I thought he was. God, I'm just so damn stupid when it comes to guys I fall in love with.

"I've had enough," I say, changing my mind about a hot bath. Hell, I'm hot enough. I need to cool off. Instead of a hot bath, I go for a cold walk, leaving my purse behind, and just taking some money with me in my pocket.

I walk down the street where the courthouse stands now, unusually peaceful in the twilight, with no sign of the drama that took place earlier. I walk down Main Street and look into the store windows. I stand in front of one window, wishing that I could be one of the mannequins, frozen in an impossible pose. They are mere life-sized dolls in the guise of human beings, standing as silent, unmoving vigils, sporting the latest winter fashions. They have no hearts, beautiful or otherwise. I envy them in all their plastic ignorance.

I go past a place with loud music coming from the door and I go in. The crowd pushes and shoves against each other, and I elbow through to an empty booth where I order a Coke. Everybody looks so happy, bumping against each other on the dance floor, not always on purpose, but always laughing. There's a couple kissing enthusiastically in a booth across from mine. Would that teacher call this inappropriate and illicit behavior? I guess it's okay to be inappropriate in a dance hall, but not in school. That's all that teacher caught me doing is kissing this guy, and it wasn't even a tongue-in-the-mouth kind.

A little guy, comb in back pocket, not even as tall as I am, swaggers over and asks me to dance. He looks like a kid for God's sake, but then I guess, after Jerry, anybody my age or thereabouts looks like a kid. I think of how Jerry has condemned me without even hearing my side of the story. At first, I'm tempted to say yes to this short, pimply-faced kid standing in front of me, but then I remember that my trying to get even with Erik was what got me in that "inappropriate" mess in the first place. I've learned my lesson. It's just too bad I didn't learn all of it. Like, don't trust a guy when he promises to be true. I get up and elbow my way back out the door into the wave of cold, fresh air that washes over me in a refreshing blast. It's starting to snow and the wet flakes stick to my eyelashes, or maybe it's the tears that I try to blink back that is making them wet. I can't tell.

I pass houses with their televisions on and get a

glimpse through one window of some horses racing across the screen in some old cowboy movie. Joey watches that kind of movie when he isn't watching *The Three Stooges*. I remember where Joey is now, how he just wants to go home, and I do a quick wipe at my eyes with one of my coat sleeves. I walk some more, until even the houses are dark inside. I have no idea what time it is or where I am. As far as I'm concerned, I'm the only person in the world. No one exists but me. Not even a mannequin. The ones with plastic hearts, who have no compassion for people like Joey.

They are frozen in one place. Me, I just keep walking. It's starting to snow harder, and with the snow comes the realization that I'm cold, lost, and alone. It's just me and the hurt inside, and no matter how fast or how far I go, I can't seem to walk away from it.

"Freddy! Wait," I hear a voice, at first thinking it's my imagination. Then the voice repeats itself, only this time louder and more insistent.

"Freddy! Please wait."

I turn around and see Jerry jogging toward me. I wait for him to catch up.

"Where's your car?" I ask when he's finally standing next to me, his breath coming in short pants, making little white puff balls in the frigid air.

"It's back there," he says, gesturing behind me. "I parked it when I saw you walking."

"How did you know it was me?"

"I know you, Freddy."

"No, you don't, Jerry. You don't know me at all."

"What happened to your cell phone? I tried calling you all night, then I went out looking for you."

"Okay, you found me, now go home," I say, picking up the pace as if what I want more than anything is to get away from him when in reality I want the opposite. But I don't know what to do. I can't deal with this right now, so my feet start to move away while my heart wants to stay.

"Freddy, don't do this. Don't lock me out."

"Tell me something, Jerry. When you were in college, did you ever screw around? Was I the first girl you ever went to bed with?"

"That's a hell of a question to ask me," he says, a baffled and almost hurt look on his face.

"Well, that's a hell of a question to ask me, too, but that's what you did when you walked out of that courtroom. When you wouldn't even kiss me when you dropped me off or walk me to the door."

"I never said anything, and I didn't kiss you because of your parents," he tries to plead with me, keeping pace with me, not letting me escape.

I stop walking and bend down to pick up some snow, wanting to shove it in his face.

"I don't think a kiss is considered inappropriate. Even in front of my parents."

Jerry takes my hands and brushes the snow off them, like maybe he knows what I'm planning to do.

"I'll kiss you now, if that's what you want."

"I want you to love me and trust me. After Erik, I messed around some, but that was only because I wanted to get even, because he hurt me so bad. I don't want to get even anymore."

We stand together, Jerry holding my hands, silent like he has to make a decision and I say, "Go home, Jerry."

"Not without you," Jerry says, then kisses me, and it's not the kind a person would do in front of her parents.

"What kind of inappropriate behavior did the teacher accuse you of, anyway?" Jerry asks, walking back to his car with my fingers entwined in his.

"He caught me kissing some guy in the hall. Hell, everybody did it one time or another. I just got caught."

We are on our way to Jerry's house when he tells me my parents left for home.

"Your dad isn't feeling well at all, Freddy. I'm worried."

"Me, too. And today didn't help. What happened after I got kicked out, anyway?"

"Nothing, really. The judge said what you did in school wasn't relevant to the case. So that was the end of it."

"But not for you?"

"All I know is that I love you, and when I couldn't find you, I got scared. I was afraid I'd never see you again. I imagined all kinds of terrible things happening to you. I couldn't help it."

"The only terrible thing that almost happened to me is getting stuck on some dance floor with a pimply-faced kid that might want to bump me inappropriately while we danced."

I squeeze his hand and give him a little smile. Jerry looks at me as if I've lost my mind. I wouldn't be surprised if I had.

Later, I'm lying in bed next to Jerry, back to living with him again, when I say, "About those girls in college? Were there a lot?"

"I don't know. I didn't keep count."

"You mean you can't remember?" I ask, raising an eyebrow, even though it's dark and he can't see me. "Why did you do it?"

"Because everybody did," he replies simply.

"At least I did it to get even. You just screwed around because everybody did."

"Is that what you meant? I thought you meant kissing. I kissed a lot of girls," he says, giving me his most innocent look. I can't see that either, but I'm sure he has that look. After all, his voice doesn't lie.

I take a pillow and hit him with it.

"Damn you, Jerry. You got me to confess, but you won't."

"I'm just not the kind to kiss and tell, that's all," he replies coolly, a smug little grin playing across his lips. I imagine the grin, too. I'm not in the mood for his trying to be cute. I move away from him, ready to turn my back when he pulls me over to his side of the bed.

"I will confess one thing, though," he says, his hands tugging my nightshirt up and slipping it over my head. Now this is real. His hands mold around each breast. First kissing them, then letting go. It's hard to talk with a mouth full.

"I've never told a girl before that I loved her except, of course, for that time when I was five years old."

"Did you kiss her too?"

"Are you kidding? And get all those girl-germs on me?" He nuzzles my neck playfully, gently.

I think of all the girl-germs I'm getting on him as I kiss him full on the mouth, but he doesn't seem to mind, not even when my lips move lower.

CHAPTER 15

About the same time that the prosecution and defense are ready for their summation Mom calls to tell me that Dad is in the hospital.

"Just for some tests" she says. "He doesn't want you to worry, though."

Telling me not to worry is like me telling Joey not to worry. There is emptiness to those words. I mean them and Mom means them to give comfort, but they just don't. Maybe it's because we said them so often that they have long since lost their meaning. I think that's why I don't tell my mother that I'm going to testify. She won't believe me when *I* tell her not to worry.

I will be the last person to testify. Mr. Baskins needs another character witness to add to the small list of those who have already testified on Joey's behalf, especially after the last testimony. Miss Evelyn Harris, one of our customers, meant well when she said she would trust Joey any day. But then the prosecutor asked if she would trust him with her grandchildren. She didn't exactly say yes, just that she was never married so she didn't have any, but she did trust him with her prize rose bushes, which were like her children. Well-meaning, but not at all helpful. I read somewhere that the road to Hell is paved with good intentions. I didn't know what that really meant until now.

I'm at the courthouse early the day I testify, a lot earlier than necessary, but I couldn't sleep anyway. Jerry sits next to me in the hall outside the courtroom, yawning and tapping out an irregular rhythm with his fingers on his laptop case.

When the court convenes, I'm brought in to testify.

I state my name, my relationship to Joey, and it proceeds much the same as everybody else's testimony for Joey until the defense asks me, "How old were you when you first realized that your uncle was different?" He pauses for effect before adding, "Mentally challenged?"

I want to protest; we never call Joey anything like that, even if deep down we all know that's what he is, but we never put a label on him. To us he is just Joey.

"Around the time I started school. When I could read, and Joey couldn't."

"Did you remain close to Joey as you had been before you understood about his being different?"

"Just because Joey is different doesn't mean I stopped loving him. Maybe Joey couldn't read and think like my friends, but he was smart about other things. I bet he knows the name of just about every flower there is."

I want to say more about Joey, but the judge looks impatient and Mr. Baskins interrupts.

"Did you ever see Joey hurt anyone?"

"Joey would never hurt anybody, not even an animal." I think of that time with the mosquito; how he would literally never hurt a fly.

"Did Joey ever hurt you?"

"No. Never!" I answer, my voice stern, my expression growing dark at the mere thought of something so ridiculous.

Mr. Baskins says, "No further questions," and I think that I can get out of the witness chair, when the prosecutor steps up and stops me dead in my tracks. I remember how Mr. Baskins told me that this guy would rip me to pieces, and I stiffen in my seat. "Bring it on," I think defiantly.

"Did Joey ever expose himself to you?"

I have to catch my breath to think of the best way to put this. I'm under oath so I have to tell the truth, but I have to do it in such a way that doesn't make Joey sound bad.

"If you mean, did he go to the bathroom sometimes when we were outside working? Yes, he did, but I never watched. Joey has a hard time holding it when he has to go, and there was no place else to go, so he just went."

"I'm afraid you misunderstood the question. Did your uncle ever show himself to you?"

"I said I never looked." I can feel my fists beginning to clench into tight balls, and I taste blood. I think I bit my lip, but I take a deep breath. I have to stay calm and collected. My stomach is making knots in my guts, but I have to protect Joey at all costs.

"Did he ever touch you indecently, in the private areas of your body?"

"No, never!" I answer with indignation. I want to slap the prosecutor across his smug, inappropriate, stupid face. But it wouldn't help Joey one bit if I just got thrown out of court again, so I behave myself.

It's obvious that the direct approach is getting the prosecutor nowhere, and it seems to me that he's trying to accomplish something in a more roundabout way when he asks, "Were you popular in school, Miss Harrison?"

Mr. Baskins is up on his feet, before I can even begin to answer.

"Your Honor, we have already been through all of this."

"Your Honor, I'm simply trying to establish credibility of the testimony," the prosecutor cuts in, smoothly.

The judge overrules Mr. Baskins' objection, and I answer. "I had friends, but I wouldn't say I was especially popular. There was a group that used to hang around together at lunchtime. I sat at the table sometimes with them."

"Were they considered popular?"

I know what he's trying to do. Next he's going to get me to define *popular* and all what being popular in high school entails. I'm not going to lie, but I sure as hell not going to define *popular* to this jerk.

"I sometimes sat at a table with Judge Ryan's

daughter, and I think she was popular. I know the teachers liked her." I turn to the judge, conjuring up the most innocent look I ever had in my life.

"Maybe you know her, or at least her father?"

By now the prosecutor is turning red, and Mr. Baskins is on his feet objecting. I think the judge is objecting, too, because he says to the prosecutor, "Please bring this back around to the point. As the defense pointed out, we've gone over this before."

The judge sustains Mr. Baskins' objection and the prosecutor sits down, finished with popular and with me, with nothing to show for his trouble, and I get to sit back down by Jerry. I've won a small battle, but the war is still being fought.

Before the attorneys give their summation, the court takes an hour for recess. Jerry and I go for the breakfast we missed because I was too nervous to eat. I'm still too nervous to eat but Jerry isn't. While he eats bacon and eggs, I sip coffee and nibble on one of his pieces of toast.

"Was that judge's kid really one of that group?"

"I never said she was part of the group. I just said I sat with her sometimes. I worked on a project with her and a couple of other kids. We even worked during some of our lunch hours. I wouldn't lie, Jerry, on or off the stand."

Jerry looks at me like I'm incredible, and then goes back to eating and I go back to sipping and nibbling. It's quiet, really quiet, when Jerry suddenly looks up at me from his plate and asks, just like that, like he's asking me to pass the salt.

"Will you marry me?"

I'm used to Jerry saying crazy things at crazy times but this is the ultimate crazy, or so I think, until I answer with an even crazier "Okay. When?"

A smile spreads across his face. He picks up the glass and washes his eggs down with some orange juice.

"Next week sound good?"

"Why so soon?"

"Because I've just been offered a job in New York and I want to take you with me."

"Can I wait until my dad gets back on his feet before I go to New York?"

"How long will that take?"

"The last time his ulcer acted up, it took him about a week. It will take another two weeks before he can go back to the store. "

"Okay, here's what we will do. We'll get married, and I'll go on ahead to my job alone. I don't think it will be much of a honeymoon, though, with you here and me in New York."

"I think we already had the honeymoon, if that's what's bothering you." I rub the inside of his calf with my foot under the table and smile, but his expression is serious.

"What is bothering me is the idea of a month without you. How in the hell am I ever going to get through it?"

"You'll be so busy, you won't even know I'm not there."

"You wanna bet?" Jerry asks, pushing his plate

aside, and picking up the bill.

We are outside, walking to the car when Jerry says, "I'll be making a lot more than I do here, and after I sell the house, maybe we can buy a house there. I don't think it will be as nice as the one I have now. Real estate is a lot higher out East. The important thing is that we have a yard for Joey to grow his flowers, and a place for our kids to play."

That catches me a little off guard. Flowers for Joey, okay, great. Kids? What? I look at him, slightly bewildered.

"Just how many kids are we talking about?" I ask as I slowly inch across a patch of ice on the sidewalk next to the car.

"At least four. I'm an only child. I always wanted a big family," Jerry says, taking my hand to guide me across a snow bank piled up on the curb, then opens the car door for me. Now we're in the car, keys in the ignition and seatbelts ready to buckle, but before Jerry starts the engine he makes the point that if his impromptu marriage proposal was lacking in romance, he makes up for it in passion when he kisses me. And once again, I find myself engaged, but this time, although less formal, it's a lot more genuine.

The attorneys give their summation, the prosecutor saying over and over that even if Joey is mentally challenged, he still knows the difference between right and wrong, and should be held accountable for what he did. Mr. Baskins counters with the fact that a child's perception of right and wrong isn't the same as an adult's, especially when the child has an adult's body.

"Besides," Mr. Baskins tell the jury, "the prosecution hasn't offered any proof that the defendant did anything wrong. This assumption is based only upon theory, but with no hard evidence to back it up."

While the jury files out of the courtroom to go and deliberate, I go to talk to Joey.

"I wanna go home," Joey says to me in that heartbreaking way he always does after court is adjourned and I'm allowed my little bit of time with him.

"Soon," I tell Joey, taking a deep breath and squeezing his hand. "Don't worry, everything is going to work out." This time I mean it, and I elaborate.

"Jerry and I are going to get married and live in New York. We want you to live with us when this whole thing is over with. Would you like that, Joey?"

"Will there be flowers in New York?"

"Jerry's going to buy a house with a yard, and there'll be lots of flowers, and someday, lots of kids. You can teach them all the names of the flowers and how to take care of them. How's that sound?"

"Will Mom and Dad live with us, too?"

"I think maybe it's time Dad retired. If he sells the business I bet he'll have enough money to retire. I think Dad will like having some time to go fishing. Who knows, he might even take up golf."

"I don't think Dad will want to go golfing. Maybe fishing, but not golf," Joey says in his matter-of-fact way.

"Why not golf?"

"Because he won't like it," he states, as though it's the most obvious thing in the world.

"Why won't he like it?"

"Because of the shirt."

"What shirt?"

"The golf shirt, Freddy! Dad always says he wouldn't be caught dead in a golf shirt."

I just shake my head and smile. Sometimes talking to Joey can be tiring. Especially after being questioned by the prosecutor. I think I've done enough explaining for the day so I hug Joey good-bye, telling him, "It's going to be okay, Joey. Jerry's a wonderful guy, and everything is going to be just great."

For the first time in what seems like forever, I'm actually able to stand behind words that no longer taste like an empty lie. They finally mean something again.

Jerry is waiting for me in the hall, and when he takes my hand and squeezes it, it just confirms my feeling that everything really is going to be okay.

"I'll drop you off at home and then I have to go to the paper, but I'll be back in a little while. I want to go to bed early tonight. We have a lot of plans to talk over."

I know that look on Jerry's face; it isn't talking that's on his mind, but loving, and now I'd be willing to bet my life that everything's going to be okay.

That feeling of everything turning out great lasts about as long as it takes for Jerry to drive away after dropping me off. Through the living room window I watch the car turn the corner, then I stand in the middle of the room listening to my heart beat so loud that it scares me. What if I'm having a heart attack? What if the jury doesn't find Joey innocent? What if my dad doesn't get better and doesn't want to take up golf, shirt be damned? With coat still on, I break out in a cold sweat.

Finally I give myself a mental shake, take off my coat, and go to the kitchen to prepare supper.

I'm just finished with putting in the meat loaf along with the potatoes when Jerry walks in.

"Well, I just gave my notice. This trial is the last thing I'll ever write for a paper until I go to New York. When you leave with Joey for home, I'll go with you. We'll tell your parents our plans together. Is that okay with you, honey?"

I can't help the great big smile that spreads over my face from ear to ear.

"Yes. It's great."

Before we go to the bedroom, Jerry shuts off the oven. He's not interested in supper. Now he wants to 'talk.'

CHAPTER 16

In the morning I wake up with a stiff neck, along with an aching head. On top of that the floor is cold on my bare feet as I make my way across the kitchen to the coffeemaker to brew a fresh pot. The smell of spoiled meatloaf wafts from the oven when I open it, and I take out the intended supper, dump it in the garbage, and finish making the coffee. I take a couple of deep breaths as the satisfying aroma of coffee fills the kitchen. With the sound of the water dripping steadily into the glass pot I pad back to the bedroom to take my shower and get dressed. I want to be ready to go with Jerry when his paper calls telling him to get over there, that the jury is back with the verdict. I have to be there for Joey. I have to be there for me. God it's hard this waiting.

I stand under the water and let it run down onto my head, letting the warmth massage my stiff neck. The soap-scented steam is soothing. I take in another deep breath and let it out slowly, sliding the bar of soap absently up and down my arm.

Last night was another sleepless night. It's all so

151

unreal lately, waiting for a jury to exonerate Joey from a crime I know he didn't commit. My dad is sick in the hospital and the worry in Mom's voice is impossible to hide. Taking a shower in this house doesn't feel right, and sometimes neither does the man I've been sleeping with. It was barely a month ago the first time we made love, a stranger if time is a factor. I don't really know that much about him, except that my mother likes him. Of course, liking him isn't enough. She thinks he's too old for me. Sometimes I find myself wondering whatever happened to the girl who dreamed of one day marrying Erik? Is she a stranger, too? Lately it seems I don't know who I am anymore.

"Honey, do you want me to pour you some coffee?" Jerry asks through the fog on the shower door.

"Yeah, sure," I say, ready to step out of the comforting, warm cocoon of the shower and into the cold reality of waiting. Will the jury have a verdict soon? Within the next hour? The next couple of hours? Will it even be resolved today at all? I shiver, vigorously rubbing myself dry with a towel and pray that this nightmare of waiting will soon be over.

Jerry already has the table set with two bowls and a box of cereal. He pours the coffee the minute he sees me.

"You had a bad night again, didn't you?" he asks, sitting down at the table.

"Uh-huh," I mutter, taking the cup he offers in

both my hands and relishing its precious warmth.

"What's wrong with your neck?" Jerry asks, giving me his reporter look, the kind reserved for someone he's about to interview. I pull the robe up around my neck just to make sure that there isn't too much showing for this "interview."

"I must have been lying on it wrong, or a draft got to it during the night. I'll be fine," I say with a shrug, thinking this is one hell of a boring interview, not at all worthy of the intensely quizzical look I received from the man sipping his coffee across the table from me.

This man, my fiancé, replies, "It's probably from stress. Honey, you have to relax a little," Jerry says, coming over to rub my neck, and I get the feeling that this interview is about to get more interesting. He kisses the back of my neck, my shoulder.

"Oh, damn," I say and Jerry pulls away.

"What?"

"I forgot to take my pill last night and the night before that. I'm just so crazy lately. I'd forget my head if it wasn't attached."

"So what's the big deal?"

"The big deal is, I could get pregnant."

"We'll have a honeymoon baby," Jerry says with a laugh, not seeming to mind the very real possibility I could have a bun in my oven. A second later, he's back to kissing and rubbing my neck and shoulders.

"We might be able to get away with a honeymoon without a wedding, but not a baby, too."

"In a week, we're getting married. Do you think a week is going to make that much difference when people start counting?"

Maybe that's the strangest of all the strange things in my life lately. Me getting married, especially when in my heart, deep down inside, I'm not even sure I'm completely over Erik.

By noon the jury still hasn't come up with a verdict, and Jerry suggests that if he's going to sell the house we should get it ready.

"We can start in the attic," he says.

"Why the attic? Aren't attics usually dusty and dark?"

"We can do the basement then."

"Oh, damp and dark, that's *so* much better," I say sarcastically and Jerry smiles, then settles it.

"We can do the attic."

The attic is dark, and when Jerry hooks up a lamp overhead the dust disturbed by our movement dances in the beam of light. There are trunks of stuff, boxes of stuff, and stuff just lying in stacks on the floor. Your typical attic, I suppose. I walk over to a stack of old comic books and pick one up.

"Jerry, you're not so old that you used to read this stuff, are you? Where did they come from?" I ask, dusting off the cover of an old Superman comic with the hem of my shirt.

"My dad collected them. He liked collecting things."

"I can see that," I say, wondering where to start.

Jerry opens a box and a kaleidoscope of color tumbles out. Bright crayon-colored pictures that a mom would tack up on a refrigerator until the kid brought new ones home from school. When she would throw out the old ones to make room, except Jerry's mom never threw them out. She just put them all in a box. I kneel down by the box and lift out one after the other.

"You had quite an eye for color. How come you ended up a reporter instead of an artist?"

I touch the drawing in my hand only by the corners, handling it like a precious relic as I study the bright, childish scribbling with wonder.

"Because the stories I wrote were even better."

"Did she save those, too?" I ask, pulling another box close to where I kneel, working the cover off. No one has opened it in years.

"Hell, my mother saved everything I ever did. You'll probably find a baby book here somewhere, with some hair from my first haircut."

"She sounds wonderful. I wish she were still alive so I could get to know her. Do you think she'd like me, Jerry?"

"She'd love you," he replies, like he knows.

"How can you be so sure?"

"She loved anything I brought home. Even a little mutt that followed me home once, and all my mother said was, 'You can keep it, but you'll have to take care of it.'"

I give Jerry a playful shove.

"Are you saying I'm a mutt?" I ask, falling on top of him. A small struggle ensues for a while until he wraps his arms around me, pinning me down to the dusty floor.

"Well, I did love that little mutt, and I did take care of it."

I start to pull away like I'm insulted, when Jerry pulls me back, and somewhere in the middle of the unzipping and unbuttoning, his cell phone rings.

"Damn it," he curses under his breath, fishing in his pocket. Another *damn* when he finds it. "I knew I should have left it downstairs," He's ready to shut it off without answering.

"It could be the jury reached a verdict," I say, moving to stop him.

With obvious reluctance, Jerry answers the phone and after a couple of, "Yeah, sure," then an "I'll be right there," he hangs up, and I stare at him, expecting to jump up and go with him to court. Jerry says, "That's the paper. There's a story they want me to cover."

"I thought you were through there. That the trial is the last story."

"So did I, but this won't take long. I'll be back in a little while," he says with a quick kiss and a pat on my rear.

He's halfway across the attic when I ask, "Jerry, about that mutt, how long did you keep it?"

"Not very long. I took it back to its owner after it bit me."

"I thought you said it followed you home," I say, moving the papers scattered around me. The dust motes back to their dance in the beam of light.

"It did, after I opened the gate."

"Sometimes, Jerry," I say, punctuating my

sentence with a little sigh, "I think I want to bite you. You're so damn impossible."

"Maybe," he agrees, laughing, those cute little lines appearing in the corners of his eyes. "But I'm not giving you back."

I think I know what he means, and I tell him that I love him. For a minute it's like the world is standing still; even the little dust dancers settle on the boxes where they'd been resting for years before we came up and disturbed them.

"I love you too, Freddy. More than I've ever loved anyone or anything in my life," Jerry says, holding my gaze with equal warmth and affection. Then, looking down at his watch, he adds, "I've gotta get going. I'll see you later."

After his footsteps on the pull-down stairs fade into silence I go back to sorting, and the dust goes back to dancing. The minutes tick away into first one, then two hours of uncovering the mystery of past lives lived in this house.

There are pictures of Jerry as a baby, his first birthday, his second birthday; there are photographs documenting important events all the way up to his graduation from high school.

Somewhere in the box of pictures is a yearbook where a girl named Janet signed it, 'To Jerry: I promise to be true, always.' I stare at the words for a long time. Such unique words; at least, they were for me. At the time I thought Erik and I had invented them, yet here they are, some girl promising the man I'm going to marry (in a week!) that she'll be true, always. I wonder if Jerry made that promise, too. I hope not. I don't want to be the cause of breaking some poor girl's heart. But this was a long time ago, likely ancient history to Jerry. I trace the words with my finger. With one last long look at the neat, loopy cursive writing, I close the book and stop thinking about it.

The box no longer holds the rapture of discovery it did only a couple of minutes ago and I move to a big trunk tucked away in a corner under the rafters. I move the light closer to it, then with a puff of dust I open what must have been closed for a very long time. There is the notion of peeking into somewhere I have no right to peek, but curiosity gets the best of me. The letters are tied in the traditional blue ribbon, and I don't have to read them to know that these are love letters. I put them down to examine the rest of the contents of the trunk.

There's a picture of a young girl and boy, and as I continue my rummaging, I discover a lot of pictures of them. Visual love letters of an unspoken love that jumps out with every look, every touch between them. The boy looks so much like Jerry that at first I think it is him, until I see the wedding picture, and I know it's his mother and father. I touch with careful hands a wedding dress I find on the bottom of the trunk, packed in blue tissue paper. I hold it up against me, wishing I had a mirror to see how it looks. Finally, I pick up the letters and, sitting cross-legged under the hanging light, I begin to read:

My Darling Eleanor,

I started the new semester, and so far so good. It's hard to concentrate though, because I keep thinking about Christmas break. Remember how it snowed on Christmas Eve and we managed to get away from the family for a while, and went for a walk? I think I will always remember how you looked in the moonlight, with the snow sparkling in your dark hair, like you were wearing a veil studded with diamonds. You are a beautiful Snow Queen, and I, your humble servant. Tell me, my darling, what did I ever do to get someone so beautiful as you? I ask myself this every day. I love you and miss you so much. I can't wait until we can be together always. I love the watch you gave me and never take it off. I hope you love the ring I gave you and never take it off, either. I guess I have to get back to studying now, but I'll write you again tomorrow. I love you, and promise to be true forever.

Love always, Patrick

At first I think that I shouldn't read anymore, that I've already intruded upon a sacred privacy, but curiosity gets the better of me and the need to know keeps me reading. What I need so desperately to know is, did the letters always stay filled with such sincere expressions of love, or was it gradually lost in football games, parties, and eventually, did they sound like letters to a friend instead of to the girl he loved? I read the whole stack and the love remains constant from top to bottom, and I know that sometimes words are unique, invented by the two people saying them when they're said with a true heart. I take one more look at the wedding picture,

159

then pack everything back in the trunk except for the wedding dress. I take it downstairs with me and carefully try it on. When I marry Jerry, I will wear this dress and carry the legacy of his parents' love into our marriage: a legacy that someday we will hand down to our children.

When Jerry crawls into bed next to me sometime around ten at night, I snuggle up to him and whisper, "I'm going to wear your mother's wedding dress when we get married."

"Won't it be too big on you? And out of style? I thought my mother was bigger than you."

"It's a little dated, yeah, but still gorgeous. And besides, I'll grow into it, along with that legacy she left behind."

"What legacy?"

"Of love. Your father and mother loved each other so much, Jerry."

Jerry starts to laugh and says, "You found those letters of theirs, didn't you?"

"Yes, but how did you know?"

"Because I found them once and read them, too."

"Didn't you think they were beautiful?"

"No, I thought they were dumb."

"How can you possibly think they were dumb?" I ask, irritation creeping into my voice.

"Because when I read them, I was still into mutts, and not girls."

Sometimes I want to kill him. I want to take this pillow and hold it over his face until he smothers; then he kisses me, making all traces of my frustration melt away into the darkness of our shared room, and all I want to do is smother him with love. Forever and always.

CHAPTER 17

We're still in bed when the phone rings and the paper calls Jerry to get over to the courthouse right away; the jury has reached a verdict. We jump up out of bed in a daze, not talking or paying attention to each other as we go about our morning routine. Like two robots we dress and brush our teeth automatically in a mechanical silence. It's not until we walk into the courtroom that it hits me why we're here; now I'm very much human again and I need Jerry to be with me, because without him to hold me up I think I will crumble.

Joey is already in court, fidgeting in his usual seat beside Mr. Baskins. He looks so scared, this little boy in a man's body. I feel the pull of Joey's need for me tug sharply at my heartstrings, and I want so much to go to him, to hold and comfort him. But that's not possible, so I sit holding onto Jerry's hand so tight I think I might break his fingers. He doesn't pull away or give any indication that he minds at all.

When everyone is finally seated the jury files in with identical solemn looks on their faces. The silence stretches on forever before the judge finally asks them, "Have you reached a verdict?"

I hear the foreman say they have, handing the

bailiff the sheet of paper that holds Joey's fate. I hold my breath as the judge looks at the paper, hands it back and asks the foreman to say the words. At least I think he says the words, but how can he? There *are* no words to describe what is happening; they haven't been invented yet. Only the sobbing has been invented to drown out the sound of the words. I hear a scream and I know it comes from deep inside me.

"Oh God! No! Please don't let this happen!"

Joey is yelling, "Freddy, what's happening! I wanna go home! Freddy, I wanna go home!"

The judge bangs his gavel and he's yelling, too, "Quiet in the courtroom! Bailiff, I need order!"

Joey is found guilty, and there is nothing I can do. I can't scream at the jury; the judge won't let me. That they're wrong, because according to the system, juries are never wrong. I can't tell Mr. Baskins that he's not a lawyer because his degree says he is. All I can do is sob in Jerry's arms as they lead Joey away, looking back at me bewildered, saying, "Are you okay, Freddy? Are you okay?" They take him away in handcuffs to spend the rest of his life paying for something he didn't do, while the real criminal responsible for the crime remains free and anonymous. I sob in Jerry's arms.

"It's not fair, Jerry. It's not fair." He holds me tight like if he doesn't do tight, I'll break into pieces.

"I know honey, I know."

I can only see Joey for a few minutes before he is taken away to serve his sentence, and before I go to him I struggle to get myself under control. I don't want him to see how upset I am. I forgot that in court but now I need to be strong for him.

"I will be waiting for you right here, sweetheart," Jerry says, giving me a tight hug. Because Jerry is a reporter covering this trial he cannot come in with me, and I wonder how in the hell I can walk through the door without him to hold me up.

"What am I going to say to him? I can't just tell him that everything will be okay, not anymore. Oh God! Jerry, what am I going to say?" I ask, the tears I've struggled so hard to wipe away returning, the lump I thought I'd swallowed rising rebelliously back up into my throat. I take a crumpled, damp tissue back out of my purse and pat my eyes dry.

"Tell him that we'll appeal. We'll get a new lawyer and appeal as soon as we can."

"He doesn't understand what that means. He doesn't even understand what's happening now. How can I make him understand, Jerry, when I don't understand it myself?" I sniffle into the tissue wadded up in my hand.

"Then just tell him that you love him. Just say that until you figure out the right words to say to him so he'll understand that this isn't the end of it."

"There are no words," I practically whine, feeling so hopeless that I can't handle it. "There never will be. What can I say?"

Tears are spilling freely down my cheeks again, my hand holding the tissue unable to keep up with catching them, so I just give up and let them fall.

The guard is beckoning me to come. With one last look back and one last effort to dry my eyes I take a deep breath and follow him to where Joey sits in the back room where we always meet, handcuffed, ready to be led away.

"I wanna go home," he pleads pathetically, and my heart breaks for him, still more tears beginning to sting my eyes, but I can't cry, not in front of Joey. He has to believe the next words I say. It's important.

I take a shaky breath and put my hand on his slumped shoulder before saying, "We're going to appeal the case, Joey. We're going to make these people let you go home, but not right now. It's going to take time."

"How much time? How long, Freddy?"

"Soon...very soon," I tell him with as much conviction as possible, giving him one last, long hug. Just before the guards start to lead Joey away he looks back at me, his eyes shining with unshed tears, a variety of unexpressed emotions swirling within their blue depths.

"Promise, Freddy? Cross your heart and hope to die?"

His voice is so small I wish I could hug him again and never let go, so that the guards standing on either side of him cannot take him away.

"I promise," I say to the retreating group, then say more quietly to myself, once Joey's turned to face forward, "Cross my heart and hope to die."

When we get back to Jerry's house, before I call

my parents and Jerry sits down to type up his column, I cry within the protective circle of his arms, and he cries with me, his broad chest trembling with silent tears against my flushed and damp face. God! I love him.

Later Jerry turns on the evening news and Mr. Baskins is bragging that at least Joey will not go to a regular prison but to a mental institution for criminals.

"And the judge agrees, handing down the sentence. It is a place where his special needs can be attended."

"That bastard," I curse at the television screen. "He disgusts me. It's not even about Joey. It's about him and his precious reputation, and the money he's made off us. I tried to tell Dad that as soon as I went into that courtroom and saw what a shitty job that leech was doing, but Dad said it was too late. Well, this time we'll get another lawyer when we appeal. Someone who actually gives a damn. Someone with compassion, who isn't just in it for the money and trying to make a name for himself."

"Sweetheart, appeals take a long time."

"I don't care, Jerry. I'm not going to let Joey stay in prison. I don't give a rat's ass what Mr. Baskins calls it; when it comes right down to it, it's still prison," I say, venom seeping into the last word and leaving a bad taste in my mouth. I continue to glare daggers at the television, even though the news has moved on to the next story.

"Let's go to bed. We can talk about it in the morning," Jerry suggests a little too calmly for my taste, walking over and switching off the television, but I can't let it go, and continue to stare at the blank screen. I can't just go to bed as if this night is like every other night, because it isn't, not at all. I have to know if Jerry is with me in this.

"What's your problem, Jerry? Is it the expense or what? You don't sound as sure about all this as you did before, when you were comforting me back in court."

"I'm just thinking about us, Freddy. Where does this leave us?"

"Maybe it leaves us not getting married, after all. Maybe it leaves us not as much in love as we thought we were. Is that how it is, Jerry? Because I don't know anymore. I'm only eighteen. What the hell do I know about love anyway?"

"I can tell you that it sure as hell isn't being popular, Freddy. Not the kind of popular the prosecutor talked about," he says, his voice harsh, condescending. I hate condescending.

"And it isn't two people promising to be true to each other either, because I did, I kept that promise, but Erik didn't."

When I mention Erik's name it's like I just slapped Jerry in the face. He turns sharply on his heel, grabs his jacket from the hook by the door, and walks out, slamming the door as he goes.

I listen detached from the sound of Jerry's car exiting the driveway, the beams from his headlights throwing sharp shadows onto the walls of the dimly lit room, then nothing.

Like a robot again, I get up from my seat on the couch and shuffle into the bedroom to start packing. I do so silently and methodically, thinking that I should be feeling sad, probably even crying, but all the tears were sucked out of me earlier at the courthouse and all I feel now is numb. I gather my things together and arrange them in my suitcase.

By the time Jerry comes back I'll be gone. It's best this way. I'll go home and maybe someday I'll learn what love really is. Maybe someday I'll meet someone like Jerry's father, who will teach me all about love and write me beautiful letters that I can tie in a blue ribbon and pack in a trunk up in the attic. I sit down on the bed and imagine my grandchildren opening a dusty trunk some day and reading the letters Grandpa once wrote to Grandma.

Hugging a pillow to my chest I lie down and close my eyes, and dream a dream I'd never dare to dream while I'm awake.

The sun is shining bright through the window when I wake up. I blink, sleep still in my eyes, and glance at the almost-full suitcase, still lying open on the floor beside the bed exactly where I left it before I accidentally fell asleep.

Sometime during the night Jerry came home, but I never heard him, never even felt him crawl into bed beside me, I had been sleeping so soundly. I prop myself up on my elbow and watch him sleep. I memorize every detail of the way he looks. The thick, dark lashes curling softly upward from the bottom of his closed lids. The color of his hair, kind of a sandy color, not exactly curly and not quite straight either, just tousled. Mom was right; he is good-looking. I reach across his rising and falling chest to touch the cleft in his chin with my fingertip, then pull my hand back at the last minute, not wanting to wake him. It will be better if I leave while he's still asleep. He's so beautiful and peaceful, the anger of yesterday erased from his face. In my heart is a surge of tenderness toward him but I have to stand by my decision to leave, no matter how my heart protests. It's the best thing for both of us. Jerry has a new life in New York waiting for him, and I have to go home to God only knows what's waiting for me. I move my legs to the side of the bed, then carefully swing them over, peeling the covers slowly away from my body, trying hard not to disturb the man sleeping next to me.

It will only take me a few minutes to finish packing and to get dressed. My car is in Jerry's garage, where it's been ever since I moved in with him. In roughly fifteen minutes it will be like I was never here. All traces of me will be gone except for the tiny things Jerry's bound to notice, like the depression my body made on the mattress next to him and the little bits of hair in the bathroom wastebasket from after my showers. I wonder if he'll be sad or angry, but I don't have much time to think about it. In the car on the way home I'll cry, but not now.

My plans are interrupted and my feet never touch the floor. Jerry wraps his arms around me and pulls me in close to him. He holds me close, his breath warm and familiar against my neck and ear. I lay quiet against him until he pushes himself up onto his elbows and looks down at me. I look up at him, our eyes lock, not exactly sure what to think or say when he says, "I'm sorry," giving me a look like a little puppy that has just piddled on the floor, his eyes so huge I think they will swallow me up. I have to say something.

"Where did you go last night?" I ask, but that's not what I wanted to say. I can't even forgive him without making it sound like an argument.

"I went for a couple of beers," he says, pushing himself up higher over me. "Hell! I went for *a lot* of beers. I guess I got drunk," he says a little sheepishly. "But, before I got *too* drunk, I knew that no matter what, I still want to marry you."

He pauses and scratches the back of his neck like he does when he's nervous or unsure about something. "Do you still want to marry me?"

"Even if I do it still doesn't change anything. I can't let Joey stay in that place. I promised him. I even crossed my heart and hoped to die. Do you want me to die, Jerry?"

Jerry falls back on the pillow with a little laugh, his arms pulling me with him.

"No, I don't want you to die. I want us to live a long and happy life. I want us to celebrate all those wedding anniversaries together that my parents never got the chance to celebrate. I'll do anything you want, Freddy, just don't go and die on me."

I lay my head on his chest and listen to his heart. I think of his parents, who will never get to see their grandchildren like Jerry and I will get to see ours, and the thought prompts the question.

"You never talk much about your parents. What were they like? Were they always as much in love as they were in those letters?"

"When you're a kid you really don't pay attention when your parents are getting along; you just notice when they're not. I never really paid attention because my parents never argued. My mother said that it didn't pay because my dad always made a joke out of it when she tried. My dad had a real sense of humor. I know they wanted more kids. They even talked about adopting, but they never did. I guess after me they decided not to push their luck. I wasn't exactly the little angel those pictures in the attic portray."

"You mean you were a little devil?" I ask, and I can't see it but I feel a grin tugging at my mouth.

"I was hell-on-wheels," he replies, imitating my grin, only double.

"At least I know what I'm in for when we have kids. Out of four, I figure there's going to be at least one that takes after you," I say laughing, even though yesterday, I thought I would never laugh again. But that's Jerry. I guess it's kind of, '*Like father, like son,*' Jerry can always make me laugh. A stellar quality in a man, and I like that.

"Then you still want to have our kids?"

171

"Hey, I stopped taking my birth control pills. That should tell you something."

We wrestle, pretending to pin each other down, and as usual, I end up on the bottom. Just before Jerry takes advantage of the situation, he asks, "About this Erik, were you in love with each other?"

"I never really loved him. I realize that now. And as far as Erik is concerned, I don't think he could care any less if I lived or died" I answer, thinking that at least part of it is true. Erik doesn't care if I live or die. If he had he wouldn't have broken my heart the way he did. People who love each other-- *really* love each other--they don't do that kind of thing.

CHAPTER 18

We have one day to get everything sorted and packed before we go home to my parents' house. Jerry will drive my car, then take a bus back for his car. He'll leave directly from here to go to New York and his new job. I'm going to stay home for a while to help Mom run the store until Dad can take over again. Like Jerry says, "It's not going to be much of a honeymoon, but at least there will be a wedding."

I stand in the middle of the kitchen, dictating to Jerry what we'll take along in the car and what will go to the antique store. Most of the stuff is old, so antique sounds good. The things Jerry's father collected, picture frames, old radios--some working and some not--and old tables and lamps. There's even an ancient treadle sewing machine, and you sure don't see those anymore. There is also old furniture that was stored in the basement and attic after his grandparents died. Jerry says his mother didn't have the heart to throw anything away. Jerry doesn't take after his mother. He was ready to throw it all out but I managed to stop him in the nick of time and called Carl, who is an expert at pricing antiques and old comic books. He certainly talked enough about it at work, complaining all the time that they don't make things the way they used to.

Now Carl's friend from the antique store is coming to pick up most of the things, except for the comic books. I intend to give those to Carl so he can sell them at one of the collectors' shows he's always going to. He says he can get more for them that way, and I think we're going to need all the money we can get our hands on once we start looking for a lawyer to appeal Joey's case.

"I don't think we can fit any more in the car," Jerry says with an exasperated look as I try to hand him the box of pictures and old love letters that I rescued from the attic before they were tossed out.

"These *have* to go," I insist. "Even if you have to leave our clothes behind, these are going."

"If we leave our clothes behind, we won't need these," Jerry says taking the box with a grin.

"Huh?" I ask, with no idea what he's talking about.

Sometimes there are no right words invented yet when it comes to talking to Jerry, and all I can do is look at him like he's from another planet.

"If we're walking around naked we're going to have all the pictures we want, and they'll be a hell of a lot better than these," he says, and I think he must be more like his father every day. I turn back to my work, trying my best to ignore what he just said, but damn...sometimes it's impossible not to laugh.

About the time Jerry is finished packing the car the antique guy comes and Jerry starts packing all over again, this time filling up the dealer's truck. The two of them huff and puff everything out except what I want to keep. Those things Jerry will store in one of those rental storage places before he leaves for New York and puts the house he was raised in up for sale.

"Are you sure you want to keep this junk?" Jerry asks, holding up a box of old copper utensils.

"I'm sure."

"Why? They're not good for anything."

"Once I polish them up I want to hang them on a rack in our kitchen."

"First we have to get a kitchen. In the meantime we'll be paying to store this junk."

"I want to keep some things that belonged to your family."

"You've got the pictures and the letters, isn't that enough?"

"No," I say, finding it rather odd that I'm the one fighting to keep his family's heirlooms even if they aren't of any monetary worth. You would think they'd at least have some sentimental value to him.

Jerry just walks outside with the dealer, mumbling under his breath, "Well, I tried."

Later we go out for pizza, then come back to our empty house where we end up on a mattress on the floor; even the bed we used to sleep in was an antique. We make love so wild, so passionate, that when it's over Jerry says with a contented sigh, "We should do this more often."

"Jerry, if we had sex more often we'd never get anything else done."

"I meant sleep on the floor."

I turn my back on him, pretending to ignore his last remark. I don't want to encourage this nonsense, but sometimes it's just *so* hard not to laugh.

I'm just starting to doze off when Jerry asks, "Do you think they'll like me, Freddy?"

"Who?"

"Your parents."

"They already know you. Believe me, if they didn't like you they would tell me."

"Yeah, but they know me as a friend. Now I'll be their son-in-law."

I turn back to face him, putting my arms around him. I kiss that little cleft in his chin, then reach down to touch what gave me so much pleasure only a little while ago.

"What's not to like?" I ask, feeling it harden in my hand, and I think I've just started something again.

Despite our wanting to sleep late, we're up early. It's still dark when Jerry pulls the car out of the garage, then does a last check of the house, walking through each room, turning down the heat and turning off the water.

"Are you going to miss it?" I ask, when at last he turns the key in the lock.

"No."

"Not even a little? There has to be something you'll miss."

"I'll miss that mattress on the floor."

"Well, after we get through paying for those

lawyers, we'll be sleeping a lot on the floor. I just hope we have a roof to go with that floor."

I think that has a sobering effect on Jerry because we're driving for almost a half-hour and he still hasn't said anything, nonsense or otherwise.

Finally, unable to stand the silence any longer I say, "Maybe we shouldn't get married before you go to New York, Jerry. It's not like I'm pregnant or anything, so we can wait if you want."

"What I want is to marry you and take you with me to New York, but that's not going to happen, at least not right away, so I'll be patient. Just don't ask me to be too patient, Freddy. A man can only take so much."

I turn my head and look out the window. The world flies past so fast from behind a car window. I think of Joey and how slowly the days must go, looking out a window with bars, not going anywhere. No flowers or butterflies to enjoy, and it hurts so much that I start to cry, and Jerry says softly, "Honey, don't cry. I'll be around for as long as you want me around. I love you."

"I love you, too, but when you said that a man can only take so much, it just made me wonder how much Joey can take. Will he have the patience it's going to take before we can get him out of that awful prison?"

"As soon as I get to New York, I'll start checking out some lawyers' names. I'll be working for a big paper, and I think I should be able to find something in their files that will help."

"A lawyer from New York? That could be

expensive. I don't think Dad has that kind of money anymore. He's mortgaged our house, and I know for a fact he had to buy the Christmas inventory on credit. Grandpa left Dad everything free and clear, so he's never had to borrow before."

"I'll sell the house, and I have some money saved. If I have to, I'll take out a loan."

"I owe you, Jerry, big time. I just hope you don't expect me to sign over my firstborn to you," I say with a little laugh, because if I don't laugh I'm sure as hell going to start crying again.

Jerry gives me this look, like I just hit a nerve and says, "That's not funny."

"Sorry," I say, wondering what put a bee in his bonnet, and I don't open my mouth again until we stop for breakfast.

We're sitting in a booth, studying the menu when Jerry says, like he's reading it off the menu, "There are too many firstborns being fought over by their parents. I don't want that for our kids, Freddy."

"Neither do I," I say, and then we drop the subject, like those words were never invented.

By the time we're served breakfast we're back to the magic of last night. We hold hands and look secret little looks toward each other. Under the table I rub my foot against Jerry's leg, and he pretends to drop his fork. On the way up after reaching down for it he runs a hand up my leg, and I just hope that the teacher who almost got me suspended isn't lurking behind one of these booths, taking note of this "inappropriate behavior."

When we get back to the car, Jerry gives me a tongue-in-the-mouth kiss, and I'm glad the windows are steamed up and we're the only ones in the parking lot. We don't exactly do it, not right away, but before Jerry slips a hand down the front of my jeans, I glance back, just in case that pesky teacher is hiding somewhere in the parking lot. I decide that if I'm accused of inappropriate behavior I'm going to make the most of it. By the time Jerry and I are through rubbing and fingering the car windows aren't the only things steamed up. We do it, and I'll be damned if I know how in a little car with bucket seats, but the wet between my legs tells me that Jerry was in and out. I take a tissue and wipe before putting on my appropriate clothes.

"What if I just got pregnant now? What if your seed just linked up with my egg and right now they're doing a little dance inside me?"

"A little dance?" Jerry is clearly interested, so I explain.

"My mother described it that way. I was around five and I saw two dogs doing it and she said they were dancing."

"If you are, it won't be a puppy we'll be having."

"Hell-on-wheels," I say, "Conceived in a car, he will be hell-on-wheels."

Jerry laughs; he understands crazy and I think I just said the ultimate crazy. Sometimes I think I've been around Jerry too much. I'm beginning to think and talk just like him.

It takes us longer to get home than we expected. With all our happy talk about apartments we'll be renting and plans we make, Jerry gets distracted and makes a couple of wrong turns and we have to do some back tracking. I think we're back on track now, though, with our plans. Maybe we won't have the house and garden or even Joey right away, but as far as the kids, well, I'm sure doing my part. Before we pull into the driveway, I warn Jerry, "Mom and Dad don't know we're sleeping together, so we're going to have to cool it, okay?"

"You mean your parents never did it before they were married?" he asks, incredulous.

"Of course they did it, but not in the house. They did it behind Grandpa's barn," I reply matter-of-factly.

"I don't mind doing it behind the barn--do you?" His grin is full of boyish mischief, and I can tell he's picturing the whole thing in his head. Hay to roll in, to discover new positions. Hay might be better than floor.

"The barn is torn down. There's a greenhouse there, now."

"So we'll do it behind the greenhouse."

"That's not funny," I say, leaving Jerry looking confused, but I'm not about to explain why it isn't funny. Not now! Not ever! Before I open the door I warn, "And no swearing."

"You swear all the time," Jerry says.

"But not in the house."

"So what do you do in the house?"

"We eat, we sleep, all kinds of boring stuff," I say as I open the door, almost pulling Jerry in with me.

As soon as we set foot inside my house and I see the look of barely suppressed anxiety on my mother's face, I know something is terribly wrong. After she takes our coats and sits us down around the dining room table to tell me about Dad, my sex life doesn't matter anymore. My wedding doesn't matter anymore. I'm not even sure that Jerry matters anymore. The only thing that matters is that my dad has cancer of the stomach, and right now the possibility of recovery doesn't look good.

CHAPTER 19

After going through the hell that was Joey's trial, always waiting and worrying and having to tell him day after day that everything is going to be okay even when I knew it wasn't, I thought there was nothing I couldn't handle. I thought I had suffered the ultimate, but there is no ultimate when it comes to suffer. There is only the depth one sinks into, like falling into a black hole, and there is no scrambling out, just falling ever deeper into despair. I thought nothing could hurt so much as when the jury found Joey guilty, but I was wrong.

Mom doesn't come with Jerry and me to see Dad. She tries to warn me about how sick he is but there is nothing anyone could possibly say to prepare me for this.

I walk silently into the hospital room and look at this barely recognizable figure of my father lying in bed, his body ravaged by the illness he must have carried with him long before there was any visible sign of it.

"Daddy," I say like I always used to when I was little, before I got too old, too sophisticated, and started calling him Dad like I thought a "big girl" should. I lean down over the bed and kiss him gingerly on his forehead.

"Honey," he says, managing a little smile as he winds his arms around my shoulders, even though it's painfully apparent that it's difficult for him.

It's hard to be brave, to pretend everything is okay. I'm learning though, because even when my eyes sting with unshed tears I manage to be bright when I announce, "Jerry's here with me."

Jerry walks over to the bed, not shaking my father's hand, instead putting his strong one over my father's frail one. I can't bear to look at the contrast, to remember how my father's hands used to be like that, big and strong, and capable of just about anything. I take Jerry's hand in mine, and for the rest of the visit I hold it.

"How's Joey?" Dad asks, like it's something he wants to know but is afraid of the answer. My hand digs into Jerry's.

"He's doing okay," Jerry answers for me. I think Jerry senses that lying to my dad is something I cannot do, and I squeeze his hand to tell him, "Thank you," without words.

"We're going to appeal the verdict, Daddy. Joey's not going to have to stay there."

"Honey, I don't have the money for an appeal. If I weren't sick, I could manage it, but now..."

There is so much heartbreak, so much defeat in Dad's voice that again, the words haven't been invented yet for me to explain to him, but Jerry finds them and says, "You don't have to worry about the expense, sir. I already have that taken care of. We just want you to get well."

183

My dad smiles, and it's not a strong smile, but it gives me the courage to invent words again, and I taste the sweetness of them when I say, "Daddy, Jerry and I are going to get married."

"That's wonderful, honey! When?"

"Just as soon as you can walk me down the aisle," I say, and I don't think Jerry is too happy with the words. There is silent disapproval in the tightening of the hand I'm holding. There is no way my father will be well enough in one week to walk me down the aisle. He's barely strong enough for this visit. He looks so tired, and I tell my dad that we'll be back again tomorrow to see him.

"I'll take care of the store so that Mom can come see you tonight. I love you, Daddy," I say kissing my father, swallowing the tears I know are trying to come out.

We're in the parking garage, sitting in the car when Jerry says, "I guess that's how it's going to be then, right?"

"What?" I look at him in confusion.

"Our getting married. We're not, are we, Freddy? I can't wait around here until your dad is well enough to walk you down the aisle. Married or not, I have to leave next week."

"I'm not calling it off. I'm just postponing it."

"For how long are we postponing it? Because I'm not sure your dad is ever going to be well enough to walk you down the aisle."

"I know," I say, with tears in my voice. "But I can't tell him that."

I cannot keep the tears just in my voice. I can't pretend anymore, not for Jerry's sake, not for mine. I sob the next words.

"I can't tell him he'll never see his grandkids, that he'll never take them fishing. Who is going to teach them to bait a hook if their grandpa's not here to teach them, Jerry? Who is going to teach our kids?"

I'm crying so hard now that I am scaring Jerry.

He says, "Honey don't; please don't cry."

But I keep crying. Those unshed tears that I pretended weren't there for my dad's sake spill out. The words have to be said, to tumble out as if they were invented in my head, before I started pretending for Joey's sake that everything is okay.

I can't stop crying and I can't stop asking, "Who is going to teach them the names of flowers and about butterflies and how soft a caterpillar feels when it crawls on your arm? Who, Jerry? Who is going to teach our kids that stuff if Dad dies and we don't get Joey out of prison?"

I'm almost hysterical. I know I am because I'm practically screaming and it's really scaring Jerry, and he promises, "Honey, we'll get Joey out."

"Who is going to teach them to have a beautiful heart, Jerry, if Joey isn't here? Who is going to teach them that? Tell me, who?"

I can't stop; the black hole of despair is sucking me in deeper and I can't scramble out.

"You will teach them, honey, because your dad and Joey taught you. We will tell them about their grandpa and how he loved to go fishing, and Joey will teach them about butterflies. And the beautiful

185

heart they will inherit from their mother," Jerry says, reaching over and pulling me towards him. "Because you do have a beautiful heart, Freddy."

I wipe at all those unshed tears that I didn't dare let my Dad see but are so real now and yield to the comfort of Jerry's arms, like I've been doing ever since his arms have been here for me.

"Will you take our kids fishing, Jerry?" I ask.

"Honey, I don't know how to fish. My dad liked to golf. I can teach them to play golf." I pull away, and Jerry says "I'll learn to fish, honey. I'll teach our kids how to fish." Jerry's arms are around me a long time. I like his arms around me, even in a parking garage, even in a car.

His arms aren't here for me at night, though. After a lot of complaining from Jerry about the sleeping arrangement, I lay in the familiar bed in my old room, and Jerry sleeps in Harry's old room, down the hall. I pull the covers up close around me and remember the night this all started. How Dad knocked on my door and asked if he could come in. How he sat on my bed and talked. There were so many times that I talked to my dad.

Especially when he would take me fishing. We'd talk a lot then, sitting in the old rowboat, line in the water, waiting for the fish to bite. We have this special thing between us, a sense of humor that only we understand. I will miss my dad.

There will never be another man in my life like him, and I already feel the hole in my heart that will always be there once he's gone.

By the time I fall asleep my pillow is wet from my mourning the loss of my father before he's even gone

I wake up to the muffled sound of voices just outside my bedroom door. I recognize my mother's voice saying, "It was hard for her, wasn't it? She didn't say anything, but I could see it in her eyes. Felicia and I never got along especially well. She was always her father's child more than mine. He understood her; I guess I never did. I wanted to, but it was her father who would say when things got too tense here at home, 'I think it's time I take a day off and go fishing,' and when he came back, and maybe the two of them didn't catch anything, he'd always say the fishing was great."

"I don't think it was the catching that mattered." Now it's Jerry's voice, deep and quiet. "It's been hard all along for her. Sometimes I'm not sure what to say to her myself."

"Felicia can be difficult to get along with, but don't give up trying."

"We're going to get married."

"That's what she told me, but are you sure? I mean, the difference in age..." the sentence trails off for a moment before Mom finally concludes it with, "She *is* only eighteen."

"There's a seven-year difference, only two years more than between you and your husband," Jerry says in our defense.

"I thought it was more--you seem older."

Jerry laughs and I imagine my mother blushing. She sure put her foot in it this time.

"I guess I'm more mature than most people my age, but I've had to be. My parents died when I was pretty young."

"Felicia needs someone like you, Jerry. Someone mature, with a will as strong as hers."

"I'm afraid I'm not as strong as you think," Jerry replies in his serious voice. Then, with a little laugh he adds, "Freddy can pretty much wrap me around her little finger sometimes."

I think of how Mom must be cringing right now; even the man I'm going to marry calls me Freddy.

To show just how much I've matured these last months, I'm already showered and dressed when I walk into the kitchen. My mother and Jerry are sitting at the table, and my mother has a surprised look on her face. My usual attire for breakfast in this kitchen is my nightshirt and bare feet, except for when I was going to school. I think there were days my mother would have preferred I went to school in my nightshirt, and I have to admit there were days when my ass really was hanging out.

"Hi," I say casually--at least I try to make it sound casual. I don't want to scare my mother into thinking I'm back to argue and this is the first phase. I've been known in the past to set little traps. Catch her off guard, then hit her with, "I won't be home from school until late. I'm working on a special project."

Of course, my clothes usually told her the project I was working on. I come up behind Jerry, wrap my arms around his neck, and kiss him on the cheek. That's another thing that surprises my mother: me being cheerful in the morning and even kissing someone. I have never been known to kiss in the morning, not even when I was little and she wanted to give me a hug before sending me off to school. I decide it's the least I can do to make up for all those missed hugs, and I give her a tight squeeze, too.

My cheery mood doesn't last though. By the time I get back from the store and looking over the books, I'm that person Mom and Jerry talked about this morning, thinking I couldn't hear them.

On our way to the hospital, I say to Jerry, "I don't know what the hell Mom did with those books. For an intelligent woman, she can't add worth a damn. Even with an adding machine! I don't know where to start."

"Your mother's never run a business before, Freddy. You have to be patient."

"You're a hell of a one to talk about patience, Jerry. You can't even get through one night of not fucking without complaining."

I have never said that word before to Jerry, and when I look at his face, I know I've gone too far. Jerry says very little during our visit at the hospital, which isn't any easier for me than the first one, and after supper he dutifully retires to his bedroom. He makes sure I hear the click when he locks the door, and I roll my eyes, exasperated but too sad and worn-out from the visit with my dad to start an argument.

For the next two days I work like crazy trying to get the books in order, only to arrive at the grim realization that the numbers don't lie. If we don't cut back on expenses, we'll lose the business.

"We have to lay off some people," I tell Carl when the store is empty of customers. "And cut back on inventory, too."

"I don't know, Freddy. With spring right around the corner, we have to be ready."

"That's what happened at Christmas; we were *too* ready. How come we're stuck with so much stuff?"

"There was nobody here to arrange the sales. You know how we always have a big Christmas sale? Well, this year it just never happened," he explains, the tired look in his eyes adding about ten years to his actual age of about forty.

"We'll make it happen, Carl. We need some money for spring stuff, okay?"

"Will do," he says, and I leave him to start selling marked-down Christmas leftovers when we're supposed to be selling Easter stuff.

Between the store and visiting my father, I don't notice just how bad my relationship with Jerry is until we're in the car on the way home from the hospital.

"I'm leaving for New York tomorrow, Freddy," he says, his voice devoid of any tenderness or any detectable emotion.

"I thought you didn't have to leave for another couple of days," I press, the hurt and confusion I've been keeping in coming to the surface.

"I don't, but at least there I won't be in anybody's way, complaining about all this fucking I'm not getting."

He stares straight ahead at the road like he's trying to freeze it with the ice in his eyes, and his knuckles are gripping the steering wheel so hard they've turned white.

"Jerry, I'm sorry I said that. I didn't mean it."

"Yes, you did. I don't even know you anymore."

"I don't even know me anymore," I reply sadly, and we drive the rest of the way home in silence.

The chill between us is so obvious that even my mother notices it and says, "I think I'll spend the night at the hospital with your father, Felicia, and leave you two alone."

I can't believe it! My mother is actually giving me permission to sleep with Jerry, in her house. I could never even swear in this house before, but now I can sleep with a man in it, and I'm not married to him? As I watch my mother get up from the table and put her coat on, I think how much has changed in such a short time.

Before she leaves, she asks, "You don't mind doing the dishes, do you, Felicia?"

"No, Mom," I reply, trying to keep shock out of my voice; I still can't believe it. My mother just gave me her blessing to have sex in her house, and instead of asking me to make sure I practice safe sex or some such other maternal advice, all she asks is that I do the dishes. I don't know what to say, so I just finish my sentence with, "I don't mind at all."

While Jerry goes to his room to pack, I take care
of the dishes. I even wipe down the cupboards. I
leave the kitchen spotless in an unspoken thank-you
to my mom, then I go into Jerry's room to help him
unpack.

He's almost finished, ready to zip up the bag,
when I walk in and stop him.

"Don't go." my voice sounds a million miles away.
"Not yet," I plead, biting my lower lip.

"Give me one good reason why I should stay. I
know coming home has been hard for you, and
there's a lot of pain in your life right now, but
hurting me isn't going to make that pain go away,
Freddy. Maybe one of these days you'll realize that.
Feel free to give me a call when you do," he says,
zipping up his bag with a finality that makes my
stomach hurt and my heart heavy.

Moving slowly, almost as if in a dream, I go over
to the phone on the dresser, push random buttons,
then begin to speak into the receiver that I never
bothered to turn on.

"Jerry," I say, silently praying that my little joke
will work and I'll have the man I love wrapped back
around my little finger, like he said. "I'm calling you.
Can you hear me? If you can you better get over
here fast, because there's a guy in this bedroom with
me that I think wants to go to bed with me, and he's
really cute."

I smile up into Jerry's eyes and am relieved to find
the ice from earlier has melted into twin pools of
warm blue, and a smile identical to my own begins to

spread across his cute face. He walks over, takes the phone out of my hand, then leads me over to the bed. He pushes the heavy suitcase onto the floor where it lands with a loud thump, and within moments, it's a contest of which of us can get out of our clothes faster.

We don't even bother to wrestle this time. I concede right away and let Jerry on top, but after the first round, I get my turn, too. I've always felt that balance is an important factor in any healthy relationship.

I'm still on top, my legs spread apart over his hips, not quite ready to lift myself up and off him, when he runs his hands along my back and says in a breathless voice, "Don't ever pull that shit on me again, Freddy."

"What shit?" I ask, truly bewildered. That really came out of nowhere.

"Treating me like I'm one of those boys you used to kiss in the halls at school, because I'm not. I love you, and if you don't know it by now, then when will you?"

My answer is a tongue-in-the-mouth kiss.

"I never kissed boys in the hall like that, Jerry," I tell him once I'm through kissing him. "Only my husband. When you come back we'll get married, even if we have to have the ceremony in the hospital. Maybe my dad can't walk me down the aisle, but I'd like him to be there, regardless. A girl likes her father to be at her wedding. Especially when she has a father like mine."

After that night we sleep in the same bedroom until Jerry has to leave. If my mother is aware of it she never says a word about it to either of us.

CHAPTER 20

I'm working at the store, going over the books, and double-checking just to make sure I didn't enter something wrong into the computer. Mom doesn't understand computers and I had to decode her scribbling in the books. I guess all those years of trying to read Mom's notes on the refrigerator paid off because after a while the scribbling in the books start to make sense, but the math didn't. The computer took care of that. I entered the scribbling along with receipts and it all came out right. I stare at the computer screen with the neat debits and credits, and I thank God for technology.

I'm still not sure how we pulled it off, and I look around the store with childlike wonder at the complete lack of wreaths, ornaments, and fake evergreens. All that remains are a few items in one box marked 'An Extra 50% Off.' Maybe it was the ad Jerry put in the newspaper; being a journalist he does have a way with words. Maybe it's just my luck looking up for a change, God giving me a break from all the trials I've been through lately. Whatever it is, by some miracle our store has successfully rid itself of all excess Christmas inventory, turning out a sufficient profit in the process. I am relieved and for a change it's a feeling, although foreign for a long time, I thoroughly enjoy. Now that I know we have the money, and even though there is still snow on the ground, I flip through catalogues and order our spring stuff. I wonder if the people on the other end of the phone can hear my smile. Of course, having such a huge sale meant keeping the store open longer than usual, leaving Jerry and me very little time to spend alone together. It's not exactly the way we wanted to spend Jerry's last days here before going to New York; I think he was a little disappointed, but I more than made up for it in bed. Jerry can't complain. And he didn't; he only said, "I guess you gotta do what you gotta do." I'm happy he understood.

I wish he were still here now that the sale is over, and I could do more making up to him and not just in bed. He sure was a big help, fixing all the leaky faucets, changing the furnace filter. Mom showed her appreciation by staying with Dad at the hospital all night. She might have given us permission to do it in the house, but she sure wasn't going to be there when we did.

It's Wednesday, the day after Jerry left to pick up his car and drive to New York. I tell Carl that on Monday I'm going to go visit Joey.

"It's four hours of driving each way just to spend one with him, but I'll be doing it every Monday from now on." I don't mean to complain, but it must sound like it, because Carl tells me the same thing

Jerry told me "You gotta do what you gotta do."

I worry all week about my first meeting with Joey. When I'm not worrying about Joey I worry about money, or else about my dad. It's always something.

I don't tell anyone but Jerry about my constant stressing, and even though his arms aren't here to comfort me I find my solace in just talking to him, just being able to hear his voice soothing me through the phone. It's not enough. I miss him. I need him. And he's not here.

"Dad wants to come home, Jerry. Of course, we would all like that, but I'm not sure that's the best thing for him. What do you think?" I ask him when he calls, chewing nervously on my pinkie nail.

"Honey, if that's what he wants, I think that's what he should do. What do the doctors say?"

"The same thing you just did, but I'm not sure Mom can take care of him. I have to run the store all day, so I can't always be here to help."

"Hire a nurse," he suggests.

"I don't know if we can afford it. The money's really tight."

"I'll send you as much as I can, but I have to save the money from the sale of the house for an attorney."

"Did you find one yet?"

"I haven't had time, but just as soon as I'm settled, I'll get right on it."

"I know, but I have to have something to tell Joey when I see him. What should I say, Jerry?" I ask, my voice beginning to tremble, like I'm on the verge of tears.

"Tell him he'll come home after the appeal."

"Mr. Baskins still wants to do it. What should I tell him?"

"Tell him we don't want him, that I've already found a new lawyer, and a better one."

"But we haven't."

"We will, though. It's just going to take some time. But I don't want to talk about Mr. Baskins. I want to talk about us. Do you miss me?"

"God, I miss you so much. Especially at night."

It's true. My bed is so cold and empty without Jerry in it. I roll over, expecting to see him there, looking so beautiful and peaceful in sleep, but the space beside me is always empty. I always end up crying and asking God why it has to be like this? What happened to our plans for a house and four kids? Why do I feel so old, and I'm only eighteen. Sometimes I'm angry with God. I don't think I have such a beautiful heart anymore.

I don't tell Jerry this, though. I don't want to sound hysterical again so I struggle to keep my voice level when I suggest, "Maybe you can come home, next weekend."

"Freddy, I can't afford to fly home every weekend, you know that. Besides, I have to work weekends."

"I thought you said you never work weekends. Remember, you told me that the first time I met you," I say, trying not to sound like I'm complaining, just joking.

I think it sounds like complaining, because Jerry says, "That was then. Now I have to."

"I know," I say, combing my fingers through my tangled hair in a show of exasperation the man on the other end of the line can't see. "I just wish we could be together all the time."

"I do, too."

"Sometimes I think I'll go crazy, I want you so bad, Jerry."

"Sometimes I think I *am* crazy to be here, with you there. Maybe I should just quit and find another job closer to home."

"Where?"

"I don't know. Some small paper like the one I left."

"But this is your dream job. I don't want you to give it up just for me."

It's real quiet, like what can I say? What can Jerry say? I have just put Jerry's dream ahead of ours, and I think one of us should say something, but right now I can't and I'm sure that Jerry won't.

"I love you, Jerry," I finally say, before reluctantly hanging up.

"I love you, too," he says, and I'm left with only a buzzing phone in my hand and an ache in my heart.

I take Jerry's advice and bring my father home, but I don't hire a nurse; I hire Agnes instead. Agnes is in-between jobs, and after two days of helping us out, she's back to being in between jobs. I fired her after Mom complained that Agnes does more watching television than she does watching my dad.

"I guess I wouldn't mind so much, Felicia, but all she watches is those stupid talk shows. You know the kind, where all they talk about is sex, and walk around on stage almost naked."

"You mean with their ass hanging out?"

My mother doesn't comment, but I think she gets the point.

Poor Mom! It must have been hard raising me, another 'hell-on-wheels,' as Jerry described himself as a child, and I can only wonder at the kind of offspring we'll produce. I think about that for a minute, then go to the calendar and look, but heck, I've been late before. It's not unusual for me to miss a period or two.

The night before I go to see Joey, I go into my dad's room to talk to him. I'm glad he's back at home; I really missed our talks like this. Even though I usually feel pretty crummy at the start of them, by the end I feel at least mostly better.

"What should I tell him, Daddy? I can't lie anymore."

"Then tell him the truth."

"You mean that there are some people in this world who are prejudiced against people like him? Is that what you want me to tell him, Dad?"

"Tell him that after we prove his innocence, he'll be able to come home."

"But not if Mr. Baskins stays his lawyer. Dad, Mr. Baskins is insisting that he should follow through with the appeal. That time is running out, and he already knows the case."

"But you said Jerry is looking for a new lawyer."

"Sometimes I wonder if Jerry's ever going to find one, or if Joey's ever going to come home."

"You have to have hope, honey."

I look at my dad. So weak and frail that he can't even get out of bed by himself. The doctors have estimated less than a year for him to live, and he's talking about hope.

"Freddy, life goes on no matter what. You and Jerry have your whole lives ahead of you. Don't lose what you have with him by trying to always be there for everyone else. Be there for him first. Be there for *yourself.*"

Now I understand my dad. The hope he has is not for himself, but for me, for my future.

"I love you, Daddy," I say, my eyes filling with tears

"I love you, Freddy," he replies with a tired smile, his eyes possessing just a hint of their former gleam. But it's there. It's still there.

As I get ready to leave so he can rest, I turn and say, "You know what I'm going to tell Joey tomorrow?"

"What?"

"I'm going to tell Joey that the next time he sees Mr. Baskins, he should pee on him."

I see the little smile soften those lines around Dad's mouth when he asks, a hint of the old mischief in his weary voice, "Are you saying, that Mr. Baskins pisses you off?"

"Well, maybe Mr. Baskins will understand that

kind of talk. He sure as hell doesn't understand lawyer talk."

"Good night, Freddy," Dad says. "And I'd think twice about telling Joey that; he just might do it."

Now I'm smiling broadly, unable to stop the grin spreading across my face.

"Yeah, but at least we'll be rid of him."

Mom walks in and asks, "What are you two grinning about?"

"Nothing," I say and make a hasty retreat out the door. Mom never understood our kind of humor, my dad's and my special brand. I'm still smiling when I crawl into bed remembering all those times I used to kid around with my father; we would laugh over nonsense that only we understood. Then I remember what the doctors say, and fall asleep crying.

In the morning I get up early. There's still moonlight shining through my window, but it's at least a four-hour drive, and I want to get an early start. I dress in wool slacks and a sweater, then I walk downstairs in my stocking feet with boots in hand. Mom is already in the kitchen when I get there, making breakfast. I tell her, "You didn't have to get up, Mom. I'm not hungry this early anyway."

"Your father had a bad night last night. He just went to sleep a little while ago, so I thought I'd wait until you left before I go and get some rest."

"You should have woke me up, Mom. I would have sat with him for a while."

"No! You have a long drive ahead of you. I don't want you dozing off at the wheel. Besides, it snowed last night and it's slippery out there. You could get into an accident. We've got enough troubles around here without that."

I agree with her on that one, but I don't say anything as I go to the window and look out. The moon is twice as bright, shining down on all that sparkling white.

"It sure is beautiful. It must be real wet because it's sticking to the trees. I hope I don't have to shovel."

"You shouldn't be shoveling, Felicia."

"Why not? I always did before."

"Because you're not a little girl anymore."

I've been hearing those words ever since my introduction into womanhood by getting my period. I respond with my usual answer.

"Gee whiz, Mom, I'm sure glad you told me. Does that mean I can go out with boys now?"

"I don't want you hurting yourself, just in case."

Now that's different, and I have to stop and think for a while, just what in the hell she means? Then I catch on, and am quick to correct her.

"I'm not pregnant, Mom. I'm not even married, so how can I be pregnant?"

My mother gives me this look, like she always did before she told me to go upstairs and change, that I wasn't going to school "looking like that."

I decide to let it slide. It's much too early in the morning for this conversation. Besides I don't think I'll win this argument, especially since I still haven't gotten my 'little friend' this month.

"I'll see you tonight," I say, lacing up my boots and putting on my coat.

"Drive carefully and give Joey our love," Mom says to me just before I walk out the door and into a world of white. It is so bright that I don't even need the yard light to find my way to the garage. Then after about twenty minutes of shoveling despite my mother's warning, I'm on my way.

I drink coffee, listen to the radio, then put an audio book in the tape deck, trying anything to stay awake. I think of having to do this every week and try not to groan. I tell myself that after a while I'll get used to it.

By the time I finally stop in front of the iron gates my muscles are stiff from the long drive, and the snow has become a gray slush that matches the depressing gray of the prison.

Despite everything the judge and Mr. Baskins say I still think of it as a prison. It's somewhere Joey was sent to against his will and can't leave. There are iron bars everywhere, and razor wire on top of every fence. Uniformed guards are posted everywhere. It's a damned prison!

I pass through the heavy metal gates that open like jaws ready to grab and swallow me, but not before the guards do everything but strip-search me. I do think that one guard got a little too thorough about patting me down; it's no way to treat an almost-pregnant woman, that's for sure. After being all but fondled by the guards I drive to the designated area for visitors and park the car. Off to one side is a little fenced-in area where I figure the visitors can meet with the inmates when it's nice outside, because there are some picnic tables under the trees. It's only the beginning of March so the trees are still bare, but I can't wait until summer so I won't have to visit with Joey inside. But by summer Joey should be out, so to hell with the trees, the picnic tables, and especially that perverted guard. This is all just temporary, a nightmare that will soon end.

If I think the outside is a nightmare, the inside is a horror show, because real life can't possibly be like this. Everybody except the staff shuffles around here like a bunch of zombies. They stare at me, but I don't think they really see me. Their eyes are blank holes in their head. While I'm waiting for those guys in white coats to bring Joey to me, (guards here wear white coats, to give the name "Institution" credibility, I suppose) I go and sit down at a table in the recreation room.

Impatient to see Joey, I sit anxiously tapping my fingers on the bare table. I look around and study the room, but there isn't a whole lot to study. Headache-green walls and drab gray furniture. If *this is* recreation, I'd sure hate to see the rooms.

At first, I'm alone in the room until a woman comes in, sits down at a table next to mine, and looks at me with one of those blank, hollow stares. She stares a long time and I shift uncomfortably in my chair, wishing she would go away and stare at somebody else. I'm not used to such creepy scrutiny. When the boys at school stared, they saw what they were looking at and I knew what they wanted. Finally, she shuffles over and hands me a Kleenex tissue that she's just used to blow her nose in.

Trying hard not to have that 'this is gross' look on my face, I say, "Thank you," like she's just handed me a present. I hold the crumpled tissue gingerly between thumb and forefinger and carry it over to the wastebasket, then toss it in, hoping she won't notice. She doesn't.

When I return to my seat she's sitting at my table talking to a doll like it's her baby. Now I'm the one staring, fascinated with the way she fixes its hair, smoothes the wrinkles in its little dress, and strokes its unfeeling plastic cheek. She fusses and croons, even holding it to her breast like she is nursing it. Not even a real baby is fussed over this much. Suddenly she starts shaking it violently, screaming over and over, "I told you! Didn't I tell you?"

It all happens so fast. A man in white comes and leads her out of the room, and I'm still feeling the shock of it when Joey's brought in only a few moments after the woman was taken back down the long hall to her room.

After the strange outburst, I'm not surprised at how thin Joey is, or how his hair sticks out like someone took scissors to it and cut chunks out of it. I'm just glad that when he looks at me, he sees me.

After we hug, Joey says, "That was Helen. Helen

thinks that doll is her baby."

"It's a good thing it's not, or she would have killed it."

Then I realize what I just said, but Joey doesn't seem to notice--or maybe he does, and just accepts it as part of prison.

"I brought some cards. Do you want to play Old Maid?"

Joey's face brightens up and for the rest of the visiting time we play Old Maid, while around us the room fills with other people: either visitors like me, or 'patients,' but I see them as prisoners like Joey.

Before I go home, Joey says what I figured he'd say, and even though I'm somewhat prepared for it, my heart still has to catch up with what my head knows, and I'm back to pretending again. "I wanna go home with you, Freddy. I don't like this place," Joey pleads.

"Soon, Joey. Jerry is working on it. We're going to get you a really good lawyer and he's going to help so you can come home."

"When, Freddy? When can I come home?"
"Soon, Joey. Real soon."

"That's good, Freddy, because I'm not crazy. Norman says only crazy people live here, and I'm not. Am I, Freddy?"

I look at him and now I'm not pretending. I answer, "No, Joey, you're not crazy." I mean what I say. Because anyone who knows Joey like I do knows damn well he's not crazy. But still, I have to wonder exactly where the line between sanity and madness is drawn, and how much of an in-between is there, and if one exists at all. Society put Joey here, a society that can't, or won't, understand about people like Joey. And it hurts to think that it can't, or won't, understand about different. It's really hard driving home because the tears keep blurring my vision.

When I get home, Mom tells me that Jerry called, and I ask her if he said he'd call back later tonight.

"No," she answers a little distracted, busy with fixing a tray to take in to Dad.

"Did he tell you why he called?"

My mother is acting like she doesn't hear me, and it scares me when she ignores me. There were times when I tried to sneak out of the house in one of my trashy outfits, when I thought that she had eyes in the back of her head. My mother has always worked hard at not ignoring me.

"What did Jerry say, Mom?"

For some reason, the little tea bag in her hand is more interesting than me. She is studying it, turning the little tag at the end of the string that says 'Lipton' over and over with her fingers, twining the string around her finger as she dunks the tea bag in and out the cup of steaming water.

"He said he'd call tomorrow," Mom finally says tonelessly.

"Is that all?"

Mom's full attention remains on the tea, staring at the tag that says 'Lipton.' It's starting to scare me. Her vacant stare is eerily similar to the shuffling patients at the place where they are keeping Joey, and I suddenly want to take that tea bag out of her hand and rip it to shreds, tag and all.

"He said that he'll be home at the end of the month to marry you," she answers in a tired voice, after what seems like forever.

For a brief, blissful moment, the euphoria I feel when I think of Jerry's and my wedding is all I know until I look at my mother. When she looks up at me, I can see that her eyes are red; they have dark circles beneath them, and I want to hug her, but something stops me. Suddenly, I realize that she's crying; tears she is trying to hold back are running down her cheeks, and I know it has nothing to do with tea. Her youngest--her baby girl is getting married. Not only am I old enough to shovel the driveway by myself, but now I'm old enough to belong to someone else.

"Mom," I begin quietly, coming to stand beside her and resting a reassuring hand on her shaking shoulder.

"I'll always be your daughter. Nothing can change that."

"I know," she says with a sniffle, putting the teacup onto the tray beside a spoon, a napkin, and a couple of sugar cookies.

"But you'll be his wife first."

"Like you are for Daddy," I say, trying to make her feel better but not at all sure that I am.

"Yes," she says, drying her eyes with the corner of a napkin and picking up the tray to take into my father's room. "He always comes first with me."

CHAPTER 21

After what seems like ages it's finally decided that Jerry and I will be married on the first of April. I keep expecting that he'll call me that morning as I'm getting ready and say, "April Fool's! I was only kidding." But Jerry wouldn't kid about getting married; at least I don't think he would.

It's the day before Jerry comes home and three days before the wedding. I'm working in Mrs. Davis's yard, pruning some bushes before their buds begin to form, when she comes up from behind where I'm bent over a branch, checking what to cut away and what to keep. Sometimes pruning can be tricky. It takes a good eye, and I have a good eye. That's what Mrs. Davis usually says.

She compliments, but today she scolds, "This could have waited a couple of weeks. Shouldn't you be home getting ready for that young man of yours?"

"I am ready," I say, pushing a stubborn lock of hair back behind my ear. "Besides, in a couple of weeks these will be all budded out."

Mrs. Davis moves closer, stoops down and takes one of my hands in her own, giving it one of her purse-lipped, appraising looks. Mrs. Davis' hands are soft, manicured, and polished. They are impeccable.

That's Mom's favorite word for hands like Mrs. Davis has. When I was little and she told me to go wash my hands, she'd use that word, how they should look. I didn't know what the word *impeccable* meant then; I only knew what it didn't mean *dirty*. Poor Mom, after all those years of raising me and now she's losing me. No wonder she was crying the other night.

"My Lord, girl!" Mrs. Davis exclaims, turning my hands over in her impeccable ones, shaking her head. "These are not a bride's hands."

Embarrassed, I pull them abruptly out of her impeccable hands and hide both of mine in my pockets. Mrs. Davis sounds just like my mother.

"This is my job, Mrs. Davis. I can't afford to take time off or have beautiful bride's hands," I say, trying not to sound judgmental. I'm not rich, Mrs. Davis is. Mrs. Davis, I want to say, give me a break! I don't, of course. I go back to cutting away the dead from the living, cutting a little more off than is necessary.

"I didn't mean anything by it, child. I just thought, since this is a once-in-a-lifetime thing, getting married, you should enjoy every minute of it. Of course, these days it's not once in a lifetime. Sometimes it's hard to keep track of what invitation it is I'm getting. Is it the first or second wedding, or sometimes even the third? I always give a gift though. I'm not one to judge."

I wonder if she would judge sex before marriage? I wonder if she and Mr. Davis did it before they were married?

I keep the wondering to myself and say, "I'm only getting married once, so this is the only invitation you will be getting from me."

"I can see that."

"How?" I ask, the pruning shears held in midair, ready to strike.

"By the way you handle those shears. No man would dare divorce you," Mrs. Davis says, laughing.

Before I know what's happening I find myself laughing right along with her. I have always liked Mrs. Davis. She just pissed me off with that comment about my hands, but I'm over it now.

"Come on up to the house for a glass of iced tea," she says, beginning to toddle off toward the house. When I don't make a move, she turns, motioning enthusiastically with her impeccable hands to follow her.

"Come on, girl--I won't dock you for taking a little time off."

I put down my shears and follow. She has a commanding force about her. Besides, she's one of our best customers; I can't afford to piss her off. While Mrs. Davis pours the tea out of a clear glass pitcher at a table in a breakfast room flooded in sunlight, we sit and talk.

"Is your father better now? I hear he's going to give you away."

"I don't think he's better. He's just pretending he is. He will be in a wheelchair, and the ceremony will be short."

"I wish it were summer. You could have your wedding here in my garden. It would be beautiful. I give really beautiful garden parties."

"Even if it were summer, we would still have to have it at home. Dad would never be able to make the trip to your place. We'll be lucky if he can sit long enough for me to wheel him into the living room where Jerry will be waiting for us," I say, trying hard not to let Mrs. Davis see my lips quiver just before I put the glass to my mouth and take a sip of tea.

"I still wish my garden were in bloom. I would at least be able to send you the flowers to decorate with."

I start to laugh. Poor Mrs. Davis. She wants so much to show off her garden, even if only the flowers.

"You forget that we own a garden store. By the time Carl is through bringing in flowers from the greenhouse, I think the house will look like a garden. But thanks, anyway."

"Well then--maybe for a baby shower. The garden will be ready by then, and I'll throw you a baby shower."

I stop sipping, almost choking on tea. Has Mrs. Davis been looking at my calendar, too?

"What makes you think I'll be pregnant by then?" I ask, kind of suspicious-like.

"Because you're young, and young people get pregnant on their honeymoon."

"Not if they're taking the pill," I say, finally bringing the glass back up to my mouth, taking

213

another sip.

"I don't believe in the pill. People should have their babies when they are young. I just wish I had been young enough to have a baby when I married."

"How old were you?"

"Too old to have babies, but Mr. Davis and I wanted them. He loved kids, you know."

I don't know. I didn't even know Mr. Davis. I was just a kid when Mr. Davis was still alive. I think that when Mrs. Davis gets through talking though, I will know him better.

"I was a nurse and Mr. Davis came in with what he thought was a heart attack, but actually it was just indigestion. He stayed a couple of days for tests, and I must have taken good care of him, because on his way out of the hospital, he proposed. I didn't accept right away. It took six weeks for him to talk me into it. He was a lawyer, and lawyers are good talkers." Her voice trails off, remembering Mr. Davis.

I remember Mr. Baskins and wish to God he were a better talker, or a better lawyer, or something better than a stupid jackass.

"I met Jerry in court. He was covering the story of Joey's trial. I guess your meeting is more romantic than mine."

"Romance is where you find it, honey, just like love. I've seen you with Joey, and maybe some people might not love him but you sure do. That's why I know you'll never get divorced. For you, love comes first."

"The problem is," I begin, staring into my glass,

wishing there were tea leaves at the bottom and I knew how to read them. "Which love do I put first?"

"Your husband's," Mrs. Davis says, filling my glass with more of the iced tea. "Always, your husband comes first."

"You sound like my parents."

"It's the voice of experience."

I get up from the table, ready to leave.

"Thanks for the tea and all that experience talk," I say, kind of joking, but kind of serious, too. "And I'll remember what you said about the honeymoon, Mrs. Davis. Maybe you will be having a baby shower in your garden, after all."

"Call me Elizabeth," she suggests out of the blue. "Or better yet, call me Liz. That's what Mr. Davis used to call me. And just to set the record straight, the first time I saw Mr. Davis he was sitting on a bedpan. They wouldn't let him out of bed, and he rang for a nurse to help him, and that nurse was me."

I'm back to pruning when I turn around and there is Mrs. Davis again, standing behind me, watching my every move.

"Where did you say you were going on your honeymoon?" she asks, real blunt-like. I don't usually mind blunt, but when it's about something as personal as a honeymoon I do.

"I didn't say."

"Well girl, where are you going?"

I want to say "none of your business", but she did give me tea, and she did share personal stuff with me when she told that bedpan story, so I share, too.

215

"Nowhere. Jerry and I can't afford a honeymoon just now."

She tries to hand me a key but I hold back from taking it, and I think maybe I should wash my hands first. Impeccable shouldn't be touching dirty, even though there are some that would argue opposites attract. Ours must attract, because Mrs. Davis grabs my hand and presses the key firmly into my palm.

"This key is to our cabin. My husband and I used to go there all the time, but I don't go there anymore, not by myself," she adds. Her voice trails off again, remembering.

"Mrs. Davis, I really appreciate the offer, but Jerry and I can't go anywhere because I can't leave Mom alone to care for Dad all by herself."

"I'll come and stay with her," she insists.

"You would stay? In our house, to help take care of Dad?" I ask, my words as unsure as I feel, and it's a good thing I don't have the shears in my hands anymore because I just have to hug this woman with such beautiful hands, and I think she has a beautiful heart to go with those hands.

"I'm a nurse and I'm qualified. I'm not so old that I can't handle a patient anymore."

"But you don't have to work. I mean, Mr. Davis left you well provided for."

"All except for the loneliness. He couldn't provide a solution to that in his will. All we ever had was each other, and now--well." Mrs. Davis is losing herself in memory, then comes back to the present. "I won't mind helping your mother. I'll feel useful again."

"Thank you, Mrs. Davis. I mean, Liz," I correct myself, smiling broadly at her and pocketing the key. I really want to hug her but my hands are dirty, and she looks so very impeccable.

Then I think, what the hell, and I hug her anyway.

When I'm ready to leave, Mrs. Davis comes out again and inspects what I've done. Just before I get into the truck to drive home, she says, "Enjoy the cabin, Freddy. My husband and I always did. And remember what I said about not taking the pill. That cabin is the perfect place to make a baby."

I drive away, watching in the rear-view mirror as Mrs. Davis walks up the path to her house, and I think of all the times Mr. and Mrs. Davis went up to the cabin. Did they try to make a baby there? Will Jerry and I, or have we already? Cabin or not, when you're young and forget to take the pill sometimes a baby can be made even somewhere as seemingly unromantic as a car or a mattress on the floor.

Later that evening I go to Joey's little house to get it ready for Jerry. The sleeping arrangement is Mom's idea. Both my brother and sister are coming home for the wedding, and since Mom has Angela's old room, I'm stuck with sharing my room with Angela. I don't argue. I've sneaked in and out of the house before. This will be a little harder, but if Angela wants to tattle, well--I still have that birth control pill discovery to use as blackmail.

After hours of dusting, scrubbing, and making the

bed up with special sheets I brought from home, I sit down and admire my handiwork. It looks cute, and if Mrs. Davis hadn't offered us her cabin this is where we'd be spending our honeymoon. But cute or not, I'll take the cabin over this any day. I put the yellow daffodil plant I brought with me from the store on the table, scatter a couple of green plants around the room, and then, for the finishing touch I lay a red rose on the pillow.

The next morning I go to the airport to pick up Jerry, and despite the plane being late and worrying that maybe all this really is an April Fool's joke, Jerry's homecoming is perfect. There's nobody around when we get home. Dad had an especially rough night last night, and both of my parents are sleeping. We go right to Joey's little house, and before I even help him to unpack we make love. We take our clothes off in between kisses. I don't even have to feel first to know Jerry is ready. We move with the pent-up need of being apart for so long until finally, after a climax that is totally self-fulfilling, still breathing hard, we lie holding each other, saying, "I love you," over and over, just in case the action wasn't proof enough.

"I smell roses," Jerry says, lying on his back with me cuddled up close.

I look around, like maybe or maybe not Jerry is right, then I spot the crushed rose among the sheets and with a little flourish, I hand it to Jerry.

"It was supposed to make you passionate," I say,

pulling off the petals and letting them flutter down to his bare chest, one by one.

"It worked," Jerry says, taking the rest of the rose, mostly just a stem now, and passing it between my breasts. Then after teasing he tastes, not the rose, but me.

We make love again, only this time we take our time. Then, after a little nap we get up and go to see if Dad is awake.

Jerry hasn't officially asked my dad yet for my hand in marriage. I don't think that will be a problem, though, considering that Jerry's already tried out the merchandise and knows for sure that he wants to buy.

The next two days go by in hectic confusion with my brother and sister arriving home, along with the news that Harry's computer business is bankrupt, and Angela's boyfriend isn't the prize she thought, and as a result, Angela has called off her wedding. I just shrug it off as something I expected anyway. But when Jerry tells me that he's accepted an assignment to go to the Middle East to report on the war there, I'm pissed and ready to call off the wedding, even if it does disappoint Mrs. Davis. Maybe the wedding is at our house but half the wedding has come from her house. Mrs. Davis loves to plan parties, especially weddings, and through all the chaos of bad news, it's Mrs. Davis who finally brings good news into the house with her announcement that she's found the perfect attorney for us.

"He was once a protégé of Mr. Davis, and now

one of the leading defense attorneys. If anybody can get Joey home, he will. And as a special favor to me, he's offered to do it pro bono," so Mrs. Davis says. I cross my fingers and say a silent prayer that she's right.

CHAPTER 22

The chair in my parents' room is big and overstuffed. It's the chair I used to curl up and fall asleep in when I was little. Now I'm bigger, and it's not as comfortable as it was then, but it's still better than having to share a bed with Angela. My sister snores--not soft little flutters of air like Jerry does sometimes when he lies the wrong way. She all but brings down the roof with her racket. I try getting her to move on her side, shoving as gently as I can at the dead weight next to me, but the only move that helps is when I give up and move out of the room. I gave up on the idea of sneaking out to Jerry. I haven't let him touch me since he told me about his assignment. That's how upset it makes me.

Mom comes into the room one more time before going to her room and whispers, "Are you sure you want to sit with him, Felicia? Tomorrow's the wedding. You should look rested for your own wedding."

"I want to do this, Mom," I answer, pulling my feet up in the chair and tucking them under me.

"But in that chair, Felicia? It's not very comfortable."

"It's okay, Mom. Just go, please."

She walks out of the room and I shift positions in the chair, trying to make myself comfortable, then cover myself with the afghan Mom left behind. I listen to Dad's steady breathing. It's a comforting sound to me. He'll be okay for a while after his shot, but if he wakes up, if he needs something, I'll be here.

I curl my legs up into the chair like I used to when I was little, and I wonder if getting married is the right thing to do. Jerry and I are barely talking to each other the night before our wedding. Is that really any way to start out a marriage? What about when we promise to be there for each other? How can we be, when Jerry will be in the Middle East covering the war, and I have to be here to help take care of Dad? And what about Joey? I tell myself that in the morning Mrs. Davis can take all her dishes and silver back home. There will be no wedding or honeymoon, but I'm not sure about the baby shower yet. I fall asleep dreaming of fat-cheeked babies: four of them, just waiting for Jerry and me to make them.

I wake up to the sound of soft moans coming from my father's bed.

"Are you all right, Daddy? Can I get you something?" I ask, going over to his bed, dragging the afghan with me and hugging it around my shoulders.

"I'm okay, but I could use a drink of water," he says, and I take the glass of water sitting on his nightstand and hold it to his lips while he sips. When I lay him back on the pillow, he gives a little groan, and I know he's got to be hurting pretty bad.

"Do you want another shot, Daddy? It's time."

"No," he says, but I think he does and just isn't admitting it, so I get the needle anyway. When it's ready and I'm about to swab his arm with an alcohol pad, my father pushes my hand away saying, "First we have to talk, Freddy, then the shot."

"Okay, Dad," I say, lying the needle down beside the water on the nightstand.

"Sit here!" he say, exerting obvious effort as he pats the edge of the bed with his hand.

"I don't want to hurt you, Daddy. I can sit in a chair."

"Sit!" he commands. I haven't heard so much life in my father's voice in a long time, and I sit.

"What's hurting me, Freddy, is what I see in your eyes."

"What do you see, Daddy? Because sometimes when I look in the mirror, all I see is nothing. A great big nothing, that goes on forever. Without you and Joey, that's all there is left, a great big empty hole in my heart, and I don't know how to fill it."

"You have Jerry."

"I used to have Jerry. He's going far away and I'm not even sure if he'll come back. There's a war there, Daddy, and I'm just so scared that something will happen to him."

"Is that why you're planning on calling off the wedding? Because you're afraid, kitten?"

My father hasn't called me that since I started first grade, and even then I told him I was too old to be called a kitten. I don't say I'm too old now.

223

"I never said I was calling off the wedding," I say, wondering if maybe I talk in my sleep.

"Your eyes tell me you are."

"Jerry and I have nothing in common, you know that, Dad. He wants to be off reporting on some war, and me--I just like digging in a garden. I don't think they have gardens where he's going. Just a lot of sand and graves."

"You know, that's what I thought when I first met your mother."

"You mean that she wanted to be a reporter? Because I already know how much you love digging in the dirt," I say with that teasing voice I'm famous for. A flicker of smile flashes across his face and now it's that special humor between us again.

"Your mother is Jewish and I'm a gentile, Freddy. Have you any idea how many problems we faced because of that?"

"You mean Marvin Lowenstein? Come on, Dad, how much competition is there with a guy named Marvin Lowenstein?"

My dad smiles again, and I think I'm on a roll.

"Besides, Mom would have never been able to call me Felicia, and you know how she had her heart set on naming her daughter that."

"You don't like the idea of being called Felicia Lowenstein?"

"I don't like the idea of being called *anything* Lowenstein. I'm glad I'm a Harrison, but I'm still not real crazy about the Felicia part."

"If her parents had their way, you would have

been a Lowenstein, a little rich girl who never had to dig in dirt or work for a living."

"And I wouldn't have Joey either. I can't imagine my life without Joey, Dad. Can you?"

"No, kitten, I can't imagine life without Joey or without you. I can't imagine my life without my family."

"I can't imagine my life without you, Daddy," I say, laying my head down on the pillow next to him and wiping my tears on the afghan beside me. My father touches my hair, smoothing it back from my face.

"Freddy, it wasn't Lowenstein money your mother gave up. Her parents disowned her when she married me. She didn't give up a career or a garden. She gave up everything she had ever known. Family, money, even her religion, to marry a struggling gardener."

"I didn't know. I just thought she never talked about her parents because they were dead, and it hurt too much to talk about them."

"When her parents said she was no longer their daughter, it hurt her more than any of us can possibly imagine."

Now I'm really crying, and I sit up to get a tissue from the box on the nightstand when Mom walks in.

"What's going on here? Why are you crying, Felicia?"

"For you, Mom," I say, getting up and giving her a hug. "I'm crying because I'm just so happy you married Daddy and not Marvin Lowenstein."

"My God, James, you didn't tell her about that

little wimp, did you?" she says, releasing herself from my hug. "Felicia, I wouldn't have married him if he were the last man on earth."

"I know, Mom, and lucky for me he wasn't or there never would have been a Felicia anything."

Dad grins and I grin, while Mom just looks confused. I go to the window and look out. The sky is just starting to get red in the east. It's going to be a beautiful day for a wedding.

"I think I'll go for a walk," I say, ready to leave.

"Don't go too far. In another four hours, you'll be getting married."

"I won't be long," I say, leaving Mom to give Dad his shot while I go and make sure there is still going to be a wedding.

I breathe the fresh air in deep, clearing my lungs of the sterile, pungent smell of disinfectant, medicine, and sickness. I walk over to Joey's house and, before going in, I stand looking out past the trees where the greenhouse once stood, before Dad had it torn down. I remember a time when I laid right on that patch of grass with Erik, and we promised always to be true. I take another deep breath, clearing my head of the past to make room for the future.

Once inside the little house I tiptoe silently into the bedroom and undress, then slip into bed next to Jerry without a sound. At first he shudders with the cold of my body against his, then wraps his warmth around me with a grateful moan.

"I love you," I breathe, reaching down to touch him under the blanket, feeling him come to life.

"I love you, too, Freddy. I should have asked you first before taking that assignment."

"Would you have said no to them if I told you that I didn't want you to go?"

"I would have lost my job if I had."

"You really love that job, don't you?"

"I love you more," he says, closing his eyes as my hand continues its business below the covers, picking up speed a little.

"You don't have to choose, Jerry. I guess I can't really speak for your job, but at least you have me for as long as you want me."

Now Jerry is on top of me, fully awake and fully alive. Before we come together to validate our agreement I say, "I heard that it's bad luck for a groom to see the bride on the wedding day, before she walks down the aisle."

"I heard that it's bad luck for a bride to keep her husband out of her bed. Don't ever do that to me again, Freddy. I've told you how I feel when you treat me like that."

"That's not bad luck, it's bad judgment. And I'm sorry."

"I'm sorry, too, sweetheart," Jerry says. Then we stop talking and start doing.

We both fall asleep, and if not for Angela banging on the door, we would have missed our own wedding.

"Damn it, Freddy, Mom's been going crazy looking for you," Angela says as she all but marches me back to the house. We leave Jerry behind to get ready.

"Look, I'm sorry. It's just that I had to discuss something with Jerry before the wedding."

"Discuss something, my ass. You two were in bed together. How long has he been banging you anyway?"

"It's none of your business, and if you say anything to Mom, well, I can always find a way to bring up those birth control pills I found in your bedroom."

"When did you find them?" she asks, looking at me with a hint of fear.

"A while ago," I reply with a triumphant grin.

"Before Jerry, right?"

"Yeah, before Jerry. What's it to you?"

"It's nothing to me, but a lot to Mom and Dad. How many guys have you fucked, Freddy?"

"How many have you, Angela? Don't tell me old money-bags didn't get you into bed a couple of times."

"No, actually, he didn't."

I stop dead in my tracks and stare at my sister.

"Not even once?" I ask in disbelief.

"Hell, he couldn't even get it up once. He's impotent. Why do you think I called off the wedding?"

So that's it; it all makes sense now: Angela's jealous of me. Beautiful, sexy, feminine Angela can't get her guy's soldier to stand at attention, while all I have to do is touch my guy with one of my un-bride-like hands, and he's hard as a rock.

"Jerry has no problem in that department. I guess it's just a matter of inspiration," I say with a wicked little grin, picking up the pace so I can get ahead of my sister.

I shouldn't have said that, I know. It's not nice to rub it in, but then I think, why the hell not? And I walk into the house humming the traditional wedding march. I still can barely believe that in about an hour it'll be playing as I walk down the aisle to my waiting groom.

Mrs. Davis did a good job having the dress Jerry's mother wore for her wedding altered and is determined that when I walk down the stairs in front of the guests, everything will be perfect, including my "impeccable bride's hands." A little reluctantly, but admittedly with some excitement, I had a full French manicure at the same salon where I got my hair done. It's the first one I've ever had in my life, and probably the last, since I'm not planning on needing bride's hands ever again after today.

"Let me see," Mrs. Davis says, fussing over my crepe-thin veil of snow-white netting, fastened to a wreath of baby's breath. Little white flowers in a circle on top of red hair. It sure beats a baseball cap. She turns me around to face her and gives me the once-over from head to toe. Really, this should be my mother's job, placing the veil on my head and whatnot, but Mom has her hands full getting Daddy ready, which is fine with me.

Mrs. Davis is fastening the string of pearls she's

lending me around my neck when Mom walks in. It's the part of "borrowed" from the "something old, something new, something borrowed something blue" tradition.

"Are you ready, Felicia?" she asks.

"I think so," I say, and then turn to Mrs. Davis. "Can I be with my mother alone, please?"

"Of course," Mrs. Davis says, making a quick exit.

"I love you, Mom," I say, the threat of tears ready to ruin the make-up that Mrs. Davis has just so painstakingly applied to my face.

"I love you, too, Felicia," Mom says, wiping at her own eyes with the lace handkerchief that she's not supposed to use until later when Daddy gives me away.

"I'm sorry for all those arguments we had. You were always right. You know that. I just hope that someday I can be as good a mother as you are."

"You will be, Felicia. I have never doubted that."

"And a wife too, Mom. I want to be as good a wife to Jerry as you are to Dad."

"You will be, Felicia," she assures me again, sniffling.

"I don't know, Mom. Sometimes it scares me."

"You will be a good wife and mother, Felicia, just like you've always been a good daughter and sister. There aren't too many people who could accept Joey the way you do. You were never ashamed of him. Not even in front of your friends."

"Not always," I correct her. "Sometimes Joey embarrassed me."

"But you never let him know, and that takes a lot of character. Even more than I have, I'm afraid."

"Oh, Mom, I wish Joey were here now. I miss him so much."

"I know, I know," she says in her way, and I know that when my mother starts repeating herself, it's time to drop the subject.

My mother walks with me down the stairs to where my father is waiting for me, and from there on it's just my dad and me. I don't see the guests seated on folding chairs on either side of me. I don't see Angela or Harry, just the top of my dad's head as I push him in front of me. When I look up, Jerry is standing next to me, tall and good-looking in his tuxedo, and I take his hand as Mom pushes Daddy to sit next to her.

The ceremony is short and simple, but somehow I know that behind me, my mother and father are crying. Their baby is now a wife, and I think when I turn to look at my dad over my shoulder that there's no more empty sadness in my eyes. I'm pretty sure he likes that, because despite his tears he's smiling broadly.

My dad and me—I can always make him smile, no matter what.

CHAPTER 23

By the time Jerry pulls the car into the driveway next to the cabin the sun is already sinking in the west, and the lake is ablaze with bright fire from the reflection of the crimson sky. Even before checking out the inside of the cabin we go to stand at the edge of the water, not daring to miss one minute of the spectacular completion of this special day.

"What a view," Jerry says, putting his arm around my shoulder.

"And it's all ours, at least for a week," I say, wrapping my arm around Jerry's waist. We stand together in awe of nature's way of saying "Good night." Finally the sun dips down behind the horizon, making the bare branches of trees, yet to get their spring leaves, only a shadowy outline in the descending darkness.

"It's getting late," Jerry says, looking at his watch, and I decide to get this honeymoon back on track.

In the dim light of dusk, we go back to the car and take out the groceries. Then while Jerry unlocks the door I brace myself for the tradition of carrying one's new bride over the threshold, wondering if Jerry will bother or will he want to get right down to checking out the bedroom. I wait while he carries the groceries in, and then sure enough, he lifts me into his arms, hugging me tight against his chest and steps through the door, careful not to bump any part of me. I hug his neck and tell him to put me down before he drops me.

He twirls me around once and I give a girlish little squeal, then to my amazement (after all I am the gardener not the ballerina in the family), I land with my feet on the floor. We laugh, we hug, we even kiss one of those tongue-in-the-mouth kisses, but we don't go into the bedroom and I wonder what the hell is wrong with him. When I try to reach down to make sure that everything is in working order he gently brushes my hand away, then walks over to check out the fireplace.

"I think I'll make a fire," he says, and I wish he would--but not in the fireplace. I put the groceries away, all the while marveling at the wonder of the kitchen, the whole cabin, and I can't wait to see the bedroom.

"Would you mind carrying the suitcases in first?" I ask, figuring that if he doesn't have the idea yet, once we are in the bedroom he will. I walk in behind Jerry and then when he puts the suitcases down, I kind of nonchalantly go over to the bed and lay across the quilt made from patches of different materials, all formed into a kind of star pattern.

"Boy, is this mattress ever comfortable," I say, stretching myself out on the quilt. I give him what I hope is the most come-hither sexy look he's ever received in his life, patting the empty space on the bed beside me, an open invitation to get it on, to consummate this marriage. We did it before, but now it's legal. There certainly won't be any parent busting the door down demanding him to do the honorable thing.

"Come on and try it out," I say, my voice low and husky in an attempt to sound seductive.

I don't think Jerry understands seduction because he says, "Later, but first I have to make a fire."

I sit up and stare after my husband with disbelief as he walks out the door, and I want to yell after him, "What the hell is wrong with you?"

I don't though, and I feel a hot blush blossoming over my cheeks. I can't possibly be having the same problem Angela had because Jerry has never missed an opportunity like this before, but that was before we were married. Maybe he has a complex about sex after marriage? I once read something about that in a magazine. I worry about that all the while I unpack, throwing on the bed a lacy white negligee that Mrs. Davis bought me as a special present.

"Now that's no way to treat a present," I hear my mom say. Even on my honeymoon I have Mom in my head and I pick it up and fold it, then throw it on the bed. Mrs. Davis is under the same fashion-related delusion that Mom is. Mom still thinks girls wear plaid skirts and sweaters. Mrs. Davis still thinks girls wear negligees. I packed it though, just so I wouldn't hurt her feelings, figuring like I did with the skirts and sweaters, that I'd never wear it. Now that

Jerry's sexual appetite needs a little boost I'm starting to reconsider Mrs. Davis' gift, wondering if some skimpy lingerie will do what my come-hither look could not.

When I go back into the living area Jerry has the fire going and is sitting in a leather chair in front of it, gazing silently into the dancing flames.

"What do you want for supper?" I ask, opening the cupboard door and taking out a can of soup that I had just put in a little while ago.

"I already put a pizza in the oven," Jerry says, still staring at the fire. I pull up a chair and gaze, too, thinking, *this is going to be one hell of a boring honeymoon.*

After we eat we gaze some more at those dancing flames, then with a loud yawn I get up out of my chair and announce, "I think I'll go to bed."

Jerry stays in front of the fire, and now I'm starting to get scared. Maybe there was something in that punch that Mrs. Davis mixed up, but I drank some of that punch, too. Even little Rose did, along with her parents. If there were something wrong with it, they sure wouldn't have let her drink it.

"Jerry!" I begin, inventing the words as I go. "Are you feeling okay?"

I wonder if I should go and check his forehead for a fever. This isn't at all how I imagined our honeymoon would be and I'm really starting to get upset, but I hide it for his sake. I've heard stories of women pretending on their honeymoon, but they pretend they want it when they don't. I'm pretending I don't when I do. I'm back to pretending again, but I don't want to scare him away should there still be any chance for romance.

"I'm fine, sweetheart," he answers without looking at me.

"Aren't you coming to bed?"

"In a little while."

Disappointed but still unwilling to give up hope I go into the bedroom and take my shower and brush my teeth in the adjoining bathroom. When I come back into the bedroom Jerry's still in the living room, probably still staring at that damn fire. I go to the window and look out at the dark. I am on my honeymoon but I think I left the guy I'm supposed to be with a t home, and I have this tight little knot in my stomach.

Just before my feelings of negativity have the chance to get the better of me I have a sudden fit of optimistic inspiration that keeps the tears at bay. I shimmy into the white negligee, liking the cool silk on my skin, then I position myself in what I hope is a provocative pose to wait for Jerry. He finally comes into the bedroom after I don't even know how long, and I stand up. I think I might yell, "Surprise!" and with the old Jerry would be there-- the Jerry I used to know. The one I lived with when my mother thought I was in some room in a boarding house, reading a book. I don't say a word, but just stand in front of him; the soft light from the bedside lamp filters through the transparent folds of material, revealing a silhouette of mysterious proportions.

I can see myself in the dresser mirror across the room, and I think I look pretty good, possessing just enough feminine mystique to tempt him. He stands there in the doorway, looking like he sees me for the first time since we came on this honeymoon. Finally, his eyes have lost that empty, blank look that had me so worried. He crosses over and slowly slips the straps over my shoulders, letting the flimsy garment slide silently to the floor, his lips following the descent of material. I'm thinking that maybe girls still do wear negligees, when he suddenly pulls himself up and says, "Do you think we should be doing this, Freddy? We already did it once today, this morning."

"So? Who's counting?" I say with a feeble laugh.

"But I don't want to hurt you."

"Jerry, if you hurt me, I'll let you know."

"But, I don't want to hurt the baby."

It suddenly dawns on me that somehow Jerry got the idea that I'm pregnant. Maybe Mom said something, but I better set him straight fast. I go over to the bed and throw myself on it, covering some of the stars on the quilt.

"Jerry, if I'm pregnant, it's news to me."

"You mean you're not?"

"I mean that maybe I am and maybe I'm not, but either way, sex has nothing to do with it."

Then I think of what I just said and decide to rephrase it. "Okay, sex has something to do with it, but it sure doesn't hurt anything. Where in the hell did you ever get the idea it does?"

"From my grandmother. She always blamed my mother's miscarriages on that dirty old man she was married to, who couldn't keep his hands off her when she was pregnant."

I think I might laugh, but when I look at poor, miserable Jerry's face as he sits on the bed with his hands between his legs like a penitent little boy, I say instead, "That's an old wives' tale. Besides, I'm not pregnant, anyhow."

He looks disappointed, so with a hint of mischief in my voice I add, "But who knows? Maybe I will be after our honeymoon. That is, if you're willing to cooperate."

As things turn out he is, and I am so relieved.

Once we get rid of all Jerry's pent-up desire, not to mention mine, and just before we fall asleep, I ask, "Who told you I was pregnant, anyway?"

"I heard Mrs. Davis tell your mother she's going to give you a baby shower."

"She's just counting on me getting pregnant on our honeymoon, that's all. Kind of like counting your chickens before they're hatched." We both laugh at that, then fall asleep in each other's arms.

After that, the rest of our honeymoon is great, or as Mrs. Davis would say, "Have your babies when you're young," and I would tell Mrs. Davis if she were here--but thank God she's not--"We're trying."

Some days we go into town to rummage through the small shops and have scones and coffee for breakfast. We even go to a nice restaurant to eat a couple of times, but we always come home early enough to see the sun set over the lake. It's early spring, and in the evening the cabin is chilly, so Jerry always makes a fire. We don't sit in chairs and gaze at the fire like we did on that first awkward evening. We lay on the rug in front of it, and after making love we cover ourselves with the quilt made of stars. It rains for most of one day, but other than that the weather is beautiful. By the time we leave Jerry and I have walked around the lake at least a dozen times and discovered all the little paths in the woods within a five-mile radius. We laugh, we love, and, if only for a little while, forget about what is waiting for us back home. I call my mother once and she tells me that Daddy is doing okay and that she and Mrs. Davis are getting along really well. Jerry doesn't call his paper. Right now, they have no idea where he is, and that's just the way we want it.

On Saturday, exactly one week from the day we got here, we pack the car and clean the cabin even though Mrs. Davis told us not to bother, that she has a couple to take care of it for her. But I figure, she let us stay here for nothing; the least we can do is clean up our mess.

By the time we're through polishing and scrubbing, the cabin sparkles. It's in better shape than when we first set foot inside, and we don't dare light a fire in the fireplace nor do any cooking. After going out for something to eat we watch the sun go down over the lake, then go straight to bed. It is still dusk, but we want to get an early start in the morning.

Sunday morning we make love one more time

before I strip the bed and wash the bedclothes. Mrs. Davis said I didn't have to do that either, but there's no way I want anyone checking the sheets for signs of our passions. Or checking to see if this bride was really a virgin? Finally, with one last look around, we lock the door, get in the car, and leave the cabin by the lake.

Jerry has to take the seven o'clock evening flight to New York, so when we get home there's no time to dawdle or for me to dwell on the pending separation. I do that later, after our tearful good-bye at the airport where we cling to each other and share one last kiss before Jerry has to go to his gate. Just before he gets in line to go through security, he says, holding up his hand with the wedding ring on it, "You can trust me, Freddy. I will always be true."

"Me, too," I say, holding up my hand, the gold band a symbol of our trust. I believe Jerry. I believe me. I believe in our marriage.

It's late when I get back from the airport and I tell Mom to go to bed, that I'll keep watch. I sleep in the chair again in Daddy's room and do the same shifting and moving to get comfortable. The shots for Daddy's pain are coming more frequently now, and it seems like I barely doze off when it's time to give him another. Mom comes into the room a couple of times during the night to sit next to his bed and hold his hand. I can only imagine how hard this must be for her. She gave up everything for this man, my father. Now she has to give him up, too. I see the pain in her eyes and I wonder where is the justice in this?

In the morning I go to see Joey, but this time we don't play cards; we color instead. I bring a stack of coloring books, a tablet of plain paper and crayons with me, and it doesn't take long before we have quite a crowd of art enthusiasts coloring with us. I leave the books, tablet, and crayons with Joey. It beats trying to put together a puzzle that by now everyone has memorized and know where the pieces fit. Where even the missing pieces fit.

Joey begs me again to come home with me, and when I say, "You can't," I look into the emptiness of his eyes and try my best not to cry. When he hands me a paper torn from the tablet covered with brilliant squares of color and tells me he colored it for me, I take it.

"It's a butterfly, Freddy. Remember that day when I waited for it to rest so it could fly away."

I remember and it does look like that butterfly. It has all the colors.

"I remember," I tell Joey, and then he hits me where it really hurts.

"I wish I was a butterfly, Freddy, because I'm tired of this place, and I want to go home."

I hurry out of the room; I can't pretend anymore, and holding the picture close to my heart I go to the car. On my way home, the tears I was able to keep from falling earlier spill out, and I think the same thing I did when sitting with my father last night. Where's the justice in any of this?

241

Two weeks later on the nightly news, I see a reporter, my husband, on television reporting on the war. He's standing amongst the rubble of a bombed-out building, explaining what happened, but the people around him do not understand. I see the dazed helplessness in their eyes. They don't understand war; all they understand is death. Once again I find myself wondering about justice.

I worry about Jerry's safety, because death is a part of war, and now he is a part of it. I turn off the television and I go to bed only to toss and turn, worrying, and loving, missing Jerry so much that the tears wet the pillow and I have to turn it over before I can even think of sleep. I lay in the dark wondering how I will raise our baby without Jerry, because by now there is a real possibility that I am pregnant.

If something happens to Jerry our child will grow up without a father and a grandfather, and I wish that I had been a little more careful about taking the pill. Now is not a good time to be having a baby. I do not think about justice anymore, I think about my baby. I worry about my baby. I remember when I was little and Dad would come in to listen to my prayers, and I'd ask him why bad stuff happened to nice people.

He would tell me, "We can't always figure out the reason for what happens, Freddy. All we can do is pray for God to help us through it."

I get out of bed and kneel down beside it, clasping my hands over my blanket and bowing my head so that it almost touches the mattress. I haven't done this since I was a little girl, when my dad told me that sometimes when things are real bad I need to have faith that it will get better. I close my eyes, still wet with tears, and pray in a whisper, sure that now is the 'sometimes' that my dad was talking about.

CHAPTER 24

By the middle of June the temperature is already in the mid-eighties, and when I walk into my father's room from outside the cold blast from the air conditioner is a welcome change.

I've been working in our yard, fighting a battle, trying to get rid of some of the weeds, but for some reason this year the weeds are winning.

"Hi, Daddy," I say, still wiping my face in the towel I brought in with me. I feel his eyes follow me as I walk over to the table by the window to look out at the yard, hoping to admire my handiwork, but even though I've been at it for hours the yard looks barely touched. There's a fly buzzing on the window, bumping obnoxiously against the glass, and I take a quick swat at it with my towel before draping it over the back of the chair.

"Can I get you something, Daddy?" I ask, my usual words upon entering the room.

My father just shakes his head "no," like the pain is so bad that he can't talk. God, it hurts to see my father like this. It takes everything in me to play our little game of pretending. The game goes kind of like this: I pretend that he's not going to die, and he pretends that I'm not pregnant. Every day we play this game even though my dad gets weaker and my belly gets bigger.

I play the game of pretending with my parents, but not with Joey. He comes right out and asks me on the last Monday in June when I visit him. I'm shuffling the cards, and by now Helen has joined us, her doll propped up in the chair next to her while she waits for me to deal.

After studying my stomach a while, Joey states in his blunt way, "You're getting fat, Freddy." Even in a baggy shirt, my growing belly is hard to conceal.

"I got fat just like that when I had my baby," Helen chimes in, all matter-of-fact-like.

"Are you having a baby, Freddy?" Joey asks.

F or the first time I utter the words that I haven't dared to say before: "Yeah, I'm having a baby."

"How come?" Joey asks, all innocent.

"Because I'm married. I told you I was marrying Jerry...remember?"

"I remember," Joey says, and I think that's the end of it, until Helen starts laughing.

"You don't have to be married to have a baby. All you have to do is let a guy poke you with his thing," Helen says, like she knows all about guys' things.

Ironically, Joey, who has one, has no idea what we mean, because he asks, "What thing?"

Before I can give a suitable answer without embarrassing him or myself, Helen points to Joey's crotch, saying, "You know, his *thing*. He puts it in and makes a baby in you, and sometimes the baby won't stop crying."

By now Helen is talking in a loud wail as she takes the doll and starts rocking back and forth with it clutched tightly to her chest. A guy in white comes over to take her away. On the way out she shakes the doll like she did the first day I met her and once again, repeating in the same loud screams, "I told you to stop! Didn't I tell you to stop?!"

We can still hear her as she's led down the long hallway back to her room, and it takes a while for me to calm down enough to go back to my cards. Around us the others in the room go back to their activities as if this happens all the time and is normal. Maybe it is normal for them because the only ones in here, except for me, are inmates and the people who work here. I'm the only visitor, today. I usually am.

"Are you going to deal the cards, Freddy?" Joey asks, impatient to continue our game.

I reach over to deal Joey a card even though my hands are still shaking.

We are about fifteen minutes into the game when out of the blue, Joey tells me, "I think Norman is trying to put a baby in Helen."

I look past the cards in my hand and stare at Joey, like maybe, I didn't hear right.

"What did you say?"

"Nothing, Freddy, just take another card, because I don't want to be the Old Maid."

I take the card that I think he wants me to take by the way he holds it out to me in his hand. I let Joey win, because it makes him happy. It doesn't take much to make Joey happy: not getting stuck with the Old Maid and going home. At least I can give him one of the two.

On the long drive home, I think of what Joey said about Norman. Although I've never met Norman I know he works on the night shift. He's one of those white coats who takes care of Helen when she goes crazy, and I wonder just how in the hell does Norman take care of her? I've read about abuse in places like this, but should I say something to someone about it? I don't even know what I would say, or to whom. After all, even I have to admit that what Joey says doesn't always make sense. Besides, there are others working on the night shift, too, some of them women. If anything is going on, they'd know about it and tell the right person to make it stop.

I just wish Jerry were home so I could talk to him. It's hard to write about worry in a letter. It's hard to write that I'm going to have a baby in a letter, too. Maybe one of these days he'll call, and then I'll tell him, but talking about life when we're both surrounded by death doesn't make much sense.

Neither does having this baby, now, and I wish I had said to hell with Mrs. Davis's advice and stuck with those birth control pills.

When I get home, my mother is in the kitchen. As I come closer, I can see that her eyes look red, like she's been crying, and she says to me, "You have to tell him it's okay, Felicia."

"Who do I have to tell that it's okay?" I ask, a little confused as I rummage around inside the refrigerator for sandwich fixings. Mom has already eaten her dinner, and I have to fend for myself.

"You have to tell your father that it's okay."

I slam the refrigerator door shut, making the little magnets on the front fall to the floor. I'm ready to walk out, the unmade sandwich already forgotten. Suddenly I'm not hungry anymore.

"He needs you to forgive him so he can go in peace."

I stop dead in my tracks and stare at my mother

"Forgive him for what?"

"For dying."

I stare at my mother like she has just said there will not be a tomorrow. That this is the last day, and there is only an eternity of lost hope to look forward to.

"He can't help it he's dying," I say, the words taste bitter and my mother understands the bitter.

"No, Felicia, he can't help it, but you're angry with him for not being here for his grandchild and to help you with Joey."

My mother has just uttered the words that I dare not think. The weight of her words suffocates me and I have to go outside for some air. I start to walk, for how long or how far I can't say. I just walk until my legs ache and my head feels like it's going to burst with the knowledge of what I have to do.

Before I go to bed, I go into my father's room and my mother walks out, saying that as long as I'm sitting with him, she'll be getting some sleep, or at least trying to.

"I love you, Daddy," I whisper, taking his hand in mine.

In the dim light next to his bed, I notice his eyes flicker, and then with effort, they flutter open. I take a deep breath. It's going to be hard, really hard to do this, to stop pretending, but I have to.

"Daddy, do you remember that time when my kitten Sammy died, and a couple of days later you brought another one home?"

My father doesn't say anything, but I can tell he remembers.

"And do you remember that I pretended it didn't exist, because I still wanted Sammy? Well, that's how I feel now. I don't want the baby, Daddy. I just want you."

My father still doesn't say anything, but I know he's with me on this remembering trip.

"But after a while, I did love the new Sammy," my father squeezes my hand, like he's agreeing with me.

"But you're not a kitten, Daddy...you're my father, and I'll never have another one. I'll never be another man's little girl again."

"But you'll be a mother," my father says, his voice so low, I have to strain to hear.

I sit on the edge of his bed and lay my head on my father's pillow, while he touches my hair, my red hair that I never liked but he loved, at least he always said he did when I'd complain.

"Sometimes I feel like one already, that I'm Joey's mother."

249

"Forgive me, Freddy," and in those words are all the heartbreak of knowing how hard it's been for me.

"It's not your fault," I assure him, and I know this is the forgiveness my mother was talking about.

"It's okay, Daddy, It's not your fault. It's my heart. In my heart, I feel like Joey is my child. I love him, Daddy, just like I love you and Mom, and sometimes even Harry and Angela. I still need you, Daddy. Not for Joey, or for the baby, but for me."

"You have Jerry now, kitten," my dad says with so much effort that I know I have to end this conversation, because if I say one more thing, I'll be back to pretending again, and I dare not utter what I'm thinking. Because the truth is, it's not all that good between Jerry and me.

Instead of admitting this, I say, "I'm going to name the baby James, after you." Then, lifting my head to look at my father, I add, "Unless of course it's a girl; then I'll call her Jamie."

I see that little smile on my dad's face, and I think of how I can always make him smile, no matter what.

I go over to the chair beside the bed and sit for a long time, holding my father's hand and letting the peace of knowing that even death will never change what is between my father and me. I will be the same loving parent to my baby that he has always been to me. This, I have learned. This, death cannot take away.

"I love you, Daddy," I say, getting up from the

chair by the bed and going to settle into the big one. Daddy is tired and I'm tired.

I'm asleep with the quilt wrapped around me when the soft words of my mother wake me. She's holding my father's hand, and in a whisper, tells him she loves him. I'm pretending again, this time that I'm still asleep and let my mother be.

Her voice is so low that I have to strain to hear, but I do hear and I finally learn the whole story about my mother and Marvin Lowenstein. She talks to my father, and holding his hand remembers how it used to be.

"I remember that first time I saw you. My father came to talk to your mother about roses. Do you remember how your mother loved roses? She was the expert and my father was planning a special garden of all roses, many of them hybrids. We were supposed to stay one day and ended up staying a week, and while my father talked about flowers, we talked, but it wasn't about flowers, that's for sure."

My mother laughs this little intimate laugh, and I think I shouldn't be here listening but I can't bring myself to get up and interrupt this remembering. My mother's "Goodbye" to the man she once gave up everything for.

"We came to the store, and I saw you, and I fell in love, James, just like that. I was only seventeen and I fell head over heels in love. Your mother invited us to stay at your house.

"This house, James, because there was a lot more she wanted to tell my father about the garden, and a lot more she wanted to sell him for the garden." There's the little intimate laugh again, a private joke between two people, but I'm awake so I guess it's between three. Mom doesn't know that, or I don't think she'd be saying, "And while you slept in Harold's room, I slept in Felicia's," and I imagine my mother sleeping in my room in my bed at seventeen. I can't even imagine her being seventeen, so I stop imagining, and listen.

"I couldn't sleep that night, knowing you were just down the hall. James, I felt so many things that night, and I knew that I had found the man I wanted to marry. I even dreamed about marrying you. Can you believe it? I just met you and was dreaming about marrying you?"

My mother pauses for a while, like she's expecting her husband to agree with her, but I think I wore Daddy out with my forgiveness speech but I agree with Mom. I used to dream about marrying Erik. Mom continues her love story, and I am eager to hear more, and boy, is there more.

"That night you went out to the barn, remember you went there because you thought you left the water running in the tank of plants, and I followed you, James. I heard you get up and I followed you. I was dreaming about you, I heard you get up, and I wasn't sleepwalking, just so you know. I knew what I wanted, James. I knew, James, so what happened wasn't just your fault. I wanted it, too." And I think this is the part I don't want to hear, but Mom doesn't go into detail, so I guess a daughter can hear what she says next.

"You asked me to marry you, and I wanted to, but I was only seventeen. My parents would never let me. Then when they found out I was pregnant," and I think, Oh my God, Mom and Dad had to get married. I guess I should have done the math between Harry's birthday and their anniversary, but what kid wants to do that with their parents? I sure don't.

"They wanted me to marry Marvin. I was pregnant with our child and they said I had to marry Marvin Lowenstein. I couldn't stand him, James. I wanted to marry you, and once I told you what they were trying to do, well, you just came marching over there."

And Mom laughs a little.

"Actually you flew in an airplane with a one-way ticket in your hand for me. You didn't argue or anything; you were very respectful, and I thank you for that, but you made it plain that Marvin Lowenstein could just go...well, you know where you told him to go. I don't have to repeat it. You asked me to marry you again. I said yes, and you took my hand and led me right out of that house. I was eighteen by then, so they couldn't stop me. I have never been sorry, James, that I went with you that day my darling, never."

I think my mom is crying now. I know I am, but I cry quietly. Mom is sobbing and I want to go to her and hug her. To tell her I'm glad she went with my dad that day. Eventually Mom gets the crying under control, but me, I have this big quilt and it's almost choking me, I'm holding it so tight against my face. I can hide my tears but not the shaking of the quilt, as I quiver under the stress of pretending sleep. My mother is talking again and I listen, especially when I hear her mention my name.

"I think Felicia is going through what I was going through when I was pregnant with her."

Mom is quiet again and I hang in suspense. What did she go through? What am I going through? *Come on, Mom! Don't do this to me.* And I want to sit up and ask, but I am supposed to be sleeping. Then Mom is back to talking and I'm back to listening.

"I didn't want her either," I hear her say, and now I really want to sit up and give her a piece of my mind. You didn't want me! What a terrible thing to tell your daughter, but she's not telling me. I am supposed to be sleeping, and that hug I wanted to give her after that Marvin Lowenstein story, well, I take it back.

"We were just getting Joey and I was worried that it wasn't a good time, but you told me time had nothing to do with it. You told me how special this baby would be, and every night before you fell asleep you'd kiss my stomach and say, "Good night."

I loved when you did that. I felt so special and I felt the baby was special, and she is special. James. She is so special."

I'm really crying now, and I give back that hug to her, and there is so much more I want to give her, but the thing she wants most is her husband and I can't give her that. I just hope that in some small way I can show her my appreciation for marrying my dad and not Marvin Lowenstein.

My mother stands up, then with one last loving look at the man she gave up everything for, my dad, she walks over to my chair, and quietly, so quietly I can almost hear my father breathing. "Good night, Felicia," she says, patting the now sobbing quilt and walks to the door, then comes back to the chair.

"But to be fair to my parents, Felicia, your Grandma and Grandpa Harrison wanted your dad to marry Patricia. But he chose me." She walks out and I think, *Oh my God, I almost had a mother named Patsy.*

And I know what my mother was trying to tell me with her love story between her and Daddy. That mothers aren't really all that different from their daughters. The only difference is that when Mom didn't want her baby, Daddy did, and that makes all the difference in the world to me. After that I cry some more, but not because Mom didn't want me, because I know that deep down she did, she was just scared. I cry not because I don't want my baby, because deep down I know I do. I cry because my mother had her husband to kiss the baby inside her, even while it's being formed, and I don't have that. My baby's father doesn't even know he is going to be a father. He doesn't even call so I can tell him.

I fall asleep in the chair, the quilt covering me. The soft sounds of my father sleeping in the same room with me. He is not struggling like he usually does to catch his breath. I think he understands what my mother and I said to him. He knows there are some things not even death can take from him: a wife's love and a daughter's forgiveness. In the early morning, I get up from my chair, ready to turn it over to my mother who has just walked in. Giving him a lingering kiss on the cheek, I say, "Thank you for being my dad."

It's my pleasure," my father says, and I know he means it with all his heart, because I'd be able to tell if he felt differently. That's how it is between my dad and me.

After I go to my room, I pick up the letter from Jerry that came in the mail yesterday and read it again. It sounds a lot like the letters I used to get from Erik, the ones at the end when he wrote more about his life and less about his love.

"I'm not sure I have Jerry anymore, Daddy," I say sadly to the picture of my father on my nightstand that's always watched over me as I slept. No matter where I go, even long after the man in the picture is gone, he always will be there. I turn out the lights and cry myself to sleep.

A week later my father dies a peaceful death, with me, my brother, my sister and my mom gathered around his bed to be with him up until his last second on this Earth. Later, after they take my father away, while Mom and my brother and sister sit around the kitchen table drinking coffee and mourning my father in silence, I go for a walk to mourn, too.

But I'm not alone, because baby James is already

kicking inside of me. I've been to the doctor and had an ultrasound, so my father knew before he died that his first grandchild would be a boy and would carry his name, just like I'd promised. I walk a lot, first talking to my father, "I love you, Daddy." I say it like a mantra, like a beat to keep my feet moving, to keep my heart from breaking and falling to the ground. I'm not sure when the daddy part changes to Jimmy, and I know that one life has ended, but inside me is another, and somehow that gives me comfort.

It's a bright sunny day, predicted to get up into the nineties when we stand at the grave to say our last good-bye. The minister says how James Harrison would have loved a day like this, how as a gardener he loved working to make this world a more beautiful place to live. I remember that as a father, my dad did make this world a better place to live for me. I start weeping again, even after I thought I had no more tears to shed.

It's a big funeral with a lot of cars lined along the little road through the cemetery, and it takes some doing to get all the cars cleared out afterward. Everyone at the store, all the people who knew my dad are here. Everyone but Joey and Jerry, the two people I wish could be here with me now more than anything. I know Joey wanted to be here, that he cried because he couldn't be. I don't know about Jerry, though, because I sent him a message through the paper where he works, and I haven't heard anything yet. I worry about that, but I have no one to express this worry to. Not for another two weeks, when Jerry is supposed to be coming home.

It's a Sunday afternoon when he walks through the front door, just like that. No phone call, no letter. We didn't even hear the sound of his rented car pulling up in the driveway. He just stands in the living room, calling out, "Is anybody home?"

My mother gets to him first because she's in the kitchen. I'm upstairs taking a nap when I hear his voice call out, so it takes me a little longer. Still half-asleep, thinking that I must be dreaming, I come down to his open arms. I hug his neck and kiss him over and over, until finally we move apart and he takes a good look at me, a really good, long look and says, "You're pregnant."

"I sure am," I say with a little laugh, holding my shirt up to show him my bulging belly.

"Why didn't you tell me?" he asks.

"Why didn't you call me, so I *could* tell you?" I answer, putting my hands on my hips, except I don't have hips. Pregnant women have only butt and belly, with belly bigger.

"You could have written me in one of your letters."

"But I didn't want to write it. I wanted to say it."

Jerry pulls me back into his arms and I relish the feeling of safety within that protective circle. His face is buried in my neck and I think that maybe he's crying. When at last he pulls away, my suspicion is true. Wiping his eyes with the back of his hand, he says, "Damn it, Freddy, what if I hadn't been able to get home in time? When would I find out, when it's old enough to tell me?"

"He, not it," I correct him. "Our baby is a boy." This just starts the crying and wiping away of tears all over again, this time for both of us.

For the first two nights that he's back, Jerry and I share the bed in my room, but after a little coaxing from Mom and Mrs. Davis, Jerry and I go back to the cabin to spend the next ten days there. It's a lot like our honeymoon, only this time we don't walk around the lake. We ride in a little boat, circling along the shore. The five-mile hikes are reduced to somewhere nearer to two. We still make love on the floor in front of the fireplace, though. That part hasn't changed, but now when I get up Jerry has to help me. I also find myself making more trips to the bathroom than last time. We laugh together and love together, and when we're in bed together, Jerry always rests his hand on my belly, hoping to feel a little kick now and then.

"I've got him back, Daddy," I whisper into the darkness after Jerry falls asleep. "At least for now."

CHAPTER 25

For the next couple of months life settles into a period of waiting and expectation. Mrs. Davis has the baby shower in her garden, and I've gotta hand it to her, she's outdone herself this time. I receive so many gifts for the baby that I write and tell Jerry there's enough for twins. Jerry just writes back and tells me to hang onto everything, because we can use all of it for "the next one." He's back to writing love letters again, and in between letters he calls. I don't tell him about my worries though, because everything is fine. The store is making money, the mortgage on the house is being paid off, and on top of that, the attorney for Joey's appeal holds out a lot of hope that this time we'll win.

I work with Brian, Carl's youngest, raking leaves and covering plants in preparation for the upcoming winter. I continue to work until a week before I have my little James. Jerry doesn't make it home for the birth of his son, and I can't blame him for that; it was the doctor's miscalculation. Instead of being born on Thanksgiving, the scheduled time for Jerry to come home and when I was due, James comes two weeks early.

"He's beautiful," I tell Jerry when he calls me in the hospital the day after Jimmy is born.

"I can't wait to see him," my husband says. "I wish I were with you now."

There's a wistful sadness in Jerry's voice that I can hear in his wishing, and before we both start crying, I say, "And can you hear him, Jerry? He's got a set of lungs on him."

"A regular little hell-on-wheels," Jerry says, and we both laugh through our tears. It's so strange to be crying and feel both happy and sad, all at the same time. I am happy having my husband back, having my baby, but sad that my dad isn't here to be happy with me. Sometimes I think I'm almost used to it, but I'm not. I figure that I probably never will be.

"I love you, Freddy," Jerry says before he hangs up. "I'll see you in two weeks."

"I love you, too," I reply, and while Jerry goes back to reporting on the war, I go back to nursing my baby.

Traditionally the day after Thanksgiving is the big Christmas Open House at our stores, but this year I put Carl and Brian in charge of setting it all up. Brian is a godsend for us, even though his father doesn't see it that way. Carl lost his wife when his children were still young, and having to take on the dual role of both father and mother, he has high hopes for his two sons and daughter. I guess two out of three isn't bad, considering that Mark, his eldest, is in medical school and his daughter, Jane, is in law school. Brian likes digging in dirt, like me.

When Jerry comes home I'm visiting Joey, so I'm not around when he sees his son for the first time. This time it is Jerry's fault. He wasn't supposed to come home until the next day.

"I took a transport home instead of waiting for the flight I was suppose to take, so I could get home to my family sooner," Jerry explains when I walk into the living room to find my husband rocking our son.

"But I wanted to be here when you saw him for the first time," I say, trying to keep the disappointment out of my voice, but who can blame me for feeling this way? After all I did all the work of having this baby.

"I'll make it up to you," Jerry says, that little grin I love playing across his lips.

"How?" I ask, taking off my coat after I give Jerry a kiss.

"By not going back until after New Year's."

Now, that is some making up, and instead of hanging up my coat I toss it onto a chair and throw my arms around Jerry's neck, kissing him until the baby wakes up and starts to cry.

"I think he's hungry. I held off giving him a bottle so you could nurse him," my mother says, walking into the room. I take the baby out of Jerry's arms, open my blouse and maybe I wasn't here when Jerry saw our son for the first time, but I sure am when, for the first time, Jerry sees me feed his son. He watches with that little grin on his face, not saying a word, but his eyes are saying a lot.

By Christmas our sex life is back to normal, and if it weren't for those empty places at the table where Joey and Daddy used to sit, our lives would feel normal, too. During Christmas dinner we all share something about our lives. Jerry talks about the paper, Angela talks about the part she got in a stage play in New York, and Harry talks about how his business has taken a turn for the better, that he thinks he'll be able to close the books for the year in the black.

Mom and I just listen. What can we really talk about, anyway? Mom is still in the throes of sorting out Daddy's things, and she has no intention of depressing everyone by talking about that. My life centers on little Jimmy, and I would love to talk about him, but right now he's suffering from a rather nasty case of diaper rash, and that definitely is not table talk.

The whole day isn't all about catching up on what is happening to whom. When we exchange gifts, like the empty places at the table, there's the memory again of the gifts that should be under the tree. When Mom plays the piano for our usual carol singing, there's the big empty hole that my father's baritone used to fill, and it just doesn't sound right. In the evening Mom puts out some leftover ham for sandwiches, and we all sit in front of the television eating and watching A Christmas Carol.

It's a Christmas Day tradition for as long as I can remember to watch the video of Charles Dickens' famous novella. It just wouldn't be Christmas without it.

It's late by the time we go to bed, and even later by the time Jerry and I are ready to go to sleep. Jerry has no trouble falling asleep, but it's not that easy for me. It's almost like I am being haunted by my own personal 'Ghost of Christmas Past.' The memories play in my head like the video I just got through watching.

There were the Christmases when Joey, Angela, Harry, and I were kids. When we all got ice skates and Dad took us to the pond just down the road from our house, and we skated, but some of us fell more than we skated.

There was Christmas Eve, right after coming home from church, and the snow was just right for making a snowman, so that's what we did, even Mom. All those Christmas mornings we got up so early, Mom and Dad still yawning, and we kids tore into the presents.

God, it was so wonderful! Why is it that we don't recognize wonderful when it's happening, but only when we look back?

And how about that Christmas Day Dad and I drove for hours just to go see Joey in jail before his trial? That wasn't wonderful, but Dad and I did have a meaningful conversation on the drive there. I remember the Christmas that I found out Erik wasn't coming home--definitely not wonderful. But what if he had come home? Then there wouldn't be a Jerry lying next to me, or a James sleeping in the bassinet next to our bed. I get up and take from the dresser drawer the ring and a locket, along with a watch engraved: *'To Eric, forever and always.'* I don't know why I do this, except that it wouldn't be Christmas if I didn't.

The winter drags after the New Year and Jerry leaves, but before he goes he promises me that this will be the last year he's going overseas. I hang onto that through all these cold, dreary days, when it seems every time I look out the window it's snowing. I'm back to running the business again, and I go to the store every day while Mom babysits for me. Brian helps me pack away the Christmas inventory we don't sell at our big post-holidays sale, and at the end of March, we set out our spring inventory.

Jerry comes home again for Easter, but this time when he leaves, there's a part of him left behind. I'm pregnant again.

"That's wonderful," Jerry says when I tell him, and I think it's wonderful, too. When Jerry calls or writes we talk about wonderful. Not just about my pregnancy, but our plans for after the baby is born. We're back to our original dream of a house, four kids, and Joey living with us. Mom isn't coming with us, though, because she and Mrs. Davis are planning some bus trips around the country once the business is sold.

I'm not sure exactly when our 'wonderful' goes awry, when our dream becomes a nightmare. I think it all starts when we learn that Joey's appeal has been turned down. Telling Joey that he'll never be able to come home is about the hardest thing I've ever had to do. I put it right up there with that night I had to say good-bye to my dad. There is a vague look in Joey's eyes after that. It's like the one thing he's been living for was finally taken from him, and now there's just nothing when I look into his eyes. Any of the joy that was once Joey is gone, and I was the one who had to tell him.

Since Joey can't come home that means moving is out of the question. Without those Monday visits I'm not sure Joey will make it, and that's when the second part of our wonderful life disappears. Jerry comes home for the birth of our second son, Ben, and tells me that he's decided to continue with his overseas reporting, only this time it will be for one of the big networks. Instead of writing about the war from New York, he'll be back talking about it on television.

"What's the difference if I'm alone in New York or in the Middle East?" he asks with a hint of bitterness.

I can't argue with that, so while Jerry reports about the war I stay home to take care of Jimmy, who is now one year old, and baby Ben. Jerry still calls, and his letters are still about love, only now it's about how much he loves and misses his sons.

The final blow to our dream comes when Angela calls to tell me that she's seen Jerry with another woman.

"It was probably a business acquaintance." I shrug it off, wondering why Jerry didn't even tell me he was back in the States.

"Business acquaintance, my ass," Angela says. "You don't cozy up to a business acquaintance the way those two were. He didn't even notice that I was in the restaurant, and I sure as hell wasn't trying to hide."

When Jerry comes home for Jimmy's second birthday I confront him, and he doesn't deny it. All he says is, "Maybe a part-time marriage is okay with you, but it's not for me."

"Then quit and get a job here," I argue, but I think that was the wrong thing to say, because next thing I know, Jerry's stomping out of the living room, and I'm locking my bedroom door. For the rest of the time that Jerry is home, we sleep in separate bedrooms. Two months later he asks for a divorce and I agree. After that the only time we see or hear from Jerry is on the television when he's talking about the war.

CHAPTER 26

There is an old saying that time marches on, but I think in my case it's marching backwards. I am single again, and a disappointment to my mother again because she still really likes Jerry. Even though she doesn't say it, I think she blames me for not hanging onto him. But I do have the kids now, and that's something I didn't have before.

By the time Jimmy is five and Ben is four, the suffocating pain I first felt after my divorce has lessened to a dull ache that I've kind of gotten used to. Like a toothache it hurts only when I bite down wrong. The rest of the time it's just aggravating, but I survive.

On the other hand I get the feeling that Jerry isn't aching. Angela keeps me posted about his life, even though I don't want to know. I keep trying to tell her but she always manages to worm it into the conversation anyway.

"I saw him with this other woman, some blonde," she says to me on the phone, crunching noisily on something that sounds like a carrot.

"I think he's living with this one," she adds, chewing. And I think Mom how always telling us not

to talk with our mouths full never got through to
Angela. I think there is a lot of stuff Mom said
never got through to her. Especially, about throwing
the first stone.

"Look, Angela," I say, trying to sound like I mean
it. "I really don't give a damn what Jerry is doing."

"I just thought you'd like to know what the father
of your children is up to, that's all," she says, trying
to sound innocent, but Angela and innocent don't
read well. They are two different books, and Angela
doesn't read innocent books. Kind of like the parts
she plays in all those off-Broadway shows she's
always bragging about. But she is my sister and I
don't think she is giving me a play-by-play account
of Jerry's love life to hurt me. She knows that I'm
hurting enough without her help.

"Obviously *it's* up," I say, remembering that
conversation I had with Angela about getting it up.
How I bragged that all I had to do is touch Jerry
there to get results, and I find myself wondering
against my will if his new blonde girlfriend has the
magic touch, too.

"I just wonder why he doesn't get married again?"
Angela says, making a little clucking noise like a
mother hen, but there is no 'mother' in her laugh.

"Well, Jerry and I still have that in common,
Angela." I'm matching her laugh now, though it
lacks the enthusiasm of hers. "Because I sure have
no intention of marrying again, either."

Angela laughs again, I laugh, too. She hangs up,
and then I want to cry.

I mean it when I vow never to marry, or even go

269

out with another man again so long as I live. The week following Angela's call, while Brian is helping me plant some shrubs, he asks me if I'll go out with him. Without even thinking about it for a fraction of a second, my answer is no.

"Give me a chance, Freddy, that's all I ask," he protests, wiping his dirty hands off on the front of his work jeans.

"The only men in my life now are my two sons, and that is how it's going to stay," I say, a note of finality in my voice. I hold a shrub in place while Brian shovels the dirt around it. He throws in the last shovelful, taps it down, looks up at me and asks, "And what about when they grow up? What then, Freddy?"

"Then I'll raise cats. I'll probably shrivel up and die, just like this plant will, if you don't put some more ground around it. Half the roots are showing."

Brian shovels some more, taps some more, then asks some more. Every day for a week he asks, until finally I give in and go with him to a dinner and movie. We do this every weekend for a month until I hire Lauren. Then Brian starts taking out Lauren.

I'm in the office working on the books when Chris, our floral arranger, walks in. After watching Brian and Lauren at the cash register, Brian patting places he shouldn't while Lauren giggles, it's obvious that I've become the woman scorned.

After a few moments of awkward silent staring, Chris leans over and says to me in a hushed voice, "I guess he's lost interest in you."

"I seem to have that effect on men," I say with a little sigh before going back to working on the books. After that, I work alone while Brian works with his father. Lauren just works on my nerves. She's cute and sexy, but really dumb, but if I fire her now, I'll sure as hell look like the woman scorned.

That is the end of my dating life, and once again the only two men in my life are my sons. And even though the movies are mostly cartoons and the dinners out are usually McDonald's, I can honestly say I enjoy going out with them more than I ever did with Brian.

I love being their mom, and I wonder if Jerry knows just how much he's missing by not being here. I know that Joey enjoys them, and I take Jimmy and Ben with me on Mondays as often as I can.

The women's recreation center is finally finished, so Helen is no longer around when I visit Joey, and I'm glad of that. Now it's just Jimmy, Ben, Joey, and me, and we color more than play cards, which is good because Ben has a hard time just holding the cards, let alone figuring out what they're for. Joey has a lot of patience, though, and even if Ben can't always tell which card is the Old Maid, Joey always does everything he can to make sure Ben gets it.

I like visiting with Joey the best when it's warm enough outside for us to go and sit at the picnic tables, or better yet, on a blanket under the trees. There isn't a bug hiding in the grass that Joey hasn't discovered, that he hasn't explained to the boys. He's so happy when we visit. It's only when we're ready to leave that I see the sad emptiness return; the raw fear in Joey's eyes that never completely went away after the day I had to tell him he wouldn't be able to come home. I had to stop pretending, and not pretending is worse than the pretending. He doesn't beg to go home anymore, but I know he wants to. Just like I don't cry driving home anymore, but I want to.

I take the boys with me when I go to work, too, especially on the days when Mom goes to bingo with Mrs. Davis. They always go on Wednesdays, and my mom always asks before she leaves, "Are you sure it's okay, Felicia?"

"It's okay, Mom," I always say, but today I add, "I'm working in Mr. Larson's yard, and I don't mind taking them there. Mr. Larson still has that kiddie gym set up that used to be Erik's. They love crawling around on it." Mom's conscience is clear, but mine isn't; I'm back to pretending again. I just told Mom I don't mind, but I *do* mind taking the boys there. I mind taking *me* there, because there are just too many memories, and lately I avoid memories with a passion.

I'm dragging my feet as I half-heartedly get the boys ready to leave. I've been known to put off the unpleasant lately. You could say that's become one of my passions, too. Then just before I'm about to walk out the door Angela calls and that is the most unpleasant thing of all.

"Hello," I answer, thinking that it's Mom, that she forgot her lucky pin and wants me to drop it off by Mrs. Davis' on my way to the Larson's. Daddy bought it for her on their honeymoon. It's in the shape of a four-leaf clover, and coming from a gardener it seems appropriate, but Mom thinks it's lucky. I don't share her opinion because she wore it to Joey's trial, and it didn't help one bit.

When I realize it's Angela on the line and not Mom, I want to hang up, but it's too late. She's already begun her broadcast about Jerry the News Reporter. When I tell her I don't need a blow-by-blow account she thinks it's funny, but I don't.

"He's buying a house. Did you know that, Freddy?"

"No! Is there some reason why I should?" I ask, irritated as I set the backpack full of toys for the kids down onto the floor, hoping to make this a news brief.

"It's a real expensive house. Doesn't it bother you that he's spending his money on this woman?"

"The only time it would bother me is if he stopped sending me child support checks."

"But he could be giving you more. That new job of his with the network must be paying him more than when you first got your divorce. You should definitely take him to court to try and get more."

"I don't want more. I'm doing fine," I insist.

"It's not fair, Freddy, that you're stuck raising the kids while he's out chasing other women. There aren't many men who want a woman with two little boys. I bet it doesn't do much for your sex life."

"What sex life?" I ask, and before we get into that old story I hang up, leaving Angela, I'm sure, with a whole lot more to say, but it won't be to me. I trip on that damn backpack, swearing, but I can swear as long as the boys aren't around to hear. And I wonder what Jerry is doing with that new girlfriend of his in that new house he's buying. I'm sure it's something I don't want the boys to see.

It's noon by the time I get the van loaded with everything I need and I pull into Mr. Larson's driveway. Jimmy and Ben run for the gym set while I get busy cutting the lawn and clipping the hedges. After a while, the boys tire of climbing and swinging, and join me in helping to pick up branches and grass clippings.

Along the edge of the garden, Jimmy discovers something and hollers out to Ben and me.

"Come and see this!"

"What is it?" I ask, dropping the armful of branches in the wheelbarrow and walking over. Curious as usual, Ben is already there.

"He jumps," Ben says.

"He hops," Jimmy says, like big brother knows more than little brother. That's been a thing with Jimmy lately.

"It's a froggy," Ben says. "It's a toad," Jimmy argues.

"Mommy," they say in unison, and now it's up to me to settle the dispute, so I tell them, "It's a jumping, hopping, froggy-like toad."

We watch this froggy-like toad hop and jump for a good ten minutes, until a car pulls into the driveway, and then that is more interesting. I watch as a man gets out, stands for a minute to look around, then, spotting the three of us staring at the bright red sports car, he begins to walk toward us. He's dressed in pressed tan khakis and a sports jacket, and at first I don't recognize him. But when I do, I wish I could hop or jump, or run like hell away from here. The man walking toward me is Erik, and if I had hoped that by now he was fat and balding, well, my hopes are dashed with one glance. If anything he's better looking and fitter than ever. We stare at each other for a while before Erik finally asks, apparently as surprised as I am, "Freddy! Is it really you?"

"It's really me," I say, rubbing at the smudge I know must be somewhere on my face. I put my hair behind my ears and tug at the bottom of my shirt, tucking it quickly back into the waistband of my jeans. Then with a quick wipe of one of my hands across a denim-covered leg, I put it out for him to shake. But instead of the one 'clean' hand, Erik takes both, and for a moment the familiar feel of him makes me dizzy, and I sway first toward him, then away.

All the while Ben and Jimmy are looking on as if Mommy has suddenly lost her marbles. Maybe they are not too far from being right. They're not accustomed to a strange man holding onto Mommy like this, and they come to my rescue by grabbing onto one leg each, as if Erik is going to carry me off.

"My boys," I say, and Erik bends down to ask their names.

"I'm Ben," the one on my right leg says.

"I'm Jimmy," the one on my left leg says.

"I'm Erik, and I'm pleased to meet you both," the big guy bending over in front of me says with a smile before straightening up to his full height again.

"I heard you got married to a reporter."

"Then you must have heard I got unmarried, too."

Erik starts to laugh. I remember that laugh, and how I used to love it so much.

I say, "If you're looking for your father, he had to leave, but he said he'd be back in a little while."

Erik looks at his watch, swears under his breath, and then says, "Well, it's been great seeing you, Freddy. Maybe we can get together sometime. Maybe lunch?"

"I don't think so," I say.

"Why not?" he asks.

And I don't think Erik is used to having someone say no.

"Well first of all, I haven't heard that *you're* unmarried."

Mr. Larson pulls into the driveway and his son goes to give him a hug, and together they walk toward the house. Erik turns and looks at me, moving his hand in a little wave, then follows his father into the house.

I clean up the yard in record time, then leave, eager to be gone. On our way home, I stop at

McDonald's as a special treat for my two special guys.

For the next couple of days, I work at the store helping Chris with some of the displays. I dress up every day, telling myself that it's good for the store's image, but I've never worried about things like image before, not until Erik came back. Secretly I hope that maybe he'll come into the store one of these days, at least once before he leaves.

Christine and I are working on a patio display, using some of the new furniture that just came in. I'm directing her to move some of the plants from around the fountain and put them on the other side when Erik comes up from behind me and says, "It's beautiful just the way it is. I wouldn't change a thing."

I turn, and once I'm over the shock I manage to ask, "You like the flowers the way they are?"

"I wasn't talking about the flowers," he says with that grin of his, same as it always was, and I think that if I don't back away he just might take hold of my hands again, but at least this time they're clean.

"Can I get something for you?" I ask, and it's probably the dumbest question I've ever asked in my whole life, considering that once Erik had all the "something" I could give.

"You can go out to lunch with me," he answers, and there's that damn grin again.

"I can't. I have to finish this display."

"It looks finished to me," he says. Then, turning to Christine, he asks, "Doesn't it look finished to

277

you?"

"I thought it was finished a half-hour ago, but hey, I only work here," Christine says, walking away to go back to her floral arrangements.

"I won't go out with you, Erik. I told you that the other day, and I haven't changed my mind."

"I'm not asking for a date."

Now I feel that dumb just happens to me when I'm around him and start to walk away, my face almost as red as my hair.

"It's a business lunch."

I turn to look back. I give him my 'queen' look; that's what Daddy always called it when I was really pissed but wouldn't stoop to their level. I ask, and it's like ice on a cold day, a really cold day, and it's not going to melt, "What kind of business could I possibly have with you, Erik? I'm just a lowly gardener. We can barely afford to support a family, let alone buy a sports car. So you see, Erik, we have nothing in common. Not anymore, so why should we talk business?"

And I think I finally got to give Erik that slap in the face I always dreamed of, and I relish the feeling until I hear what he has to say next.

"We have Joey in common."

The feeling of satisfaction quickly dissolves and I sound like that innocent little seventeen-year-old again when I ask, "What do you mean?"

"Come to lunch with me and I'll tell you."

I panic. How can I possibly trust him enough to

get into that car with him? How can I trust me? I have to think, but Erik doesn't want to think. He never has. He wants action, and in an impatient voice, I hear him say, "Let's go. Or aren't you interested in what I have to tell you about Joey?"

"I'll be back later," I holler out to Christine as I walk out the door with Erik.

He leads me to his sports car and we head out of town. "I thought we were going to lunch," I say, watching the houses disappear into large fields, with mostly farmhouses and barns dotting the landscape.

"We are, just not around here."

"The only reason I came with you is because you said something about Joey. Either tell me, or take me home."

"Don't worry, I'll tell you. But first I have to relax a little."

"Take me home first, then you can relax."

"I'm not going to hurt you, Freddy, if that's what's worrying you."

"You already hurt me, Erik. It's your wife I don't want to hurt. I know how it feels to be replaced by the other woman. I don't want to be one of those other women."

Erik pulls the car over onto the gravel shoulder of the road. He gets out, turns to me, and says, "I'm unmarried, too, Freddy. I just don't have the paper to prove it like you do."

He goes over to the trunk, pulls out a blanket and a basket, and then motions for me to follow.

"I think that tree will be just perfect," he says, pointing to a tree about a hundred yards off the road. I nod in silent agreement and begin to follow him. I help him spread out the blanket, then hold the two glasses while he pours the wine. We eat cold chicken, potato salad, and drink almost a whole bottle of imported wine, and it's obvious Erik enjoys expensive.

Finally, he says, "I've been reading over the transcript of Joey's trial and I want to try to overturn the verdict."

"If you had been at the trial, you wouldn't have to read it." And there is no denying the accusation in my words.

"Then it wouldn't have made any sense. Now it does."

"Erik, there is no sense to what happened at that trial."

"I know, and that's why I'm going to reopen that case."

"We've already filed an appeal and we were turned down."

"I'm not talking an appeal; I'm talking about proving his innocence."

"How?"

"Through DNA. There are a lot of innocent people getting out now because of DNA."

"So let's do it then," I say, lifting my glass in a toast.

It's not that easy. We have to have some evidence first that there was a miscarriage of justice when Joey was convicted."

"In other words, we're back to an appeal."

"No, we're back to proving Joey's innocence," he corrects. I take a rather large drink of the wine like I need it, because none of this makes any sense to me, but right now getting drunk does.

"Why are you doing this?" I ask, totally confused, sure that even drunk won't help.

"Because once I ran out on you and Joey, and I haven't been able to look in the mirror since. When you wrote me and asked me to come home, I was afraid that I'd be stuck here."

"So you married someone else instead."

"But I still loved you."

I swirl the wine around in the glass, gazing at the sparkle of red splash against the crystal.

"Okay," I say after a little while of gazing and swirling, taking my eyes off the glass and looking at Erik. "I'll help you in any way I can, but I'll pay you your regular fee."

"I don't want your money."

"That's how it has to be, Erik. A business deal and that is all, nothing more."

We pack up the lunch and Erik drives me back to the store. Just before I get out of the car, he leans over to kiss my cheek and says, "Okay. It's just a business deal."

I stare after his car as he drives away and I wonder just what in the hell am I getting into anyway with this so-called 'business deal?' If I ran the store like I run my life, we'd be broke in no time.

CHAPTER 27

It's late by the time I get home from taking my
mother to the airport. As I'm pulling into the
driveway I tell Ben and Jimmy, "You guys have to go
right to bed."

"But can't we have something to eat first?" Ben
has this little way of getting what he wants. He
pleads, "Please, Mom," but this time it doesn't work.

"You just got through eating."

"But we always have a snack first."

That's Jimmy's way of getting what he wants, He
argues, but that doesn't work either.

"Your ice cream cone was the snack," I say,
almost out of patience.

My mother took care of what little I had, telling
her over and over and over that we would be okay.

"When is Grandma coming home?"

Ben changes the subject after it's plain I'm in no
mood to argue. Sometimes little kids are so much
smarter than most grown-ups. They sure knew how
to get their grandma on that plane. After the last
"We'll be okay. After Jimmy and Ben have their last
argument. After the last person shakes his head
when these two little hells on wheels rolled

Grandma's suitcase over his foot, Mom looked relieved to get on the airplane.

"Grandma will come home after she gets tired of visiting Aunt Angie," I say, and I think to myself, when she forgets what is waiting for her here at home.

"That will be a lo-o-o-ong time," Jimmy wails putting emphasis on the *long*.

"Not so long," I assure him, remembering the last time Mom went to New York. She was ready to come home after a week, but this time depends on what is worse, arguing or drinking. My sister is known to tip a few-sometimes more than a few.

"Why did she go away? Doesn't she like us anymore?" Ben asks, and I think he's going to cry if I don't say something fast.

"Grandma went to see a play that Aunt Angie is in," I explain in the most excited tone my tired self can muster.

"Is Aunt Angie an actress?" Jimmy asks, like this is really something.

I respond, "Kind of."

I'm in the boys' bedroom helping Ben put on his pajamas, while Jimmy is busy picking out a book for their bedtime story when the phone rings.

"You guys get into bed and I'll be right back to read you your story," I yell over my shoulder, almost breaking my neck to get to the phone before the answering machine kicks in. I have this image of me going back to pick up Mom, thinking maybe her flight was cancelled-but no, we waited for it to take off.

Okay, maybe it had to turn back because of trouble, and knowing my mother, even a suggestion of trouble will make her change her mind. I swear under my breath, thinking how I'll have to go through that whole convincing conversation again to get her back on the damn plane. I pick up the phone and my "Hello" isn't nice.

"Hi! It's me," the voice says, and for a while, I have to really think to figure out who *me* is.

"Oh, Erik!" I breathe into the phone, relieved, and my voice reverts back to nice.

"Did I get you at a bad time?" he asks, and I wonder what Erik considers a good time.

"I'm putting the boys to bed. We just got back from the airport."

"Were you meeting someone or taking someone?"

"I took my mother. She's going to visit Angela."

"Ah yes, Angela. The birth control sister," Erik says with a laugh. I start to blush, grateful he can't see it over the phone.

"Erik, I have to go. The boys are waiting. Is there something you want?"

The minute I say it, I know it's the dumbest response yet. I know what Erik wants. I saw it every time he looked at me the other day. No matter how he's changed over the years, that part of him is exactly the same.

"I want you to go with me to the town where the trial took place. I want to see the court records, the newspaper stories; everything I can get my hands on."

I decide against letting him get his hands on everything, especially me, and say, "I can't. My mother isn't here to take care of my boys."

"We can take them with us."

I think of how I don't want to have my boys hear me swear. I think of what Jerry is doing in that house of his, and I think what Erik is thinking about. I sure don't want them to see that.

"I don't think it's a good idea to take them with us."

"Why?"

I sure can't tell him the truth, so I say, "Because with kids there's a lot of stopping, and they are noisy."

"I'll make a reservation to stay overnight. That way we won't be driving both ways in one day."

"No!" I say with such intensity that it scares even me. "Freddy, you said you'd do everything you can to help. Either we're in this together, or I forget all about it."

"I just don't want to stay overnight."

"You'll be safe with me."

"That's not what I mean."

"Yes, it is, but you don't have to worry. I won't ask you to do anything you don't want to."

That's what scares me. Erik has never had to force me. I always wanted it as much as he did, but if I back out of this now I'll be letting Joey down.

"Okay," I finally say. "What time should we be ready?"

"About eight o'clock. Or is that too early?"

"No, it's fine. But we'll have to use my van. I don't think a fancy car will fit all four of us."

"I'll use Dad's Cadillac."

Then, just before we hang up he says, "Freddy, it's going to be fine. Trust me."

Walking back to the boys' bedroom I think of how I once trusted him. How he said he'd be true.

"Guess what?" I say to the boys, who are already in bed waiting for their story. "Tomorrow we are going to visit the town where your daddy grew up."

"Will he be there?" Jimmy asks. Both boys have that look of expectancy in their eyes and it nearly breaks my heart.

"No, but we'll see his house," I say. I wish to God that Jerry could see their faces now. Just once I'd like him to see that disappointed look that I have to see every time I have to tell them they won't be seeing Daddy.

I snuggle with them, tickle them, and even giggle with them. It's just another way of Mommy showing just how much she loves them. Then I read a story about dinosaurs, working a couple of frogs among the prehistoric animals. But heck, they can't read yet, so how do they know where the story ends and Mommy's begins?

After good night kisses and a couple of hugs, I leave the boys to dream about friendly dinosaurs, little froggies, and an absent Daddy. I go to bed and don't so much as dream as lie there and worry. Am I doing the right thing for the boys? Am I doing the right thing for me by getting mixed up with Erik again?

In the morning when Erik pulls up in his Dad's Cadillac the boys are ready and anxious, bouncing around like the frogs they're so fond of. I'm ready but not exactly anxious--more like apprehensive, or maybe even scared.

While Erik puts our suitcases in the trunk, I help Jimmy and Ben in, making sure they buckle up. Just before we take off, Erik turns and asks, "Everybody okay back there?"

My two sons nod, sitting with their little shoulders hunched together, Ben clutching his stuffed green Froggy, and Jimmy holding his picture book of dinosaurs. They look scared to death. I think they sense what Mommy is feeling.

When Erik asks, "Is everybody okay up here?"

I want to say, "Hell, no," but instead just nod.

I've brought snacks, toys, and even some juice boxes with me, but I think I've just left my brain behind because if Mom knew what I am doing right now she'd turn right around and come back home.

We're not even an hour into the trip when the first argument breaks out.

"Mommy! Jimmy took Froggy," Ben complains.

I say, "Jimmy, give Ben back Froggy."

"But he took my book!" Jimmy complains back, but his complaint sounds like an argument in the making.

"Give him back his book," I say, and they obey, but not before Ben hits Jimmy with his book, and Jimmy hits back with Froggy. I reach back to stop

287

the flailing arms.

Then with a sigh, I say, "This is only the beginning. Are you sure you don't want to turn back?"

Erik just laughs, and I remember how I used to love the way he laughs, so easy and carefree.

"I said we were in this together, Freddy."

"But I didn't think you meant my kids."

"You're a package deal now. I knew that before I asked you to help me."

"Erik, I don't know what you're thinking, but..."

I don't get the chance to finish because he reaches over, takes my hand into his own, and says, "Relax, Freddy. Can you do that for me, please?"

"I'll try," I say, and I really do try. I try so hard that after the boys doze off, I doze off, too.

When we wake up, it's time for a stop at a gas station for a bathroom break and to stretch our legs, and then it's back in the car and on the highway. Erik doesn't say much, just kind of glances over at me and smiles every once in a while. Especially after every argument I settle between my two sons, like he approves of the way I handle things, or maybe he's just glad that he's not the father of these two little 'hell-on-wheels' kids.

When we finally arrive at our destination, Erik asks, "Where is the courthouse?"

I direct him there and we drive by, but Erik doesn't stop.

Then he asks, "You don't happen to know where the library is, do you?"

"Yes, but why?"

"Because I want to see some of the old newspapers with the story of the trial."

"I was there. All you have to do is ask me and I can tell you."

"I will, but first I want to see what the papers wrote. Sometimes a reporter sees things the average person doesn't. And sometimes they take pictures."

"What do you expect to see, Erik?"

"Maybe the real murderer."

"Are you serious? You sure don't expect to see it written on his shirt. I think you're barking up the wrong tree."

"Freddy, let me do this my way, okay? Just trust me on this?"

"I thought you said we were in this together," I reply, crossing my arms over my chest and staring at him with a look that demands an answer. I've perfected that kind of thing over my years of being a mother.

"Yes, but later. The together comes later."

I'm left wondering just when later will be? I hope not at the motel.

After Erik parks, he goes to one area of the library and I take the boys to another.

"Come on, boys," I say, taking them both by the hand. "Let's find you each a book."

I'm in luck. And I think maybe luck has nothing to do with it but the fact that both Ben and Jimmy have a nose for a good story. They have that in common with their dad. It's story time in the children's section, and while I leave Jimmy and Ben to listen to a nice lady read all about trains and airplanes, I go to find Erik.

He's hunched over a screen, pulling up page after page about a trial that I experienced first-hand. I feel the helplessness build inside of me again with every word that flashes in front of me.

Finally I say, "I can't take this anymore."

Erik prints some of the pages we just read, then goes to collect them from the printer. We go together to collect my two boys.

"We did enough business for today; now what do you guys want to do for fun?" Erik asks.

Before I can say that we're hungry, Jimmy pipes up with, "We want to see Daddy's house."

I direct Erik down the familiar streets, my heart aching with every turn. We pass the park where Jerry first kissed me, and in my mind I again see the snow falling on our heads when he shook the branch. We drive down the street where Jerry and I walked the night that he came looking for me, and again I can hear him saying he was worried when he couldn't find me. We even drive by the drugstore where I bought the birth control pills that I 'forgot' to take. I look back at my firstborn and remember how Jerry said it didn't matter, that he wanted four kids anyway, so we might as well get started on them. I didn't know then that we would never get to four.

When we drive down the street where Jerry lived I point out the house and remember how it used to be.

I say to Erik, "Let's get out of here." I think he knows what I mean, because he makes an illegal turn, then heads down the street away from the neighborhood full of memories.

For the next hour while we are eating at a restaurant that has no connection to my past with Jerry, all the boys can talk about is Daddy this, Daddy that, and I wish to God that Jerry could hear what they say. Just once I wish he could hear how much they love him, and I could tell him how much I hate him for not being there for them.

At the motel, I leave the boys in the room to watch television and I step outside for a minute to talk to Erik.

"I'm sorry," I begin, a sad little sigh somewhere in the *sorry*."That you had to listen to all that talk about Jerry. But he is their father, and they want to know everything about him."

"Don't worry about it, Freddy. I'm old enough to handle it, but those two little guys? What the hell is the matter with that jerk to walk out on them anyway? And for that matter, how could he walk out on *you*?"

"I don't know, Erik. You did once. Maybe you can tell me?"

"You weren't pregnant then, Freddy, were you?" he asks, a look of real fear on his face.

"No, I wasn't. But would it have made a difference?" I ask, and I'm ready to walk back into the room when Erik answers by taking me in his arms and kissing me. It's a long and passionate kiss, and I don't move to stop him.

"Good night, Freddy," he says as he releases me, starting to go in the direction of his room.

"Good night," I reply, my voice shaking. My legs are like jelly, but I manage to walk away and into my room, where I flop down onto the bed and pretend to watch television with my two sons.

"Mommy! What did Daddy look like when he was little?"

"You've seen the pictures of him. Remember, I said he looks like you, Jimmy"

Jimmy has a self-satisfied look on his face, but Ben has a problem with that.

"Do I look like him, too?" he pipes up, sounding worried.

"You have his eyes," I reply, smoothing my younger boy's hair.

"Dad wears glasses," Jimmy says, like eyes and glasses have nothing in common.

"You're right, but when he takes off his glasses, his eyes look just like Ben's."

Jimmy is smug. Ben is satisfied, and I remember the times Jerry would be reading in bed. When I came in after getting ready he'd take off his glasses and put them on the stand next to our bed, and we'd make love. I fall asleep thinking of Jerry. I dream we are making love, but then it's Erik. I wake up more confused than I have ever been in my life.

The next day, while Erik goes to the courthouse

and to Jerry's old workplace, I play in the park with Jimmy and Ben. We go round and round on the merry-go-round that I have to push. I help them go up the slide, and then catch them when they come down. I even push them on the swings, taking turns by first pushing one, then the other. Now we're in the sandbox, and I'm settling an argument about who threw sand at whom when Erik walks up and asks, "Are you guys ready to go home?"

I say, before the two little arguers can protest, "You bet I am."

The drive home is pretty quiet. I guess I tired those two little hells-on-wheels out, but I think I'm more tired than they are. We only have to stop once and that's to eat. After that, it's pretty much naptime for everyone but the driver.

When we walk in the door at home the phone is ringing. I run to answer it, thinking it's probably my mother. Instead it's Jerry, and I wish to God that Erik had just dropped us off and not come in. I don't want him to hear this conversation and I definitely don't want my sons to, either. Not after Jerry tells me he wants me to bring the boys to New York.

"You can see them any time you want, Jerry, but not in New York. Not until Mom can take them. You can come here."

"How in the hell can I do that? I'm still working. I can't get away."

"Well, neither can I."

Then before we say anything more that we might be sorry for later, I turn the phone over to Jimmy.

"We saw your house today, Daddy," Jimmy says, and I stand helpless while my five-year-old spills the beans about why I can't go to New York. Mommy's friend Erik is taking them all kinds of places. Ben only adds to the detail, describing the motel we stayed at while visiting Daddy's house.

After the two little informers are done talking, Ben holds the phone out to me and announces, "Daddy wants to talk to you, Mommy." I take the phone and hang up. When the phone rings again, I ignore it and pull the plug from the wall.

"Time to go to bed, guys," I say, leading them upstairs and leaving Erik to stand looking after me with his mouth hanging open. Later when I come downstairs, I find him sitting on the porch.

"I didn't mean to ignore you when I took the boys up, but when Jerry makes me mad, it's best I keep my mouth shut until I cool down," I explain, going over to the top step and sitting down. Erik comes and sits down next to me.

"Do you know why I never came back here, Freddy? Why I broke it off between us?"

"You found somebody you liked better," I say simply.

"I got scared, that's why."

"Of me?"

"Of being stuck in this town forever. I knew you would never leave. Then after you wrote that letter, I panicked. If I came home for Christmas, I'd end up staying, and damn it, Freddy, I'm just not a gardener."

"Take a good look around you, Erik. This is still a small town and I'm still a gardener. Nothing's changed."

"But I have," he says quietly.

"Yeah, you're married. Why did you come back anyway? You're not the only one who has changed. I'm older now, and I want more. Damn it, Erik! I'm tired of feeling older than I really am. I love my boys, but I want more than just being a mom."

I'm ready to get up and go inside, leaving Erik still sitting on the steps, but he doesn't want me to leave. He stands up, blocking my exit, then pulling me into his arms says, "I have some unfinished business here, that's why."

Then he kisses me like that first time he kissed me on a table covered in plants, and like that first time, I don't protest when Erik leads me upstairs into my room and lays me down on the bed. When he enters me, it's even better than the first time. I'm not a virgin anymore, not by a long shot.

Judging by his performance, he most definitely is not either. It's both different and yet so very familiar all at once.

Just before we fall asleep, I say, "You know this is the first time we have ever done it in a bed."

"If you want to, we can always go behind the greenhouse."

"We can't, actually," I say, fitting myself against his body, his breath warm on the back of my neck. "Dad had it torn down right after it happened."

I don't have to explain what I mean by *it*. Erik read all the papers, the transcripts of the trial. He knows what happened that night in the greenhouse.

"When you read about the trial, did you also read about my father's testimony?"

"Of course."

"It wasn't like the prosecutor tried to make out. I was just trying to get even."

"Sweetheart, I knew about your getting even before I came here."

"How?"

"I met the son of one of the detectives who questioned you. He's a detective now, too, and he's the one who told me about how they had Joey convicted before they even went to trial. There's a lot of evidence they never followed up on that they should have. They were just so sure it was Joey from the beginning that they didn't even bother."

"Was the detective's name Frank?"

"Yes."

"Is his son the one who told you about me?"

"Yes."

I lay quiet against Erik, vaguely curious about what exactly it was that Frank the detective's son told him, until I hear the steady sound of Erik breathing in his sleep. Then I fall asleep, too, and it doesn't matter anymore.

CHAPTER 28

It's gotten to the point that Jerry and I can't even talk to each other anymore without fighting, and I dread every time the phone rings. I've always tried to get along with him for the boys' sake. There were times when I wanted to say something but would always keep my mouth shut. Now that I'm not keeping it shut, there are problems.

Ever since Erik has come into the picture, Jerry's become possessive. I can understand his concern for the boys, but it's really none of his business if I'm sleeping with another man. I don't ask him who *he's* sleeping with. It's none of my business and frankly, I really don't want to know. I try not to add fuel to the fire, so when I talk to Jerry, I don't volunteer any information about home, but the boys do. They don't exactly tell their father that Erik is living with us, just that he eats at our house, even breakfast.

The two little motor-mouths usually eat breakfast with us, but Erik is going back to New York to the home office, so we're up extra early. Today it's just the two of us at the table drinking coffee as we talk.

"While I'm gone, I want you to go back to the place where Joey said he found Karen's body and see if you can find something," Erik says, reaching for the cream.

"But it's been so long since it happened. What could I possibly find now?"

"I don't know. But look for anything that might prove that whoever killed Karen brought her there."

"We searched that area by the creek, and there was nothing there. I know because I helped with the searching. They even brought in search and rescue dogs and they led us there. I even stood by the bank and watched them drag the creek."

"But wasn't there a drought? Didn't the creek dry up?"

"Well, yes, but the rain took care of that."

"It didn't rain until after Karen was missing for a while. That means there is a time lapse between, when the creek was dry and it rained." he says, stirring his coffee slowly, deep in thought. I just sip my coffee and wait. I listen to the clock chime in the living room, and still I wait.

Then suddenly--and it scares the hell out of me-- he says, "Right! So where was Karen, while you were searching? And tell me this," Erik says, shaking his spoon at me, like I better answer or else. "How can dogs pick up a scent after the rain washes everything clean?"

"I don't know," I say, making a helpless gesture with my hands. If Erik is after a confession, I give up. But whatever I have to confess I've already told him.

"Maybe they figured that she was lost and

wandered back toward town, after it rained, and fell in on her way home. I only know there was water in the creek, and that's all there was in it."

"Or maybe she never left home."

His expression is intense as he looks at me across the table, and he's scaring me again; it's not his voice but what he says. We are drinking coffee and talking murder. It is definitely not table talk, but it is eerie. The realization of what he's trying to convey hits me hard, like a slap across the face.

"My God, Erik! Are you saying that someone in her family killed her?" I ask, raising my eyebrows along with the pitch of my voice.

"Statistics tell us that most cases of child molestation are committed by someone who knows the victim. By someone they trust, like a teacher or relative."

"But they said she was raped, so it can't be them," I say, shaking my head, like this is totally unbelievable.

"But they never came up with any DNA to prove it. Why didn't your lawyer want samples of Joey's semen if he was accused of raping her?" Erik asks, and I'm glad the boys aren't here to hear me swear, but it's worse than swear.

"Because he was a fucking jackass, but I know that family. Accusing them is as ridiculous as accusing Joey."

"But they did accuse him, didn't they?"

I get up from the table. I don't like when Erik questions me like this. I feel like he's accusing me, but right now the only thing I'm guilty of is using the

F word. I don't think they can put me in jail for that. I make myself busy with clearing off the dirty dishes.

"Sweetheart, there're just so many discrepancies."

"Like what discrepancies? And how come the other lawyers didn't find them?"

"Because they weren't looking for them. I believe Joey is telling the truth when he says he found Karen by the creek. And that means Karen had to be put there after it rained, and before the dogs led you there. After it rained the scent was still there. If she had been brought there before, the scent would have been washed away. It's simple logic."

"Then how come we didn't find her?"

"Because Joey found her first."

I feel my head explode with the craziness of it all, and I set the dishes down on the counter before I drop them. Erik doesn't seem to think it's crazy, though, and continues with his theory. The more he talks, the more I'm beginning to think that all lawyers, both the prosecution and defense, have a theory.

"Personally, I think the person who killed Karen had her the whole time in the beginning when you were searching, then after it rained intended to make it look like an accident by throwing her body into the swollen creek."

"Then why didn't he?"

"Because Joey just happened to come along before he could do it. Another fifteen minutes and Karen's body would have been in that creek."

"Are you sure?"

"Not until I have proof. That's why I want you to look around the whole area, not just on the bank of the creek. One thing I'm pretty sure of is that the cops never did. Hell, they had their killer, and as far as they were concerned, they weren't about to make waves by turning up evidence that might prove they were wrong. One thing I've learned as a defense lawyer is that prosecutors don't like to be wrong."

It seems logical, at least more logical than the prosecutor's theory when he explained it to the jury, but I'm still not totally convinced. I wish Erik didn't have to leave so that he could convince me some more and preferably not with theory.

"Do you really have to go?" I ask him.

"Yes."

"But I don't want you to."

"I'll be back. I promise."

"You promised before."

"But that was before last night," Erik says as he gets up, bringing his empty cup with him to put on the counter where I'm rinsing the dishes and putting them in the dishwasher.

"Last night was nice," I say, adding the cup to the load in the washer. Then I turn and wrap my arms around his waist, squeezing him in a bear hug, thinking that *nice* is too mild a word to describe last night. It was more along the lines of *amazing*. Erik must think so too, because he throws back his head and laughs.

"Nice enough for me to come back for more," he says, untangling himself from the hug before he ends up wanting a repeat of *nice* and being late going to the airport.

"I love you, and I meant everything I said last night," he tells me before giving me one of his 'I'm in a hurry' kisses, then makes a quick getaway while I go back to the dishes and wait for my two sons to wake up.

With my hands in the hot soapy water, I think of last night. I smile to myself, scooping some of the soap bubbles into my hand and blowing them into the air. I watch them scatter and dance. A rainbow of color floats, then bursts into soapy little spots on the floor, like I used to do when I was a kid, and it was my turn to do dishes. Doing dishes can be fun, even when you're a kid. You just have to be inventive. Last night, Erik and I were inventive, and later we even renewed our promise always to be true to each other. I think that maybe it won't be long before we'll be getting married.

I feel a twinge of guilt that, in order to get married, he first has to get unmarried. I remember the pain I felt when Jerry asked me for a divorce, but I tell myself that this is different. I'm not stealing another woman's husband, because she stole him from me. He belonged to me first, and I just wish I knew how in the hell Jerry ever figured into the equation. Why did I marry Jerry? Was it because Erik rejected me? And if I didn't marry Jerry on the rebound, why wouldn't I go to New York with him? But I'm willing to follow Erik to the ends of the earth if he asks? I decide that from now on, I'm going to try harder to get along with Jerry. I might even take the boys to New York to see him. I'll stay with Mom and Angela. I'll even suffer through the show Angela is in. I figure punishing myself like that should ease my guilty conscience, at least a little.

I finish the dishes, and while the boys are busy playing, or more likely, fighting, I call Jerry and tell him I'll bring him his sons.

"When?"

"In a few days. There are some things I have to do here first."

"I'll be leaving in a week. Can't you bring them earlier?"

"I have to go see Joey on Monday, then I'll bring them."

"And Joey always comes first, right?"

"Somebody has to put him first."

There's this long pause, like suddenly the line went dead, but then Jerry asks, "Could I talk to my sons, Freddy? I'd like to talk to them before I leave. I don't know when I'll be back."

Maybe it's the way he said it, but I think he's sensing that maybe he won't be back, and I'm not sure how I feel about this.

"You're going back to the war, aren't you?" I ask, my concern sounding more like accusing than concern.

"Yes," he answers, his voice very quiet, and I can tell he's downhearted.

"But I thought you were through with that? You were even buying a house," I say, confusion part of the question.

There's a pause where I can hear him sigh on the other end of the phone, then he says, "It didn't work out." He sounds even sadder, and for a minute I wish he were here so I could give him a hug.

"Be careful, Jerry." And I really mean it.

"Would you miss me if anything were to happen to me?" he asks, and I choose my next words. A long time ago I told Jerry I loved him. The other day I told him to go to hell. How do I tell him I care, when we crossed the line of not caring years ago?

"Your sons would," I finally settle on. "They miss you, Jerry. They talk about you all the time."

"That's funny; when they're talking to me, all they seem to talk about is Erik."

Now I want to take back the hug and I say, "Oh, go to hell."

Jerry pretends he didn't hear and says in a tired voice, "Just let me talk to the boys, okay?"

I call for them. "Ben, Jimmy, your father wants to talk to you." There is the sound of feet running down steps and then landing in front of me. I hand them the phone and walk away. I don't want to listen when they talk about Erik to their father. No matter how innocent their intentions.

It's raining by the time I finish with the housework, and I decide the walk to the creek will have to wait. Instead, I go to the store to work on the books while the boys work on doing their best to destroy the place. After about an hour of doing more damage than good, I pick up the books, saying as I leave, "I'll do these at home."

I can't be sure, but I think I hear a big sigh of relief just before grabbing the two little troublemakers, half carrying and half pulling them out to the van.

On the way home I stop at Mrs. Davis'. While Jimmy and Ben play with her two cats, Mr. Peepers and Mrs. Nosy, and her dog, Charlie, we adults talk at her table and drink coffee.

"Erik thinks that whoever killed Karen still had her while we were searching. That the dogs picked up the scent after it rained, so there was about a week in between."

"How is that possible? The way I understand it, every conceivable place was searched. They even knocked on my door and asked if I saw anything suspicious."

"But they didn't search your house, did they?"

"Not without a search warrant they weren't going to. I was married to a lawyer, remember?"

"Well, maybe someone had her in his house."

"It would have to be someone who lived alone. You can't hide a body in a house where people are going in and out all the time."

"So who do we know who lives alone?"

"Old Mr. Moses, but he walks with a walker."

"This person would have to be strong enough to carry a body."

"This person would have to be sick enough to hurt a child."

"In other words, all we have to do is find a strong,

sick person who lives alone...Right," I say, thinking how crazy it sounds. Just like how my going to the creek to look for something we couldn't find almost seven years ago. I ponder this while Mrs. Davis pours more coffee in my cup. It takes time to ponder, and I like to drink coffee while I'm doing it. Somehow it helps the thought process.

Suddenly from the living room, we hear a bark, a loud meow, and then all hell breaks loose. Jumping up, I run into the room and lying on the floor is a lamp, a framed picture, and the overturned lamp table.

"What happened?" I ask, putting the table back on its legs and putting back the lamp, now with a lopsided shade, and a picture that should have a smiling face on it, but now it's not smiling.

"They were fighting." Jimmy says, the very picture of innocence. I know that look, and I know that these pets always get along. They wouldn't just start fighting; not unless they had some help.

"Why were they fighting?"

Jimmy just gives me that big innocent look again and says, "I don't know. Mrs. Nosy just scratched Charlie's face."

I figure that I'm not going to get anything out of Jimmy, so I turn to Ben.

"What happened, Ben?"

"Jimmy put the kitty on top of Charlie's back so he could give her a horsey ride, but I don't think Charlie wanted to, because he bit kitty's tail."

"Did not!" Jimmy argues, pouncing on Ben.

"Did too!" Ben insists.

I grab their two wriggling bodies, one under each arm. With an apology, I leave Mrs. Davis' perfect house, which isn't so perfect anymore.

On the way home I think that maybe I should just take the boys to see their father tomorrow. He's used to wars, so let him put up with this one for a while.

While the boys are taking their nap, I pull out the books and start working. I'm adding up debits and subtracting credits when the phone rings.

"Hi, it's me," and this time, I know right away who *me* is. "Do you miss me?"

"Of course," I say, a smile on my lips and in my voice. "Erik, Jerry wants me to bring the boys to New York, but I want to know when you're coming home. I don't want to leave if you're here."

"It'll be a while yet."

"In that case, I'll bring the boys to New York, and while they visit Jerry I'll be with you."

"Freddy--you can't."

"Why not? Would that be too inconvenient, too weird, having your mistress and wife in the same state?"

"You're not my mistress, sweetheart."

"Then what the hell am I, Erik? Tell me, because right now I feel like nothing. A great big zero, who's sleeping with one guy and fighting with another; I'm not a wife and not a mistress."

Erik hangs up, just like that. I pushed for an answer and I got it. I go back to the books, only now the credits and debits are all blurry. I can't tell the assets from the liabilities, and the tears are making the page wet. I know what I am: a bitchy single mother of two. That's it, and that's all.

Fifteen minutes later, the phone rings again and it's Erik saying, "You're the woman I love and intend to marry."

"I know," I say after a pause. "But you never say anything about when. That first day when I told you I wasn't married anymore, you said that you weren't either. That you just didn't have the paper to prove it. I want to know when you're planning on getting that paper, that's all."

"Soon, I just can't yet."

"Why?"

"Because I just put my wife in rehab. She's an alcoholic. She has been ever since college. She drank then; I just didn't know how much until I married her."

"I'm sorry," I say, wishing that Erik were here so I could give him the hug I took back from Jerry.

Erik continues, his voice tired. "I'm sorry that I never came back that Christmas, and I'm sorry I married Diane instead of you. I just wish I could go back and change things."

"We can't go back, but we can change things. I guess I have to be patient, that's all."

"I love you," he says, and I tell him I love him, too.

Then, just before hanging up, I ask, "Is that why you came back? Was it for me? Or was it really for Joey?"

"After I talked to Frank's son and realized how the system had screwed Joey, I came back for him. Then when I saw you again, I knew I would stay for you."

We're quiet for a while, giving his words some time to sink in.

"Hurry home," I finally say. "I'll leave a light on."

"I'd rather you warmed up the bed," he says. We both laugh and then hang up. I love to hear Erik laugh. I want to spend the rest of my life making him laugh.

In the afternoon, the rain stops and the sun comes out long enough for me to take Jimmy and Ben for a walk.

"Where are we going, Mommy?" Ben asks as we leave the road and walk toward the woods.

"We're going to the creek," I say, holding both boys by the hand.

"Are we going fishing?" Jimmy asks, pulling his hand out of mine.

"No, not for fish," I say.

"For what?" Jimmy asks, picking up a stone and throwing it at something that only he sees. He's the active one today. Ben is content just to hold my hand and walk.

"We're going fishing for clues. For something that maybe somebody lost a long time ago."

"You mean like the time I lost Froggy?" Ben asks, and I remember that day Ben left Froggy at a booth in the restaurant and the frantic return to find it. Without Froggy, it would be hell trying to get Ben to sleep. I'd rather lose a thousand dollars than lose Froggy.

"Kind of," I say. "But instead of a restaurant, this time it's in the woods by the creek, and I'm not sure what we're looking for."

"You don't know what's lost?" Jimmy asks, like I should know because Mommy knows everything. Unless Mommy is fighting with Daddy, then Daddy knows everything. Or so Jimmy thinks, and I pretend not to hear when he says, "Daddy would know."

Before we get into that old song-and-dance about how Daddy is smarter than Mommy I explain, "We'll just find anything that we think might be lost, then let the person who lost it choose what it is."

The whole thing sounds crazy, and I'm beginning to think that maybe Daddy really is smarter than Mommy. How can I expect a five-year-old and a four-year-old to make sense of it? But I say the magic word, and that they understand,

"We will call it a treasure hunt, and Mommy will pay for the treasure."

"How much?" Jimmy asks.

"A nickel."

"That's not much," Jimmy says, and I up the offer.

"If it's real good, I'll pay a quarter."

I think I struck a deal, because before we even get to the creek, they're picking up stones, scraps of paper, even a black plastic pocket comb, and running to me with their treasures. I take everything they pick up, but so far the only things that don't belong in the woods are the paper and comb, and I don't think they have anything to do with Karen's murder.

Jimmy finds a penny, and that definitely doesn't belong in the woods, but I don't know who it belongs to, so it goes in my pocket. Jimmy thinks it's worth more than a quarter, and to settle the argument, that it's really worth only a penny, I up the prize.

"Fifty cents," I offer, and Jimmy accepts. I think he will someday be a shrewd businessman.

"We better go home," I say, noticing how long the shadows are getting. In a little while it will be twilight, and this place gives me the creeps during the day. I sure don't want to be here at night.

We're all hungry when we get back to the house, so I put a pizza in the oven. It is the fourth this week for our supper. I'll be glad when my mother gets home so we can start eating real food again.

We go through our usual ritual at bedtime. One hour of arguing to get them ready and a half-hour of reading, praying, and snuggling.

"Okay, everybody in their own bed now," I announce, putting down the book and pulling myself up out of Ben's bed where I did the reading and the three of us did the snuggling. Bending down for one last hug from Ben, I say, "How would you guys like to see your daddy?"

"In New York!" Jimmy yells, and then says, "Daddy, Daddy, Daddy" over and over in rhythm while he jumps up and down on his bed.

311

"While you guys visit with Daddy, I'll visit with Grandma and Aunt Angie."

"Yippee!" Ben shouts, and now both of them are jumping on their beds.

"It will only be for a couple of days because Daddy has to go away for a while," I say, loud enough to be heard. They just can't stop celebrating, and they celebrate loud.

"Is he going to a war again?" Jimmy asks, and Ben stops jumping. Tears fill his eyes, and he starts to sob.

"I don't want Daddy to go to the war. He might get hurt."

I hold Ben in my arms, and I wish to God Jerry were here to see his son crying for Daddy.

Of course, this is an open invitation for Jimmy to start his own war, and he sounds absolutely convinced when he says, "They're going to kill Daddy! The bad guys are going to kill him and then come and kill us!"

"Stop saying that!" I yell at Jimmy, cradling his little brother against my chest.

Ben cries harder and Jimmy jumps higher, pointing an imaginary gun at us and screaming, "Bang! Bang!"

I yell louder than I've ever yelled before. "Stop it, Jimmy! Stop scaring your brother! Daddy is *not* going to be killed, so just STOP IT!"

Then Jimmy grabs his pillow and throws it at me, making a whistling sound to go with the imaginary bomb. I stop yelling and start grabbing. The imaginary gun is taken away, and the imaginary bomb is back on the bed. The war is over.

I finally get Jimmy to surrender by threatening him with no television for a week. I calm Ben with hugs. I even hug Froggy. If Froggy is happy, so is Ben, and Froggy is happy when I give him a hug. Finally, peace reigns in the boys' bedroom, and before I go into mine, I make sure I give Jimmy a hug, too.

I take out the box I have so carefully kept hidden all these years, even from Jerry. I line them up on top of the dresser: the ring, the locket, and the watch. Somewhere still in the box is the broken toy car I found forever ago in the Larson's yard, and I take that out, too. I read over the letters that Erik sent when he was in college. When my strange little ritual is complete, after reading the last letter and tracing the engraved words on the watch, I return each item back to the box and I put it away again.

Just before closing the drawer I notice the box with Jerry's love letters. I don't read those, not anymore. I stopped about a year after the divorce. Now I just keep them around to remind myself that once upon a time, we did get along. Maybe someday my daughter-in-law will discover them in an attic and will tell her husband how it used to be between his mother and father. He already knows how it is now. I fall asleep on the side where Erik sleeps now, and where Jerry used to sleep.

Sometime around two in the morning, Jimmy

comes running into my bedroom, screaming. "Mommy, Mommy! Ben can't breathe again!"

I jump up and take Ben into the bathroom, close the door and turn on all the hot water faucets until the room is full of thick steam. Then I sit on the toilet seat cover, sweat dripping into my eyes, holding my younger son on my lap and listen to his labored breathing. And I wish again, like I do so many times, that just once, Jerry were here. I wish he could see what I go through when Ben gets so upset that he can't breathe, when his little son fights for each breath, when it usually has to do with his father.

Once Ben is breathing normally again, I carry him back into his bedroom, and plug in the vaporizer. I lay down next to my son, singing him a song I made up about frogs. I sing it over and over again, until I can tell by his steady breathing that he's okay. I fall asleep with Ben in my arms and Froggy in Ben's arms.

CHAPTER 29

I'm still in bed when the sound of the ringing phone wakes me from a deep sleep. Still groggy, I fumble for the phone, surprised to find that it's Erik on the line.

"Are you still bringing the boys to New York tomorrow?" he asks without even saying "Hello" first, and I wonder why he's calling so early.

"Yes." I answer, my voice still half asleep, my eyes trying to register on the clock on my nightstand, hoping I didn't oversleep. Today is Monday. It's my day to visit Joey.

"I have to. The boys miss him, and to tell the truth, it might be a while before they see him again. I don't know when he'll be back."

"If you still want to get together, we can go to Angela's play."

"I'd like that, even though I'm not crazy about going to the play."

"Neither am I, but at least we'd be together."

I smile kind of a half yawn and half smile into the phone and ask, "What time will you pick me up?" I try to figure things out in my head. If I leave on the seven A.M. flight instead of the one at ten like I had planned, what time would I get to New York?

315

Maybe the show isn't all we can see.

"I'll meet you there. Have Angela reserve two seats together. But have her reserve them under our separate names."

Well, there goes my figuring. It suddenly dawns on me that I'll be sitting next to Erik, but he's really supposed to be a stranger.

"Should I introduce myself when you sit down, or should I just ignore you?" I ask, the bitterness inside me creeping into my voice, and I want to spit out the taste of it.

"Freddy, don't do this, please?" Erik begs.

I can't help myself when I ask, more bitter than ever, "Will you be able to stay for the party after, or will that be too obvious?"

Erik answers my question with a question of his own. "Did you go down to the creek yet?"

It's plain that Erik is trying to change the subject. It's too early to argue. Besides, I'll save that for Jerry. Jerry likes to argue. I answer Erik's question with another, and I wonder just how long we can keep up this game of question but no answer. He's a lawyer so he'll probably win.

"Erik, what am I looking for anyway?" I ask, and this time I get an answer.

"For one thing, a belt. The coroner's report says there were marks on her wrists. That indicates her hands were strapped together, probably with a belt, but there wasn't one in Joey's greenhouse."

"Joey doesn't wear a belt. He wears those overalls all the time. You know he has a hard time with buckles and buttons."

"Exactly, and that's another thing that I noticed on the report. Karen's back had some marks on it, like the kind you get from a rug burn."

"They didn't say anything about marks on her back at the trial. There even wasn't anything about a belt. All the coroner said was she was tied with a rope like we have at the store."

"There was a lot that didn't come up at the trial that was in the police report."

"Like what?" I ask, sitting up in bed and running a hand through my tangled hair, completely awake by now.

"For example, it showed that the buttons on Karen's dress, all but the one missing, were buttoned, all perfectly straight. I saw that on the pictures taken after they found her."

"That doesn't necessarily mean anything. I'm sure Karen knew how to button her clothes."

"But she couldn't after she was dead. The marks on her back are indicative that sometime during her kidnapping, she was undressed and dressed again. Have you ever tried buttoning up a lot of buttons on a kid who's struggling?"

"I try not to buy clothes with too many buttons. I just have to sew them on when they come off."

"Is that why your mother bought clothes without buttons for Joey?"

"Erik, stop playing lawyer with me. I don't like being cross-examined. What's your point anyway?"

"My point is, when was the last time Joey buttoned a row of buttons and matched up the right buttons with the right buttonholes?"

"Never," I say. "That's why Mom always bought him the kind of shirts that pull over the head and don't button."

There's a pause to let my brain catch up with what I just said.

"There's no way Joey could button Karen's dress, struggling or not. Erik, are these the discrepancies you were telling me about?"

"Yes, and that's why the other attorneys never noticed them. They don't know Joey the way I do. That's why I want you to go to the creek. Maybe somewhere in all the brush, there's still a belt or even that missing button. I need to prove that Karen was taken there, that Joey is telling the truth when he says he found her."

I marvel at the intelligence of this man, and I can't stop myself from asking, "At the play, would it be all right if we hold hands? I mean, as long as we don't make it too obvious."

"We can do better than that. Maybe we can't go to the party, but we can go to a hotel. I'll make a reservation."

"I guess we're back to sneaking around again. But at least this time, I get to sleep in a bed."

"I'll pick you up after the show."

"Where?"

"Don't worry, I'll find you."

"How?"

"I'll be walking out right behind you. You don't think I'm going to let you wander around at night by yourself, do you? Not in New York City."

"I love you, Erik," I say, sorry that I was so bitter toward him earlier.

"I love you, too. Call me when you get here."

After hanging up I look at the clock again and wonder why Erik is up so early. Then I roll over and lay in bed for another half an hour, hugging my pillow the way Ben hugs Froggy. Even a pillow can be comforting when you're all alone and scared.

After my shower and breakfast--I know I can't do this on an empty stomach--I call Jerry to tell him that I'll be bringing the boys to New York tomorrow morning, and I have to confess, our first words are quite pleasant. We should have quit right after "Hello," because by the time we get to the "picking us up" part, we're fighting.

"I thought you'd spend the day with us. We can take them to the museum and the Statue of Liberty."

"I have other plans," I say. "And I can't break them."

"And they're more important than your two sons."

"No, but I spend all my time with them, now it's your turn. Jerry, Why are you being such a jerk about this? I'm bringing your sons to you because you don't have time to come to them, ever. I'm seeing you even though I don't want to. What more do you want from me?"

"What I want, Freddy, you won't give me."

"But I'm sure there are plenty of other women who will. Damn it, Jerry, why does every time I talk to you lately have to turn into an argument?"

"Maybe it's because all those women that are supposed to be making me happy aren't," Jerry says with a sarcastic laugh. I don't like that laugh, and I hope that I never have to hear it again.

"I'll be coming in on the ten A.M. flight," I say, then slam the receiver down.

"Was that Daddy?" Jimmy asks coming into the kitchen, still in his pajamas and rubbing the sleep from his eyes with his fists.

"Yes," I say, getting out bowls, milk and cereal.

"I wanna talk to Daddy." Now Ben is in the room, wailing along with Jimmy about wanting to talk to Daddy.

"You will see him tomorrow," I say, pouring cereal in the bowls and adding milk. "We're in a hurry, so eat and get dressed. Today we go to see Joey."

"But I want to see Daddy," Ben protests, ignoring his cereal. I'm beginning to lose my patience.

"I said tomorrow. Today we're seeing Joey," I say leaving the two to eat while I get their clothes ready for them to wear. As I rummage through their drawers, the familiar wish that Jerry could be here comes to my mind, this time so that he could see how good I am with his sons. Only a mother's love could put up with 'hell-on-wheels' day after day.

Joey's already outside waiting for us to arrive, sitting by one of the picnic tables when we walk over to the little park for visiting. He looks so thin, so old. Once he was a tall man like my father, but now he looks like he's shrunk into himself. Even his hair is beginning to turn gray, and he's only seven years older than I am. His once-bright blue eyes have taken on the same dull gray of these depressing buildings. Sometimes when I catch him staring into space, it's like looking into an empty room where Joey once lived. I notice the shirt he has on is buttoned crooked. A small flaw in Joey's habit of dress. Something nobody would notice except Erik and me. Before I do anything more I re-button Joey's shirt for him.

Joey takes the cards I always bring with me and is starting to deal them out when I say, "Let's not play cards. Let's go for a walk instead."

The boys look at me like I've really lost my marbles and think that now for sure Daddy is smarter than Mommy. Even Joey thinks he's smarter than me. In a place like this, a walk means going about two hundred feet to the end of the fenced- in yard and sitting at a table under a tree.

While Jimmy and Ben run back and forth from the fence we left to the fence we walked to, I question Joey. "When you found Karen, it was by the creek, right?" Joey looks startled by the question. It's been so long since we talked about the reason he's here that I guess it does seem a bit surprising, so I do my best to make sure he understands that the reason I'm bringing this up now is because I want to help him.

"Joey, Erik is working on an appeal for you, and I

think this time there's a good chance we're going to win," I explain.

"Why?" Joey asks. I wonder if he's asking why the appeal or why we're going to win. I answer two questions with one answer. And I think I must be getting good at this game because the way Joey's eyes brighten up, I think I'm getting through to him.

"Because you're innocent, and Erik has found some evidence that the other attorneys never did. Erik believes in your innocence and he'll prove it. I just know he will. You're going to come home, after all."

I think I've lost the game, because maybe Joey understands too much, and his eyes are empty again.

"This is my home, Freddy," Joey says with such finality that it scares me.

How can Joey possibly consider this fenced-in yard and a collection of drab, lifeless buildings home? Has he forgotten our white house with the big front porch where we used to sit on the bottom step, licking popsicles on hot summer days? Joey would always have a red one, and I liked orange. Has he forgotten the hill behind our house where we used to go sledding in winter? That was covered in a rainbow of wildflowers in the summer? Maybe he forgot what it was like when I was growing up with him, but what about his little house down the road from us? The grass and trees overflowing into both yards, filling the air with the smell of fresh green life in spring, and then in the fall, the way the green turned all gold and rust colored.

The leaves we'd rake up and, even when I was old enough to know better, would pile into and we'd have a leaf fight. Joey can't possibly have forgotten the red seven sisters roses Mom has growing on a trellis against the house, covering the bright white with deep red when they're in full bloom. And what about the lilac bushes that Joey always trimmed to keep them from getting so tall that they threatened to engulf his little house? God, they smelled so good, almost like dessert after a meal.

There are so many bugs out there, so many little creatures, and so much of nature that my sons have no idea exists. This place can't possibly be Joey's home. He still has so much to teach us.

"This is not your home, Joey," I say in a voice I reserve for when I'm being a no-nonsense mother.

Joey doesn't argue, just says like it is God's truth: "Norman says this is my home, and I have to do what he says."

"Well--Norman is wrong."

Joey gives me a little smile, a Joey kind of smile that I haven't seen in a long time and says, "Maybe you should tell Norman he's wrong."

"Maybe I will, then."

"Norman isn't here now. He comes to work at night."

"Well--when Norman gets on days, you can introduce me, and I'll tell him," I say, thinking I'm off the hook for now, at least until Norman starts working the day shift. I should write down all the things that I've promised Joey that I'd say to Norman when he starts being here during the daytime.

"When you found Karen at the creek, were her hands tied?" I ask, coming back around to the original story. The one I wanted to get Joey by myself to talk about without little ears hearing any details. The boys are still running off their excess energy.

Joey looks puzzled for a moment before answering, "No. Why should they be tied?"

"Because the person who hurt her didn't want her to fight back."

Joey jumps up and starts pacing, saying over and over: "I didn't hurt her, Freddy. They said I hurt her, but I didn't."

"I know you didn't hurt her, Joey, and so does Erik. He's going to prove you didn't. We believe you. We always have."

"I carried her real careful. I even wrapped her in the blanket so she wouldn't get cold."

"What blanket, Joey? Do you mean the one you covered her up with in the greenhouse?"

"No! No! No!" Now Joey is pacing and shaking his head, looking more and more like he's ready to flip out, and it really scares me. "The blanket I found on the ground, right there next to her by the creek."

I feel suddenly very lightheaded. If Joey found a blanket by the creek, someone had to drop it there after we searched that area right after Karen was missing.

"Where's the blanket now?" I ask, my heart beating so hard and fast, I can hardly catch my breath.

"I don't know. I think I left it in the house when I got a bigger one. It was too small to cover her with, anyway."

I remember cleaning the house just before Jerry came for the wedding, and I didn't find anything that I didn't recognize. Joey has to be wrong.

"Are you sure, Joey? Maybe you left it outside. Maybe you threw it away."

By now Joey is hitting his forehead with open palms and saying, "I didn't hurt her. I didn't hurt her," and I realize if I'm going to get any answers out of him, I better calm him down first.

"Joey, come and sit down here next to me," I demand. When that doesn't work, I beg: "Please." When that still doesn't work I threaten, "If the guard thinks you're having a fit, he'll take you inside and then we'll have to leave."

That works, and Joey comes and sits down, but he is still hitting with his hands. Not on his head, but the table. I take hold of his hands, saying, "That's better, Joey, but you still have to calm down."

"Why are you asking me these questions, Freddy? I don't like your questions."

"I don't either, but I have to tell Erik everything, Joey. You don't want me to lie to Erik, do you?"

"I don't want you to lie, Freddy. I just don't remember. Besides, it was really small. Why do you want it when it's too small?"

"I just want to see it, that's all. Maybe it was Karen's blankie. Like the one I used to have when I was little. Remember how Mom put it away as a

325

remembrance of me as a baby? Maybe Karen's parents want it as a remembrance of her."

"If I remember, I'll tell you, okay, Freddy. Her parents should have a remembrance of her."

Joey stops hitting the table with his hands, and I let go of him. We sit real still for a while and take deep breaths.

"There's a caterpillar in the grass right next to you," I say to Joey. He stares at it for almost ten minutes, with his empty-room eyes, then, bending down, he picks it up and places it gently on his arm. He lets it crawl up his arm almost to his elbow, then takes it off and puts it on mine. I watch the inch-long line of green fuzz make its way slowly upward. When it gets almost to my shoulder, I carefully take it and put it back in the grass to continue on its journey. We watch the caterpillar slowly crawl away, going over small obstacles in its path, and when it can't go over, it goes around.

"Let's play Old Maid," Joey finally says, and while I deal the cards Jimmy and Ben fight over where they are going to sit. I think that it's too bad Jerry can't sit down and play a game with us without a fight breaking out between us. If I thought it was possible I might even consider spending the day with them, going to see the Statue of Liberty, the museum. Just so long as I'm back in time to go to the play and meet up with Erik.

Jimmy takes Ben's cards and Ben is quick to report it, whining, "Mommy, Jimmy has my cards."

"Give Ben his cards," I say flatly.

Jimmy argues, "They're mine."

"Are not," Ben protests, sticking out his lower lip in a pout.

"Are too," Jimmy say, still holding the cards, but using his other hand to hit.

"Now they're mine," I say, taking all the cards back and dealing again, but not until I place myself between the two feuding brothers, and that takes care of that.

I decide that tomorrow when Jerry picks us up I'll go as far as Angela's with him, but that's all. Experience has taught me that anything after "Hello" usually ends up in a fight. I guess we're too much like our kids. But at least they get along with each other some of the time.

When I get home, I go over to Joey's little house and turn it inside out looking for the blanket, but it's nowhere around. Joey has to be wrong, and I wonder if maybe he's wrong about where he found Karen, too, and how he said her hands weren't tied. After all, he's only a child. Jimmy and Ben put their things away all the time and can't remember where they put them. Even Jerry and I do, and we're supposed to know everything. I just wish we knew how to get along.

CHAPTER 30

When I hear the wheels of the airplane hit the runway I start to panic. For the entire duration of the flight I have been thinking of how I will defend myself in the war between divorced Mommy and Daddy, and I hope we can call a truce for the sake of our two sons. It's been a long time since I've talked to Jerry face to face, and I won't be able to hang up on him when the battle gets too nasty. On the telephone a simple "Go to hell" usually cuts him off at the pass. I have always sent my mother with the boys, but Mom's already here, and I wish to God that I weren't.

When we finally get through the gate area Jimmy spots Jerry first, and the two go running to him. I stand at a safe distance while they hug, then with a bright smile that has nothing to do with the way I feel, I say, "Hi."

Jerry says "Hi" back, and I think, so far, so good.

"We don't have any luggage to pick up in baggage. We just brought carry-on with us," I say, daring to venture a little closer to Jerry.

"Then we can go right to the parking lot. Or should I get the car and pick you up outside?"

"No, we can walk, right, boys?"

"We can walk, Daddy," Ben says.

"Yeah, we can walk." Jimmy agrees.

With our two sons between us we head to the parking lot. But first we have to take the escalator. Ben is scared of the moving steps, and Jerry picks him up, then waits for me to get on first with Jimmy.

Jimmy hesitates but he sure isn't going to say he's afraid. Holding tightly to my hand he steps bravely on with me. Jerry is right behind breathing down my neck, and I want to say, "Back off." There is no place to back or go forward. I wish I had taken the elevator and let Jerry deal with the escalator and two scared little kids. Hey, I've been doing it. Now it's his turn.

We get off and continue with the boys between us. Anyone who sees us would probably think that we're a perfectly happy family, and I think, little do they know. Just like the jury only knew the picture the prosecutor painted of Joey. They didn't know Joey like I do. Mrs. Davis called it "circumstantial evidence." I call it "appearance versus truth." And I pray to God that we get Joey out of that place before his appearance matches the place.

Once in the car, Jerry asks us if we had a good flight. "Yes, very good," I answer, wondering if maybe I should thank him for asking, but I don't want to overdo the fake politeness or I'll make myself sick.

"Are you sure you don't want to go with us to see the Statue of Liberty?" Jerry asks.

"No, thank you." There, now I did thank him, kind of.

"Please, Mommy?" Jimmy begs and Ben is quick to add his plea.

"Pleeeeease?" he whines, drawing the word out, his voice getting higher in pitch as it goes on.

I look at their hopeful little faces and I think that maybe I should reconsider, until Jerry says, "Your mother has better things to do than go sight-seeing with us."

And it was all going so well, too. In my head, I hear a toilet flushing as our attempts at being civil toward each other go down the toilet. I'm trying to think of something to say, not wanting to swear in front of the boys, when Jerry, without even giving me the chance, says, "Besides, it's going to be fun. We don't need Mommy to have fun, do we?"

That's it. I can't hold back anymore, not even for the sake of my children, and the words, "Go to hell, Jerry!" come flying out of my mouth. He gives me a mean look, and I think it would have been best if we'd stopped talking right after that "Hi" at the airport.

I decide to keep my mouth shut before we get into a war of words. I might say that F word again, and I sure don't want to do that in front of my kids. And I remember how Jerry doesn't like me saying that word, but if it weren't for my sons, well, who knows.

We agree on a silent truce and until we get to Angela's, we both keep our mouths shut. I feel only vaguely victorious that I got the last word in as Jerry silently drives, his knuckles on the steering wheel white with anger.

While Jerry waits in the car, I take Jimmy and Ben up to see Angela and Mom. Angela falls all over herself trying to please Jimmy and Ben. Like your typical doting aunt she spoils them with candy and soda, giving them each a present, making a big deal out of missing their birthdays. And I wonder which one she means?

Mom falls all over herself to please the boys, too, but she doesn't give them presents. She never misses their birthdays.

For at least the next twenty minutes the boys eat, drink, and open their presents. Both of them get a pair of roller skates, and I wonder, who is going to take them roller skating? It sure won't be Angela. By the time she sees them again they'll be going out on dates and won't want their aunt tagging along. I tell the boys to thank her, and they do. I tell the boys to thank Mom for the chocolate cake, and they do. I tell the boys to get ready to leave, and they don't want to.

"Daddy's waiting in the car for you," I say, looking out the window at Jerry. He looks impatient, like there's a war still going on inside him. I wonder if it's the one he covers as a reporter, or the private one he has with me. I try to remember that long-ago time when we lay by a fire during a snowstorm. My head hurts trying to remember, so I stop trying.

"Tell Daddy to come up and wait," Angela

suggests without asking Mommy first, and I give her a '*look.*'

"Get ready, or I'll tell Daddy to go see the Statue of Liberty without you," I threaten, and the boys hurry to put their new skates back in their boxes, and then hug their aunt and Grandma.

After I wipe the chocolate frosting from Jimmy's face and tell Ben he'd better go potty because of all the soda he drank, I tell Mom to take them down to their father. Jerry and I have never made it all the way to a 'Good- bye' yet in our conversations, and I decide that I'm not in the mood to bother with trying now.

While I'm giving Ben a final hug, he whispers, "You don't really want Daddy to go to hell, do you?"

"No," I whisper back, wishing to God that I had kept my big mouth shut in front of the boys.

"You love Daddy, don't you?"

"Yes," I lie, saying a silent prayer that I won't burn for all eternity for lying to my little boy.

"Be good for Daddy," I tell the boys.

"Have fun," Angela adds with a wave.

"Let's go," Mom says, taking the boys by the hand.

The minute Mom walks out the door, Angela asks, "How did it go? Does he still have a beard?"

"Who?" I ask, going over to the window to watch my mother give Jerry a hug, then hand the boys over to him. Sometimes my mother falls all over herself to please Jerry, and I think if we were still married she'd definitely fall under the category of "doting mother-in-law."

"Your ex. You know, the guy who has no trouble getting it up."

"I didn't notice," I say, turning my back on the window and walking over to the bar, where Angela is stirring up a couple of drinks. I take the one she hands me and take a big swallow that burns all the way down.

"Don't give me that bullshit, Freddy. You noticed." "Did not," I say, and I think that maybe I'm beginning to sound like my sons, so I add, "What's it to you anyway?"

"Nothing; except that maybe you're not the only inspiration around. I hear that Jerry has a lot of 'inspirations' all flocking around to inspire him."

"Good, and I hope one of them will make him happy."

"Bullshit," Angela says, downing her drink in one gulp, then walking to the bar to make another. If she weren't my only sister, I'd think she was maybe a lush. But I'd hate to think that of my sister.

"There's only one man I want to inspire now, and I'm doing a damn good job of it, too. So let's just drop the subject of Jerry, okay?" I ask, swirling the ice cubes around in my glass before taking another swallow. Sometimes it takes a lot of swallows to talk to Angela, and I thank God that she lives in another state from me. That way I can always hang up the phone.

"Who's the new guy in your bed these days?"

"Erik," I say, finishing my drink, picking up my

bag to take into the bedroom.

"You're kidding! Not the Erik you stole birth control pills from me so that you could fuck," Angela says like she can't believe it. And she follows me into the bedroom.

"The one and only. And just to keep the record straight: *you* fuck, *I* make love."

"What's the difference?"

"The difference is, I love Erik, and I want you to get him a ticket for tonight's play. A seat right next to mine, but put our names separately on the reservation like we don't know each other."

"Complications with the wife?"

"For now," I say, hanging the dress that I brought with me for tonight in the closet. "But we're going to get married as soon as his divorce comes through."

"Except his wife doesn't know about the divorce yet. Sound familiar?"

I go into the bathroom and close the door behind me. It's not exactly the same as when I'm talking to her on the phone and I hang up, but by the time I come out Angela is gone.

I figure that Mom should be through with talking and spoiling Jerry by now so I go back into the living room. Angela has a fresh drink; Mom is making lunch.

"He's such a nice man, Felicia. I can't understand why you can't get along with him."

"That's because you've never been married to him."

"He still loves you. You know that, don't you?"

334

Angela starts to laugh a cackle of a laugh, a drunk kind of laugh. Lifting her glass, she says, "Here's to love. Long live love, and may we Harrison girls always be an 'inspiration,' no matter who we're sleeping with."

Mom gives Angela a mean look., like she just might take that glass out of her hand, and tell her to go to her room. Instead, she changes the subject. "You didn't eat yet, did you Felicia?"

"No, Mom. And I am starved for your cooking."

Mom smiles, Angela sips, and I eat everything my mother puts on my plate and more.

After lunch, Angela excuses herself and goes to her room for a nap.

"If I don't, I'll forget my lines," she explains, putting aside her empty glass. I'm not sure how many drinks she's had, but I am sure that if she doesn't take a nap she sure as hell won't remember her lines.

"You should take a nap, too," Mom says to me after watching Angela walk, and I'm happy for Mom's sake it's not a straight line to her bedroom.

"I'll help you with the dishes first," I offer, taking my dishes to the sink, but Mom kind of pushes me aside.

"Felicia! You need a nap, or you'll fall asleep at the play."

"It's that bad?" I ask, "that I'll fall asleep?"

"It's not exactly a Broadway show, Felicia."

I want to say to my mother, "It's not even an off-Broadway show," but that would hurt Mom, and I

think Angela is doing a good job of it without my
help. I don't want to argue with my mother.
Compared to Jerry, arguing with her would be
boring.

"I'll take a nap, Mom, if it makes you happy," I
say, going to the bedroom that Mom and I will share
tonight. I just hope she doesn't wait up, though,
because she's going to have a long wait--most likely,
all night.

Mom's earlier prediction that I might fall asleep
during the play if I didn't have a nap was correct,
because I do, even with the nap. I wonder why Erik
was so worried someone would recognize him. The
people he knows wouldn't be caught dead here.

The play is halfway through when Erik finally
comes and sits next to me. I pretend I don't notice,
partly because I'm supposed to, and partly because
I'm angry. He sure wasn't in a hurry to get to me,
and when he reaches to take my hand, I pull it away.
After I'm sure he has my message, I rub my leg
against his, and it's a lot more than once. Maybe he
wasn't too anxious to be with me before, but by the
end of the last act, he is.

When I get up and walk out of the theater, Erik is
right behind me. He stays so close, I can feel his hot
breath on the back of my neck, and that makes me
anxious, too.

The minute we hit the street he hails a cab.
Without any warning he guides me into the
open door where I sink into the upholstery of the

back seat. We're still among bright city lights when he kisses me, and it's one of those 'tongue-in-the-mouth' kisses. The kind kids at school used to call a French kiss. When he lets me go, I ask, "Aren't you afraid someone might see us?"

"Hell, no," Erik replies, kissing me again, even more passionately.

We kiss a lot until I finally pull away to say, "Then why all the intrigue?"

"I didn't want to go to the party. Can you think of a better excuse?"

"You could have just said you didn't want to go."

"But then I would have to tell you the real reason."

"What is it?"

"I can't stand your sister."

When the cab stops, Erik walks around and opens the door for me. I take the hand he offers and I let him help me out of the backseat. I look around, and I'm surprised. It's completely unlike anything I had imagined. I stop imagining and start enjoying.

"Wow! Some hotel!" I say, still being guided by a gentle hand at the small of my back as we go through the front door and into the lobby. I hope to God Erik knows what he's doing because this is the kind of place where people he knows would come all the time.

"It's not exactly a hotel," Erik says once we get to the elevator.

"Then what is it?" I ask, confused.

"My apartment."

The elevator door opens with a dinging sound,

and I'm relieved to find it empty.

"We're going to the top," Erik informs me, stepping into the elevator and standing so close behind me that I can feel more than just his breath against the back of me.

I'm sure it's a beautiful apartment. I think that maybe it's even the penthouse, but I could never testify to it if my life depended on it. Before I get a chance to get a good look around, Erik takes me into the bedroom, and I spend the rest of my night in it, a lot of which isn't spent sleeping.

I do get to talk to Erik, though, in the morning, when we take his car to Angela's. But first we take a little ride.

"I didn't know you had an apartment. I thought you lived in a house," I say, seeing from a distance the Statue of Liberty and hoping the boys had a good time with their father. I sure did, but not with their father; that stopped a long time ago.

"I moved out of the house. I have no intention of sharing a house with Diane anymore."

"You mean a bed, don't you?"

"We stopped sharing that a long time ago," Erik says.

There's no bitterness in his voice, and I marvel that he can be so forgiving. Or maybe there's simply nothing to forgive. She's an alcoholic, and isn't that kind of a sickness? He can't rightfully be mad at Diane for being sick, just like I can't be mad at Angela. But I sure wouldn't want to live with her

"So, when did you move out?"

"Yesterday. Last night was my first night in the apartment, too. After our phone call, I decided I wasn't taking you to a motel or a hotel or anyplace else."

"You rented an apartment for us? I can't come here to see you, Erik. Once the boys go back to school, I'm stuck at home."

"But I'll be coming to see you to talk to you about Joey and to visit my sick father."

"I didn't know your father is sick," I say, and I really am concerned. I like Erik's dad. He looked really sad that day he had to tell me Erik wasn't coming home for Christmas. Sad and embarrassed-and I wonder how he'd feel if he knew I'm sleeping with Erik again. Probably not sad, but I think embarrassed. We live in a small town and I wonder how long we can keep this up without people talking.

"Not now, but he is getting up in age, and what kind of a son would I be if I didn't come and see my old dad?"

"I don't know, but you never came before."

"But I wanted to. You have no idea how many times I wanted to come and see you. I just didn't think you would want to see me. Not until I talked to Frank Jr. I knew you would talk to me if we talked about Joey."

I lay my head back and close my eyes. I need to think about this for a while. Does this mean Erik is just using Joey to get to me? Kind of like, "Hooray for me and to hell with Joey"? But I promised Joey that he would come home, that Erik would get him

339

out of prison. I don't like lying to Joey.

"Do you still want to hear what Joey told me when I visited him the other day?" I ask, kind of testing the water to see if Joey is still a priority.

"Yes."

"Why?"

"Because he's innocent, and because I love him. You're not the only one who does, Freddy."

"Sometimes it feels like I am," I say, wishing we were still in the apartment. We'd go right back to bed, and I'd thank him the way I want to.

"Joey told me that when he found Karen, he found a blanket, too, next to her body."

"What kind of a blanket?"

"He was kind of vague when I asked, but he did say it was small. He said it was too small to cover her with. I suggested that maybe it was her blankie, and I should find it so that I could give it back to her parents."

"Did you find it?"

"No."

We don't talk about Joey, anymore. We just drive past tall buildings, through underpasses and overpasses. I see buildings with graffiti on them and buildings that house rich people. I have no idea where we are, but as long as Erik does, I don't care. Finally, we stop at a little park with a fountain, and Erik guides me to a bench near to it, where we sit and watch the water pour out of cement statues. There are a couple of boys hanging around, tempting fate by leaning over the edge and splashing each other, laughing.

"Stop pushing," one of them says.

"You started it," the other one says back, and I think maybe I should step in to settle the argument, if only out of habit. But, I don't have to because someone else does.

"Stop it, you two!" a woman yells, pulling the fighting boys apart and giving us an apologetic look. I return it with one of understanding, thinking that maybe my two sons aren't the only "hells-on-wheels".

"Freddy! Do you know what this means?" Erik asks right out of the blue, and I think he lost me right after my name.

"What!" I ask in the same startled voice I use when my sons suddenly scream, "Mommy!"

"It substantiates my theory that Karen was taken from her house."

"Not really. She went to school and never came home. Her parents even testified to that."

"How many kids take their blankies to school with them?"

"None. Especially once they reach third grade, like Karen,"

I say the last part slowly as realization washes over me like a cold wave. If that blanket were Karen's blankie? And if that blanket came from home, she had to go home first to get it.

We both sit in silence, and the two boys walk away, tired of splashing. I guess they'll find something else to do. Something that is more exciting. Like trying to catch one of the pigeons feeding in the grass, which I really hope they'll decide against. Even a pigeon isn't safe when 'hell-on-wheels' is around.

"Do you want a hot dog?" Erik asks, getting up from the bench to walk to the vendor on the other side of the fountain.

"Sure," I say, letting him take me by the hand.

We're stuffing our faces with hot dogs when I tell him, "You're good."

"You should know," Erik answers with a little grin, and I think we're talking about two different things. But I don't argue. He is good at both.

"What time does your flight leave?" he asks, "This afternoon," I answer.

"Why so soon?"

"Because Jerry leaves tomorrow, and I don't want to hang around Angela's any longer than I have to. But I can hang around yours. Jerry didn't take the boys everywhere. I think we can find a few places to take them." I watch as a big blob of mustard plops onto my dress, right where it's most likely to be noticed, and I curse.

"I don't think that's a good idea, right now. We can be together when I get to my dad's."

"But I thought that after your declaration of separation by moving out that it wouldn't matter," I say, wiping at the mustard with a napkin, but it's no use. It's going to stain, for sure.

"Freddy, I haven't declared anything yet. Some of the married lawyers in the firm have apartments in town so they don't have to commute every day."

"And some of the married lawyers have girlfriends, too, but I bet the girlfriends don't bring their kids with when they stay overnight, do they?" I say, continuing my struggle with the stubborn spot of mustard, even though I know it's probably ruined. But then, what the hell? So is my day.

"Want another hot dog?" Erik asks, clearly trying to avoid the issue, and I answer him politely.

"No thanks." Polite is good when you're mad, I think.

We finish our hot dogs, wipe our mouths, and head back to the car. I find myself wishing that Erik and I were married so we didn't have to sneak around like this. And as long as I'm in a wishing mood, I wish Angela would stop drinking, and I wish Jerry would give up on his war to stay here for our sons. But if I can't have all three, I'll settle for the first one.

It's noon when Erik drops me off at Angela's apartment and kisses me good-bye.

"I love you," he says.

"I love you, too," I reply.

"You just have to be patient, sweetheart"

"I know, I know," I say as I'm getting out of the car And I figure it's time to go when I start repeating myself.

Instead of taking the elevator, I walk up the stairs. Ready to do anything to postpone seeing my mother's disapproving face. I try to sneak in, but Angela's already up.

"So the prodigal daughter returns. Where were you all night? Was it a motel or in his car? Or maybe there's a greenhouse somewhere around? He sure wouldn't take you home."

"Go to hell," I say, getting a cup of coffee while Angela makes herself a Bloody Mary.

"I just don't want you getting hurt again, Freddy," she says on her way to the toaster. Toast with a Bloody Mary to wash it down. That is Angela's lunch when Mom isn't around. I wonder where she went off to, so I ask, "Where's Mom?"

"She went to church."

"During the week? Mom never goes to church during the week unless Christmas falls on a weekday."

"She went to pray for you. I told her why you didn't come home last night."

"You could have told her I was staying overnight with a friend or something."

"That is what I told her. You met an old friend from high school at the play, and you were spending the night with him."

"You know, Erik's wife probably has Bloody Mary's for breakfast, too. Then martinis for lunch, maybe a couple of Manhattans for dinner, and by then, she's so smashed that for a nightcap she takes it straight. Is that what you do, Angela? Because if you do, you just might end up like her-in a rehab for alcoholics."

I take my cup and start toward the bedroom.

"I don't want you to end up like her, Angela. I

really don't," I say, going into the bedroom and closing the door behind me.

I'm almost done putting my things back in my overnight bag when Angela walks in.

"How come every time we get together we end up at each other's throats? Did we ever get along, Freddy?"

"Maybe when I was a baby," I say with a shrug. I really don't want to analyze my feelings toward my sister right now. I'm confused enough as it is with my feelings for Jerry and Erik.

"You're my sister, but we can't stand to be in the same room with each other. Do you know why that is, Freddy?"

"Maybe I'm still pissed off because you're the one who started calling me Freddy after a boy in your class when you were little."

"But I liked him."

"And you don't like me."

"I didn't say that."

"Well, maybe I don't like you, Angela. Ever since I can remember, you've always been held up to me as an example. It's always been, 'Why can't you be more like Angela?' Well, you want to know the truth? I don't *want* to be like you. It's Mom who always wanted me to be like you."

"That's not true."

"The hell it isn't. The only ones who liked me just the way I am are Daddy and Joey," I say, shoving a shirt into my bag without bothering to fold it, I'm so mad.

"And I always envied you because of that."

I turn and stare at my sister, thinking that maybe my ears played a trick on me.

"That's a joke. You're the one who always got the boys, while I was the little red-headed Orphan Annie."

"You have to admit, you were perfect for the part until they asked you to sing," Angela says, flopping down onto the bed and laughing like, even after all this time, it's still hilarious.

"I don't think that's funny," I say, zipping up my bag and standing over her.

"I do. I can still see you up on that stage, your red hair like a curly mop on your head, belting out that song, 'Tomorrow, tomorrow, I love ya, tomorrow.'" She mock-sings between giggles.

"I guess I was pretty bad," I admit, sitting down on the bed with a little laugh that's ready to become a big laugh any second.

"Bad! Freddy? You even scared Sandy the dog. I can still see Mom's face!"

Now I'm on the bed laughing my head off, too. "*I* can still see the director's face."

By now, both of us have a pillow in our arms, rolling on the bed and laughing like two jackasses, hee-hawing at each other until tears roll down our cheeks. Finally we sit up and, wiping at her eyes, Angela says in a serious voice, "The truth is, Freddy, I was always jealous of you."

"Of me?" I still can't believe it. Angela being jealous of me is like Beauty being jealous of the Beast.

"You always got the boys, Freddy."

"The only two guys I ever got were Erik and Jerry. You got all the rest."

"But Erik and Jerry are the only two good ones, and you got them both."

"I had them both, but now I've just got Erik. Jerry was the one who cheated on me, remember?"

"Maybe you shouldn't believe everything you hear," Angela says, walking out of the bedroom, closing the door behind her.

I wonder just what in the hell she means by that. She's the one who told me he was cheating. And I ask myself, was she lying? It wouldn't be the first time. No wonder Jerry was so mad when I accused him. I would be, too. I straighten the pillows on the bed again before carrying my overnight bag into the living room where I sit down and wait for my ex-husband and children to come and take me to the airport.

Before I leave Mom comes back,. She doesn't say anything about my not coming home last night. Maybe she's finally realized that I'm a big girl, now.

I'm watching out the window when Jerry pulls up in front, and I waste no time in leaving. But before I can make my getaway, Mom hands me a box, saying, "Something I baked for you and the boys."

"Thanks, Mom," I say, giving her a hug.

Angela hugs me, too. I guess in a way, it's kind of an "I'm sorry" hug. But I think she should be hugging Jerry instead. He was the one she hurt. At least I ended up with Erik.

In the elevator on my way down I take a peek in

the box and recognize my favorite cookies. I love chocolate chip. Ever since I was a kid they've been my favorite, and I think that maybe I'm not really such a big girl after all.

CHAPTER 31

On our way home from the airport I stop at the store to make sure Carl has everything under control. The first thing Carl asks me is, "How's your mother?"

"Good," I answer, and Carl looks pleased.

"I'm glad. I know how hard it is after losing someone you love. My kids were still young when I lost my wife. At least she doesn't have that to deal with."

"No, she just has to deal with my little boys. I think this vacation did her a lot of good, but she's ready to come home."

Now Carl looks really pleased, and I'm beginning to think that all this concern about my mother has nothing to do with her being his boss.

"I was thinking, Carl. Now that Brian is married and you're alone, maybe when Mom gets home you might like to come to dinner sometime? I'd invite you now, but she's a better cook than me."

"Just let me know when and I'll be there," Carl says with a big grin. "I never pass up a good meal."

I watch Carl walk away. He's a tall man, almost as

349

tall as my father was, but not as good-looking. There's nobody in this world as handsome as my father was before he got sick. Carl's been a friend of our family for years. We kids grew up with Carl's kids, and I think that was the problem with my going out with Brian; it was too much like going out with my brother. Mom and Dad were there for Carl when his wife died and left him to raise three small children on his own, just like Carl is here now for Mom and me. There were a lot of women after Carl, but he always insisted that his kids were enough for him. Honestly, though, I think that ever since Brian married Lauren, Carl has been lonely.

It's still light out after I leave Carl to line up the landscape jobs for tomorrow. I park the car on the road next to the woods and say to the boys, "Come on, guys, let's go look again by the creek."

"But we looked the other day. I don't want to look anymore," Jimmy protests, refusing to budge.

"I don't want to look no more, too," Ben says, hanging onto his older brother's arm, sticking out his lower lip as only Ben can. Kind of like he might cry, or he might not. I can see that it's going to be two against Mommy: the only time they get along.

"Okay, you go ahead and stay here while I look, but if you don't look, you don't get paid."

I knew that would get them, and in no time flat they're out of the car and running ahead of me. When all else fails, bribing tends to do the trick.

"How much?" Jimmy asks when we get to the

creek.

"I'll give you a dime for anything you find, but stones or sticks, stuff like that doesn't count."

"That's not much," Jimmy says after weighing his options, and starts to drag his feet. I think he must take after his father more than me, because when I was his age, a dime sounded like a lot.

"I'll give you a quarter if it's really interesting," I bargain.

Ben wants to know, "What is interesting?"

"Anything that's unusual," I explain.

"What's un-us-ual?" Ben asks, and I think that he must take after his father, too, because when I was a kid, I never asked complicated questions like that.

"Just find it, and I'll decide how much it's worth." I finally concede. I'd have to be a lot smarter than I am to outwit these two.

While we look under branches, kick up old, dry leaves, and push aside bushes, the three of us talk. They were quiet on the airplane and in the car on the way home. It was hard for them to leave their father and I want them to talk about it.

"Did you guys have a good time with your dad?" I ask, sitting down on the bank by the creek. Ben comes and sits down cuddling up against me.

"I wish Daddy could live with us," Ben says.

"Honey, your daddy has to work in New York, and I have to work here."

"But Daddy would come and live with us if you wanted him to," Jimmy says, coming to sit on the other side of me, but he doesn't cuddle. Jimmy doesn't cuddle that easily anymore, not since he started blaming me for Daddy not living with us.

"Look, you guys, your daddy and I love you very much."

"But you don't love Daddy. You love Erik," Jimmy says, getting up and standing in front of me like he's accusing me.

"Is that what your daddy said?" I ask, suddenly furious with Jerry.

"No, but I can tell. You're nice to Erik, but not to Daddy."

"That's not true. I am nice to Daddy," I say in my defense, but it's a weak defense. I see the truth as my children see it, and I ache for them.

"I love you guys," I say, hoping for forgiveness, and Ben gives it to me with a kiss on my cheek. Jimmy just starts going, "Bang! Bang!" with his imaginary gun at everything that moves.

I'm just glad there are no pigeons around. I sit on the creek bank, holding one of my sons against me while I watch another try to destroy the world. I worry that maybe I've got a troubled little boy and that I haven't found the right words yet to untrouble him. I decide to share my worry with Jerry. It's been a long time since I've shared with him. I can only hope and pray that I still remember how.

"Let's go," I say, getting up, taking Ben up with me. "But we didn't find anything un-u-sh-aal," my youngest protests, sounding out the word one awkward syllable at a time, and it makes me smile.

"I know, but it's getting late and I don't know about you guys, but I'm getting hungry. How about

McDonald's for supper?"

"Yaay!" Ben cheers, while Jimmy just keeps shooting and running ahead of us. We're almost to the car when he comes running back.

"Is this worth a quarter?" he asks, holding out a small key. I take the key and rub it on my shirtsleeve until it shines.

"This is worth a dollar," I say, recognizing the key.

"How come?" Ben asks.

Jimmy answers for him. It's older brother explaining to younger brother, and if it sounds a little like bragging, well, that's what older brothers do: "Because it's unusual, right, Mommy?"

"Yes, it is. I lost this key long before either of you were born. I had it on the key ring to the company van, and it ended up here."

"How come?" Jimmy asks.

"I have no idea," I say, putting it in my pocket. "Maybe the Key Fairy took it," Ben suggests, and I start to laugh, but only to myself because he's so serious.

"What makes you think the Key Fairy took it?"

"When we lose a tooth, you always say the Tooth Fairy takes it. Maybe the Key Fairy took it."

"But the Tooth Fairy doesn't throw away teeth. She keeps the teeth and pays us for them," Jimmy says, looking around just in case there really is a Key Fairy lurking somewhere in the woods, flitting from tree to tree.

"Oh," Ben says, satisfied.

Then the three of us go to McDonald's, but we save room for the dessert Mom sent home with me.

Chocolate chip cookies are a favorite of all three of us.

Just before bedtime Jerry calls to see if we got home okay and to say good night. I let the boys talk to him first, then while they're upstairs brushing their teeth I talk to Jerry.

"I'm worried about Jimmy," I say, and I think, so far so good.

"Why?"

"He's so aggressive lately. He wants to shoot everything in sight. He always makes his hands into the shape of a gun and makes the sound of a gun shooting."

"I used to shoot everything in sight with my bow and arrow. Lucky for the birds, I was a poor shot."

"I think I should take Jimmy to a child psychologist."

Jerry explodes, "What the hell for?"

"Because he blames me for you not living with us."

"Well--" Jerry says, and it isn't what he said, but how, that makes me explode.

"Damn it, Jerry, this is our son I'm talking about. Can't we stick together on this?"

"What do you want me to do?"

"I want you to explain to him that the reason we aren't living together is because we don't love each other anymore. We still love them, but not each other."

"I can't do that, Freddy."

"Why?"

"Because I'd be lying."

"You mean you don't love them."

"I'm not talking about loving them. It's the not loving you that I'd be lying about. Good God, Freddy, don't you think I know what's going on with you and Erik?"

"Jerry, don't! Please, don't."

I slump into a chair and I wish it were the big chair in Mom's bedroom so I could sink in further.

"I know you love Erik, but will you tell me one thing? Did you ever love me, or was it always him?"

I think I might start to cry. I don't want to hurt him, but I can't lie either.

"I don't know, Jerry. Please don't ask anymore."

"But you love our two sons, don't you?"

"Of course, they're my children. They're a part of me."

"And they're a part of me, too, so at least you love a part of me, right?"

God, he sounds so heartbroken. I feel a guilty knot twist painfully in my stomach, and I want to take back every 'Go to Hell,' I ever said to him.

"Yes, Jerry. I love a part of you, and I always will," I answer fighting to keep my voice from crying.

"Thanks, Freddy, for at least that much. And if you think Jimmy needs help, get it. I'll do everything I can to help."

"I know you will, Jerry," I say, and now there are tears in my voice. I want to hang up before I lose it completely, but I say, "Jerry, please be careful. I don't want anything happening to you."

"Because of the boys."

"Because you're their daddy, and I need you to help me raise them."

"Those letters I sent you in the beginning—do you still have them?"

"Yes," I say, wondering what letters have to do with Jimmy's problem.

"Hang on to them for my sons, will you? If anything happens to me, I want them to know how much I loved their mother. I want them to know that they are loved; that they were, even before they were born."

Then, before I can say anything more I hear the click and the monotonous, empty sound of an empty line, and I know for sure that Angela lied to me. Jerry would never cheat on me. He's just not the type.

For the rest of the week, I live in limbo. I know Jerry can't call because he's en route to his war, but I wonder what Erik's excuse is. I begin to have doubts about him. That maybe he isn't telling me everything, or he might even be lying to me. How convenient for him to have a mistress here and a wife there. You would think I'd have learned my lesson the first time. My phone sits silent, a reminder of how lonely life can be, and I think I understand Carl's loneliness. Maybe I should invite him over for dinner. I'm not that bad a cook. I just don't like cooking.

By Tuesday, I'm desperate for a phone call, willing

the phone to ring every time I pass it. I'd even settle for a call from Angela with some gossip about Erik, and that's really lonely.

After dropping the boys off with Mrs. Davis I go to work at the store. Carl is already gone to work on the new subdivision just outside of town. He'll be pushing and tilling dirt with heavy equipment all day. I don't think Carl will be in much of a mood for talking, even if he does stop by before closing shop. I decide that Christine is my best bet to talk to about my worry. Christine has been an employee for years, but she isn't lonely--not with a husband, six kids, and half a dozen grandkids. But still, Christine has experience in the love department. With six kids, a couple of them must have had some problems.

"I'm not even thirty," I complain to Chris, "but sometimes I feel like forty."

"Right now, forty looks good to me. I wouldn't mind forty again," she replies with a little laugh.

"Sometimes I feel like I'll never make forty."

"Yes, you will. By that time your kids will be in college and you'll be wondering if you'll make fifty."

"At least you had a husband to help."

"You still have Jerry. He hasn't divorced the kids, has he?"

"No, but a dead father isn't much help," I say, and walk away, leaving Christine to wonder just what in the hell I meant by that. About an hour later, after giving herself some time to think about it, she comes over to where I'm watering the plants in one of our greenhouses.

357

"What exactly did you mean when you said that about Jerry being dead? He isn't suicidal, is he?"

"If you mean, is he planning on shooting himself? No, but I think someone else will do it for him. He keeps going back to the war."

"It's his job, and I hear he's good at it."

"But he was going to give it up. According to Angela, he was going to buy a house. She even hinted that he might be getting married, but I guess the relationship didn't work out."

"How come?" Chris asks, like she's writing a book and taking notes.

"The last time we talked, he told me that he was still in love with me."

"That's too bad," Chris says, walking away, shaking her head. And I just hope to God that when she writes the book or tells the story that I don't end up the villain.

After supper, I try calling Mom and Angela answers, telling me that Mom isn't there, and then hangs up. Now that's a switch, Angela hanging up on me, and I wonder if I've done something that is making people shun me, besides causing Jerry to feel suicidal. But my boys don't shun me, and neither does Mrs. Davis. I decide that if this keeps up by the time the weekend comes, instead of sitting here doing nothing, I just might go with Mrs. Davis to church. Lord knows she's been asking me long enough.

But before I tell Mrs. Davis the good news, I tell

Carl the bad news that Mom won't be home for a while yet. He looks so disappointed that I ask him over for dinner on Sunday, and he declines. Now I know it's not just the cooking; it's the company. Carl said he never passes up a good meal, and if I put my mind to it, I am capable of cooking a good meal.

On Sunday morning, I get the boys up and explain that we're going to church.

"Why?" Ben asks.

"Because we should keep the Sabbath holy?" I say, not really knowing how to answer since I'm new at this whole church thing.

"What's the Sabbath?" Ben asks another one of his complicated questions, and Jimmy answers for me.

"It's a day that we don't have to go to school, because God said we should rest."

"Where did you hear that?" I ask.

"From Mrs. Davis. She knows all about God."
"Yes, she does," I agree. "She reads the Bible."

Ben is taking all this in, like he's taking notes, too, and says, "I'll read in school, but I won't read on the Sabbath."

"We'll pray," I say, "to keep Daddy safe."

And I must say, the boys do pray. For about fifteen minutes they're perfect little angels, and after that they're back to hell-on-wheels. I'm glad when we say our last "Amen" and leave.

On our way out of church, I see Mr. and Mrs. Clayton. They have a new baby now, a little boy, and I go over to say, "Hi." They both turn away, leaving me standing with my mouth open and my heart aching, and I wish they had listened to the sermon. It was about forgiveness, even though there isn't anything to forgive, and if Erik ever calls me again, I'll prove it.

Mrs. Davis insists on taking us out to eat to a really nice place, and eating is a lot like church. After we pray, it's hell-on-wheels all over again. I look at the destruction behind us as we leave the restaurant. I still haven't figured out how two glasses of milk can be spilled at the same time by two separate kids at the same table. I have a feeling we won't be welcome here again for at least another ten years-- after my kids have grown up.

We get in the van and start driving with no particular place in mind. It's a beautiful day. The sky is clear with no clouds over us until an airplane crosses overhead and cuts a white streak through the perfect blue. We have the air conditioning off with all the windows open, the way I like it, and our hair blows around our faces. Mrs. Davis takes her hat off and lets the air blow her hair, too.

"Have you seen that new subdivision yet?" I ask loudly, trying to make myself heard above the kids' fighting and the wind blowing into the open windows.

"No, but I hear it's quite interesting."

Anything that doesn't have a medical term or legal term is interesting to Mrs. Davis. I suggest we go see the subdivision.

The dirt blows in our faces from the big piles that

haven't been pushed yet to where the dirt belongs. I don't think the boys belong on those piles either, so I yell, "Get off that dirt! Do you hear?" They do hear, but they don't get off until I yell a second time. And I do not want to make light of what Jerry's doing, but sometimes I envy him.

"It's a shame what they did to this land," Mrs. Davis says. "There should be a law against it."

"I'm sure if there were, you would know," I say, in my heart agreeing that taking a once-fertile field and scraping off all the topsoil to be pushed into piles is a shame. But if there were no pushing or tilling, or even planting afterward, we'd be out of business, and my head says, "But that's progress."

We go through some of the model homes, but Mrs. Davis doesn't like any of them and I can't blame her. They aren't perfect like hers. The boys want to move in right away, and I guess I can't blame them, either. Not with those big recreation rooms in the basement, filled with games they don't understand.

But they *do* understand the pool table. There are sticks and balls, and everybody knows you bat a ball with a stick. You don't just kind of push it into one of the holes on the table. I take the sticks away and put all the balls into the holes in the table and tell the boys that Mommy won. Mommy always wins, and they lose interest in pool. There is a big television screen and it makes you feel like you are watching a movie in a theater. Myself, I'd settle for any house, anywhere, as long as I lived in that house with Erik and my kids. But I don't think that's going to happen--not anymore.

After the fourth house both Mrs. Davis and I have had enough, and I promise to stop on our way home for ice cream. That is, if we go right now.

When we get home, I check the answering machine for messages. There are none, and I wonder if maybe it's not working. I call Mrs. Davis and ask her to call so I can make sure. It's working, and I feel like a teenager waiting for that call so I can go to the prom.

We have peanut butter sandwiches for supper, then it's pillow fight time, and that really wears them out. We end up cuddling and tickling. Of course, the tickling turns back into a pillow fight and they giggle some more. They gang up on Mommy, and I giggle. When one of the pillows starts losing its feathers, we go back to roughhousing without pillows. I think of Jerry and his war and I don't envy him anymore. It's late when I read a bedtime story. I'm not even finished with the story when I have two little sleepyheads, yawning and asking, "Can we finish it tomorrow?" Of course, I never refuse an invitation like that, so I kiss them good night and go downstairs.

I'm watching a documentary on television when the phone rings. I tell myself that it must be Angela, because she would call during a documentary and give her own idea of news. I don't kill myself getting to the phone to answer.

"Hello?" I say, with one ear still listening to the

documentary.

"Hi, it's me," the familiar voice says, and I turn my full attention to the telephone. I don't want to miss one word of Erik's defense when I ask him about why he hasn't called for almost a week, but I don't get the chance.

"I'll be home tomorrow," he says, a smile in his voice.

"What is your flight number," I say, forgetting all about asking why he hasn't called. I'm just happy he's coming home. "I'll pick you up."

"I don't have a flight number. I'm flying my own plane."

"I didn't know you were a pilot."

"A private pilot, and a damn good one, too. I want to take you up in my plane."

"I'm not sure I want to."

"Yes, you do. You'll love it."

"How do you know I'll love it?"

"Because there's nothing in the world like being up in the clouds and the freedom of all that empty sky. I want you to feel that with me, sweetheart."

"Is it better than sex?" I ask, twisting the phone cord around one finger.

"Nothing's better than sex."

"In that case, I'll just stick with sex."

Erik is laughing, and I think again how much I love to hear him laugh. It's a lot better than crying, and that's all I've been doing lately.

"Guess what the boys found down by the creek?"

"What?"

"The key to the shed behind the greenhouse. You

know where we used to go when it was raining out?"

"You mean when we couldn't do it outside on the grass."

"At least we had a blanket."

"How did the key get there?"

"It was on my key ring to the company van. We used to store some things in there for the lawns we worked on. Remember those bags of fertilizer we once did it on?" I ask with a giggle.

"Was that what it was? I thought it was grass seed."

"Does it matter?"

"Not anymore."

We say our usual "love you" before hanging up, and now I'm looking forward to tomorrow, willing it to get here as fast as it can.

I fall asleep dreaming of Erik and of airplanes, all circling around my head. Then the airplanes are keys shaped like question marks, asking me why the 'Key Fairy' threw away a perfectly good key. The key sprouts wings like a mosquito and is chasing me. I'm running away from it, my feet like lead, running over pillows all filled with letters tied in blue ribbons. Then the pillows break open and the letters float away. The mosquito makes a noise like a bomb, and I run trying to get away until it settles on my arm and starts to suck out my blood, but I dare not hit at it because Joey will go to jail if I kill it. I wake up soaked with sweat and trying desperately to remember when was the last time I saw the key chain; wondering why it's even important that I do.

CHAPTER 32

When I pick up Erik at the small private airport outside our town it's like he's a little kid showing off his new toy. I planned on asking him why he didn't call all week, and then decide that now isn't a good time…maybe it never will be. I leave the boys with Mrs. Davis, but not without some worry. What if something happens to me, and to Jerry, what then? I sure don't want Angela to get the boys, and as the closest living relative, it is a possibility. I can't expect Mom to raise them.

"Erik, I'm not going up with you," I say, my feet firmly planted on the ground.

"Honey, it's safe. In fact, it is a lot safer than driving in a car. More pedestrians are killed just crossing a street than passengers are killed in airplanes."

"I'm still going to walk," I say as I start to turn away, but then I think that at least he wants to share this with me. All those months in college when he bragged about his quarterback skills, it was the other girls who got to share the excitement while I read about it in his letters.

"Okay, I'll go," I say, turning around, stepping up the ladder and settling into the seat next to the pilot's.

"Atta girl," Erik says, getting into his seat. When he starts the engines, I have this crazy urge to jump out.

"When did you start wearing a baseball cap again?" he asks, like checking me out is all part of taking the plane up.

"I always had it. I just found it again."

"I like it."

"Since when?"

"Since that day I saw you pull that cap out of your book bag and take off on your bike for home."

"I remember that day. I almost ran you over with my bike."

"See!" he exclaims with a grin, "What did I tell you? Flying in an airplane is safer than walking on the street. You never know when a girl on a bicycle will come along and kill you."

I get the feeling that I walked right into that one and pull my cap down over my eyes. When Erik revs up the engine and we start to move, I close my eyes tight and start praying the rosary, and I'm not even Catholic. But Mrs. Davis, who is Catholic, told me that, when facing death to pray the rosary; it'll help you go straight to heaven without any detours to purgatory.

We're about ten minutes in the air, when Erik shouts to me over the noise of the engine, "You can open your eyes now." Reluctantly pushing back my cap, I obey.

At first the sun is so bright, I have to adjust my cap back down and peek out from under the visor.

It's breathtaking. The world around me is a mixture
of gold and blue, dappled with white clouds floating
lazily around us. We fly into a cloud, and for a
minute I see only white mist until we break through,
and then it's sunshine again. Another cloud crosses
our path, but we don't fly into it, and the whole
cloud looks like it's lit up. I feel like part of the sky, a
sunbeam that floats among clouds.

"It's beautiful," I say, not even aware that we're so
high up.

"I told you it's wonderful, didn't I?"

"Yes, you did," I admit. "There's such a sense of
freedom. Like there's nothing to tie you to the
earth."

"There isn't," Erik says, making a big circle over
the town and I look down at the toy cars on little
strips of highway.

"See that down there? That's your house."

I take in the whole neighborhood at once, trying
to locate my house. Then, with a dip of the wings, I
see it.

"It looks so small from up here."

"You've flown in planes before. Didn't you ever
look out the window, Freddy?"

"I always ask for an aisle seat."

"Then you don't know what you're missing.
Would you like to fly the plane?"

I suddenly panic, as if he'd just asked me to jump.
I start making up excuses as I go along.

"I think I'm getting airsick. I might turn the wheel
the wrong way. Besides, I have no idea what all these
gadgets are about. Shouldn't I learn that first?"

"I was just going to let you take the controls for a while, not land the plane." Erik laughs, and maybe I love to hear him laugh, but laughter has a time and place, and this isn't it. I turn a bright red and pull my cap down over my face again.

"I was only teasing, sweetheart. I'm not about to turn the controls over to you. Not yet, anyway."

I push my cap back on my forehead and take a good look at the man flying this plane and see that he's grinning from ear to ear. Now that I'm off the hook, I get brave and do a little teasing myself.

"What's this?" I ask, reaching to touch one of the handles like I'm going to pull on it. Erik grabs my hand away.

"Lesson number one: Don't ever touch anything in the cockpit of an airplane that's up in the air. Not unless you know what it does."

"What does it do?" I ask.

"It releases the landing gear."

"I guess we're not ready to land yet?" I ask, hoping that we are.

The sun is starting to turn red now. The sky is streaked with pink and orange, and Erik heads back to the airport.

"We're running low on gas," he announces, checking the gauge. "But before we go back, there's something I want to ask you."

"I hope it's not directions to the nearest gas station," I say.

"Will you marry me?" he asks as casually as if it were directions, and I don't have to think; I know the direction I want to take. I've been thinking about it a long time, especially this last week.

"Yes," I answer, moving out of my seat to hug him. The plane dips and Erik shoves me gently away. Then when the plane is steady again, he says, "Lesson number two: Never hug the pilot when he's flying the plane."

We circle the airport once, and then after clearance to land, he lines the plane up to the runway, saying, "Now you can pull the handle." I pull it, and with the landing gear down, we glide back to the ground.

"Now you can hug the pilot," he says, and sometime during the hug, Erik pulls out a ring and puts it on my finger.

"See, we're safe back on the ground, just like I promised," he says, helping me out of the plane.

"We certainly are," I say with relief, but I don't think the relief is because we're safe on the ground; At least not all of it.

On our way home, I ask, "What about the divorce?"

"What about it? I'm getting one and that's it."

"But you work for your father-in-law. Does this mean you're out of a job?"

"It would if he were the only partner, but he's not. The others want me to stay. I'm a good lawyer, and they're businessmen first."

"A good quarterback, a good lawyer, a good pilot. Tell me, Erik, is there anything you're not good at?"

"I don't do windows or cook," he replies, and he's back to grinning again.

"Neither do I," I say, returning the grin. "So on our way home, can we stop for some chicken at that take-out place?"

"Sure, but what about when we get married? Who's going to do the cooking, then?"

"What do you want, a good cook or good lover? I'm not good at everything like you."

"We'll just have to eat out all the time."

"Or have my mother come and live with us."

First we pick up the boys at Mrs. Davis's, then, while Erik goes in to get our supper I wait in the car with Jimmy and Ben.

"Did you guys have fun with Mrs. Davis?" I ask, turning back to look at them.

"Uh-uh," Jimmy says, ducking his head down, so I can't see the guilty look on his face.

"Jimmy spilled his juice on the living room rug," Ben tattles, and Jimmy denies it.

"Did not! Mr. Peepers did. He knocked it out of my hand."

"What kind of juice?" I ask.

"Grape," Ben says, and I close my eyes to imagine this big blotch of dark purple on light beige. Mrs. Davis's perfect house is beginning to look like our not-so-perfect one.

I turn to stare out the window and see Ellen, one of my high school classmates, go into the restaurant. Ellen has put on a few pounds since she was a cheerleader. The only thing big on her then was her bust. She sure knew how to make a sweater look good. I hear she's a good cook now. I guess even good cooks settle for take-out sometimes. In a little while she's back out, carrying only one bag. I guess good cooks don't buy everything take-out, just the main course.

She comes over to the car and, standing by the open window, she says, "I didn't notice you at first. How is everything going at the store? Did your summer sale start yet?"

Ellen is a regular customer at our store. She's a lousy gardener and needs all the help she can get.

"Next week," I say. "You'll be getting a flyer in the mail."

At first I think she's going to walk away, but then she turns back like she forgot something and asks, "Guess who I just saw in the store?"

"Who?" I ask.

"Erik. You know, the sports jock, the football hero that all the girls at school were crazy about, and used to brag that they slept with him?"

"I never bragged that I slept with him."

"Well, some girls just weren't his type, I guess."

"I guess," I say, and again I think she's going to leave when Erik comes out and Ellen stops leaving and starts smiling.

"Hi, Erik," she says.

He looks puzzled for a while, standing there with our bag of food while Ellen explains herself.

"I'm Ellen. Remember? I was a cheerleader, and the Homecoming Queen? I was your date."

"Oh, yes, I didn't recognize you. It's been a long time," Erik says, coming around to the driver's side and opening the door.

"Honey, I didn't know what vegetable to get for the boys so I got corn. Is that okay?"

Jimmy and Ben say in unison, "Vegetables--yuck!" Erik says, "No vegetables, no dessert."

"Good-bye, Ellen," I call out the window before I roll it up, while she stands like a statue looking after us. She may be a good cook but she knows nothing about men, saying I'm not Erik's type. Ha!

"How come you never asked me to go out while you were still in high school?" I ask, finally out of the eyesight of Ellen. "I wasn't your type then, was I?"

"Because you tried to kill me with your bicycle?"

"I didn't do it on purpose."

"And I didn't ignore you on purpose, but to make up for it, I'll ask you to the next Homecoming dance," he jokes.

"Sorry," I say, "but I'm already spoken for and engaged to be married." I wiggle my ring finger at him, making the diamond on it sparkle in the setting sunlight, and I think maybe I'm bragging.

"Can we stop for an ice cream?" Jimmy asks, and I usually remind the boys that it's not polite to interrupt when Mommy's talking to someone, but this time I'm grateful.

"We've got chocolate chip cookies for dessert."

"Again!" Jimmy says, and I guess cookies don't stand a chance against ice cream. Not even chocolate chip.

"I thought you liked Grandma's cookies."

"But she makes so many," Ben says, and it's hard not to laugh.

"I'll take you for ice cream after supper."

Erik asks, "Will you take me, too?"

"Are you asking me for a date?"

" Only if you're paying."

"You paid for the main course, I'll pay for the dessert," I say, and both boys yell, "Yaay! We're going for ice cream!"

"But only after you eat your vegetables," Erik and I both say, and the shout of joy turns into another "Yuck." We eat our chicken and corn out on the screened-in back porch, and it's already dark when we go for our ice cream. As usual, the boys drip as I wipe. I remind myself that one of these days, we will be past this phase of spills and drips. But if Erik and I have kids, I'll be getting these two out and the others in.

"Do you want kids?" I ask him, after I send the boys back into the ice cream place to get some more napkins.

"I never really thought about it," he says, taking a long lick from his chocolate ice cream cone.

The boys come running back with the napkins, and I go back to wiping. I look at Erik over Jimmy's head and say, "How about four?"

Erik takes another swipe at his cone with his tongue before saying, "Four sounds about right."

"I don't want to wait too long, though. I'd like to have them as close to the boys' age as possible."

Erik licks his cone again, studies it for a while, and then says, "Can I finish my ice cream first?"

I throw the wadded-up napkin at him.

While I oversee the boys' bedtime, Erik cleans up the porch from supper and is already in bed when I walk into our room.

"That didn't take you long," I say, pulling off my T-shirt and slipping out of my jeans.

"I only had to throw away the paper plates."

I go into the bathroom, and when I'm in the shower, I think about Jerry. Maybe it's because of my saying I wanted four kids. That's what Jerry wanted. I don't want to think of Jerry with Erik waiting for me in bed. With a quick rinse, I step out and wrap a towel around my still-damp body. I don't take off the towel when I come into the bedroom. Erik does it for me, pulling me into bed next to him. He takes my breasts into his hands and I wonder if he ever did this to Ellen, and the thought makes me jerk away.

"Did I hurt you?" he asks, all concerned, and I say, "No, I thought I heard one of the boys call my name."

He picks up his head, listens for a while then says "I don't hear anything. You locked the bedroom door, didn't you?"

"Yes," I say, pulling his head against me, my arms around him, my hands caressing his back. He kisses my lips, moves to my throat, then after each kiss moves down a little farther, until I no longer care if the boys are calling, or what Erik used to do to the other girls. It's what he's doing now that counts, and

I love every minute of it.

Later, when I'm back to thinking again and Erik has his back to me, I tell him, "The girls in high school used to brag about going to bed with you."

Erik turns to face me and says, "Freddy, I never ask you about the guys who came before me, so do me the same courtesy, okay?"

"There were no guys before you."

"After me, then."

I remember my past after Erik left and I wonder, just what is it that Frank Junior told Erik? And for a while, I shut up long enough for Erik to turn his back and start to doze again.

"I think those girls at school were wrong about a lot of people. Remember how they used to pick on Roger Crandon? They used to say he was weird. He worked for my dad that summer you were gone, and Carl said he was a good worker."

Erik turns again, propping himself up on an elbow and says, "Honey, he *was* weird."

"Why do you say that?"

"One day, I bumped into him in the hall and knocked him down. I helped him up and was picking up his book bag when one of those magazines fell out."

"What kind of a magazine?"

"A porn magazine, and it wasn't the kind like all us guys looked at, once in a while. It had a naked girl right on the cover."

"So? *Playboy* has the naked girl as the centerfold. I mean, naked is naked, right?"

"But this girl wasn't like the others. She didn't

375

even have breasts."

I remember Ellen again and say, "Yeah, well, everybody isn't built like Ellen."

"Freddy, you have nothing to be jealous about. I love you."

"Is that why you didn't call all week?" I ask, not meaning to start anything, but it has been on my mind a lot. He sighs and his head drops off his hand and into the pillow.

"The reason I didn't call is because I was busy," he says, his answer muffled. He moves his face to the side and continues, "I talked to Frank Jr. again, and we were looking at some old photographs."

"What photographs?" I ask, not without some worry. Did Frank actually take pictures? No, he was too busy. I don't think taking a picture was a priority.

"Some pictures taken of Karen. There were marks on her neck that still remain a mystery."

"They were rope marks. That's what the coroner said."

"They weren't rope marks, but right now, I want to go to sleep."

For a while, I lay quiet against Erik, but I can't sleep so I say, "But you could have called. How much time would that take?"

Erik turns to me again and this time his voice sounds like he's out of patience.

"The reason I didn't call is because I needed time to think."

"About us?"

"Look, Freddy. When I said you were a package

deal, I didn't mean just the boys. I meant Joey, too. And right now, without any hard evidence, if I can't get Joey out of that place so he can live with us I'm going to have to live here, or at least close enough so you can visit Joey all the time. That means I'm going to have to stay at the Chicago office. I'm not crazy about the Chicago office. I like New York."

"But we're going to prove Joey is innocent, right?"

"I hope so," Erik says, and for the first time I hear doubt in his voice.

I sit up in bed, and say, "You sure know how to tell a bedtime story." I get up and put on my nightshirt.

"Where are you going?" Erik asks.

"To make myself some tea."

I fumble my way into the dark kitchen, shading my eyes against the brightness after turning on the overhead light. There's a whole shelf of teas to choose from. I collect the stuff. There's some to sip hot and some to drink cold. There is some to put me to sleep and some to wake me up. I stand gazing at all the boxes and wish that I didn't have so many to choose from.

Suddenly a shrill noise shatters the quiet. There is no explanation for what happens next, except that maybe divine providence has a hand in it. Anytime something happens that can't be explained, Mrs. Davis calls it divine providence, even a smoke alarm going off when there is no fire. I sniff to make sure there's no smoke, and then grab the kitchen stool to get to the ceiling to take out the battery.

"Damn," I mutter, as the little junk dish I have sitting on the counter falls, and I watch breaking glass mixed in with junk litter the floor. My head hurts with the ear deafening noise, and I'm tempted to pound the damn alarm into submission with a hammer, but I don't have a hammer

There's another "Damn" when I can't get the cover off the alarm. I pry with my fingernails, break a couple, then another "Damn" along with a "Son of a--" I don't finish the sentence. Instead I grab the first thing I can get my hands on to pry the thing off the ceiling just so it will shut up.

By now, Erik is downstairs with the boys in tow and I'm standing in my nightshirt, up on a stool, holding a battery in my hand, screaming for them to watch out for broken glass with their bare feet. They stand in place and stare.

"The smoke alarm went off," I say, like they didn't already know.

"How come? Did you burn something?" Erik asks, his gaze drifting around the kitchen.

"I didn't even turn on the stove. I was just standing here, trying to decide if I wanted chamomile or Sleepy Time, and it went off."

"As long as there's no danger, I better get these two off to bed," he says, herding the boys toward the door.

"I'll be up as soon as I clean up the glass," I say, looking down at my hand holding the battery, then at the key that I used to pry off the cover and my legs start to tremble. I taste bitter rise up in my mouth, and I think I might pass out.

"Erik wait, stay with me," I say stepping down off the stool and sitting on it.

"Let me get the boys off to bed first, then I'll come back down."

"No!" My voice is shrill; I'm shaking so hard I think the floor might come up and swallow me. "Don't leave me."

"Is Mommy okay?" Jimmy asks, sounding scared, and Ben starts to cry.

"Mommy's okay. Go up to bed and we'll come up in a little while to tuck you in," Erik reassures them. They stay for a few moments, scared expressions on their faces, not sure if Erik will take care of Mommy. Finally Jimmy tugs at Ben's pajama sleeve and leads him away.

As the two boys go upstairs, Erik comes and kneels down beside me, putting his arms around me.

"Honey, you're shaking. What's wrong?"

I hold up the key and say, "I think we found the evidence you were looking for."

Erik looks as confused as he did when Ellen said "Hi" to him earlier. I try to explain, but instead end up babbling.

"I gave this key to Roger. Remember, I said he worked for my dad, and that I didn't think he was weird, but you said he was because he had this creepy magazine..."

"Honey, what does the magazine have to do with the key?"

"I just told you. I gave it to Roger and he was the one who lost it."

"When did you give it to Roger?"

"Just before he quit. He was having trouble with his car, and Dad said he could use our company van until he could get it fixed, but it took a week before he could, so he had it all the time. That whole week we were looking for Karen." I finish with my nonstop explanation, and take a deep breath.

"Maybe he lost it while looking for Karen?" Erik asks and I shake my head.

"But he never helped look for her. I don't remember seeing him all that week."

"What are you trying to say? That maybe Roger didn't look because he knew where she was?"

"I don't know, Erik. I don't know what I'm thinking or saying. It's just that when Roger brought the van back, the key was missing off the key ring, and the blanket was missing in the van. The one I'd always sit on to keep the seat from getting dirty from my work clothes."

"Was it a small blanket?"

"It was one of my old crib blankets. Mom was giving some of the stuff to the church bazaar that she had stored in the attic, and I grabbed it out of the box to put in the van. It had these little white sheep on it, with little clouds, but by the time I got through sitting on it in the van, the sheep and clouds were black."

I have no idea why I said that, except when Erik interrogates, it's hard to leave anything out.

"Honey, the key and the blanket don't prove anything."

"But he was into child porn. You even said so."
"Okay, I admit it all seems to fit, but it's still circumstantial. We need hard evidence."

I pull away from him and stand in the same kitchen I stood in the day after they took Joey away, and I say, "God, I hate when you talk like a lawyer."

"Freddy, I just don't want you to get your hopes up, that's all."

"Well, at least it's some hope," I say and head for the stairs.

"Shouldn't we clean up this mess first?" Erik asks, starting to pick up some of the glass.

"Tomorrow," I say. He stops picking up glass and follows me.

"Will you check on the boys?" I ask going into the bedroom. "I'm going to take a bath. Maybe it will warm me up."

I have the water running in the tub, my nightshirt off, when it hits me, what if Roger was the one? If it was his hands that did what the coroner and the prosecution said happened to Karen? His hands touched the same steering wheel I touched later when I moved it out of the lot where Roger left it. Just a half-hour later of him touching it, I drove it to the garage where we keep our equipment, when I realized it sounded funny. Was there blood on his hands? Was any of it still on the steering wheel? What else was on that steering wheel, on the seat? Oh God! What happened in the back of that van? I'm sobbing and shaking, bitter bile choking in my throat and I swallow hard to keep it down. I remember, my mind vivid with the picture of that night I saw Karen lying in the greenhouse with flowers banked around her. I'm on my knees sobbing, living it all over again: the eerie light, the smell, all of it. Erik comes and shuts the water off and leads me to the bed.

"I'll warm you up," he says, cuddling me under the covers, saying, "Sweetheart, I'm here."

We don't make love, he just holds me, and when I finally stop shaking he says, "What happened to the van, Freddy? Do you still have it?"

"Carl bought it for his son. When Roger brought it back, the transmission was acting up and Dad gave Carl a good deal on it. Mark was good with cars, but before he got a chance to fix it up, he went to school. I think it's still stored in one of Carl's sheds."

"I'll check it out tomorrow," Erik says with a yawn. "You just have to trust me, sweetheart. I want to get Joey out as much as you do."

I lie in Erik's arms and listen to the sounds of the old house creak, like it's settling its bones from the strain of keeping up with all the generations that have slept under this roof.

"You don't know what it's been like. He was nobody's child after Grandma died, yet he loves everybody and every creature. He asked for so little and got even less. Children like Joey are children of the heart. Sometimes you just can't help loving them. I can't stop loving Joey. I just can't." I say softly to Erik, but only the house hears me; Erik is sound asleep.

CHAPTER 33

The breeze drifts through the open bedroom window, moving the lace curtains like delicate dancers in white ruffles, their long dresses swaying to the slow beat of the music made by the rustle of leaves on the trees outside the window. With each movement the pattern of light and dark changes. I breathe deep the fresh clean air to clear the cobwebs, woven so intricately in my brain by the spider of memory. It was a long night of waiting for morning, visiting the dark places of my mind where I'm too busy to go during the day. I yawn and then stretch. I try to connect the dots of everything that has happened lately, but the dots aren't always clear. Erik is already up and I can hear him in the shower.

In our house there are four bathrooms: one for boys, one for girls, and one for our parents. The one downstairs belongs to everybody. The boys' bathroom that Harry and Joey used to share is at the far end of the hall. The one that Angela and I used is between our rooms. It used to be a storeroom until Daddy had it converted into a bathroom. He got tired of us kids fighting over who got to go first. We still fought, though.

Angela kept forgetting to unlock the door to my

side when she was through. Now Jimmy and Ben have what used to be Harry's and Joey's and I have the other one all to myself. The one off Mom's room is still off limits to the kids. It's always been that way for as long as I can remember.

Suddenly from my bathroom comes a burst of song, and I have to admit it is a happy song, but it's loud, and I jump up to stop Erik; even happy has its limits. He sounds almost as bad as my impersonation of Little Orphan Annie.

"Erik! You'll wake up the boys," I say over the sound of the running water and out-of-tune song. He sticks his sudsy head out and squints at me.

"What did you say?" he asks, dripping water on the floor.

"I said, you'll wake up Jimmy and Ben."

"Sorry," he says, then, closing the shower door, he goes back to music. This time he hums more quietly, but still out of tune. That's another thing Erik and I have in common. We don't sing or hum very well. I walk out of the bathroom, shutting the door behind me.

I'm making the bed up when Erik comes into the room with a towel wrapped around his bottom half.

"I think I'll stop by the store and talk to Carl about that van," he says, letting the towel slide from his hips and drop to the floor before fishing for a clean pair of underwear from the dresser. I watch him as he digs around in the drawers, and I'm really wishing I hadn't made the bed yet.

"Is this what you're looking for?" I ask, shutting

the drawer he has open and taking his boxer shorts from another.

"You keep changing my stuff around," he complains.

"You keep bringing more stuff for me to put away. I had to make more room," I explain, closing the drawer with kind of a bang, but I didn't mean to.

"Are you saying you want me to move out?"

I turn to him and put my arms around his neck, burying my face in it, breathing in his clean, fresh smell. "No. Never! I don't ever want you to move out. Not unless I move with you."

"We'll just have to make sure when we build our house to have room for all our stuff."

"And our kids' stuff, too."

"And your mother's and Joey's stuff. I think we're going to need a hell of a big house," he says.

I hug Erik tighter. I love when he talks like this. Not like a lawyer, but like my husband, and I'm about to say to hell with the bed being made up, that I'll make it up again, when Erik takes my arms from around his neck and holds my hands in his.

"I think we better get Joey out first before we start building the house," he says, moving toward the closet to get his pants and shirt.

"Can I go with you to talk to Carl?" I ask, opening a drawer and pulling out shorts and a top for me.

"Honey, taking the boys with us will only make talking impossible. Besides, I want to have a good look at that van."

"I'll get Mrs. Davis to babysit."

"Don't you think Mrs. Davis is getting sick of

taking care of them?"

"I don't think she will ever get sick of being with those two. But this time, I'll ask her to watch them here, while she still has a house left," I say. The image of a big dark stain on her once-immaculate rug crosses my mind as I recall the grape juice incident.

"How soon can you be ready?" he asks, slipping into his underwear.

"In a half-hour," I say, a little disappointed that just when my interest has reached its peak, he covers it up, but one opportunity missed is not all. We got a lot of important work to do. We can play later.

"First, I'll make some calls while I'm waiting," Erik says, all dressed and heading for the door.

I pick up the phone by the bed and call Mrs. Davis, who is now Grandma Davis as far as the boys are concerned. By the time I'm through with my shower and come downstairs she's waiting at the kitchen table, drinking coffee with Erik.

"That was fast," I say on my way into the room. "I hope I didn't interrupt your plans for today," I add as I pour myself a cup of coffee.

"Even when I have nothing to do, I still get up early," she tells me, taking a sip from her mug and smiling at me over the rim of it.

"I really appreciate your help. And Ben told me that Jimmy spilled some juice on your carpet yesterday. I want to pay for having it cleaned."

"Nonsense. I was thinking of having it replaced anyway. Something a little darker that spills won't show on."

I can't believe it. Mrs. Davis is planning on childproofing her perfect house. But then, Mrs. Davis was never a grandma before either.

"Erik tells me you're onto something that might clear Joey's name."

"Yes, and that's why I need you. I want to be with Erik when he looks at the van. I'm the one who used to drive it all the time. I'd know if anything's missing, or even if something's in it that doesn't belong."

"Honey, I don't want to disturb anything. I've already called forensics to meet me at Carl's place."

"But you don't even know if Carl still has the van."

"I called him, and he still has it. He'll be waiting for us when we get there."

"You're really on the ball," I say, impressed.

"Good lawyers are supposed to be on the ball," he replies, getting up from the table and putting his empty coffee cup on the counter near the sink without rinsing it. I notice it but don't say anything; he's so good at the big things so I figure little stuff doesn't matter.

"The boys will probably sleep for a while yet. They woke up last night and didn't get to sleep right away," I tell Mrs. Davis, but don't go into detail about why they woke up. Right now I can't even explain last night to myself, and I certainly don't have time to listen to a sermon about divine providence or divine intervention. I hear plenty of bible stories after the boys have been with Mrs. Davis. I just wish she'd work in a couple of stories about turning the other cheek; it would sure help my intervention when I have to break up their fights.

Carl is waiting for us when we get to his place, and the first thing he asks is, "How's your mother, Freddy?"

"I think she's coming home in a couple of days. She hasn't told me about any specific flight yet, but I can tell she's had enough of New York."

"She's a small-town girl, Freddy. You can always tell a small-town girl."

"Yes. Mom likes a small town," I agree, thinking that Carl likes them, too. Mom and Carl have a lot in common.

Erik and I follow Carl to a big red steel shed that's really more like a barn, which he has at the back of his property. Carl lives on the outskirts of our small town and owns three acres. His job is landscaping, but his hobby is collecting, and when we step into the red barn, I take a look around and find that it's overflowing.

We step around an old cultivator and some old tires. It's hard to distinguish what is treasure and what is trash, but Carl pushes on like he knows exactly where he's going. I hang onto Erik, afraid that at any minute the jaws of some big machine will come to life and take a bite out of me, or at least snag on part of my clothes.

"There it is," Carl says, pointing at the familiar shape in the dark corner. I haven't seen this van in years. Once I considered it mine. Now I shudder to look at it.

Erik goes to the back, opens the double doors, holding a rag in his hands and peers in. I think of all the times I opened these doors to move things in and out, and I wonder if Karen was moved through them. I'm past just shuddering, and now I'm about to throw up. To turn my attention away from the horrific idea of what might have happened inside the empty space in front of me, I step to the side, brushing against a small garden tractor.

Startled, I jump away from one and almost fall into another, and that's when I notice a dent in the front fender.

"When did this fender get dented? I don't remember one when I had it."

"It was there when Roger brought it back," Carl explains. "Your dad gave me a hundred off because of it."

Erik comes over to where I'm standing, and without touching it, bends down to take a look. After inspecting it for a few moments, he says, "It looks like he ran into something with white paint on it. See where the white rubbed off?"

Carl comes around to where Erik is crouched down and looks. "It sure looks like it. You know, I drove it in here, parked it, and this is where it's stayed. Mark was going to work on it, but once he decided on medical school, well, a surgeon's hands shouldn't be messing with tools, so this is where it's been sitting. I thought of getting rid of it, but it'd be too much work to pull it out of here. I'd have to move all this junk that's accumulated around it over the years. It didn't seem worth it for the few bucks I'd get for my trouble. It was one of those things you buy and end up wishing you hadn't."

"I'm glad you did," Erik says. "If they find any trace that Karen was ever in this van, that will prove Joey's innocence.

Even the court will have to concede that Joey can't drive. And when you drove it, Karen was never in it, was she?"

"Never," I say, and I say this with conviction. Because of the liability insurance, Dad had this rule to never let the customer's kids crawl in or on our machinery, and that meant the van too. I always kept Dad's rules when it came to the business. Now my personal life, that's a different story. I think Daddy wouldn't be too happy with my lack of common sense lately.

The three of us head around to the back again, and without touching anything, we look at the empty space where I used to haul everything from tools to small shrubs.

"What's this?" Erik asks, spotting a scrap of paper on the ground just under the open doors. He picks it up, and after he and Carl inspect it, he hands it to me.

"Is this from something you bought, Freddy?"

I look at the faded date at the top, then say, "No. If it fell out of the van, it has to be something Roger bought. That was during the time he had it." Then, studying it more closely, I say, "It's for some blank videotapes. Roger was into making movies. The amateur kind where he was the director, the actor, and probably his only audience."

"What kind of movies?" Erik asks.

"Horror, I guess. Roger never talked much, but one day he asked me if I wanted to be in one of his movies. I told him if it involved singing, he could forget it. I told him about my *Little Orphan Annie* experience and we both had a good laugh, and he said that all I had to do was play dead and he would suck the blood out of me like a vampire. I told him that I was too healthy-looking to be a corpse, but if I ever saw someone who looked dead, I'd let him know. We were only joking around. I didn't think he'd take me seriously, but he suddenly got really mad, like I was making fun of him."

"And you don't think that was weird?" Erik asks, taking the receipt from me and studying it.

"No, why should I? Half the kids I knew dressed up like vampires for Halloween. Even I did, once. Mom made me this black cape. She even bought me some vampire teeth and painted red lines coming down from the corners of my mouth to look like blood."

"What kind of teeth? Were they hard enough to bite someone? I mean bite really hard."

"They were plastic and kind of hard, but hey, I wasn't going to bite anyone, so what's the big deal?"

Erik doesn't say anymore, just pulls out his cell phone and dials.

Frank," he says into the phone. "Those marks on the victims' necks you were telling me about. Could they be from a vampire's teeth?"

For a minute I think Erik is the weird one until he says, "I don't mean a real vampire, but the kind of teeth you buy in a store...you know, for a costume."

Erik listens for a while before saying "I think there's a tape somewhere that has everything on it that happened to Karen and the others."

After that, I don't stay to hear anymore, but before I leave I go around to the front of the van and notice that the blanket is gone. I don't think Carl would take a crib blanket, even if he could get those black sheep white again. I walk past the machines with big jaws, the cultivator, and trip over the tires on my way to the car. I lay my head back against the seat, taking deep breaths and wishing to God that I hadn't eaten any breakfast. Erik and Carl come out of the building and walk to the car and Erik opens the door.

"Come on inside, honey. Carl said he'll make us some coffee while we wait for the police."

"I guess we'll know more once the cops check it out. Maybe Roger killed Karen in the back of the van and there's some traces of blood in there," Carl says matter-of-factly.

"Do you have something stronger than coffee?" I ask, walking on weak and trembling legs to the house.

"I think I can dig something up. It's been a while, but I'm sure I could find us some brandy," Carl offers, and I wish he'd found another way to say that without using the word *dig*, especially after discussing corpses.

"Frank is going to meet me in Cedar Creek," Erik tells me, downing a shot of brandy while I sip mine. Carl just has a beer. I guess small town men stick with beer.

"Why Cedar Creek?" I ask, my courage restored by the brandy.

"Because that's where Roger bought the tapes. I'm going to meet Frank at the airport, after I fly down in my airplane, and we'll go together to the video store. This is the break he's been looking for, ever since he told me about the similarities of Karen's death and the others he's investigating."

"What similarities?" I take another sip of brandy and it burns my throat.

"Those marks on the neck. But I have to admit, until he actually showed them to me last week, I was skeptical. I was sure her parents had something to do with it because of the bruises."

"But they explained them at the trial. Karen fell off her bicycle, the week before she was missing."

"Bruises can always be explained away, but the marks on her neck couldn't. At least, not until now."

I gulp down the rest of the brandy with a little choking noise and Carl gets me a glass of water for a chaser.

"I'm going with you," I tell Erik when I finally get my voice back. He doesn't argue. He knows it would be just wasting his breath.

When the police come Erik goes outside with them while I stay inside with Carl.

"The less people to get in the way, the better," Carl tells Erik, and I'm not about to argue. My stomach is just starting to settle down.

"You know," Carl begins, standing by the window and watching the police follow Erik to the barn, "if those cops wouldn't have been so darn sure it was Joey in the first place, a lot of lives could have been saved. Erik says there were seven cases that fit the profile of the killer. Not all of them were as neat as just some vampire teeth-marks."

"Are you saying Roger wasn't only into vampire movies?" I ask cautiously, and Carl answers with a question.

"Did you ever see the movie *Silence of the Lambs?*" For a moment, I can just stare in horror. He nods grimly, taking another swig from his beer. My stomach does a flip-flop and I run to the bathroom and lose the brandy and coffee. With my second bout of retching, I lose my breakfast. Once my stomach is thoroughly empty, I sit shaking on the floor, my hands grasping the sides of the toilet bowl so tightly they turn the same white as the porcelain.

CHAPTER 34

When we get back home Mrs. Davis has Ben's head draped with a towel over a pot of steaming water.

"He's having a hard time breathing," she says as I take him from her lap and onto mine. Five minutes passes and he's still gasping for air, his small chest heaving with effort.

"I'll have to take him to the emergency room for a shot," I tell Erik.

"Do you want me to go with you?" he asks, and I'm already starting for the door.

"I've done this before. Besides, you have to meet Frank."

"I'll call you later when I find something out," he says, handing me his card with his cell phone number on it before adding, "If you need me, call me at this number."

He helps me get Ben in the car, buckling him into his child seat and giving him a hug.

"Take it easy, little buddy," he says to him, then turns to me and says, "Be careful, honey."

We give each other a quick hug, and I'm already down the road when I Eric pulling out of the driveway in my rear-view mirror. Ben was upset last night. I should have given him his medicine then when it would have done him some good, but I was upset, too. I look at my son, who has had a hard time breathing ever since he was a year old, most especially when he gets upset. I've always blamed it on the divorce. Ben needs his father even more than Jimmy does, but Jimmy has his problems, too. Sometimes I think I've been too protective of them. All they've ever known growing up is Mom and me. They need a man's influence in their lives. I just thank God that Erik is around to be that influence. He's a good person...just what the boys need, just what I need.

Once I get to the hospital, the routine is pretty much the same, except this time when they give Ben his shot, he doesn't cry like he usually does, but only lets out a few small whimpers. On our way home I tell him, "You were very good about that shot. You hardly cried, at all."

"Jimmy says only babies cry. I'm not a baby, am I, Mom?"

"No, you're not a baby, Ben. But even grown-ups cry sometimes."

"Does Daddy ever cry?"

"Sometimes," I reply, remembering how he used to, but I'm not sure if he does anymore.

"Do you think he cries because he misses us?"

"Well, I know he misses you and Jimmy and that he loves you guys very much."

"Sometimes I cry because I miss him. That's when Jimmy says I'm a baby."

"Jimmy misses Daddy, too. He just shows it in other ways."

"Is that why he's mean to me sometimes? Because he misses Daddy?"

"Jimmy doesn't intend to be mean. I think he's just mad and takes it out on you."

"I wish Jimmy wouldn't be mad." Ben says in a forlorn little voice, and I wish just once, Jerry could hear that sad little voice. But of course the war Jerry keeps going back to would drown it out.

Ben asks, "Are you mad, Mommy?"

I lie and say, "I'm not."

I think that Ben must be like Joey. After everything that's been done to him, Joey's still not mad, only hurt and confused, and lately, resigned to his fate. A broken child in a man's body, and I ache to think of how abandoned Joey must feel. I wonder if Ben and Jimmy feel abandoned by their father, too. I know Jerry loves them. He's just so busy telling the world about its problems, he forgets about the ones he has at home.

"How would you guys like to go to Disney World with Erik and me?" I ask on an impulse, desperate to see a smile on my son's sad little face.

"Yaay!" Ben yells, his face lighting up, and I think I've just solved one of the world's problems. I've made one sad little boy happy. Of course, I haven't told Erik yet, but he did ask me where I wanted to go on our honeymoon. What's wrong with Disney World?

For the rest of the day, while I think of Erik and

wonder if he's found anything out at the video store, the boys constantly talk about Disney World. Jimmy thinks he's an expert on Mickey Mouse, and Ben pretty much goes along with everything, until Jimmy says that froggies aren't part of the Magic Kingdom.

"Are too," argues Ben, while Jimmy argues back, "Are not!"

This goes on until I finally use my intervention, and I tell them that if they keep fighting, they'll never see the Magic Kingdom, including froggies or mice or anything else. It doesn't always take divine intervention, just the mommy kind to make it work.

After supper, Mom calls and says she's ready to come home and asks if I'll pick her up tomorrow.

"You didn't have a fight with Angela, did you?" I ask, all concern in my voice. I've just got the boys talking peacefully; I don't need another fight to settle.

"I've just had enough of the big city, that's all."

"You're a small-town kind of person, right?" I say, thinking about what Carl said.

"I guess so. I like sitting on my back porch and knitting. Apartments don't have porches."

"Carl likes small towns, too," I say, but for the life of me can't figure out why I did.

"Is that what he said?"

"That, and he always asks about you," I let slip.

"Carl's always been very nice to me," Mom says, and I can almost hear her blushing over the phone.

"I told him we'd ask him over for supper some night."

398

"That's nice, Felicia. It will be nice to have my cooking appreciated again."

"Angela didn't appreciate your cooking?" I ask, pretty sure that maybe I'm getting to the truth about why Mom is so anxious to come home.

"Angela's never around to eat my cooking. At least you and the boys are. How are they, anyway?"

"Okay," I answer, not telling Mom anything about my rush to the hospital. No sense in worrying her. But I do decide to tell her about my engagement, and about the mission my new fiancé is on. I won't tell her everything, though. She doesn't have to know how the victims died or how many of them there are. God knows, once the papers get hold of the story all the gory details will unfold in newspaper print. *I* know. Wasn't I once married to a reporter?

"Erik and I are engaged," I say, kind of matter-of-factly.

"That's nice," Mom replies in that same matter-of-fact way.

"He's working to clear Joey's name. That's where he is now, tracking down some evidence. I think this time we have a really good case. Carl still has the van that Daddy sold him right after Roger borrowed it."

"What has the van got to do with Karen's murder?"

"We think it was used in the kidnapping."

"Does Carl think so, too?"

"Yes, he does," I say.

"Well, then," Mom starts to say, like she doesn't want to discuss it anymore, "I guess if Carl thinks so, then it must be true."

After promising Mom I'll meet her flight, I turn the phone over to her grandkids, and they tell her all about Disney World. I go into the kitchen and make myself a cup of tea. When Erik calls, I'll have to tell him to forget about Mom's stuff so far as our new house is concerned. I'm sure that if Mom moves anywhere, it'll be to live in Carl's house.

For a bedtime story, I have to read one about Mickey Mouse. After giving a hug to each, even Froggy, I say, "Good-night, sweethearts."

"I'm not a sweetheart," Jimmy protests.

"Are too," Ben argues back.

"Am not!" Jimmy insists.

This will go on all night if I don't put an end to it, so I say, "Good-night, my two big strong men!"

"Good-night, Mommy," they answer. Then, after closing the door behind me, I whisper, "Good-night, my darlings."

Peace reigns once again in the big white house that has heard so many 'good-nights' in its time. I go into my room, turning on only one light by the bed. I'm undressing when the phone rings, and I flop half-naked onto my bed, reaching over to pick up the receiver.

"Hi," I answer, knowing that it's Erik calling. I pull one of the pillows across myself and hug it tightly to my chest.

"Hi, sweetheart. How's Ben?"

"He's fine. But what happened at the store? Did

you find anything out?"

"The store couldn't tell us much. After this many years, even the help has changed. Not that they'd be able to remember, even if it were still the same people."

"Then your trip was all for nothing."

"Not at all. We did meet someone who remembered Roger, a waitress at the restaurant where he ate. We were showing his picture around town, and she said she'd never forget him. Apparently, he was the only guy who ever walked out on her without paying. He had been in a couple of times before with another guy. They ordered just hamburgers then, but always paid. The last time they ordered steaks and just up and left, leaving her holding a forty-dollar bill that the boss took out of her pay."

"He was with someone else? Was she able to describe the person?"

"Right down to what he was wearing. She said if she ever met him again, he'd have the other tooth missing, right next to the one that was already out— right in the front."

"So now Frank has two suspects?"

"Not just suspects, but the place where Roger may have held Karen. It's an abandoned shack about ten miles out of town. This waitress did some asking around after she got stuck with the bill and found out that's where they were staying and decided to go there."

"My God, what did she find?"

"Nothing, really. Their car was gone and she

figured it was a lost cause. She never went inside."

"Did you and Frank?"

"Yes."

"What did you find?"

"We didn't go all the way in, but there really wasn't much to see. There was just some old furniture and papers thrown around. Frank figured we better not touch anything until the police came and dusted for fingerprints. And that dent in the van, it was made when Roger side-swiped the post on the porch, with the fender. There was just enough white paint on that post to scrape off onto the van. They're doing an analysis on the paint, too. That definitely puts the van there. Frank promised me he would share everything he finds out. I'm going back to the main office and start working on Joey's appeal. I want DNA testing done, and I want it done now."

Erik sounds so decisive, so in control, and I say, "I love when you talk like this."

"I thought you didn't like lawyer talk."

"I guess I don't feel like it is lawyer talk. I feel like it's my man talking, and I wish he were here, right now."

"Am I your man, Freddy?"

"Forever and always," I say, like I did that first time I promised to be true to him.

"Forever and always for me, too," he says, and for a minute I feel a sudden panic surge through me.

"Erik, this time you really mean it, right?"

"Yes. I really mean it. I love you, Freddy, and just

as soon as I finish up at the office I'm coming home and we're getting married."

"I love you, too," I say, lying back against my pillow and hugging the one that Erik always sleeps on. I'm ready for some pillow talk. Some nice sexy pillow talk with my man, and for the next half-hour, maybe Erik and I can't make love, but we sure talk about what we'd do if we could.

It's only after I'm in the bathroom brushing my teeth that I remember. "Damn, I forgot to tell him about Disney World," I say to my reflection, but my reflection just smiles back.

CHAPTER 35

The warm afternoon sun beats down on the trees next to the porch, dappling the lawn with shadows from the moving branches. The leaves rustle in the breeze like a soft murmur of contentment. I ask Mom if she wants something to drink, since I'm going in to get something for myself.

"Maybe a glass of lemonade," Mom answers, looking up from the crossword puzzle she's working on just long enough to meet my eyes with her own weary ones. Despite the tiring trip home from New York, Mom rejects my suggestion of a nap, and after lunch we end up here on the back porch listening to the boys playing in the yard. I bring out two glasses of lemonade, and in-between figuring out words to fit into spaces in the puzzle, we talk.

"It sure is nice to be home again," Mom says, with a heavy sigh of relief, but I'm not sure if it's because of figuring out the five-letter word that's a synonym for *content*, or if it's just being home that is the relief.

"I'm happy that you're home, too. So are the boys. They've been asking every day when Grandma's coming home."

"You should have told me, Felicia. I would have

come home sooner."

"I didn't want to spoil your vacation."

Mom just says, "Humpf," and I think it will be a long time before she goes to visit Angela again. It was supposed to be a time to relax, but now it seems Mom needs a vacation from the vacation.

"I think I'll go tomorrow and get the boys their school clothes," I say, kind of like I'm thinking out loud. I've been known to do that sometimes, talk to myself...especially when I'm the only adult around. Talking about froggies and dinosaurs is okay, but I need more stimulating conversation. At least now Mom's home, and in a couple of days, Erik should be, too.

The boys are climbing the apple tree that Daddy planted just before he got sick, and right now it's perfect for climbing.

"Be careful you don't fall," I warn them, thinking that one trip a week to the emergency is enough.

"We are," Jimmy calls back.

"Don't lift Ben," I say, going over to the tree and taking Ben down from the limb he's stuck on, afraid to jump down by himself.

"I'm strong," Jimmy insists, rolling up the sleeve of his T-shirt and showing me his arm like he has big muscles.

"I know you are, Jimmy, but Ben is too heavy for you to lift, and I don't want you to lose your balance," I explain.

"That's because he's fat," Jimmy says, and we start again with, "Am not." "Are too."

Finally I step in with, "Ben's not fat. He is just

growing up to be a big boy like you."

"I'm like Daddy," Jimmy boasts.

"Yes, you are," I agree. Sometimes it's easier to agree than argue, because right now being like Daddy doesn't exactly appeal to me.

"Ben's like Joey," says Jimmy.

"In a lot of ways he is," I agree again.

Jimmy turns to Ben and says, "You're *stupid* like Joey."

"Am not!" Ben cries, and before Jimmy has a chance to shoot back, "Are too," I grab him by the arm, the anger in me wanting to strike back. It's like a dam that bursts in me. I squeeze his arm so hard it makes Jimmy cry out and try to pull away.

"Don't you *ever* say that again!" I say. My voice is a shrewd hiss, and I'm yanking at the arm like I just might pull it out.

"Ouch!" Jimmy screams, his face reflecting the pain, bringing me back to my senses. I let go, turn my back, and walk down around to the front of the house where I pace up and down the driveway. I have to admit that for a minute I hated Jimmy, my own flesh and blood, for saying what all the kids at school used to say. All my life I've defended Joey. I put him before everyone else. My friends, my husband, and now even my own child.

After pacing, asking myself what is happening to me, I go back to the porch, and I can't bear to look at Jimmy. Mom has him on her lap, sharing her lemonade with him. Ben is drinking mine.

"I'm sorry," I say, kneeling down to kiss the red

mark on his arm, remorse replacing the anger swirling inside me, and I swallow back the tears that started when I was pacing.

When Jimmy pulls away, I'm sure I'm going to cry, and when he says, "I'm going to tell Daddy! Daddy would never hurt me," my heart breaks.

"No. Daddy would never hurt you, and I'm sorry I did," I manage to say, getting the words past the lump in my throat. "But Daddy wouldn't let you say mean things about people, either. I know your daddy, and he's a kind person, just like I know you are, deep down inside."

"If Daddy is so kind, then how come you won't live with him?"

I'm drowning in words, trying to find the right ones to save me. Just before I go under, Mom comes to the rescue and says, "Sometimes, James, it's kinder for people to separate when they can't get along than for them to try and live together."

"Why?" Ben asks, coming over to where I'm kneeling and putting his arms around me.

"Because when they're together, they hurt each other. Not the way I hurt Jimmy, but with words, and sometimes that can hurt even more."

"You mean like when Jimmy is mean to me because he's mad? Are you mad, Mommy?" Ben asks, and I'm drowning again.

My mother says, "Not mad Ben, just hurt. And sometimes when you hurt, you want to hurt back. Your mother loves you boys and your daddy loves you, too." And I take back all those times I argued with my mother growing up, thinking she hadn't a clue what I was about.

"I love you, Mommy," Ben says, giving me a tight squeeze with his arms around my neck. "I don't want you to hurt."

"How about you, Jimmy? Do you still love me, too?"

"I guess so," he says, getting down from Mom's lap and giving me a hug, too, kind of.

"Let's go for ice cream," I suggest, taking them both by the hand. "How about you, Mom? You want to go too?"

"No, I'm just going to sit here and finish this puzzle. Carl said he might stop by later."

"Why?" I ask, wondering why the rush. I know he likes Mom, but couldn't he wait another day for her to get rested up after the trip?

"I asked him over for some warm apple pie."

"We don't have apple pie, Mom. Warm or cold."

"Not yet, we don't" she says, getting up to go back into the house, taking the puzzle with her.

"I'll bring some ice cream home to go along with the pie," I say, and while Ben tugs at my hand, Jimmy shoves from behind, getting me out the door in no time flat.

On our way home from the ice cream parlor, after the boys finish their cones and I do the usual wiping away drips, we stop at a video store and I rent a movie for the boys. It takes them so long to make up their minds about what they want, that by the time we get to the car, the ice cream I bought for the pie is leaking out of the carton and into the plastic bag.

"So much for having apple pie and ice cream." I say, taking the plastic bag out of the car and throwing it into the trash can outside the door of the video store. "Next time we'll get the movie first."

"Can we stop at K-Mart and get a toy?" Ben asks. I look at Jimmy who, despite the ice cream and the movie, is still sitting nursing and rubbing his hurt arm, except it's the wrong arm. I decide Jimmy will not be a businessman, as I'd thought the other day with his negotiating over how much for what he finds. Jimmy will be a politician. Every politician knows how to work the crowd, and this crowd of one is really being worked over.

"Would you like a toy, too?" I ask Jimmy.

He stops his nursing and rubbing just long enough to answer "Yes."

So we stop at K-Mart, and I'm just lucky they each pick out something for less than ten dollars. I was ready to spend twenty. That's how bad I feel about hurting my son. But it's not just wanting to patch things up that makes this crowd of one so anxious to please. It's also kind of a bribe for not tattling to Jerry on me. God knows, we argue enough as it is. We don't have to fight over me being an abusive mother, too.

When we pull into the yard, not only is Carl's car parked in front, but Erik's is as well.

"How come he's back so early?" I ask and I'm talking to myself again, but after froggie and dinosaur talk, with Mommy doing the interpretation for two kids who can't make up their minds, talking to myself doesn't seem so crazy. I'm not sure if I run or fly into the house, but when I open the kitchen door, both men are sitting at the table, while Mom serves hot apple pie.

Erik gets up from his chair and by the time I reach him, his arms are waiting.

"God, I missed you," I say, and Erik laughs. "It's only been a couple of days."

"But I missed you anyway," I repeat, giving him an extra tight hug.

"I missed you, too," he says, kissing me, the kind you give in front of an audience. Then, spotting the boys, he releases me and reaches for them. They both give him a hug. Ben shows him his new frog, and Jimmy shows him his new dinosaur.

Before I can ask him why he's home so early, not that I'm complaining, Jimmy asks, "When are we going to Disney World?" Erik looks confused.

"I told them if they were good, we'd take them to Disney World," I explain, but again in front of an audience, I can't use other persuasion.

"When?" Erik asks.

"After we're married. For our honeymoon."

"I was planning on something more romantic, like Italy." And now I know what's wrong with Disney World; it's not Italy. I will be kicking myself for a long time, maybe until we're married fifty years and Erik takes me to Italy for our golden wedding anniversary.

"I guess it's not the place, but who you're with that counts," Erik says, sitting back down again, and

I feel a little better, kind of. We all eat warm apple pie, without ice cream since I wasn't smart enough to get the ice cream last. Just like I wasn't smart enough to ask where Erik was planning to take me on our honeymoon before I opened my big mouth. I sure hope I can keep it shut when Jimmy tells his daddy on me, or at least be smart enough to talk my way out without swearing at Jerry. I've got enough on my conscience.

After having our dessert first, we eat the main entree that seems to just happen. When Mom's around, food materializes out of nowhere. Even counting the time to do dishes, it's still early, and so we all go sit out on the back porch, even Carl.

Coaxing him to stay wasn't difficult. All he had to do was take a look at the warm German potato salad, smell the ham warming in the oven, along with fresh coffee brewing, and Carl had no trouble saying 'Yes."

Ben and Jimmy are back to playing in the yard again, only this time, instead of being in the trees, they're under them, with their menagerie of dinosaurs and frogs spread out on the grass. They are introducing the newcomers to the group, and as long as the dinosaurs don't threaten to eat the frogs, peace reigns in the backyard.

"I've filed an appeal based on the evidence we have so far and after the DNA test, I don't think we'll have any problem getting Joey home."

Carl sits back in his chair and studies Erik, measuring his words. "You're really that sure."

"I'm as sure as I've ever been about a person's

innocence. I think when this is all over, there will be a lot of embarrassed police in this town," Erik says, and that makes me feel good.

"Especially Frank Sr. and that other detective who questioned me. I just want to see their faces when the papers come out with the story," I say, getting up to stand by Erik and putting my arms around his neck from behind. He takes my hand and kisses it.

"Frank Jr. has more than made up for the mistakes his father made."

"Try telling that to the parents of the other victims," I say, going to sit back down.

"I can't undo what's been done, Freddy. I can only help create legislation to prevent this from ever happening again."

We all look at Erik expecting him to explain, and that's when he drops the bomb.

"I'm going to run for the senate. My father-in-law is ready to back me up."

"Do you think you stand a chance of winning?" Carl asks.

"I think I stand a damn good chance of winning. Especially after winning this case," Erik says, getting up from his chair and stretching before heading for the door.

"I have to get back tonight, but first I'm going to stop by my dad's."

I follow Erik out to the car, and as soon as we're out of earshot, I ask, "What the hell is going on, Erik?"

He pulls me into his arms, ready to give me a

good-bye kiss, but I pull away.

"Is that why you did it? Getting Joey off the hook, so you could get elected to the senate?"

"No," he says, looking surprised that I should suggest such a thing. "When I started this, I had no intention of running."

"But your father-in-law suggested it, right? Is this his way of getting you to stay married to his daughter?"

"Right now a divorce isn't a good idea, but I'm still going to get one. I just want you to be patient, honey, that's all."

"I've been too patient too long, Erik. Send me a bill for your services for getting Joey out," I say, walking to the house.

"Freddy, I'll meet you later. I don't have to go back tonight."

"Where?" I ask.

"You know where," Erik says.

"Go to hell," I say, and I'd like to say more, but those words haven't been invented yet, and I go into the house.

For the rest of the night, I sit in silence. I sit through the movie I rented for the kids, through Carl saying good-night. Then I take the boys up to bed, and I even sit through their prayers. I listen to them, "God bless Mommy and Daddy and Grandma. God bless Auntie Angela and Uncle Harry," then it's everybody else they can think of, including froggies and dinosaurs. I read them a story about railroads and bridges without paying attention

413

to a single word. Finally, after performing all my duties as Mommy, I go into my bedroom and cry like a woman who has just been told she's not good enough to be a senator's wife.

I lay in bed, tossing and turning. One minute I hate myself for being so stupid; the next minute I hate Erik for making me feel stupid. Then I do the most stupid thing of all, I jump up and go downstairs. I run across the damp grass in my bare feet into Joey's yard, and there, waiting for me, is Erik.

"I knew you'd come," he says, pulling me down next to him on the blanket.

"How could you be so sure?" I ask, snuggling up to him.

"Because we love each other, and nothing will ever keep us apart."

"Nothing?" I ask.

"Nothing," he says, kissing me long and hard with passion and the sweet taste of him is on my tongue, and it's not just his lips that I taste.

"Erik, I forgot to put my diaphragm in. I've been forgetting to take the pill, so to be on the safe side, I mean with everything so crazy lately," I say, but it's too late.

Nothing can stop us now, nothing.

"I'll be careful," Erik promises, but that's too late, too.

It's almost morning, and just before we have to leave Erik tells me, "I want to get Joey out of there as soon as I can. I don't like what I've been hearing about that place."

"What have you heard?"

"That there's abuse going on there. Some of the guards are stealing the prisoners' gifts that are brought in, and if anybody says anything, they make them pay."

"What do you mean 'pay'?" I ask, sitting up. Erik reaches up and strokes my back.

"There's bruises, and one of the prisoners was hurt so bad he ended up in the hospital. They said they had to restrain him, but there are ways to restrain someone without almost killing him."

I shudder, horrified at what I'm hearing, and Erik pulls me back down beside him. He rubs and soothes, but horror can't be soothed. He tells me he loves me, and I think, that the "soothe" is starting to work.

"I'm going to be true to you, Freddy. If I stay married for a while, it's only for political reasons. I'll get back here as often as I can. After all, my father still lives here. Nobody will question that."

"What does that make me, Erik? Your mistress?"

"My love," he answers. "My one and only love."

"I'll be true to you, too," I say, and it's another hour before we finally part. "Forever and always," we promise to love each other, and then we go our separate ways.

CHAPTER 36

The month of September is a busy one. The boys start school, with Jimmy in second grade and Ben in the first. On top of that, we've never been busier at the store. We really slashed the prices on our summer stock to make room for the Halloween, Thanksgiving, and Christmas merchandise that will start arriving any day now. Mom insists on helping out with the business since it's so busy, and I think it has something to do with Carl being there. He doesn't go out on the landscape jobs as much as he used to, and I think Mom has something to do with that, too.

It's kind of cute the way they flirt with each other. It reminds me of the time Erik and I worked together at the store. Looking back, it seems like a lifetime ago that Daddy was still alive, and Joey was still home.

I see the way Carl looks at Mom, and I'm sure it won't be long now before they'll be getting married. I'm happy for Mom. I know Daddy would want this for her, not to be lonely. He would approve of Carl being the one. He always said Carl was a good man and would make someone a good husband. I don't think Daddy would approve of my life, though. Not just because I'm lonely, but because he always gave me credit for having common sense, and my relationship with Erik defies any sense, common or otherwise.

I hardly see Erik, and when I do, it's just for an overnight at his father's house. It's too cool in the evenings for us to make love outside like we sometimes did in summer. I can't bring myself to do it inside Joey's house. Besides, I have it all ready for when Joey comes home. Mom was lenient with Jerry when he slept with me before we were married, but Mom likes Jerry a lot more than she likes Erik. She thinks Erik is just stringing me along ever since he announced his candidacy. I tell her that if it weren't for him, Joey would rot in jail, but she just says, "What you're doing has nothing to do with gratitude, Felicia." Mom will not come right out and say what it is I'm doing, but Jerry does.

"He's still married to her and still fucking you. If you involve my sons in a scandal, Freddy, I'll fight to get them."

"And if you would get custody, what then? Are you going to take them to cover the war with you? I'm a good mother, Jerry, and what I'm doing is no worse than what you're doing. I just do it with one person. How many partners have you had this last month? Or does it not matter, because you're a man?"

For my answer, Jerry says, "If you're such a good mother, why did you hurt our son? He told me how you almost broke his arm."

417

"Go to hell, Jerry," I say, and I don't feel guilty, not one bit. Sometimes that's the only language he understands.

After that, Jerry hangs up, and we never discuss our love lives again, only our sons' lives, and that's enough to keep us fighting.

It's early October now, and the weatherman on television is predicting a frost when Erik and I finally get to spend a weekend together. Mrs. Davis is more liberal than Mom, and she tells me to enjoy myself when I ask her if we can use the cabin. She says something about her not throwing the first stone, and I think there's more to the romance between Mr. and Mrs. Davis than her helping him off the bedpan, like maybe there was another Mrs. Davis before her. That may be why the cabin holds many secrets, but then I'm not about to throw stones either. By now, I have a little group of non-stone throwers who know of my romance with Erik but turn the other way. I trust these people. They would never do anything to hurt me.

We arrive at the cabin on a Friday evening. I took the boys out of school at noon, and they sure didn't complain. Right from the beginning, even on our way, it's great. Jimmy and Ben don't argue at all, not even when Ben knocks Jimmy's toy truck out the car door when he gets out to go to the bathroom, and we don't discover it's missing until we're ten miles down the road. "It's okay, Ben. It was an accident," Jimmy says when Ben starts to cry, saying he's sorry.

418

"Yes, it was an accident," I say, while Erik turns the car around. We find the toy lying on the pavement next to the gas pumps where we made our stop for gas and potty. We laugh and joke about how lucky we are that a truck didn't run over the truck. For supper, we stop for hamburgers and chocolate milkshakes that prove the boys' eyes are bigger than their stomachs, and I end up throwing out two half-eaten hamburgers and two almost-full melted milkshakes when we finally get to the cabin just before dark.

The trees are a glorious color, and I remember another time I came here, but that was another season and another life. And I think from now on October will be my favorite month. The boys run to the lake and shout for Erik and me to hurry when they see a ripple from a fish jumping up in the water. We stand on the pier and gaze down into the clear water and see little minnows swimming.

"Can we go fishing?" Jimmy asks, excited.

"Tomorrow," Erik answers.

"Can we eat the fish that we catch?" Jimmy asks.

"If your mother fixes them."

"I don't want to eat baby fishes," Ben says, wrinkling his nose.

"We aren't going to catch baby fish." I tell him. "We're going to use them for bait," Jimmy says matter-of-factly, and I'm glad Ben hasn't the slightest idea what bait is.

We all go into the cabin, and I unpack while Erik and the boys make a fire in the fireplace. Later, we

419

sit around the fire and toast marshmallows, putting them between graham crackers layered with pieces of chocolate bars. At bedtime I listen to their prayers, and before I can even open the book to start their bedtime story, both of them are yawning and dozing off.

I go into the bedroom that I once shared with Jerry, and if I feel even a little guilty, I remind myself that at this moment, Jerry is probably sharing his bedroom with someone else. That's just how it is. We're not married to each other anymore. It was another lifetime, and the only reminders of what we once were to each other are now sleeping in the next bedroom. I undress and stand in front of Erik with nothing on. No negligee is necessary to arouse the passion I see in Erik's eyes. When I'm in his arms, there are no regrets, no guilt for choosing this lifestyle, only my love for this man, and our passion that has no beginning and no end. It's like it's always been this way.

In the morning, we take the boys fishing in the rowboat that's tied to the pier. We all take turns rowing out to the deep water. Even Ben and Jimmy have to try it, but we don't get far, not until Erik takes over. The boat rocks back and forth every time one of us moves, making little ripples that widen as they move away from the boat. When Ben catches a fish, he gets so excited that he almost capsizes us. I grab Ben, Erik grabs Jimmy, and the fish gets away, flip-flopping right out of the boat.

"I didn't want to eat him, anyway," Ben says.

"He wasn't big enough," Jimmy says, and for the first time that I can remember, Ben agrees with his older brother.

For lunch we have hamburgers and hot dogs, then walk off our meal by taking a hike around the lake. Jimmy and Ben run ahead while Erik and I walk at a leisurely pace. Sometimes he puts his arm around my waist, but mostly we just hold hands. We feel so married, so much like a family that Erik turns to me smiling and asks, "Why can't it be like this always, Freddy? We're a family. Just look at us."

"You're the one who decided why we have to be careful, Erik, remember? I don't like hiding out like this any more than you do."

"It would be political suicide for me right now if I got a divorce."

"And that's important to you, isn't it?" I ask, moving ahead to where the boys are standing, looking down at the carcass of a dead squirrel.

"How come it's dead, Mommy?" Ben asks me.

Jimmy answers, "It probably fell out of a tree and broke its neck."

"It probably died from old age," I say, wondering if squirrels did actually die from old age. But I don't have the heart to tell them what probably did happen: that the squirrel was killed by another animal. Ben would get sick over it. I guess I'm too protective, but they're only babies. That's my job, to protect my babies.

Erik comes and stands by me, and when Jimmy and Ben are ahead of us again, he puts his arm around me.

"I love you, Freddy. You know I would never do anything to hurt you."

"It's not me I'm worried about. Jerry says that if there's a scandal, he'll fight me for custody of the boys."

"We won't let him do that."

"I won't let him, Erik. If it ever comes to that, they come first. I'm their mother. I have to protect them."

When we come around the bend I see the cabin. We've completed the trip around the lake, and for the rest of our stay we don't talk about divorce, marriage, or politics. We only concern ourselves with what we love, namely each other and the boys.

After Erik leaves on Sunday night, I have the vague feeling that my life is a dream and when Erik is gone, I wake up, wishing I were still dreaming.

Monday morning I go to visit Joey for the last time before he comes home. It starts out to be a joyous occasion. I even pack extra Hershey bars in the paper bag I call Joey's survival package. I've been doing this ever since I've been going to see him. I put in a can of peanuts, a couple of books about flowers, and of course, a couple of new CDs. I go into the cupboard and take out two packages of licorice, black and cherry, and put them in, too. Then I remember what Erik said about the abuse, and I take out the CDs and the licorice.

"I'll be damned if I'm going to entertain and feed

those fat-asses," I mumble to myself, going upstairs and putting two pictures into the package. One picture colored by Ben and one by Jimmy. The only one besides me who appreciates the boys' artwork is Joey.

On my way, I tell myself that this is the last time I make the trip. When I go through the main gate and the security guard takes the wand and pushes it up between my legs as far as he can go with my pants on, I tell myself this is the last time. There are a lot of "last times," and it sure feels good, considering that I've had to see Joey in this place year after year, with him in prison clothes and a hopeless look on his face.

Every time I see Joey he's thinner. Erik must be right about the abuse, because if he were eating any of this food I've been bringing him, he wouldn't be this skinny.

"I brought your favorite chocolate bars today. They even have almonds in them," I say, handing Joey the package.

"Thanks," Joey says, putting it down on the table without opening it.

"Don't you want to check it out? Maybe I brought you a surprise."

"I don't like surprises," Joey says

"You always used to, remember?"

"I can't remember anymore, Freddy. It's been too long."

"Well, it's not going to be long now. If everything goes right, the next time I come here will be to take you home."

For a moment, Joey's eyes light up and I recognize the old Joey somewhere inside. Almost as fast as the light is ignited, it goes out again.

"I'm never going home, Freddy. Norman says nobody here ever goes home."

"Tell Norman to go to hell because you *are* going home, Joey. I promise you."

"You promised a long time ago, but I didn't go home then."

"Now Erik is helping me, and Erik is the best lawyer in the world."

Joey smiles and says, "You like Erik a lot, don't you, Freddy?"

"A lot. And so will you when you come home. Someday I'm going to marry Erik, and you'll live with us," I tell him, taking the package off the table and pulling out the two pictures.

"The boys colored these for you, Joey."

He looks at them, studies the brown dinosaur with red blood dripping from its teeth. He turns the picture of the green frog with yellow polka dots around in his hands and says, "When I get home, I'll color flowers. Do you think you can buy me a book with flowers, Freddy?"

"I'll buy you lots of books with flowers to color, Joey.But you won't have to just color flowers. You'll be able to grow real ones again. I'll build you another greenhouse, and you can fill it with flowers."

Now the light I saw only a minute ago is burning again, lighting up Joey's pale face and I pray,

"Please God, don't let that light go out. This time let me keep my promise."

A week later, Joey is found innocent of all charges, and I think it's like Mrs. Davis always says whenever she hears the weatherman predict nice weather. "God must have heard your prayers."

In the third week of October, on a bright, beautiful fall day, I finally get to keep my promise to bring Joey home.

CHAPTER 37

The end of October turns out to be beautiful as far as the weather goes. The sun shines almost every day, and the trees in the backyard respond to the one night of frost with an array of colorful foliage.

We have a party for Joey's homecoming, inviting many of the same people who once thought Joey was guilty, now ready to celebrate his innocence. Mrs. Davis has it in her backyard and, as if specially ordered for the occasion, it's unseasonably warm. The yard is perfect, the weather is perfect, and so is the food that we have catered in.

It's during the party that I begin to think something is wrong with Joey. I go looking for him and find him back in his little house. He's doing nothing, just sitting on his porch alone, staring into space.

"What's wrong, Joey? Don't you like the party?"

"I don't like parties."

"You always did before."

"I'm not like before, Freddy."

"I know it's been hard, but you're home now. I love you, Joey, and I want you to be happy."

"You don't really love me, Freddy. Norman says that people just say they love me, but they don't."

"Norman is wrong, Joey. Now, I want you to come back to the party with me, and you'll see how much we all love you."

Joey gets up from the steps, bent over like an old man, yet he's only seven years older than me. We go back to Mrs. Davis's yard, and the minute Mom sees us, she asks, "Where have you two been? There's something Carl has to say."

"It's Joey, Mom. He doesn't like the party."

"Nonsense, it's a beautiful party. Everything is perfect and that's why we've decided   to announce our engagement, now. Haven't we, Carl?"

Carl nods in agreement, then says real loud, "You heard her, folks. Margaret and I are going to get married."

"We thought before Thanksgiving. That will still give us time to get the store ready for Christmas," Mom adds with a big smile, and it feels good to see her so happy.

"Mom, you shouldn't have to worry about the store. Just get married when you want to and go on a honeymoon."

"That's when we want to, Felicia. And at our age, we don't need a honeymoon."

"Everybody should have a honeymoon when they get married," I say and Mom blushes. Carl just stands around kind of awkward-like until the talk of marriage and honeymoon dies down, and Joey becomes the focus of attention again.

Erik and I are back to sleeping in my room, since Mom has taken a more liberal approach to sex. I'm almost positive that Mom and Carl are doing it, so it would be kind of like the pot calling the kettle black to say Erik and I are wrong when she's doing the same thing. The only difference is, Carl and Mom are getting married. Erik and I can't. Not yet. I just have to 'be patient.'

"I'm worried about Joey," I say to Erik later that night as we're going to bed. I switch off the light on my side of the bed and keep talking. "He doesn't seem well. The other day I asked if he wanted to help me rake the yard and get it ready for the party, and after a little while he got tired. He actually had to go and sit down to catch his breath."

"Take him to a doctor for a check-up if you're worried, but you have to remember that for all these years, he's been locked up without much exercise. It's going to take a while for him to get used to things, again."

"I know, but he keeps saying all kinds of crazy things that this Norman person told him. He actually has Joey convinced that we don't love him."

"It's part of the abuse, Freddy, making them feel isolated and dependent on them."

"Come on, Erik, for a few candy bars? Maybe some other stuff, too, but I don't think any of it's worth going through all the trouble of brainwashing someone."

"I'm not talking about that kind of abuse, honey."

And I think, but dare not ask, what kind Erik means. Not now, with Erik next to me in bed. I turn to him, and in his arms I forget everything but the moment.

I wake up in the morning to find Erik getting dressed. He's always the first one up and the last to go to bed. It's all part of the arrangement. We pretend that Erik doesn't really stay overnight, and I think the boys are fooled, but not Mom. She doesn't say anything, though, just plays the game like the rest of us. That Erik is only our lawyer and friend. Of course, Mrs. Davis isn't fooled and doesn't even pretend to be. Every time we go to her cabin, when she hands me the key, she says, "Have fun! Mr. Davis and I always did." Mrs. Davis never does explain what she means by fun, but I have a pretty good idea that it has nothing to do with fishing.

"I'll see you later," Erik says, bending down to give me a kiss.

"Later when?" I ask, putting my arms around his neck, pulling him down on top of me. He nuzzles my neck and just about the time I think I've got something started, he gets up.

Looking down at me, he says, "This afternoon when the boys come home from school, we'll take a ride."

"To where?"

"That's a surprise, but we'll be back late, so it'd be a good idea to tell your mother not to expect us," he says with a secretive smile. I know that smile. When he was working at the store with me, when we were meeting behind Joey's greenhouse, he would smile at me like that. Then I knew what the secret was, but now I have no idea.

"It's Saturday tomorrow. If we're going to the cabin, why don't we stay for the weekend?"

"Because we're not going to the cabin."

"Then where?"

"It's a surprise."

"I don't like surprises, so tell me," I insist.

"You'll like this one, but maybe you're right. We should stay overnight. I'll make the arrangements."

"Erik, don't do this to me," I beg, but with a quick kiss he's gone, leaving only the warm indentation where he slept next to me.

I get up and go to the window just in time to see him running down the street. Erik runs every morning, rain or shine, and everyone in town knows it. The only thing they don't know is that he starts out at my house and finishes at his father's. I crawl back into bed and snuggle under the covers, the feel of him still with me as I doze off.

The sound of a loud bang outside wakes me, and I jump up to see the garbage truck going down the street. I walk away from the window and go downstairs, still wearing my nightshirt like I always did when arguing with my mother was a morning ritual. Now I cover it with a robe, and my once-bare feet are covered in fluffy slippers that shuffle when I walk, just like slippers are supposed to. I don't argue anymore unless it's with Jerry, and what time of day or what I wear has nothing to do with it. When I get to the kitchen Mom and my sons are already sitting at the table, eating breakfast.

"You should have gotten me up," I say, moving to the coffeepot to pour myself a cup. That's different, too. Then I drank orange juice, now I drink coffee.

"Grandma wouldn't let us," Jimmy says.

Then Ben chimes in, "She said we should let you sleep. That we should stay out of your bedroom."

Mom blushes, saying, "I just meant that you probably got to bed late last night. What time did Erik leave?"

"Early," I say, meaning morning.

"I thought I heard him leaving late," Mom says, meaning last night.

"No, he left early."

I think all this double-talk has Mom confused, because she says, "It must have been someone else I heard drive away then. Erik usually doesn't drive here, does he?"

"No, Mom, he usually runs. He always runs an hour at night and an hour in the morning, and both times it's early."

"But he always stays for a while."

"Yeah, Mom, he always stays for a while." I hope I've cleared that up, because now I have to confuse her again.

"Erik and I are going to take the boys for a ride tonight, and we won't be home until late."

"How late?"

"Pretty late. In fact, it might not be until early in

431

the morning."

Now that I've added the morning part, Mom understands. Getting up to get another cup of coffee, she asks, "Are you taking Joey with you? I hate for him to be by himself while I'm at the store."

"What time will you be home?"

"Late," Mom says, blushing again. Mom doesn't have to spell it out for me. By late, she means early in the morning. After closing the store Mom is going to spend the night with Carl.

"We can take Joey with us," I say, figuring one good turn deserves another. She plays my game and I play hers.

"Hey, guys, you better hurry or you'll be late for school," I say, taking their lunch bags from the cupboard and peering in. Mom made them a good lunch, just like I would have if I hadn't slept so late. I hand the boys their lunches, kissing them good-bye. With a last-minute reminder about the trip later, I hurry them out the door. I watch them get on the big yellow school bus, then shuffle back to the kitchen.

"Does Joey seem all right to you, Mom?" I ask, sitting down at the table opposite her.

"No, Felicia, he doesn't. I think you should take him to a doctor."

"I'll call Dr. Marshall and make an appointment."

"I don't think that's the kind of doctor he needs, Felicia."

I study Mom for a while. Now I'm the one who's confused.

"I think you should take Joey to a psychiatrist, Felicia. It's not physical that's making him tired. It's mental. Joey's depressed, and God knows he has reason to be, but this moping around isn't good for him."

"Mom. What if they want to put him away again?"

"Maybe it will be for his own good."

"Don't give me that crap, Mom. I won't let them lock Joey up again. I promised to bring him home, and here is where he's going to stay."

I'm so angry that I slam my cup down onto the table and before I waste a good argument on Mom-- I sure can't tell her to go to hel--I go up to take my shower. When I come down again, Mom is gone to the store and I go to check on Joey.

Many of the leaves on the trees around Joey's house are already on the ground, and I kick through them. Sometimes I even kick in places where there are no leaves just to work off some of the anger inside me. Not at Mom, certainly not at Joey. So I save my anger for Jerry, for when I can do some real kicking, mainly his ass if he even thinks of taking my kids from me. I knock three short knocks, our usual signal, and then walk in.

Joey's sitting at the table crying, and I ask, "What's wrong, Joey? Did you have a bad dream?"

"I lost my book," he sobs, rubbing his eyes.

"What book? I'll help you look."

"The one with all those flowers. You bought it for me when I was still not home."

Joey never calls the place he was in *jail*, he just

calls it *not home*.

"Joey, you never brought it home with you, remember?"

"They took my book, Freddy. They said if I didn't do what they wanted me to, they'd take it."

"Who said it, Joey?"

"They."

"Is they Norman, Joey?"

"Yes."

"Did Norman ever hurt you, Joey? Because if he did, I'm going to tell the authorities that Norman shouldn't be working where he is."

"NO! No! No!" Joey shouts, repeating 'no' over and over, getting up and holding his head between his hands, starts to pace back and forth. I get scared, really scared, and try to calm him.

"Don't worry, I'll buy you another book, and no one will ever take it away from you."

"When?"

His voice sounds a million miles away as he stands, twisting his shirt up in his hands.

"I'll go this afternoon and get one exactly like the other one. Would you like that, Joey?"

"And nobody can take it away from me? Promise me, Freddy."

"Cross my heart and hope to die."

"Don't say that, Freddy."

"What? Why not?"

"Don't say you hope to die. I don't like when you talk like that."

"Joey, we used to say that all the time."

"Please don't say it anymore. Please," he begs, staring straight ahead at the wall in front of him.

"I won't," I say, going into the living room and picking up the clothes he left lying around. Joey never used to leave his clothes thrown around. There are a lot of things he does now that he never used to do, and I wish to God that I had the old Joey back again. I worry about him all day, so much that my head hurts.

I'm still worried when I pick Erik up at his father's house in my van. Jimmy and Ben are in the seats all the way in the back and Joey is directly behind me. The boys are busy with their hand-held computer games, while Joey flips through the new book of flowers that I bought him this afternoon. I move over to the passenger's side and let Erik drive.

"I've got a headache, and besides, I have no idea where we're going," I explain, buckling myself up.

"Something wrong, sweetheart?" he asks, concern in his voice, and I wonder if the concern has more to do with the headache I have now or the headache I might have at bedtime.

"Sometimes I think everything is wrong," I sigh.

"But not this weekend. This weekend is going to be wonderful."

"Good," I say, resting my head against the back seat headrest. "I could use a little wonderful right now."

"If not now, at least a little later," Erik says, a promise in his voice, and I wonder just what he has up his sleeve. When he says, "I sure hope that headache goes away," I know what it is. Except it's not exactly his sleeve, but more in the area below his belt.

We follow the expressway out of town, and then after we exit we drive along some country roads. I have no idea where we are, and right now, I don't care. I gaze out the window at the trees in the distance and tell the three in back to notice how the bright colors are starting to fade.

"I bet a week ago, they were perfect."

The only one who pays attention is Erik, and I wasn't even talking to him.

"They *were* perfect last week, but I couldn't bring you yet. Not until I closed the deal."

"What deal?"

"You'll see," Erik says, and I think I'd like to kill him for being so smug, but then I'd never get to see.

"You know how I hate when you do this, don't you? This whole surprise thing is making my headache worse. And you know what happens when a woman has a headache at bedtime," I tell him.

"Okay, I'll tell you. I bought us a house."

"A house?" I echo, and I think maybe I heard wrong. Erik starts to laugh.

"Not just any house, honey. It's big and comfortable and private."

"You mean private like, nobody's around?"

"No nosy neighbors. We can come and go as we please. We can sleep late, and it will be like we're married."

"But we're not married, Erik. Being like we're married isn't the same as actually being married.

Because if we were, you wouldn't have to hide me away like this."

"I'm not hiding you away. I just want some privacy for us, that's all."

"Do you want me to move here, Erik?"

"Only if you want to."

I turn my face and gaze out the window at all this privacy that stretches for miles around. I know I'm a small-town girl just like Mom, but this isn't even small town. It's *no* town.

Finally Erik pulls up to a big brick country house, surrounded by trees of all kinds. We get out and walk to the back where there's a pond, and farther in the distance there are more trees. In fact, there is a forest of trees. The boys run to the pond while Joey walks at the slow, tired pace he's become accustomed to.

I just stand up on a hill, watching the boys and Joey walk at the pond. I look with awe at the peaceful setting of nature all around me. I turn to Erik who's standing beside me, also looking, and I put my arms around his neck.

"I love it," I say. Any uneasy feelings I had earlier float away like dry leaves in the light autumn breeze. "When do we move in?"

We carry in our suitcases, but I don't make it past the entry. I stand looking to one side of the foyer into the living room, then to the other side at the dining room, both huge.

Erik explains, "I bought it furnished, but you can do anything you want with it. You can knock down walls and throw stuff away. It's all yours to do with what you will."

"It's ours, Erik," I say, "And it's perfect the way it is."

As the boys run to explore the upstairs, pulling Joey along with them, I wrap my arms around Erik again.

"I'll show you our bedroom," he says with a grin tugging at the corner of his mouth. I know that grin, but the boys and Joey don't understand what it means.

They could come bursting into that bedroom any minute, so I say, "Later. Right now I've got a headache."

We eat our supper in our new house, and by the time I wash and Erik dries the last dish, my headache is gone. "Let's go to bed early tonight," Erik suggests. I'm about to agree when suddenly from upstairs comes a loud yell. Erik and I run up, taking the stairs two steps at a time.

"Don't touch my book! It's mine and you can't have it!" Joey shouts, all the while hitting Ben with the book. Erik pulls Joey away from Ben while I take my son in my arms.

"What happened?" I ask, when Erik leaves with Joey, an arm gently around his shoulders, careful not to touch the book still in Joey's hand.

"I just wanted to look at it, Mom," Ben answers, his voice almost a sob as tears spring to his eyes. "I wasn't going to take it."

"I know you wouldn't, Ben. It's just that Joey has

a problem with people taking his things. It's not your fault, but I think from now on you should just leave Joey's things alone," I say, gently smoothing back his hair with my free hand and my other arm holding him to me.

"But why? You always say we should share. I share my toys with him."

"Of course you do, darling, but after Joey was put away, he forgot about sharing."

"What happened to him, Mom? Did they hurt Joey?"

He looks at me with such fear in his eyes that I think I might cry, and I know tears now would only make the fear more real.

"Yes, they hurt Joey, but we don't have to be afraid for Joey anymore. He's home now and no one can hurt him again. Now, why don't you go into Jimmy's room? I think for tonight, you two will share a room, okay?"

"Okay," Ben says, rubbing at his eye. After I kiss him on the cheek he runs down the hall and into the open door of the room Jimmy chose as his.

"Mom said I could sleep with you tonight," he announces to his brother.

"Okay," Jimmy agrees, adding, "I didn't want to sleep alone anyway."

"Me neither," Ben says, and I thank God that for once they want to share. I have a bad enough headache as it is.

When I walk into Joey's room he's sitting on the bed and crying, Erik sitting quiet beside him.

"You can have my book back, Freddy. Just don't

be mad at me."

"I'm not mad, Joey. I just don't understand you anymore."

"They did bad things to me, Freddy. Things I can't talk about." His eyes are fixed on the floor as he speaks, tears streaking a face that is too young to look so old.

"You don't have to talk about them now, Joey," Erik says as he hands him a tissue. "Maybe some other time you will want to."

"Maybe," Joey says, getting up and taking his pajamas out of the suitcase. "I just want to go to bed now."

"Goodnight, Joey," I say, giving him a kiss on the cheek.

"Goodnight, Joey," Erik echoes, patting him on the shoulder.

Together Erik and I go into the boys' room and listen to their prayers. We give them each a goodnight hug and kiss, and then Erik leads me to our room.

It's a big old-fashioned room, with a king-sized brass bed covered with a patchwork quilt, and for the first time we don't make love when we're in bed together. Instead, I spend my first night in our new house crying myself to sleep in Erik's arms.

CHAPTER 38

On Monday, the day after Erik and I come back from staying at our new house, I make an appointment to take Joey to Dr. Marshall. I've decided to go the physical route before the mental route.

"It just makes sense," I tell Erik on our way to the airport. I'm dropping him off to fly back to his office.

"Honey, do what you have to, but do something. We can't go on like this," Erik says. Then, with that little grin I've learned to read, he adds, "It's wrecking our sex life."

"Oh come on, Erik. Just one night, and we made up for it in the morning."

"I'm not complaining, but Joey needs help and if we don't choose a doctor, the court will."

"What are you talking about? I don't want anything to do with the court."

"I filed a complaint against the institution. Now we have no choice but to follow through. Honey, we have to stop the abuse. Joey's out of it now, but there are others like him still dealing with it. I can't just turn my back on them."

"I know you can't, and all those things I thought about you after you left for college and you didn't write, I take it all back."

"What things?"

"That you were egotistical and uncaring. I thought that playing football and making it big were all you were about. I'm sorry."

"In a way, I can't blame you. In college, I sure was into football, and if wanting to win makes me egotistical, then I guess I am. But I do care, Freddy. Don't ever think I don't."

I pull into the drive to the private airport where Erik keeps his plane. We give each other a last kiss, and I wait while the man I love walks in long strides to his plane.

"Be careful," I yell to his retreating figure, and then pull out of the driveway to go back home.

In the afternoon, I take Joey to the doctor, and while he goes into the room to change into a gown for his checkup, I go into the waiting room. I've known Dr. Marshall all my life. He delivered my brother, my sister, Joey and me, and later my two sons. There isn't much the doctor doesn't know about our family. Sitting here and looking at the newest issue of a magazine filled with flowers and gardens, I feel that coming here is the right thing to do. I flip through the magazine, not reading, just looking. Anxious to get back home in case Erik calls. I put down the magazine and take another, then another, then another, flipping through the pages. I'm reaching for one of the older issues of *House and*

Garden, when the nurse tells me that the doctor wants to talk to me, and it's a good thing, because at the rate I'm going, I'll have gone through every magazine in the place. Maybe some of them were issued before I was born.

While Joey is in the next room getting dressed, Dr. Marshall tells me about Joey.

"He's not really sick, as far as I can tell. I've ordered some blood tests just to be sure, but his heart sounds good."

"But he's always so tired, and he cries a lot. On top of that, he sometimes gets so mad. Dr. Marshall, have you ever known Joey to hurt anyone? But the other day he hit Ben really hard. If we hadn't stopped him, he could have hurt Ben."

"I think Joey is frustrated, confused, and angry all at the same time. What happened at the institution is beyond Joey's scope of understanding so he has no way of knowing how to act. I'm no psychiatrist, but I have seen abuse cases. Many that involve children, and believe me, Freddy, many of them act the same way Joey is."

"What kind of abuse are you talking about? Did they beat him?"

"Don't you know? Hasn't Joey said anything at all about it?" the doctor asks, studying me like he doesn't know me at all.

"No. He just cries and says bad things happened."

"It's not surprising. Children rarely talk about the sexual abuse they've been subjected to."

I grab hold of the arm of the chair and close my eyes. When I open them, Dr. Marshall is studying me again, but this time he knows me, and there's pity in his eyes.

"Freddy, I examined Joey and there's scarring in his anal passage. Joey has been used in the worst possible way."

The room swims in front of my eyes. The lights are too bright. The sun shining in the window blinds me and I close my eyes while the room circles around me, like I'm going to fall off this earth, or at least off my chair.

"Put your head between your knees," Dr. Marshall says, pushing my head down. "Take deep breaths."

I breathe with my head so far down, I swear I feel the floor on the top of my head, but it's really the doctor's hand making sure I don't straighten up too soon, or maybe he's just ready to catch it when it falls off. It feels like it's disconnected. Finally I get to straighten up. When I open my eyes he's handing me a glass of water.

"Here, take this," he says, and I reach for the glass in front of me. I sip slowly and feel the shudder run from my feet up to my head, escaping from my mouth in a soft moan.

"You've always taken care of Joey, haven't you? I remember the time your mother brought you in and I had to stitch up your arm because of the fight you got into when some kids made fun of him. I've always admired you for that, Freddy."

"That's because what they said about Joey isn't true. Maybe Joey isn't as smart as others expect him to be, but he makes up for it by being the sweetest,

444

kindest, gentlest person in the world. He's always been so caring, so loving. That's why I can't understand him now. He's just not Joey anymore," I say, handing the glass back to the doctor. "I guess I've always felt like I had to protect him, because he could never protect himself. He's this child that nobody wants."

"So you adopted him, right?"

"Yes, but I've failed him. What mother would let something like this happen? My God, if anybody did this to my boys, I think I would kill that person."

"You're a good mother, Freddy. You are good to your sons and to Joey. There are a lot of people who aren't as lucky as Joey."

"Joey's not lucky. Look at what happened to him."

"But you fought for him. Not just when you were growing up, but now. You got him away from the abuse. There are some who aren't as lucky."

"That's what Erik said, and that's why he's fighting for an investigation into what happened to Joey. He said he can't turn his back on the ones that are still in there."

"Erik is going to make a fine senator. I just hope this won't spoil his chances."

"What has the investigation of what happened to Joey got to do with Erik's chances for running?"

"He's stepping on a lot of important people's toes. There are people who can make or break a politician. I just hope the public is smart enough to know who's on their side and who isn't. If I lived in his state, I would vote for him." Then giving me one of his winning smiles, the kind that always makes me think of the big round smiley faces that I paste on all my letters, the doctor adds, "Hell, I'd even campaign for him."

I think Dr. Marshall really means what he says because he always says 'Hell' to emphasize his enthusiasm when he gets fired up.

The doctor walks me out of his office and through the examining room, where Joey is waiting fully dressed, sitting on the examining table.

"You can hardly see it now," I say to the doctor, pulling up the sleeve of my shirt.

"What?" he asks.

"This," I say, pointing to the faint scar where the doctor sewed me up. "That's because you do such good work." And maybe I can't paste a happy face on him, but I sure can make him smile. All the way into his office, he smiles.

At the supper table, Mom asks about what the doctor said, and I don't exactly lie. I just don't tell the truth.

"The usual. Joey should just take it easy for a while." Even if we were alone, I still wouldn't tell Mom the truth. I just can't bring myself to say it. I tell Erik, though, when he calls. I have to.

"The doctor says there's scarring. It's proof of the abuse."

"What scarring?"

"Erik, I'm not going to spell it out. Use your imagination."

There's silence for a while and when he speaks

next, I know his imagination is right on target.

"Are you saying he's been sodomized?"

"That's what the doctor said."

"Damn it, Freddy, I was hoping that what I heard wasn't true. Those bastards are going to pay. If it's the last thing I do, I'm going to make them pay. From now on, I don't care who I take down."

"Erik, what are you talking about?"

"I'm talking about going for the throat. I'll use everything I've got to make them pay for what they did to Joey. Those bastards. Those damn bastards. The abuse has been going on for years, and nobody stopped it. Well, now damn it, it's going to stop."

I know Erik means it. Like Dr. Marshall swears when he's enthused, Erik swears when he's mad, and he is really swearing.

"Dr. Marshall thinks that the investigation will hurt your chances for running for the senate."

"I don't want to be a senator that bad," Erik says, and I wish he were here right now, so instead of just telling him how much I love him, I could show him.

"I love you, Erik," I say.

"I love you, too," Erik says, and I change the subject before I start to cry.

"Are you going to make it for Mom's wedding?" I ask.

"Honey, I can't. I'm too busy."

"Jerry's coming, and I was hoping you'd be here. I need you here, Erik."

"It would be kind of awkward, don't you think?"

"Why, because I was once married to him? I'm not jealous of your wife. I don't like her, but I'm not jealous."

"That's because I don't like her either."

"I'm not in love with Jerry. You know that."

"But he's still in love with you."

"Jerry's got other women," I say in defense, but it sounds kind of lame.

"Did you make it okay? Your flight I mean?" I ask, but that sounds lame, too. Sometimes it's so hard to change the subject when desperation calls for it.

"I'm here, aren't I?" Erik laughs and I just wish to God that for once I could pull off clever.

"That was stupid. Wasn't it?"

"That was nice, to care enough to ask."

"I guess it means I like you."

"That's not what you said a little while ago. You said you love me."

"Of course I love you, but I also like you."

"I like you, too, Freddy, and I can't wait to see you again to show you how much."

"When?"

"The day after the wedding, or right after your ex-husband leaves."

"Erik, I want you here."

"Honey, I don't think your mother does, and it's her wedding."

"That's not true!"

"She likes Jerry more than me. You can't deny that."

I want to deny it, to protest, but before I can, Erik says, "I love you," and hangs up.

Just before I go to bed I do a pregnancy test, and my suspicion is confirmed. I am pregnant. That night in late August when I went to Erik, I forgot my diaphragm, and he promised to be careful and he wouldn't. Well, he wasn't, and he did. I decide to tell him when he gets here after the wedding. If a woman is going to confront a man about a broken promise, the least she can do is do it to his face.

Now I have something more to worry about. I tell myself over and over again, "This can't be happening. This baby shouldn't be. The timing is all wrong." I worry myself sick until something else happens and I forget about one worry and take on another.

The news hits the media and sets our little town buzzing. Karen's killer has been caught, and not just Karen's, but all those others who came after. It turns out that Roger got involved with an Internet group fascinated with vampires when he was still in high school. In a chat room, Roger was able to live out his fantasies of horror, until even making up stories wasn't enough. He had to make them real.

After the boys are in bed, Mom and I turn on the television. There is a reporter interviewing Erik on a talk show, and from the beginning, I know Erik is going for the throat.

"It seems to me that if the police had done their work in the beginning, that group would have been stopped before the others were killed," the host says.

"It was an election year and the prosecutor

needed a conviction. It was convenient for them to blame someone who couldn't defend himself."

"But isn't that what a defense attorney is for?"

"True, but all the evidence wasn't presented to the defense."

"Like what kind of evidence?"

"We found out after we started to suspect Roger that he had a prior offense. He was picked up for trying to entice a child into his car when the parents caught him and told the police.

There were also reports of him hanging around the school where Karen went, and he was there the day Karen disappeared. The police never followed up on any of this. Like I said, it was an election year, and all that mattered was looking good."

After that Erik starts naming names, not only about the misconduct of the police department and prosecution, but also about the cover-up concerning Joey's abuse.

When they're finished the host says, "There are some who say you're doing this to make yourself look good for the pending election."

"There are some who say that this can also hurt my chances. I guess I'll have to leave it up to the public to judge."

"There are rumors that you and your wife are separated. Are you?"

Erik hesitates for a minute and I think my heart will stop. "I don't believe in rumors. I took an apartment in town so I could be close to my office, but I still live at home in the suburbs."

After that the host turns his attention over to the jury members who convicted Joey, and I walk over to turn off the television, and without saying a word, I go up to my bedroom.

I go to my dresser and take out the watch, the locket, and the ring that I still have after all these years. I look at a young Erik's picture in the locket; then closing it, I put everything back. I go through all the drawers where Erik has his clothes, fingering his shirts, his underwear. I even go into the closet and hold his ties up to the light, like I'm choosing one for him to wear. In the bathroom is his toothbrush in a glass next to mine, and I say to the person staring back at me,

"Damn you, Erik. Damn you to hell. You rent an apartment, but you live at home, but you live here too. Or do you?"

I crawl into bed and cover my head with the blanket. It's dark under here, like I'm six feet underground. I'm dead and people are walking on my grave. Back and forth they march, like a parade, and Erik is leading the parade.

When the phone rings and I don't answer, Mom knocks on my door. "Felicia. It's Erik. He wants to talk to you."

"Tell Erik that I'm already in bed," and then adding bitterly, "Better yet, tell him that I don't live here anymore. That I moved the hell away from here."

There's silence for a minute, then I hear my mother's soft footsteps move down the hall. I don't know what she's going to tell him, but I don't think she's going to repeat what I said. Mom doesn't swear.

Erik calls again in the morning, in the afternoon, and again at night, but I still won't talk to him. Then he stops calling.

CHAPTER 39

Mom and Carl are getting married in one week, and I attack the work of getting the house ready with a fierce anger that surprises even me. I scrub, I dust, and I polish until not a single dust-bunny is under the beds or so much as one scratch is left on the furniture. When the boys walk into the house, I yell at them to take their shoes off. I yell a lot, and even Joey hides in his little house, away from my angry struggle for perfection. I drown myself in work to keep myself from thinking until Angela comes the day before the wedding--then I drown myself in fighting.

It starts the minute she walks in the door. "We should move this chair over here, and maybe the piano over there, or maybe we should rent an organ." I tell her that no one knows how to play the organ.

"Then we can hire someone."

"What for, when you can play the piano? Or have you forgotten how?" I ask, pushing the chair back to its original place and making a long scratch on the newly polished floor.

"I still know how to play. I just thought organ

453

music would be more fitting. More theatrical."

"This isn't a play, Angela. It's a wedding. I had piano music for my wedding and it worked out fine."

"Your wedding wasn't really a wedding, Freddy."

"Then what in the hell was it? A funeral?"

"You have to admit, you had to get married. Everybody knew you had to."

"How? I didn't put it on the invitation."

"You were showing. You had a big belly on you."

"No way," I say. "I wasn't that far along."

"Well, some people show early, and you're one of them."

I suck in my breath and pull my long baggy shirt over my stomach and wonder if Angela can really tell.

After supper, while Angela practices "Oh Promise Me" on the piano, I do the dishes, then go into the living room to ask her to help me get the punch bowl and cups set up on the buffet.

"Don't tell me you're serving punch!" Angela says, stopping in the middle of a note.

"That and coffee," I say.

"You mean you're not having champagne?" She looks at me as though I must be out of my mind.

"Does it look like we're having champagne? What are we supposed to serve it in, paper cups? Mom doesn't have champagne glasses, but she does have a punch bowl and cups."

Angela comes and helps me take the punch bowl down from the cupboard and set it on the buffet. As I'm arranging all the little cups around the bowl, I say, "It looks nice."

"It looks tacky," Angela complains.

"Does not," I say.

"Does too," Angela argues back.

Mom just says, "Carl was right; we should have eloped."

I wake up in the morning to the sound of footsteps going up and down the stairs and doors slamming. I look at the clock and see that it's only six, and I wonder why all the commotion this early on a Saturday.

"Put that cake down before you drop it. Right here, next to the punch bowl," I hear Mrs. Davis yell real loud. Loud for her anyway, and then I remember that today is Mom's and Carl's wedding. I get up to take my shower, but before stepping behind the glass doors, I stand naked in front of the full-length mirror. I turn and look at my stomach from every angle, then suck in my breath and turn again. Finally I run my hands across it, thinking maybe I can feel what I still can't see.

"What the hell was Angela talking about?" I ask myself in the mirror. "I don't look pregnant."

But just to make sure, I go into the closet to take out the dress I'm going to wear. It's long and straight with no waist, the kind everybody is wearing now, even non-pregnant women. I hang it back up in the closet and brush against one of Erik's suits. The familiar scent reminds me of the feel of Erik touching me: with this suit on, with no suit on, both of us with no clothes on. God, what I wouldn't give to have him here right now, touching me. Even my pride isn't worth this much agony, and I think if Erik walked in right now, I'd accept any arrangement just to have him back. I'd even settle for sharing him with his wife.

I go back into the bathroom and into the shower, scrubbing while the water mixes with my tears. When I finally step out, my body is red from scrubbing, and my eyes are red from crying. I cover most of the red with jeans and a shirt, and if Angela asks about the red eyes, I'll just tell her I'm practicing my wedding cry. Maybe it doesn't sound logical, but it sure sounds theatrical.

By the time Harry arrives around noon Angela and I have fought our way through the finishing touches of the wedding, and I go upstairs to change. Jerry still isn't here, and I think that maybe he changed his mind. I hope he changed his mind. Angela, Harry, and Jerry are more than I can take all at one time.

After a quick check in the mirror, this time with my clothes on, I still think that Angela is wrong about me showing early. Then I go to Mom's room and knock. When I walk in, Mom is standing at her dresser with her back to me. She isn't even starting to get ready and the wedding is at two.

"What's wrong, Mom?" I ask. Then she turns to me and I know what's wrong. She's holding hers and Daddy's wedding picture, tears running down her cheeks.

"I still love him, Felicia. After all these years of being without him, I still remember how it was on our wedding day. I thought it would be forever, and now--" Mom starts crying even harder, and then I start to cry.

"I know, Mom," I say, putting my arms around her to comfort her. "I know."

I think about how much I sound like her. I've always thought of myself as more my father's child, but now I know I am just as much hers. We both share the same kind of heartbreak; the only difference is that Mom married her true love and shared a home with him, and I never will. Erik's home is in New York. Isn't that what he said?

"All I ever wanted was to have what you and Daddy had, but I never found it with Jerry, and Erik doesn't want it. So count your blessings, Mom. At least you had that. Maybe not forever, but I'd settle for even that much."

Now Mom is comforting me, and by the time Angela walks in we are both crying.

"What is this?" she asks, going to the closet and getting Mom's dress out. "In a little while the curtain's going up and the star isn't ready yet."

I move away from the bustle of Angela getting Mom ready for the "opening curtain."

"Oh, break a leg, Angela," I say, thinking how I wish she really would just break her leg.

When I go downstairs Jerry is waiting, and I'm not real happy to see him. I suck in my breath, take a couple of steps toward him, then trip on the chair that Angela moved when I went upstairs, almost falling into his arms.

"You look beautiful," Jerry says, helping me to gain my balance.

I swear under my breath at Angela, smile at Jerry and say, "Thank you," real polite, like I didn't just almost fall on my face. "You look nice, too."

Jimmy comes running up to take his father by the hand to show him something in the backyard, and I thank God for small interruptions, namely my son.

I go to the punch bowl to take a sip. Next I move to the kitchen to taste the hors d'oeuvres. I open the oven to smell the ham, then tell the caterer that the cake is beautiful.

By the time I get through with all this checking Jerry is back from his excursion with Jimmy, and we're back to polite conversation again, until he says, "It kind of reminds you of our wedding, doesn't it? Punch bowl, flowers, even the chairs are arranged the same way."

"Not all of them," I say, sidestepping the only chair out of place as I walk away.

I go back upstairs where Mom is waiting all dressed and ready to meet her leading man. I take my bouquet from Angela, and then wait while she goes downstairs to play the piano. At the first strains of the wedding march, I suck in my breath and start walking. I would have made it, too, all in one breath, if I hadn't looked at Jerry. If he hadn't caught my eye, thinking the same thing I am. I let out my breath, take in another, and finish the journey to the front of the living room to stand almost in the same place I stood when I married Jerry. I step to the side and make room for my mother.

After the ceremony, I stand next to Joey, who has exchanged his usual overalls for a pair of tan pants and shirt. I can tell Harry helped him get dressed, because Joey has a belt on instead of the suspenders I bought. Joey wouldn't even know how to buckle a belt, much less get it through the loops.

"You look nice, Joey," I tell him, buttoning one of the buttons on his shirt that's undone. Even Harry misses a button once in a while.

"You look nice, too, Freddy. You look real pretty."

"That's what I just said. You look real pretty, Freddy," Jerry says, moving over to the side of us.

"You said I looked beautiful. That's not the same as pretty," I say, thinking, Where are those kids when I need them? But they're busy eating cake. It all seems so strange: me, Jerry, a wedding cake, like history repeating itself. I'm even pregnant. For a while, I soften towards Jerry, remembering how it used to be between us.

But then he says, "So, where's Erik? Too busy to come, or is this his weekend to relax at home in the suburbs?"

I know by the way Jerry said it that he heard the same interview I did, and I say, "Go to hell, Jerry." Then I walk away to join my two sons who are stuffing themselves with cake.

"Hey, guys," I say, bending down to wipe Ben's

459

face with a napkin. "Save some for the rest of us. Besides, I want you to eat a sandwich and some potato salad. There's a vegetable tray. I know you like those little tomatoes, so how about having some?"

"But they're on the same plate as the cauliflower," Jimmy argues, like the word *cauliflower* is a bad word.

"What has that got to do with it?"

"The tomatoes might taste like cauliflower," Ben explains, like it's the most obvious thing in the world.

"Fine, then take some strawberries off the fruit plate. They're just touching the pineapple, and I know you like pineapple."

"Okay," Ben agrees, moving away from the cake to the table with strawberries. Jimmy hesitates until I give him that Do-What-I-Say look.

"Okay," Jimmy says, giving me an If-You-Insist look, and follows Ben.

"I take it they don't like cauliflower," Jerry says, coming up from behind me.

"There's a lot of things they like and don't like, Jerry, but you don't know that, do you?" I say real sarcastic-like, and I see in Jerry's eyes that But-I-Wish-I-Did sad look.

"Don't do this, Freddy. Please don't," he pleads.

"I'm sorry," I say, ready to move away again, but Jerry takes me by the arm to lead me out of the room.

"We have to talk, Freddy."

"About what?"

"The boys."

"Why?"

"Not here. Please?"

"Where?"

"Outside. In private."

"It's cold outside."

"Not that cold," Jerry says, and his eyes still have that sad look. He's the father of my two sons, the man I once kissed under an evergreen of snow. The man I once was snowed in with for days and loved every minute of it. It wasn't the not finding what Mom had with Dad that made our marriage fail, because at first I thought I had found it. It wasn't even that Erik had come between us. I think it was the same thing that has come between Erik and me now. Career and ambition came before love.

Then, remembering how Daddy told me to always put my husband first, I know I'm just as guilty as Jerry. We both forgot to put each other first.

"I'll get my coat. We can go to Joey's house."

We walk down the path between the two houses with only the sound of our footsteps in the dead leaves to remind us of each other's presence. We go into the house and sit down at the table across from each other.

"Would you like a soda?" I ask, getting up to go to the refrigerator before the spell of how it used to be takes over. When Jerry was still only a small-town reporter. That used to be when our love came first.

"No," Jerry says.

"I think I'll make some tea for myself," I say, still reluctant to sit down opposite Jerry again.

"Freddy, please sit down. We really have to talk."
I sit and Jerry talks.

"I want to take the boys back to New York with me."

"For how long?"

"To live with me. I want custody."

"No way!" I say, starting to get up like I'm going to walk out of this house, this conversation.

"I mean it. I want my sons."

I sit back down and look Jerry right in the eye. "You can't have them. I won't let you take my sons."

"They're mine, too."

"But you were never around. I'm the one who raised them."

"I know you did, but now I want to raise them, too. I want to take them back with me when I leave."

"You can't. They're in school. You can't take them out of school," I say, trying my best to sound logical.

"I'll hire a tutor until the next semester, then I'll enroll them in school."

I jump up, ready to pounce on Jerry and scratch his eyes out, but instead I say, "I'll take you to court. You'll never get them with your lifestyle. For God's sake, Jerry, you're never in this country long enough to be a father!"

"I'm changing my lifestyle. I'm getting married again."

I stare at him in disbelief, thinking that what he's just said blows to hell the theory of him still loving me, and I wonder if he ever did. My voice is full of accusation when I say, "For *her* you change, but not for me."

"When did you ever say you would come and live with me?"

"You never asked."

"Oh yes I did, over and over again. In every letter I wrote, every time I said I missed you. Couldn't you tell every time I touched you how much I wanted you to live with me?"

"You were the one who went back to your war. I was going to live with you."

"But only on your terms, Freddy. And you know something? I was ready to accept them, but then you locked me out of your bedroom."

"Because I thought you were cheating on me."

"I never cheated on you. I loved you too much to do that." When Jerry says *loved*, I know that to beg wouldn't make any difference.

"You can't have them all the time, Jerry. Sometimes for holidays and maybe summer, but not all the time. We'll have to work something out."

"We'll talk about working it out when you get this mess with Erik straightened out."

"What has Erik got to do with our sons?"

"A lot, Freddy. One of these days it's all going to blow up in your face, and when it does, I want my sons out of it."

"Erik and I are going to get married," I say, trying to sound positive.

"That remains to be seen," Jerry says, getting up to go. He moves toward the door, then turns back and adds, "I'm leaving tomorrow around noon. Have the boys ready."

"Over my dead body," I say, getting up. Now I think I will scratch his eyes out.

"If you don't, I'll drag you to court. I'll expose your sordid little arrangement with Erik if I have to. I don't want to hurt you, Freddy, but if that's what I have to do to protect my sons, I will."

Jerry walks out and I sit back down again. I lay my head on the table across my arms and start to cry. I cry so hard that I make the tablecloth all wet, but I don't stop. If I lose my sons, I will spend the rest of my life crying for them. If I lose Erik over this, I don't think I'll want to live.

Joey comes in looking for me, and when he sees me crying he puts his arms around me.

"Don't cry, Freddy. Please don't cry," he begs, patting me on the head like a parent comforting a small child. It's so strange, because usually it's the other way around.

"Jerry is going to take the boys away from me."

"We won't let him," Joey says simply.

"I have to, Joey. If I don't, he's going to tell about Erik and me, and I can't let him do that. Not now." Not while I'm carrying his child.

The next day, I keep the boys home from school, explaining as I pack that they're going with Daddy for a visit. Jimmy is thrilled, but Ben is worried.

"But you'll miss us, Mommy. Maybe you can come with us."

"No, I can't," I say, kind of loud--like loud makes it definite. Then, in a softer voice, I add, "I have to stay here, but I'll call you on the telephone every day, okay? Besides, it's only for a little while, and before you know it, you'll be home again."

I finish with the clothes and then start to pack their collection of frogs and dinosaurs.

"If we're only going for a little while, how come we're taking so much stuff?" Jimmy wants to know.

"Because I'm not sure what you're going to need. I just want to make sure you have everything you might need."

"It might be snowing in New York," Ben adds, and I'm not sure what snow has to do with frogs and dinosaurs, but as long as they're not asking, I'm not saying.

At noon, when Jerry pulls up in front of the house, I help him put the boys' things in the trunk of his car, making sure Ben carries Froggy with him. I hand Jerry a little book of instructions, then tell him everything I wrote.

"If Ben gets upset he has a hard time breathing. Give him his medicine. He doesn't have to have it all the time, only when he's upset."

Jerry takes the book and puts it on the dashboard of the car. When he comes back, I continue, "If he still has a hard time, sometimes steam helps. I usually take him into the bathroom and turn on all the hot water, and then have him sleep with a vaporizer in his room. He's usually okay but sometimes you have to take him to the emergency room for a shot. I just try not to get him upset, that's all."

"I know, you told me about that once over the phone."

"Just try not to get him too upset, Jerry. If the boys fight, don't let it get out of hand. That upsets Ben a lot. If Jimmy has a bad dream, lie down with him for a while until he goes back to sleep. He'll say he's not scared, but he is. And make sure they eat some vegetables. They hate them, but tell them that they have to eat vegetables if they want dessert."

I know I'm babbling, but I can't stop. They're my babies; I've been with them every day of their lives. How do I cram all their lives into a book?

"They're going to be okay, Freddy. Trust me," Jerry says, taking my hand, and I pull away.

"I'll never trust you again, Jerry. I hate you for what you're doing."

Jerry turns away, then hollers to the boys still in the house, "Let's go, guys," and the boys come running to the car, carrying their last-minute packages of toys and things I forgot to pack. I bend down to give my sons one last hug and kiss, trying not to cry in front of them.

I wave good-bye, saying, "Be good for your father." I watch Jerry drive away. Now I can cry.

A week later, when Mom and Carl come back from their honeymoon, the one we kids insisted they take, Mom asks, "Why did you let him take them? Is Erik worth that much to you?"

"Mom, I'm pregnant. What chance would I have if I went to court? Jerry's getting married and can offer them a home. What can I offer them?"

"The same thing you've been giving them since they were born: your love, Felicia. That wonderful capacity that you have to love."

"But it's not enough, Mom. It wasn't enough to keep Daddy from dying, to keep Jerry from taking my boys, and even to keep Joey from that institution. And what about Erik? My love isn't enough for him to want to marry me. It's just never enough."

"Loving hurts, Felicia. But not to love hurts even more. I will never stop loving your father, because to stop would be unbearable. That's important, never to stop loving. You are going to get your boys back. I know it. Jerry loves you too much to hurt you like that."

I start to laugh, and it's not a nice laugh. "Jerry is getting married again. Didn't you hear me?"

"He'll never go through with it. He still loves you. I saw how he looked at you when you walked down the steps into the living room."

"You were supposed to be looking at Carl, not at Jerry."

"Well, Jerry was looking at you the same way Carl was looking at me."

"Yeah, but Carl isn't taking away your kids. You'd hate Carl if he did that to you, Mom. I know you would."

"I'd never let him take them away. I'd scratch his eyes out first."

I think Mom is right. The next time I see Jerry, I'll scratch his eyes out. Better yet, I'll find myself a good lawyer. The next time I see Jerry, it will be in court.

Before I walk away, my mother says, "You're like him, Felicia; you love so very much."

"Like who, Mom?"

"Your father. He always had so much love to give, and nothing, not even death, can take away those years he was here."

"But Daddy had more common sense, Mom. He married you and that was the most sensible thing he ever did."

"But your grandparents didn't think so. His father told him he was crazy to marry me. Felicia, I had been abandoned by my own family. I felt unworthy of love, and yet he loved me. I think that is the most loving thing a person can do."

It's quiet, like the words haven't been invented yet to fill in the gap. Then I find the words—they *have* been invented—I just don't say them often enough to her.

"I love you, Mom."

And she says to me, "I love you, too, Felicia, and if anybody hurts you, I'll scratch their eyes out."

I think I'll take my mother with me when I go to court to get my kids back. If that judge ever had a mother like mine, he or she would definitely see it my way.

CHAPTER 40

The weather is cold now. A few flurries of snow flutter past the big store window, and I remember last year when it snowed for the first time. The boys were so excited that they couldn't wait for me to take them outside to build the first snowman of the season. It was a crazy, lopsided snowman that tilted even more the next day when it started to melt. First snowmen never last, and I wonder if Jerry will build one with the boys. I don't think there are many places to build a snowman when you live in an apartment.

"I think this looks better without the garland, Mom," I say, draping the garland on the Christmas tree, only one of the many Mom and I are decorating for our annual Christmas Open House right after Thanksgiving.

"I like it," Mom says, stepping back to admire it.

"But garland isn't in this year. It's old-fashioned," I say, starting to take it off. Mom stops me.

"Then so is Christmas. It's been around longer than any of us, but we still celebrate it, right?"

"Right," I say, putting back on what I had just taken off. I put the star on top and remember how the boys fought last year over who got to put the star on our tree at home. The fight didn't last long, though. Jimmy got to do the honors because Ben was afraid to climb the ladder, and he's getting too heavy for me to lift. I hope this year Jerry will have a tree, and maybe he can still lift Ben to reach the top. But by Christmas I'll have the boys back.

It's two days before Thanksgiving, and two weeks since Jerry took the boys. As we work, Mom talks grandmother-talk while I just listen, until she asks if I've filed for custody yet. I tell her that I have to give Erik some time to contact me. After all, it's his career that I'm putting in jeopardy if I go to court.

Mom just says, "And what about your sons? If you wait too long, you'll never get them back. How many times have you talked to them since they've been gone?"

"I call every day, at least a couple of times, but Jerry's fiancée says they're gone or else they're in bed. I try, Mom, but what should I do? Get on a plane and demand to see them?"

"If you have to, Felicia, then do it."

"I don't want to create a scene in front of the boys It's been hard enough on them."

"If that woman ends up their mother, it will even be harder on them."

The thought of another woman being my sons' mother scares me, and I forget the decorating and go into the office to look in the yellow pages for a lawyer.

Mom follows me into the office and, standing

over me, asks, "Why are you looking in the yellow pages?"

"For a lawyer. Isn't that what you said I should do?"

"You already know a good lawyer, Felicia."

I look up from the telephone book and stare at my mother, shocked that she would even suggest such a thing.

"I can't call Erik, Mom."

"Why not?"

I do not answer but I get up, leaving the book open, and go back to hanging ornaments and draping garland on fake trees that look almost real.

We finish early with the decorating. In the afternoon I go home to my empty house. I wander lost in thought through the once-busy rooms in the once-noisy house, missing the 'good old-fashioned' days of only two weeks ago. I go into the boys' room and pick up one of Jimmy's toy cars. It's the one with a wheel missing, and I search until I find the wheel, and then put it back on. I flip through Ben's books, all of them about frogs, and remember how Ben always liked this page when I got to it in the story. I say, "Ribbit, ribbit," to myself, and I hope to God that Jerry has time to read them a bedtime story. I wonder if he's even home at bedtime. I put the book back exactly in the same place, and I even take the wheel off the car again and put it back on the floor. I can't bear to change anything, not even the sheets. I lie down on one of the beds and then, laying my head on the pillow that Ben slept on I cry so hard my head starts to hurt.

"How could you do this to me, Jerry?" I moan into the pillow over and over until eventually I fall asleep.

It's already dark when I wake up. I go to Joey's house where I open a can of chicken soup. Joey and I sit across from each other making slurping sounds and talking in between slurps.

"I miss the boys so much," I tell Joey.

"Me, too. Let's go get them."

"We can't, Joey. I have to wait for a judge to say that I can."

"Don't ask the judge, Freddy. Please don't ask the judge. He'll put them in a terrible place. He'll lock them up."

"No, Joey. The judge won't lock them up. They haven't done anything wrong."

"But I didn't do anything wrong, did I, Freddy?"

"No, you didn't. But locking you up was different. It was a mistake."

"Don't let the judge make another mistake. Just go take them away from Jerry. Tell him he can't have them. They belong to you."

"I just wish it were that easy, Joey," and I start to cry again, the tears running down my chin and into my soup.

"Don't cry, Freddy. Please don't cry," Joey says, getting up from the table and starting to pace. I wipe my eyes and tell Joey to sit back down and finish his supper.

After we do the dishes we play Old Maid until it's time for me to go back to my empty house, and I wish that Mom still lived with me.

When I walk into the house, the phone is ringing, and I trip on the leg of the chair that's been out of place since Angela's visit. Then, stepping fast to gain my balance, I slip on a throw rug that's covering my gleaming floors, continuing my little dance right up to the telephone table that's draped with white satin streamers left over from the wedding. The boys' bedroom isn't the only thing I haven't touched since they left. Breathless, I grab the phone, thinking it's my sons, but it's only Angela.

"Why are you calling me?" I ask, trying not to sound as disappointed as I feel.

"I'm your sister. Why shouldn't I call you?"

"Because you never do. Besides, didn't you get enough arguing with me at the wedding?"

"You never called and told me, so I have to call you and ask. What are the boys doing in New York? I go into this restaurant and there's this woman with your boys. Just what in the hell is going on?"

"Nothing," I say flatly, doing my best to sound convincing. "They're visiting their father."

"Then how come when I went over to the table to give them a hug, this bimbo gets up and takes them away? She said our family wasn't supposed to have any contact with them. Since when are the Harrisons a bad influence?"

"Is that what she said?"

"Well, she said *I* was. How come I am now when

473

I never was before?"

"Since Jerry took them away from me."

There's a pause on the other end while I can almost hear her digesting the information and trying to come up with something to say.

"You're kidding. And you let him!"

"For now, but I'm going to get a lawyer and get them back."

"How about Erik? You have him. What do you need another lawyer for?"

"I don't have Erik. Not anymore."

"Then get him back, Freddy. If you have to get on your knees and beg him to come back, then do it."

"I can't."

"Why not? You're going to have his kid, aren't you? Or is that why he left?"

"He doesn't even know yet. But how did you know? Did Mom tell you?"

"No, Mom didn't tell me. I could see you were pregnant at the wedding."

"You could not."

"Could too."

"Could not."

"Could too."

This will turn into a Jimmy-and-Ben fight unless I break it up, and I go back to why Angela called in the first place.

"The woman, Angela, is she pretty?"

"You mean the woman with the boys?"

"What other woman would I be asking about?"

"She's ugly, Freddy. She's an ugly old bag. And

frankly, I can't imagine what Jerry sees in her unless she's good in bed. A real bitch in heat."

"That's not nice," I say. Sometimes Angela's language shocks me.

"She wasn't very nice to me--acting like I was contagious or something."

I know Angela is lying about the looks part. I can tell, just like she can tell that I'm pregnant, but I still say, "Thanks, Angela, for being such a good sister."

"Hey, I'm your only sister."

"I know," I say like Mom would. "I know." Then I follow with my own words, even though they sound strange to me. "I love you, Angela, my one-and-only sister."

"I love you, too, Freddy. But get those kids away from that crazy lady before she turns them against us, okay?"

"Okay," I say, and the minute I hang up, I call Erik.

He doesn't answer his phone, so I call his service.

"Mr. Larson," I say, real formal-like, leaving a message. "This is Felicia Harrison. Remember me, a client of yours? I need some advice and would appreciate it if you called me on my cell phone or met me at my home in the country. I'm going there over Thanksgiving. Thanks so much."

After hanging up, I go upstairs to pack my clothes, then I go back into the boys' room where I sleep in Jimmy's bed until morning.

I call Mom at Carl's house before she goes to the store. "Will you take Joey for a couple of days?" I ask her, and I can tell she isn't out of bed yet.

"Why?" she asks with a yawn.

"Because I don't want him here by himself. Especially over Thanksgiving."

"I thought you were bringing him here for Thanksgiving. Aren't you coming for dinner?"

"I'm leaving in a little while for the house Erik bought me. I'll be spending Thanksgiving there."

"I don't like it, Felicia. You should be with family."

"I asked Erik to meet me. I want him to help me get the boys back."

"Is he going to be there?"

"I don't know, Mom, I just left him a message. I guess at this point it's up to him."

"What if he doesn't come, then what?"

"Then I'm going to have to fight for my sons alone."

"Not alone, Felicia. You still have your family."

"I know, Mom," I say, "I know."

I'm sure starting to take after my mother, but I don't mind. I only hope that I end up to be half the mother she is.

I drop Joey off at the store on my way out of town, and I can see the disappointment in his eyes when I tell him I won't be at Mom's for Thanksgiving.

"But this is my first Thanksgiving home, Freddy," he says, more than once on our way.

"But I have to do this, Joey. You want me to get Jimmy and Ben back, don't you?" I say that more than once, too.

"Yes," is the answer Joey always gives, right up to the minute he gets out of the car, and I give him a hug. Mom comes out and tells me to drive carefully, reminding me to make sure I have my phone turned on before leading Joey into the store where he'll help her with the Christmas decorating. I don't think he'll be much help, but Mom will find something for him to do. She always did for us kids, even when we didn't want her to.

With the map spread out next to me on the passenger's seat, I head for the expressway. When one CD finishes, I pop in another. When I get sleepy, I stop for coffee, returning the extra-large-sized cup to the cup holder after each sip. I pass big semi-trucks that make me feel small and claustrophobic when I get between two of them, then relieved when one pulls ahead, and even more relieved when they both pull ahead or exit.

The trees are all bare and there's stubble left in the cornfields after the harvest. I take the exit I have marked on the map, and now the fields are bigger and the houses are fewer and farther apart. The loneliness of a single vehicle moving down the country road creeps in, and I feel a chill as I worry: what if something happens so far out of town? I think that maybe I'm lost, and wonder how in the hell did Erik ever find this place anyway? Sometimes I have to make a sharp swerve to avoid potholes, and once, when a dog runs in front of the van I have to slam on my brakes to avoid hitting it. I think that maybe this isn't the right road after all and almost end up in the ditch trying to read the map while driving, but I catch myself in time.

I don't catch the phone though, and after making a grab for it, I pick it up from under my feet, then throw it back onto the seat beside me, all in one motion, all faster than I can say, "Damn it."

By the time I pull into the driveway, I've gone through a stack of CD's more than once, drunk an extra-large cup of coffee, folded the map, put my phone in my purse where it belongs, and all without pulling over once.

The house is cold and dark when I open the door with the key Erik gave me, and the first thing I do is flick on all the lights, even though it's still daylight. I turn up the thermostat, hoping that's all I'll have to do to get more heat. I make my way down to the basement, pushing cobwebs aside on my way to turn on the water, hoping that turning the knob connected to the tank is all I have to do. After the water heater makes a loud hissing noise, I run upstairs, praying it doesn't blow me to Kingdom Come. I wish to God that Erik were here, or at least had shown me what to do when I'm here alone.

While the house gets warm I go out to the van and take out my suitcase and one of the bags of groceries I brought with me from home. I make a couple more trips, and then go about the task of putting away what I just carried in. There is a small turkey that I will make for Thanksgiving dinner.

That is, of course, if Erik is here; otherwise I'll just make a frozen pizza.

Just before I leave to go for a walk I take a couple of slices of bread and stuff them into my jacket pocket. In my other pocket I stuff my cell phone, making sure it's turned on like I promised my mother. I walk to the pond and sit on a fallen tree. The beauty of the water rippling in the autumn wind is like a whisper from the past and it quiets my soul. The sound reminds me of when Daddy and I used to go fishing.

We'd sit in the old rowboat, Daddy casting for fish, and with each cast, it made this little rippling sound. I sat with my fishing pole, watching the cork bob up and down, but not down enough to tell me I caught a fish. We wouldn't talk at first, then we kind of worked our way into it. My father would ask about school, and my complaints depended on what grade I was in. Of course, it always ended up with me complaining not about school, but about Mom.

"She doesn't understand me, Dad. I'm not Angela."

His response was always, "No, you're not, but you're not a mother either, Freddy; she just wants what is best for you."

I'd complain some more and Daddy would always listen. But there was one time he did more than just listen; he told me that he always gave me credit for using my head, and in that instance, I definitely did not use my head.

It was the time I ended up at Dr. Marshall's office and had my arm sewed up. A guy called Joey stupid;

I called the guy a fucking asshole. He called me stupid and I said his girl was just a fucking everything, and he pulled a knife on me.

"What was I suppose to do, Daddy? I had to defend myself. Mom says nice girls don't say words like that, and I told her the hell they don't."

That's when my father gave his sermon about using common sense. Sitting on this log, watching the sun on the water, I think I've forgotten it.

If I had remembered, I sure wouldn't be sitting here, pregnant, waiting to find out if the father wants to be a father or a senator, or if once again my heart has fooled my head. The worry in my soul takes over again, and the desolation, the loneliness seep in and I think I must be the only person on this planet, or at least within ten miles..

A flock of geese lands and it's not so quiet anymore. I pull the bread out of my pocket to feed the geese. A couple of slices don't go very far when feeding a flock. I think Mrs. Davis, if she were here, would have a story about that, about feeding a flock with only a little. But Mrs. Davis isn't here, my boys aren't here, and Erik isn't here. I have never felt so lonely in my life. With a little "ah" to help push me up from the log, but feeling more like a sigh, I start to walk away. The little beggars honk after me before deciding to leave, too. With a loud honking they take flight, and when I turn back to look, the pond is quiet again.

The woods looms big and forbidding as I walk

toward it, but once I enter, I'm surprised to see a little path. It twists and turns among the brush. A branch from a tree slaps me in the face as I walk past. This path intrigues me, and if I weren't so hungry, I'd explore further.

'Tomorrow,' I tell myself, turning back toward the house.

On my way in, I pick up some wood from the pile outside the door. I'm not as good at making fires as I am at driving and folding maps, so it takes me a while to get one going.

I watch the flames lick at the wood, making shadows on the floor. I sit in front of the hissing fire with my legs bent and my head resting on my knees and feel the loneliness of the pond and woods. It's a big house, with lots of creaks and sounds like the one I grew up in, that I live in now, and if it weren't so lonely, if the boys and Erik were here, and Joey too, it would be perfect.

After a quick supper of a bologna sandwich and tomato soup out of a can, I settle down in front of the television to wait for a little while before calling my sons. I don't want to call during dinner and get turned down because the boys can't leave the table, so I wait.

There's an old *Three Stooges* movie on, one that I've watched with Joey so many times that I have it memorized. I think maybe I should change channels, but that would take more energy than I have right now. The house is warm, the fire glows red in the fireplace, and I doze during commercials. The movie is boring and I fall sound asleep. When I wake up, it's too late to call the boys.

'Tomorrow,' I mumble to myself, still half-asleep as I trudge up the stairs. "Tomorrow," I repeat, crawling into the big brass bed under the patchwork quilt. The last thought I have just before falling back to sleep is, 'Tomorrow. I'll talk to my boys, tomorrow.'

In the morning, I try to call only to discover that my cell phone is dead. I fiddle with it a while, saying 'damn it' at least three times, mentally kicking myself for not remembering to bring the charger with me. As I get into the van, I say another 'damn it' for Erik never having had a phone line hooked up, for waiting until I moved in. I decide that if I can't find a place to make a call I'm going back home.

After miles of reading the map while driving I find this little town that I'd miss if I blinked twice. There is a little café with lots of cars parked in front, and it seems like a place that would have a phone. I find an empty spot to park the van, then wait for an empty table to park myself.

After about fifteen minutes, I get a booth and order the Thanksgiving Special of turkey, mashed potatoes, and peas. For dessert, I have apple pie that's served by a woman who looks like she should be home baking the pies instead of serving them.

"I haven't seen you in this neck of the woods before," she says, pouring more coffee in my cup to go with the pie. It's finally calmed down enough, the place is starting to empty out, and she gets a chance to talk.

"I just bought a place."

"Where would that be, honey?" the waitress asks, and I wonder if I should tell her. But if I'm going to move here, I sure can't keep it a secret. Besides, I'm not going to mention Erik's name.

"It's that big farmhouse off the interstate on March Road."

"I know the place. It used to belong to the Marches. The road was named after Robert March's grandfather. They used to raise horses. Are you planning on raising horses?"

"I don't know yet," I say, thinking that right now raising horses is the last thing on my mind. I just want to raise my kids.

"How many kids do you have?" she asks, and I'm beginning to think she's awfully nosy, not to mention possibly a mind reader, but she is nice, so I answer, "Two boys. But how did you know I had kids?"

"It's too big of a place for just two people. That house was built for kids. The Marches had five, plus two dogs and more cats than is healthy."

I never knew having cats was unhealthy. We kids had cats and we're healthy, but I guess she's entitled to her opinion, and I'm entitled to mine. That is, until she asks, "So what does your husband do?"

"I'm divorced," I say, and when she raises one of her penciled eyebrows at me, I think her opinion of me is almost as bad as her opinion of cats. In this part of the country, I guess people don't get divorced.

Suddenly, there's a bitter taste in my mouth, and I push the rest of the pie away, asking, "Do you have a payphone?"

"Over there," she says, pointing with the tip of her pen to a far corner beside the door, and I feel her eyes follow me all the way.

First I call Mom, using my phone card, and I talk for about five minutes. She tells me that she has the turkey in the oven and can't talk long.

"It's almost ready to take out. It's perfect, and I don't want it to get any browner, Felicia, so I have to go now," she says, hanging up. My mouth waters remembering Mom's Thanksgiving dinners, wishing I were there to help eat it.

Next I call Jerry's number, and when the 'old bag' answers, I ask if I can talk to my sons.

"We're going to eat in a little while, and I don't want you to upset them," she says to me, her voice all snippy. I've never even seen the woman before and I hate her already.

"Get them to the phone!" I say so loud that it makes heads turn.

"I'm sorry but I can't do that," she replies in this calm voice that's so irritating I just wish I could reach through the phone and rip her tongue out.

"Then let me talk to Jerry," I say through clenched teeth, trying not to draw attention to myself, even though I want to scream some swear words. I would even use the *F* word.

"He can't come to the phone right now, either."

"Look," I say, my voice rising in anger. "You get his ass over to the phone now, or the next person who calls is going to be a lawyer with a subpoena."

My threat doesn't work and she hangs up. It's Thanksgiving and I can't even talk to my sons. I can't believe that I ever loved this man. That I ever carried his children inside of me, because I have never felt so much hate in my life as I do now. Before I go back to my table, I dial again, but get a busy signal. Five times I dial, then give up. I'm sure the old bag took the phone off the hook.

My hands are still shaking when I dial Erik's number and get his answering service. I leave the same message as I did before, only this time I tell him that I'm going home, and if he wants to contact me, I'll be there by this evening.

I go back to my booth to get the check, and I must be crying because the nosy woman who doesn't like cats says, "It'll work out, honey. I'll pray for you."

"Thanks," I say, wondering if I'll ever see her again. I hope I do. She's just so nice, and I bet she doesn't really hate cats.

On my way back to the house, I cry so hard that I get the map that's lying across my lap all wet. Folding a map and crying doesn't work, and I finally throw it on the seat next to me so I can concentrate on just crying. I have a couple of close calls on the old dirt road called March Road, almost going into a ditch again, but I don't care. My two boys are eating

485

Thanksgiving dinner with their father and his soon-to-be wife.

He's all nice and cozy in his new lifestyle, while my life is going to hell. The anger boils inside me like a volcano ready to erupt. Once I get back to the house, it fizzles out and I'm just left feeling drained, my eyes sore and red from crying.

That woman at the restaurant must have a direct line to heaven, because when I pull into the yard, Erik's car is in the driveway. I'm not sure how I make it into the house, if I fly or walk, but when I open the door, Erik is waiting with open arms.

"I'm sorry," I say first. Then Erik says it. We don't say why we're sorry; it doesn't matter, as long as we're both sorry. After a lot of hugs and kisses and a lot of crying on my part, in between sobs, I tell Erik about Jerry taking the boys. While Erik wipes my tears, he curses Jerry.

"Damn him. He won't get away with this. We'll take him to court. You're a good mother, sweetheart, and we'll prove it."

"But he said that if we say anything, he'd ruin your chances of running for the senate," I say, in a sobbing, kind of choking voice.

"I don't want it that bad, Freddy. Not enough for you to lose your boys."

I hug him even tighter, wondering if now is the time to tell him I'm pregnant. But then I start to hiccup, and somehow telling a man he's going to be a father for the first time between hiccups doesn't seem proper.

We're in bed when I do tell him. After we've made love, I say, just like that, "Erik, I'm pregnant."

"How did that happen?" he asks. Not like he's accusing me, but like he just can't figure it out.

"When you said you'd pull out, but didn't."

"I guess nobody's perfect," he says with a shrug, and I hit him with a pillow. He pushes the pillow aside, holding me down. Our mouths come together in a kiss. Then he moves down, kissing a trail from my mouth to where our child lives.

"Monday I'll file for a divorce and file to get your boys back," he says, stroking where he's just kissed, and I remember how my father once kissed me while I was still being formed. And I wonder if Erik thinks now is a good time for a baby, like my father once told my mother.

"But what about your political career? You said it would be suicide to get a divorce now."

"I never wanted to run anyway."

"You're just saying that to make me feel better."

"No, honestly, these last couple of days, I've been thinking of withdrawing from the race."

"If you don't care, then why did you run in the first place?"

"It was a challenge. My father-in-law came up with it, and I guess I couldn't resist."

"Damn you, Erik!" I say, pushing him off of me, ready to get out of bed.

"Honey, I didn't realize what I really wanted until I thought I lost you, and now with the baby. Hell, I'd rather be a father than a senator, anyway."

I crawl back into bed, snuggling down under the covers with this man who isn't perfect, but whom I love.

Before we leave for home, as we walk to our cars, Erik asks again for me to stay here until everything blows over.

"Sweetheart, I don't want to put you through this. There will be reporters waiting with all kinds of accusations. They'll say you're a home-wrecker, and maybe even worse. You have no idea the things they might say."

"They'll say them about you, too."

"But I'm used to people making nasty remarks about me. I'm a lawyer."

"And a damn good one, too. Maybe not perfect, but good."

"I can't protect you from the gossip."

"What can they say that hasn't been said about some politician already? Isn't mud-slinging part of it all? Besides, I don't want to leave Mom and Joey holding the bag. I'll be there to face whatever I have to."

"Maybe you're right. I think Joey is going to need you."

"Why?"

"Because I've got an appointment set up for him right after Thanksgiving with a psychiatrist. I want to have my people evaluate him before the court does."

"When is the court going to?"

"Right after Christmas."

"How will we ever get through all of this?

Between fighting for my kids, your divorce and, on top of that, Joey has to go through court again? I just don't know how we're going to manage."

"We'll get through it together, and you know something?" Erik says, wrapping me in one of his hugs. "We're going to win, because maybe I'm not perfect, but I'm still damn good."

We both laugh at that, and when Erik gets in his car to go to the airport and I get in mine, we're still laughing. I love the way Erik laughs. I hear it all the way home.

It's a good thing that I'm in a good mood, because when I get home, I call again to talk to my sons and Jerry answers.

"It's kind of late, isn't it? Or were you too busy to wish your sons a Happy Thanksgiving?"

"I tried, Jerry. That's all I've been doing lately is trying to talk to them, but your girlfriend or fiancée or whatever you call her wouldn't let me!"

"You mean Lisa? She's just as outraged that you don't call as I am."

I feel my good mood fading fast, and I only hope I can stay calm enough to finish this conversation before I tell Jerry to go to hell, or worse yet call him the names a nice girl doesn't know about, but I don't have to worry because I'm starting to think like my mother, and that scares me.

"Is that why she keeps telling me the boys aren't home when I call? Or when Angela saw them in a restaurant, your Linda--"

Jerry interrupts, "Lisa. Her name is Lisa."

"I don't give a damn what her name is. All I know

489

is that she told Angela that my family was to stay away from the boys. All she wanted to do is give them a hug. Since when is it wrong for an aunt to give her two nephews a hug?"

"I don't believe you," he says after a period of silence, and I can tell he's not entirely sure of himself.

"Oh, so you'd rather believe Lisa? Tell me, Jerry, how long have you known her and how long have you known me? Do you really think I'd forget my sons? If you don't believe me, ask Ben about Angela; he'll tell you he saw her. Ben doesn't lie and you know it." Another pause.

"Freddy, I'm sorry."

"No, you're not. But you will be, because I'm taking you to court. Erik and I are going to fight for the boys, and all your threats aren't going to stop us, because he's dropping out of politics. When I get my sons back, Jerry, you're the one that's going to be begging to see them."

"Freddy, I didn't know. I swear, Lisa never told me."

Where before there was accusation in his voice, now there is fear at the prospect that I might really mean business. I do, of course, but part of me still hurts to hear him so afraid that he'll lose his sons forever.

"She didn't tell you on purpose, Jerry. She's got you believing all kinds of lies about my family and me. I thought you had more sense than that, but I guess there's no arguing with a bitch in heat."

And now I'm thinking like Angela, and that scares me even more.

"Stop it. I won't have you talking about her like that."

"And I won't have her saying she's my sons' mother. You can have all the kids you want with her, I don't care, but not my sons."

"They're mine, too."

"And that's why I won't keep you from seeing them, Jerry, because they love you. I hate you, but they love you, and they're what really counts, right?"

Jerry doesn't say anything, just turns the phone over first to Jimmy, then Ben. I haven't talked to them since they left, and I have to keep from crying when they ask me why I haven't called. They tell me all the things they did with Daddy, and I think that maybe I don't count anymore, until Ben says, "Can we come home now, Mommy? Jimmy and I want to come home."

"Soon," I promise my son. "Real soon."

"But we don't like it here. Not when Daddy's at work; then Lisa yells at us all the time. You never yell all the time."

"What does Daddy say when you tell him that she yells?"

"We don't, because she says she'll spank us if we do."

I have never hit my kids in my life. Except for the time I grabbed Jimmy by the arm, I've never hurt them, ever. Now they're afraid of some woman in another state who's threatening to hit them, and there isn't a thing I can do about it.

"Let me talk to Daddy," I tell Ben.

"You won't tell, will you?" he asks, fear in his voice.

"I'm going to ask Daddy if Aunt Angela can pick you up and take you boys to lunch and out shopping. Would you like that, Ben?"

"Yaay! We're going to lunch with Aunt Angela, and she's going to buy us some toys!" Ben announces, and I think he's telling Jimmy the good news because I can hear Jimmy yelling "Yaay!" in the background. Then Jerry comes back on the phone.

"Ben says that Lisa hollers at them."

"I've never heard her."

"She does it when you're at work."

"Okay, so maybe she scolds them once in a while. You've done it yourself, sometimes."

"But I've never hit them."

"She never has either."

"But she's threatened to."

"Threatening is not the same as doing."

"And I'm not going to give her the chance. The boys want to come home. Ben just said it, and Ben never lies. I told him that Angela is going to pick them up for lunch tomorrow, and you better not stop it, Jerry. That's all I'm going to say for now. I'll say the rest with your lawyer present."

"Freddy, Lisa just believes in discipline, that's all."

"She can discipline the kids that you have with her, but not mine," I say, and then slam the phone down.

After I hang up, I call Angela and ask her to pick up the boys and take them to lunch.

"And if they have so much as a single mark on them, I want you to tell me right away. I'll come there personally and scratch that woman's eyes out."

"Atta girl. Now you sound like the Freddy I've always known."

"You mean that you've always fought with," I say.

"Somebody had to get you ready for this. What kind of a sister would I be if I didn't teach you how to fight?"

"Yeah, but what about the calling people names? Do you know I just called Jerry's fiancée a bitch in heat?"

Angela starts laughing, the same kind that always made me mad, but now I'm more forgiving and I laugh with her.

"Maybe I should have taught you more about birth control. Jesus, Freddy, I can understand once, but having to get married twice?"

"How do you know I'm getting married?"

"Because Erik just held a press conference and said he was withdrawing from the race."

"You're kidding. What channel is he on?"

"It's over now, but it was short and sweet."

"Thanks, Angela," I say. Before hanging up I add, "By the way, I promised the boys that you would take them shopping."

"And who's going to pay for all this shopping?" Angela asks.

"Their famous rich aunt, of course."

"I'm not rich, Freddy."

493

"You're not famous either, but you are an aunt."

"I'll take them shopping already, okay?" Angela says. I thank her again, and this time I really hang up. Then I go upstairs to get the boys' bedroom ready for their homecoming. I can't expect them to sleep on dirty sheets, can I?

CHAPTER 41

The open house at the store marks the beginning of the Christmas Season. Now it's okay to put up a wreath. It's okay to put the Christmas tree lights on the trees outside, or even the tree inside. If a bulb burns out, or if the old tree doesn't look the same as it did when it was stored away, all one has to do is come into our store and get new. And if for some reason a customer just wants to browse, that's okay. We have little tables and chairs set up and another table where we have coffee and Christmas cookies. The coffee and cookies are free, but the muffins and doughnuts aren't.

It's a season of getting ready and of celebration, but this year in our town some people forget what we're celebrating. Instead of peace on earth, good will to men, the whole town is locked in a bitter controversy. All Mom and I hear at the store is how the local high school won't allow any Christmas carols in their program. It's a town divided, and we at the store don't take sides, but sometimes it's hard. Mrs. Davis has her opinion, so I try to be sympathetic, because after all she is my boys' adopted grandmother. Mr. Larson, on the other hand, has his opinion, too, and it's not the same as

Mrs. Davis's, but he's the grandfather of the one I'm carrying inside me.

"What do I do?" I ask my mother in frustration.

"Just shake your head kind of sad-like, and keep your mouth shut," she answers, and I think that is good advice. I just wish I could remember it when I talk to Angela and Jerry.

I call Angela right after she takes the boys for lunch and she complains how much it cost her on their shopping spree.

"You have to set a limit," I tell her. "You just don't let them have every single thing they want."

"But we were celebrating."

"What?"

"That Jerry kicked the old bag out."

Now this *is* good news, but it would be better news if Jerry had kicked the boys out and right back home to me.

"Angela, I expect you to keep your eyes on the boys for me."

"If I wanted to watch kids, Freddy, I'd have some of my own."

"Lucky for them you don't," I say, "You'd make a lousy mother."

The minute I say it, I know I should have kept my mouth shut, because Angela says real nasty-like, "Next time, do your own dirty work," and hangs up.

I don't worry about Angela hanging up. I guess after all the times that I've hung up on her she has to have a turn, too. But with Jerry, if he hangs up, I don't get to talk to the boys. Not unless I talk to them first, but that doesn't happen very often. I try the polite treatment when I talk to Jerry.

"Can I please talk to Ben and Jimmy?" I ask in my Sunday-best voice.

"Of course," Jerry says, then calls Jimmy to the phone. "Daddy hired a housekeeper. Her name is Maria."

"Is she nice?"

"Yeah. I guess. Anyway she's a lot prettier than Lisa."

"Does she yell?"

"She's real quiet, but she smiles a lot."

"That's good."

"It's because she doesn't understand us very good when we talk."

"Does she speak a foreign language?"

"No, Daddy says it's Spanish."

After Jimmy gets through talking, I imagine a young Spanish dancer with dark hair, clicking her heels and shaking her tambourine, and I hope to God that's all she shakes in front of the boys.

After talking to Ben, I have another picture of Maria, and I like Ben's a lot better.

"Jimmy says Daddy hired a housekeeper to take care of you. Do you like her?"

"She makes cookies for us."

"That's nice," I say.

"But they're not as good as Grandma's."

"Nobody makes cookies like Grandma."

"But she *is* a Grandma."

"How do you know?"

497

"Because she's as old as Grandma."

"She is pretty, though."

"Not as pretty as you. Mommy, when can we come home? I miss you."

"I miss you, too, and I pray every day that Daddy will bring you back home."

"Will you ask him?"

"I have been asking him. Every time I talk to him."

"But maybe now that Daddy has to pay somebody to take care of us, he'll let you do it for free."

"Maybe," I say, wishing Angela could hear what Ben just said. Ben could tell her what motherhood is all about a lot better than I ever could.

Ben calls, "Daddy!" and now I have to ask for what I told Ben I was praying for.

"Ben and Jimmy want to come home. Please let them, Jerry. I don't want to go to court and neither do you."

"I can't do that, Freddy."

"Why?"

"Because you're living with Erik."

"And what exactly were you doing with Lisa, playing house?"

"That was different. Neither of us was married, and our relationship didn't cause a scandal."

"Well, pretty soon Erik won't be married either."

"We'll see." Jerry says, real smug-like, and until then I remembered what Mom said about keeping my mouth shut. I forgot.

"At least I don't have to kick Erik out because he mistreats little kids."

"I didn't kick Lisa out. We just decided to go our separate ways, that's all."

"You lying bastard," I say and slam the phone down. Now I'm going to have to pray extra hard to get those boys back, or at least pray for a judge who believes kids belong with their mother.

The peace on earth, good will to men isn't working for Erik either. Diane is fighting the divorce like she really wants to stay married. But according to Erik, it's just the benefits of marriage she wants.

"She's asking for the house, the money, even the Jag. I'm lucky if I end up with keeping the plane, but I'll probably have to sell that once everything is settled, because I'm not going to have a job either."

"Let her have the stuff, Erik. It'll be worth it to get this over with. And I don't want you to sell the plane. You're giving enough up for me; I don't want you to give that up, too."

"I thought the partners would stick up for me, but they want nothing to do with a scandal."

"It'll die down, Erik. It always does."

"I'm still a damn good lawyer."

"And I'm still a damn good mother."

"We're both damn good," Erik says, patting my thickening middle, our little Emma.

By now, I've been to see Dr. Marshal, and after my ultrasound, I've learned that we're going to have a daughter. We've decided to call her Emma, after

Erik's grandmother. She was the one who actually raised him, because his own mother was always sick.

I buy a Christmas present for Emma at the same time I buy gifts for the boys. I wrap them in bright blue paper, covered with white snowmen, and put them under the tree. The packages don't look as neat as the ones on television, but those are just square boxes. It isn't easy to wrap a football, a bat, a toy dinosaur, or a frog to make them look like a square, and that's just the little stuff. I don't bother to wrap the bicycles and sleds. I don't wrap Emma's bear either. It looks too cute sitting under the tree just as it is.

I decide to give Erik the watch I planned to give him years ago. I think he'll appreciate that more than anything else. As for me, I just want him to get my boys back home, I hope in time for Christmas.

All Joey wants is not to go see the psychiatrist, but I tell him that's not going to happen. He puts up a fuss when I tell him that Erik has made the appointment.

"I won't go. You can't make me, Freddy."

"I'm taking you, Joey, so you might as well stop fighting it. All he's going to do is ask you some questions."

"What kind of questions?"

"About what happened in prison."

"He can ask, but I won't talk about when I wasn't home."

"We'll see," I say, "We'll see."

As it turns out, I don't have to take Joey, because

at the last minute, the psychiatrist decides it will be better if he came to see Joey. And it's a good thing, too, because the morning of the appointment Joey gets sick. In between questions Joey has to go to the bathroom while the doctor sits at the table drinking coffee. A whole pot of coffee by the time he's finished with the little talk that was supposed to take only an hour, but ends up as three. After that, Joey is real quiet, like a little boy afraid of his own shadow, and I just pray to God that all this will be over soon so we can get on with our lives.

Three days before Christmas it starts to snow and doesn't quit. Our town is buried under snow, and I think the townspeople are relieved when the Christmas program at the high school is cancelled. They come into the store, those who manage to get through, and say, "I guess Mother Nature has her own way of dealing with controversy." Mrs. Davis calls it 'Divine Intervention.'

I'm glad for the snow. It keeps Angela and Harry from flying in. It's a lot easier to keep peace with Angela in New York. All I have to do is wish her a Merry Christmas and a Happy New Year over the phone. If she were here, Christmas would have to be a theatrical experience. If Harry were here, it would be a computer experience, listening to all the latest technological discoveries. After my disappointment of not having the boys and my frustration with Joey, all I want to do is spend a quiet Christmas with Erik. I thank God he was here and not New York when we got snowed in.

Mom and Carl make it over in the big dump truck that Carl uses for landscaping in summer, with a snowplow in front for the winter. They don't stay long, though, because they plan on going s t raight to church from here. I think they may be the only ones there, but Mom wouldn't miss church or coming back to the house on Christmas even if she had to walk. She piles the gifts she and Carl carry in under the tree saying, "We'll stay long enough for you and Erik to open your gifts, then we have to go."

"But there're so many," I say, watching the pile grow higher.

"They're not all for you, Felicia. I brought the boys' gifts, too."

"I know Mom, but there are still so many."

"Some are welcome home gifts," Mom says, handing me one package and Erik another. Ever since Jerry took the boys away from me, Mom's loyalties have changed. She now sees Erik in a kinder light. I open my gift first, and it's a fluffy robe.

"When you have your baby, you can wear it at the hospital," Mom says. But I don't think fluffy robes are in. Especially if it's a warm spring, because that's when I'm having my baby.

"It's so nice and cuddly, I think I'll wear it now, Mom," I say, while she just shrugs her shoulders, like have it your own way. Erik opens his, and it's a leather aviator-type jacket, and I think maybe Mom must like Erik a lot lately. Leather jackets cost more than a robe--I don't care how fluffy it is.

Erik and I give Mom a ring, set with the

birthstones of us three kids and two grandkids, leaving a place for Emma's when she comes. And I think Erik likes Mom, too, because he's the one who picked it out. He got it in New York at Tiffany's, and I think it cost more than all the gifts Mom and Carl bought, including the boys'. We give Carl a wool shirt, because he is too small-town for Tiffany's. Besides, I picked it out, and liking had nothing to do with it. I was just being frugal.

Mom is disappointed that Joey isn't here, and I say, "Joey left right after supper. He said he was too tired to wait up for Santa."

"He still doesn't believe in Santa Claus, does he, Felicia?"

"No, Mom. Prison knocked that out of him."

Erik adds: "Prison knocked a lot out of him. The psychiatrist said Joey is so depressed that he should be on medication." We all shake our heads.

After Mom and Carl leave, I put on my fluffy robe and cuddle with Erik on the couch, watching the original movie version of *It's a Wonderful Life,* with Jimmy Stewart.

"Have you ever thought of what it would be like if you had never been born?" I ask, after the movie ends.

"I think my ex-wife is wishing that right now."

"She's not your ex-wife yet, Erik."

"She would be, if she'd just sign the papers."

"You know she won't until you give her what she wants."

"I'll give her some, but not everything. I can just see her laughing all the way to the bank."

"It'll be more like her laughing all the way to the nearest bar."

"While you'll be struggling to make ends meet, until I can get my practice established, she'll be boozing it up on my money."

"And I should envy her for that? Just what do you think she's winning anyway?

"You know, you're right. All the while I'm thinking she's winning, she's actually losing. Right after Christmas, I'll give her everything she wants."

"Not everything, Erik. She can't have you," I say, thinking that this Jimmy Stewart might just have something when he said, "Every time a bell rings, an angel gets its wings," because right now the phone is ringing. I'm sure my angel has wings, because I almost fly to answer it.

"Hi, Mommy," Ben says. "We just came from church and Daddy says we should call you and wish you a Merry Christmas. Merry Christmas, Mommy."

"Merry Christmas to you, too Ben. Guess what! Santa came already and left you and Jimmy your presents."

"Did he leave me a sled?"

"Maybe, but I can't tell."

"I miss you."

"I miss you, too, sweetheart. I love you."

When Jimmy comes on, he wants to know if he got a football because Daddy got him one, and maybe Santa will exchange it for a basketball.

"Maybe," I say. "Are you having fun?"

"It's more fun at home."

"We'll celebrate Christmas here when you come home. See how lucky you are? You get two Christmases!"

"I'd rather have just one with you and Daddy together."

Despite all our fighting, all our controversy, Jimmy still thinks that someday Mommy and Daddy will live together. I don't think even Divine Intervention would help that cause, and I quickly say, "Merry Christmas, Jimmy. I love you."

"Merry Christmas to you, too, Mom. Daddy wants to say Merry Christmas, too."

I wait while Jimmy hands Jerry the phone, then in my most festive voice say, "Ben said you took them to church. That's nice."

"Did you go to church, too?"

"No, we're snowed in here."

So far the conversation is nice and polite, like people should talk on Christmas. Unless you're Scrooge, and I'm not Scrooge.

"Is Erik there?"

"Why?"

"Because I was wondering if it's as good being snowed in with him as it was with me. Is it, Freddy?"

"Better," I say, and then add, "Merry Christmas, Jerry," just before slamming the phone down, and I wonder what Scrooge would have said in my place-probably "Bah, humbug."

In bed Erik and I exchange our gifts. I sit cross-legged in the middle, opening mine, while he sits on the edge.

505

"It's beautiful." I hold up the gold chain with a single solitaire diamond dangling from it, with earrings to match. "But it must have been expensive if you bought it at the same place you bought Mom's."

"I want to give you expensive while I still can. Besides, there's less for Diane to get."

"I hope you got it for me because you love me, and not because you hate Diane."

"What do you think?" Erik asks, slipping on the watch that I gave him, the one I'd been saving for him all these years. He crawls into bed next to me and then proceeds to show me what I think.

It stops snowing Christmas morning, and while the town digs out Erik and I sleep in. Around 10:00, we're still in bed when Mom calls and wants to know if she should just bring dinner here.

"As long as it's just us, why don't I bring it over? It'll be easier for us to get through with the truck."

"It's up to you, Mom, but what if Carl's kids call to wish him a Merry Christmas? He won't be home."

"They already called this morning. Brian sounded like he's glad he's in Florida for the holidays and not here."

"If you bring the turkey and pies, I'll make the rest of the stuff."

"But that's only two things. I should bring more."

"You're bringing the hard stuff, Mom, but if you want to make the sweet potatoes, you can. I don't have any on hand."

"I'll bring everything," Mom says, and then hangs

up.

"That was Mom," I tell Erik, crawling under the covers again. "They're bringing the dinner here instead of us going there."

"How come?"

"She says it will be easier for them to get through with the truck, but I think Mom misses this house, especially at Christmas."

"If she wanted to spend Christmas here, we could have made the dinner."

"I don't think Mom trusts my cooking," I say, and then add, "Maybe you should get Joey. He still hasn't opened his presents. He used to love opening his presents. It always had to be on Christmas Eve for him."

"Honey, don't expect so much of Joey yet. It's going to take time. He's still afraid that any day he's going to have to go back."

"Talk to him, Erik, please. Tell him that as long as you're his lawyer, that's never going to happen."

"I'll try, honey, but it's going to take time for him to believe me."

"I believe you. I always did."

"That's because I can use my convincing technique on you."

"What's a convincing technique? That's not even lawyer talk."

"That's lover talk," Erik says, and it's almost 11:30 before Erik gets through convincing me with his convincing technique.

The table is all set when Carl comes in carrying the electric roaster with turkey, while Mom follows behind with the pies. It takes a couple more trips before our dinner is carried in, filling the kitchen with the smells of Christmas.

"Isn't Joey here yet?"

"Erik went to get him, Mom."

"You should have left the table for him to help with. You know how he likes to help set the table."

"He doesn't like to anymore. I can't even get him interested in flowers. The real ones."

"He's afraid to like what he used to, Felicia. He thinks it's not going to last."

"He doesn't believe me anymore, but I think he does Erik. He's the only one that hasn't broken a promise to him. Erik says we just have to be patient. That the best thing we can do for him is just let him know we love him."

I think Mom wants to say more, but Erik comes walking in with Joey, stomping snow on the kitchen floor I just scrubbed yesterday, and that ends our little discussion about what's best for Joey. The snow plow makes grunting sounds outside the big living room window, and without even looking at his presents still under the tree, Joey goes and stands by the window watching Carl plow out our driveway.

"Come on and open your presents, Joey," I say, taking his hand and leading him over to the tree. One by one I hand the bright packages to him, and I think Mom and I show more enthusiasm than Joey. Carl comes in just as Joey opens his last present, a new leather belt from Harry. Maybe Mom still has enthusiasm, but it's hard for me. Who is going to put that belt through the loops on his trousers? It's sure not going to be Harry or even Mom. I make a mental note to exchange the belt for suspenders the first chance I get.

After we pray, we eat what we just asked God to bless. While Mom and I do the dishes the men doze, and I just wish to God my two youngest men were here to doze with them. Mom looks so comfortable in this kitchen, like it's still hers, and I think that maybe Erik is right. Once we move out Mom is going to move back in. Of course, she'll bring Carl with her, but hopefully not all that junk he has stored in the big red shed.

We all play Old Maid because Joey got a new deck of cards; it's the only gift he showed any enthusiasm for. By the time Mom and Carl leave for home, we're all played out, and for the rest of the night, we watch Christmas carols sung on television. I'm thinking if they're good enough for national television, they should be good enough for our local high school.

The day after Christmas Erik leaves for New York, kissing me good-bye, telling me, "The next time you see me, I'll be a free man. Broke but free."

I don't have much time to dwell on that. We are having our after-Christmas sale, which keeps us all hopping right up until we close on New Year's Eve.

We decide to skip the celebrating, and Mom and Carl stay home to rest, while I wait for Erik.

"Tomorrow we'll celebrate," I tell Mom, just before they get into their car. Lately Mom looks so tired. I hope she's okay, but I think it's more her missing the boys. I guess I look tired, too, and I know it's from me missing my sons. After supper, I say to Joey, "Let's skip cards and watch television."

"I want to play cards," Joey says.

Frankly, I'm getting real tired of cards lately, and I bargain with Joey. "Let's play checkers instead. Mom bought you the game for Christmas and you haven't even opened it up. Let's do something different."

"I don't like different, Freddy. Norman liked different, but I don't."

I let the subject of different pass and get out the cards.

Sometime around the twentieth game, I look at the clock, wondering when Erik will be home. He called earlier, when he was leaving New York; after a quick stop in Chicago, he said he'd be on his way. He should be home by now, and I think maybe I'm getting a little angry. He probably stopped and had a few with some of his old friends. I don't mind him stopping, but he promised to celebrate with me. Around 9:00 Erik calls, and I'm not mad anymore. I just want him to come home.

"I'm sorry, honey, but I stayed at the office too long and now I'm snowed in. I don't think I'll get home tonight."

"You're stuck in Chicago because of the weather? I didn't think it was that bad."

"It's sleeting here. I should have left the work go for another time, but I wanted to be done with it."

"Where are you now?"

"At the airport, and if it clears up enough, I'll be home soon."

"Promise?" I ask."

"I promise. I want to be home too."

"I love you, Erik. Happy New Year."

"I love you, too, but I'll wish you Happy New Year in person. I'm free, Freddy. Broke but free."

"I'll wait up for you," I say, and then before I hang up, I renew my promise.

"Forever and always, Erik. I love you, and we will be together forever and always."

Then Erik renews his promise. "Forever and always, sweetheart," and then he hangs up.

"I think I'll go home now, Freddy," Joey says, real tired-like, but I don't think his tired comes from missing the boys.

"Aren't you going to stay until midnight? We can take down all the old calendars and burn them in the fireplace like we used to when we were kids. Remember how we used to celebrate then, Joey?"

"I try not to remember, Freddy."

"But those were good times, Joey. You have to remember the good times."

"It will only hurt when they're taken away again."

"Nobody's taking anything away, Joey. I won't let them. Erik won't let them. He's smart, smarter than the whole bunch of them put together."

Joey smiles, getting up to leave. He puts on his jacket, carefully zipping it up.

"I bet he's even smarter than Norman."

"Everybody's smarter than Norman," I say, going over to turn on the television.

"Happy New Year," I say to Joey just before he walks out the door. Then I settle myself on the couch to wait for Erik and the New Year.

I wake up to a loud banging on the door, and I wonder why Erik doesn't just use his key. I run to let him in, but instead it's my mother.

"Mom, what are you doing here? It's not morning already, is it?"

"I had to come and tell you before you heard it on the news."

"Is it that bad that it couldn't have waited?"

"It's bad, Freddy."

Immediately, I think of Jerry. It's the war. But Jerry isn't in the war now. Maybe it's the boys. Oh my God, something's happened to my sons!

"Is it the boys, Mom? They were in an accident with Jerry?"

"It's Erik."

"Mom, I just talked to Erik a couple of hours ago. His plane is grounded."

"No, Freddy, he left Chicago. His plane went down."

"No, Mom. It's not true. It's just not true. The news is wrong. They make mistakes all the time."

"It's true, Freddy," Mom says, and I know it is. Mom only calls me Freddy when something terrible happens. And in this dark place, I hear Mom crying, and I think Carl is, too, but I do not cry. Dead cannot cry. Didn't we promise to always be together? *'Forever and always.'* I am with Erik. I am in the plane with him and holding onto him, forever and always.

CHAPTER 42

The evening news covers the airplane crash in painful detail. It shows the divers searching for the body, but there is little hope of them being able to recover it soon. The water is too cold for them to stay down very long, and so far all they come up with are pieces of wreckage. I imagine how the icy water feels and start to shiver. I can't stop, even with Mom piling blankets on me.

There is an interview with Erik's father-in-law, who hints that maybe it was no accident; that when Erik left the office that day, he was depressed. After all, he was out of a job. Then, of course, there was the divorce that he really didn't want, but after the scandal, after finding out about his affair, his daughter wasn't about to take him back. I want to scream at the television that Erik was not depressed. That he was happy to be rid of that whole bunch. We were going to spend all our New Year's Eves together. Hadn't he said, "Lots of them?" Hadn't we promised "Forever and always?" I feel so helpless, so overwhelmed with grief that I bury the anger inside.

"The boys should be here," Mom says.

She's spent the past two days trying to console me and has finally run out of words. I cry so many tears that I can't talk, not even when my sons call. Talking to Jerry is out of the question, so Mom talks to them instead. I don't know what she says to Jerry, but the next day Carl goes to the airport to pick them up. Jerry doesn't stay, though, only long enough to hand them over to Carl, and I'm grateful for at least that much.

There is no body, and there probably won't be until the thaw in spring, when there's a chance that it will wash up on shore. Until there can be a real funeral Erik's father holds a memorial service. Angela and Harry come home and talk to me about their grief in hushed tones as though whispering lends reverence to their words. I take the boys with me to the church, but it's Mrs. Davis who takes care of them. Mom and Carl have their hands full with holding me up.

After a week of mourning, the people around me settle back into their lives. Even Jimmy and Ben go back to school. Life goes on for everyone but me. I'm still down in that cold water with Erik, and no amount of heat from the fireplace or blankets can warm me.

I go to bed after I become so weak from not eating that the doctor is afraid I will lose the baby.

"Felicia, you have to eat," Mom says, coming into my room carrying a bowl of hot homemade chicken soup.

"I can't," I say through chattering teeth.

"You have to think of the baby."

"That's all I do think about is the baby. That if I weren't pregnant, Erik would have taken me with him. He wouldn't have tried to come home if I'd been with him."

"And what if he had decided to come home in that weather anyway, even with you with him? Then you'd be dead, too."

"At least I'd be with him," I moan into my blankets. Mom just walks out of the room shaking her head, taking the soup with her.

Ben and Jimmy come in to see me. Jimmy is uncomfortable and makes an excuse so he can leave, but Ben crawls on the bed next to me.

"Are you sick, Mom?" he asks, taking my hand like he's going to take my pulse.

"I'm just so cold, Ben."

"Maybe I can take you into the bathroom, like you do when I can't breathe. It gets real warm in there then. Are you having trouble breathing, Mom?"

"That's not the kind of sick I feel, Ben," I say, wishing that he'd leave me alone because right now I can't even explain to myself how I feel, let alone to him.

"Don't you have some homework to do?" I ask, and I guess Ben can take a hint because he leaves me to my sorrow, wishing that I could fall asleep and never have to wake up.

Joey is frightened over the pending hearing and comes into my room. He just stands at the foot of the bed and says, "They'll lock me up, Freddy. Now that Erik isn't here to stop them. I know they'll make me go back to that place."

"Stop it, Joey. I can't deal with that right now. You'll just have to trust Mom and Carl, that's all."

"I trust you, Freddy. If you come with me, they won't hurt me."

"I can't come with you, Joey, can't you see that?"

"Are you okay, Freddy?" Joey asks. So simply, like he always does, and suddenly I explode.

"No! I'm *not* okay! Every day you ask me, and I tell you that I'm not, so just stop it, already!"

Joey walks out of the room, hanging his head. I'm too busy feeling sorry for my own loss to feel sorry for what I've just done.

The next day, Dr. Marshall comes into my room and threatens, "Either you start eating, or I'm putting you in the hospital and feeding you through a tube. Maybe you don't care about that baby, but I'll be damned if I'm going to let you kill her."

"I'm not trying to kill her."

"Yes, you are. Maybe not outright, but by not eating, you're starving her to death. That's Erik's little daughter you're carrying. Why don't you stop thinking of yourself and think of her for a change?"

I start to cry and Dr. Marshall pats my hand gently. "Freddy, I've known you and Erik all your lives, and neither one of you were ever quitters. Don't quit now. This is Erik's immortality you're carrying, the part of him that is still living. Don't take that away from him. Don't take that away from his

517

father."

After the doctor leaves I start eating again, and I don't have to go to the hospital. I even get out of bed, but I'm still always cold, and when someone talks to me, it's like they're trying to get my attention from another room. Mom tells me that the psychiatrist thinks Joey should be put in a hospital for a while.

"He's so depressed, Felicia. They think that if they can get him in the hospital, they can put him on medication. What do you think?"

I shrug my shoulders and say, "I don't think, Mom, because if I start to think, I'm the one they'll have to put in the hospital. But there's no medicine to help me."

"You have to think of the baby, Felicia."

"But all I can think of is Erik. Ever since I was in high school, I've loved him. Jerry wanted me to go with him to New York to live and I wouldn't leave my family or Joey, but if Erik had asked me to follow him to hell, I think I would have. Do you know what it's like to love someone so much you're ready to leave everyone you know to be with him? My God, Mom, I would have given up the boys for him if he'd wanted to stay in politics."

"I know," Mom says. "I know."

"No, you don't," I say, suddenly tired of hearing her say that.

"Yes, I do, Felicia. I left my family for your father."

"But that was different; they wanted you to marry

Marvin Lowenstein," I say with a little smile, the first since I lost Erik, and it feels strange that I still know how.

"I'll go talk to Joey, Mom," I promise, hauling myself out of the chair, putting on my coat and buttoning it across my swollen middle. I go outside for the first time since the memorial service, and I shiver all the way to Joey's little house.

There's a February thaw, and I have to be careful not to slip on the melting ice that coats the porch steps.

"Joey, are you home?" I call out as I open the door, but there's only silence.

"Joey, it's me, Freddy. You better answer me, because I don't have the energy to come and look for you."

I sit down on the chair by the table and wait. Sometimes Joey hides on me, especially when he's mad at me, and I guess he has reason to be. Ever since I hollered at him, he hasn't asked me if I'm okay.

"Come on, Joey," I say, beginning to get impatient. "I'm sorry. Will you forgive me?"

For my answer, I hear the clock chime seven times. I get up from the chair and move through the house, cradling my stomach in my arms, calling Joey's name. I go into his bedroom, and I'm ready to leave when I notice that one of the dresser drawers is open. I go to close it and then I know: Joey's run away. I go through all the drawers, making a mental note of every item that's missing. Joey packed the same things he packed before when he was going to run away, only that time, I was here to stop him.

I call Mom on the phone, and then sit down on Joey's bed and cry. "I'm sorry, Joey. God, I'm sorry. Please, forgive me."

While I sit at home holding Jimmy and Ben close to me, Mom and Carl go looking for Joey. The police put out a call for all the squad cars in the area to watch for him on the highway in case he's hitchhiking. The neighbors join in, along with Carl's son, Brian. I put Jimmy and Ben to bed, and in their prayers they plead for Joey to come home. Mrs. Davis comes and stays with me, brewing me hot tea to stop the chills that make me shake so hard that the cup clatters against the saucer.

"Drink it while it's still hot," she says. "It'll warm you."

"It's my fault," I say, staring down into my cup without drinking. I am numb, like if someone were to stick me with a thousand tiny needles all over, I wouldn't even feel it. "I should have been there for him. He was so scared of having to go back to that awful place."

"You can tell him when you see him that you're sorry, Freddy. They'll find him, don't worry," she says gently, rubbing one of my arms through the blanket draped over my shoulders.

"I'll never treat him like I did, ever again. I just want him home."

"They'll find him. He hasn't been gone long. He'll be back before morning. God takes care of people like Joey," Mrs. Davis promises, adding more tea to my still mostly full cup. I think I agree with her, and with that thought to comfort me along with the steaming tea, I manage to stop shaking. We sit and drink our tea and reminisce about Joey.

"Ever since I can remember, you two were always together. If I saw one, as sure as anything, I'd always see the other not far behind. I'd look out my window and the two of you would be working in my yard."

"He once told me I had a beautiful heart. I complained that I wasn't beautiful, but he said I had a beautiful heart. I don't think it's beautiful anymore. At least Joey doesn't think it is. I hurt him so bad."

"You didn't mean to, Freddy. When he comes back, he'll understand."

"Where do you think he went?"

"I don't know, but they'll find him."

They find Joey around midnight. When Mom comes home, she's crying.

"This never should have happened, Freddy," she sobs, shaking her head and wiping at her eyes with a tissue.

"What happened?" I ask, already knowing it has to be terrible; Mom just called me Freddy.

"He was so afraid. The doctor told me he should go to the hospital."

"Mom! What happened? Did you find Joey, but he won't come home?"

"He can't come home, Freddy." She drops her eyes to the floor as she continues, unable to meet my own tear-swollen eyes.

"He tried crossing the creek and fell through. After the thaw, it just wouldn't hold his weight. Carl said he must have been heading for that abandoned cabin on the old Forester place and tried to cross the creek. If only it wasn't so high. Why did it have to rain so much this fall and make it so high?"

"Joey's not dead, Mom. He can't be dead," I beg, like if I say it enough, it can't be true. I turn to Mrs. Davis, accusing her. "You said that God takes care of people like Joey! Is this how he takes care of him?"

Mrs. Davis only shakes her head and says, "The Lord giveth and the Lord taketh away."

"But he takes too much!" I scream.

Mrs. Davis tries to comfort me. "He's with the Lord, Freddy. God is taking care of him."

And I say again, loud--there is no reverence in my voice, "And where was God when Joey was in prison?"

Mom and Mrs. Davis just cry and shake their heads. Warm tears form but cannot escape through my frozen eyes. I am so cold...so very cold. I think there is nothing or no one who will ever warm me again.

CHAPTER 43

There is another funeral, another coming together of family to mourn. Only this time instead of just words and pictures commemorating a life, there is also a coffin where people stand around and speak softly about their sorrow, with little white balls of tissue clutched in their hands. Jerry comes and takes my cold hand in his like he's trying to warm me, but I pull away.

"I'm sorry, Freddy. If there's anything I can do, please let me know."

"It's too late," I say, turning away to stare at what was once Joey but is now only a lifeless shell lying with its head on a white satin pillow.

"It's all wrong," I say to my mother, touching the buttons on the last shirt he'll ever wear. "Joey could never button a shirt with buttons this small. And where are the suspenders? They better not have a belt on him under that blanket." Mom puts her arm around me while I weep against her breast at the sheer wrongness of it all.

After the casket is closed and we're back from the cemetery where we laid Joey to rest beside his mother and father, Jerry comes over to talk to me.

I'm not sure this is the time to talk to you, but I'd like to take the boys for two weeks in the summer," he says.

I just stare at him with a blank look and reply, "You're right, this isn't the time. I'm not sure there will ever be a right time to talk to me. If you hadn't taken the boys, none of this would have happened."

Jerry looks like I've just accused him of murder, and in a way, it sounds like I have.

"I would have never insisted that Erik get a divorce if you hadn't threatened me."

"And what about you getting pregnant? Are you telling me that had nothing to do with it?" Jerry asks, looking down at my protruding belly. For a minute, I want to put my hands across my middle to hide it from his stare, but I will not apologize for loving Erik, and I run my hands across my front in a gentle caress. The baby kicks, and it startles me to think that there is such a thing as a new beginning amid all these endings.

At first there is numbness, a surreal quality, even to routine, normally mundane things. I get the boys up for school and make them breakfast. I even listen to all their little everyday complaints and arguments. It seems always to be the same, but I know it's not. Before I cared. Now I don't. For almost a month I live in this nonexistent world I've created to hide in, until one day Jimmy scares me into caring again.

Jimmy has been a problem all along. He is failing

in school, and I've even caught him playing with matches, almost burning down the garage in back of our house. So far nobody has gotten hurt, and I don't mention anything to Jerry until Jimmy almost kills Ben.

Jimmy found a loaded gun in Mom's bedroom, aimed it at his little brother, and pulled the trigger. I'm busy in the kitchen, not paying attention to what I'm doing, when I hear the shot. When I run into the room, there's a hole in the ceiling, and a white and shaking but otherwise unharmed Ben, standing beneath it. Lucky for us, Jimmy isn't the shot that he brags he is. After hugging Ben and punishing Jimmy by telling him no television for a week, I call Jerry and explode.

"You can't dump this all on me, Jerry! Jimmy needs his father. That's what the psychologist said."

"What the hell was a loaded gun doing in your mother's room, anyway?"

"It was Daddy's. Mom must have loaded it when she was staying all alone and forgot that she did. It's still Mom's room, even though she doesn't live here anymore and they know they shouldn't go in there. We kids always knew it was off-limits."

"So now it's also my fault that your mother is forgetful? What do you want me to do anyway? When I brought them to live with me, you threatened to take me to court."

"Because I didn't like the way your girlfriend was abusing them, that's why."

"She wasn't abusing them."

"Then why did you break up with her? Ben said

you had an argument after I called and you kicked her out. If she was right, then why did you kick her out?"

"It's none of your business, Freddy. Just like Erik was none of mine. Isn't that what you said?"

"Erik is gone, Jerry, and so is Joey. All of you have left me alone with three kids to raise all by myself," I say, starting to cry. Then I am furious with myself for crying.

"Is that what this argument is about, Freddy? You being mad at Erik and Joey for dying?"

"He shouldn't have taken off in that weather, Jerry. Erik was a good pilot. Why did he have to take off just because I said I missed him and wanted him home? He didn't have to listen to me." Now I'm really crying, and I wonder if I'm making any sense.

"Freddy, it was an accident. Nobody's to blame. We all use poor judgment sometimes, but nothing happens and we just count ourselves as lucky, that's all. And how many times did you tell me when we were first married that you missed me? It's okay to want to be with the person you love."

"But I was mean to Joey. I should have been there for him."

"You had a right to be there for yourself, too. You were going through a lot. Joey understood."

"Then why did he run away? He left me, too."

"If he hadn't gone through the ice, I have a feeling he would have come back on his own."

"And what about you? Why did you leave?" I ask, thinking that this makes the least sense of all after all these years.

"You kicked me out of your bed, remember?"
"Because you started sharing yours with someone
else. At least I waited until I was divorced before I
slept with Erik."

"It always comes back to that, doesn't it? Angela
tells you I cheated and you believe her."

"Then why didn't you take that job in Chicago, if
you didn't have someone in New York?"

"Why didn't you come and live with me in New
York? I asked you to."

I don't have the energy for this, and I'm ready to
hang up when Jerry says, "I'll take off from work and
take the boys for the whole summer. That will give
you time to have the baby and get settled before you
have the boys to deal with again. When are you due?'

"In another six weeks, just before the boys get out
of school."

"I'll come and get them right after," Jerry says,
and before I can say thanks or even apologize for
the accusation I made at Joey's funeral, he hangs up.

Exactly six weeks later Emma is born. It's a warm
night in May when I go into labor. Mom goes with
me to the hospital while Mrs. Davis comes and takes
care of the boys. I hold Mom's hand, crying for Erik
to be here with me, but no amount of tears will
bring him back. I know that, but the tears keep
flowing, anyway.

When the pain gets so bad that it feels like my
insides are going to rip apart, I let out a loud scream,
sounding more like a dying animal than a person. A
couple of times I think I even say Jerry's name, and I

think I'm getting my babies mixed up, and it's Ben that I'm having. When I tell my mother that I can't take any more, she just says, "I know...I know," and I think I scream at her, too, for saying it.

Dr. Marshall comes into the delivery room with his face covered and stands over me.

"I don't want this baby. She has no father," I blurt out, as if I have a choice. She's ready to come out, father or not.

"Push!" Dr. Marshall commands, and I can tell he's not the kind that takes kindly to screaming. So I push with all my might.

Finally, with one last push, the doctor takes into his hands the baby that he once told me that he would be damned if he let starve. When he puts my daughter in my arms, I'm glad that Dr. Marshall is so stubborn. I hold the only part of Erik I still have left close to me and start to cry. Mom cries with me, and I think Dr. Marshall is crying, too, or maybe smiling; it's hard to tell with his mask on.

Emma is one week old when Jerry comes for the boys, and he sees my daughter for the first time. When I offer to let him hold her, he takes her, and I think I have never seen so much hurt in his eyes as when he says, "She looks like Erik."

"Yes, she does," I agree, and we leave it at that. I hug the boys, telling them to be good, and then watch as Jerry leaves with them for the summer. He's rented a place by the ocean, and for a second I wish I were going with them. Then my daughter starts to cry. I settle myself into the big easy chair, turn on some music, and nurse Erik's and my little girl.

For a while my world consists of feeding, changing diapers, and when not rocking, I'm walking Emma. Usually the walking is at night. She has colic and I wonder when I'm supposed to get that rest Jerry promised me. Lucky for me it doesn't last long. Within a month, Emma is sleeping all night and so am I.

At first, Erik's father visits his granddaughter, but once it's warm out and I'm feeling better, I take her to his house. While I work in his yard, he sits in one of the lawn chairs and holds her. It's wonderful to see the joy Emma has brought into his lonely life. After losing his wife and son, Emma is like a breath of hope to him, and I take her to visit as often as possible.

"She looks like Erik," he says, going into the house and bringing out the album of Erik's baby pictures. We look at the pictures together and I say, "I remember when he got this bike. He rode it all over the neighborhood."

"He was always so athletic. It was like he had to be healthy because his mother wasn't. He knew how hard it was for me."

"But his grandmother lived with you for awhile, didn't she?"

"She raised Erik. That's who this little one is named after," Mr. Larson says, shifting Emma on his lap so he can show me the picture of Erik's grandmother holding Erik.

"I remember seeing her sometimes in the store. She always bought the fertilizer for her house plants there."

"Yes, she liked plants."

"So do I," I say, thinking how I have that in common with my child's namesake.

"Erik never was much for gardening, though. The only reason he got a job in your store was because of you. He always liked you, Freddy."

"He never acted like he did. Joey and I would be working in your yard and he wouldn't even say anything. He'd just jump on his bike and ride away."

"That's because girls scared him."

I start to laugh. Somehow, Erik being afraid of girls just doesn't sound quite right.

"He could have had any girl in school. I don't think they scared him."

"You scared him."

"I guess that's because I almost ran him over one day with my bike."

Now Erik's father is laughing. "He told me about that. He asked me what he could do to make you notice him."

"What did you tell him?"

"I told him to get a job at your store."

We both laugh. It's nice to sit with Erik's father and remember with him. The hard part is when I go home and go to bed, remembering how it was when Erik slept next to me, where now there is only empty space.

I work in Mrs. Davis's yard, too. Mr. Larson's and Mrs. Davis's are the only yards I work in because she baby-sits for me.

"I remember how Joey used to like tending to that flower bed over there," Mrs. Davis says, pointing to the flowers along the fence line. Then, putting Emma to her shoulder, she gets up and pours me a glass of lemonade. I fan myself with my baseball cap, sipping the cold drink that she just handed me.

"He used to get mad at me for pulling out the flowers instead of the weeds. I didn't know flowers the way Joey did. He could tell a weed from a flower while standing at the other end of the yard."

"Joey sure had a way about him. One minute he'd be mad at you, and the next he was apologizing for being mad."

"Joey could never stay mad long," I tell her, remembering how he was always so forgiving. I like talking about him with Mrs. Davis. It's at night, after I've put Emma to bed, that it's painful to remember. Lying in bed at night I sob into my pillow, begging Joey to forgive me.

I talk to the boys every night after supper and they tell me everything they've done with their father that day. They also tell me when Aunt Angela comes to visit them.

"She's living with us," Jimmy says. "She makes breakfast for us every morning."

"She's lots of fun," Ben says, "but not as much fun as you. I miss you, Mom."

"I miss you, too, and I'm glad you're, having fun with Aunt Angela," I say with a little laugh. After I hang up, I go back to cleaning up the supper dishes, banging the cupboard doors shut after every dish I put away.

A couple of weeks later, Angela calls me and, before saying anything else, I ask her, "Did you sleep with Jerry?"

She laughs and says, "Remember the day of your wedding, when you bragged that Jerry had no trouble getting it up, and I didn't believe you? Well, I believe you now."

"Damn you, Angela!" I shout and hang up. Maybe I don't want to sleep with Jerry, but I sure as hell don't want my sister to either.

By the end of summer when Jerry brings the boys back home, I have my shape back, I have a great tan, and I look reasonably happy. Jerry tells me, "You look wonderful, Freddy."

"Yeah," I say, real sarcastic. "I look almost as good as my sister. How do we compare, Jerry? Or didn't you take notes?"

"What the hell is that supposed to mean?" Jerry asks, but I don't explain, just slam the cupboard door shut after taking out a glass to serve him some lemonade. But it's not lemons in the drink that's bothering me. It's the sour taste in my mouth I have from thinking of Jerry in bed with my sister.

CHAPTER 44

There is a healing in being busy. It seems that no sooner do I get the boys off to school, and they're back home. Between taking care of Emma and her brothers, along with working at the store, I have no time to dwell on the fact that at this time last year Erik was still with us. Joey was finally home, even if he wasn't himself, and Jerry had taken my kids away from me.

Halloween gives way to Thanksgiving, and Mom suggests we go to a restaurant this year, but we kids balk at the idea.

"We'll all bring something if it's too much for you, Mom," I offer.

Brian has just walked into the store and agrees. "I'll even make the turkey."

Maybe Mom doesn't trust my cooking, but I'm sure she's even less trusting of Brian's, because she says, "I'll make the turkey. You guys can bring the rest and clean up after."

"It's a deal," I say. Then, with a meaningful smile, I whisper to Brian, but loud enough for Mom to hear, "They have real fancy paper plates at the party store, all decorated for Thanksgiving."

"No paper plates or paper napkin, either," Mom says.

"How about plastic then? I can bring the plastic forks and knives," I offer.

Mom walks away shaking her head while Brian goes back to his truck and his landscaping job.

I remember last Thanksgiving, how disappointed Joey was because I wasn't home to celebrate it with him. I quickly wipe away the tears that well up in my eyes. Then I remember when Erik came last Thanksgiving and I smile through the tears, remembering how we celebrated, mostly in bed. Lately my life is equally full of both smiles and tears, and I'm never sure which memory will produce which until it's too late.

Jerry is back at his war, but he writes often. His letters to the boys are filled with love and promises about next summer. My letters aren't exactly love letters, but they are nice. He doesn't talk about the war. I guess he figures that if I want to know, all I have to do is turn on the television.

It's a different Jerry who writes to me now, telling me about the crazy things the guys do. The crazy things he does. Even the stuff about the people that live in the country he's in. Places I've only read about in books or heard about on television. I like the Jerry in the letters, and I think I'd like him a whole lot more if he hadn't slept with my sister.

The boys are growing so fast that it's hard to keep up with clothes for them, and when I complain about this in one of my letters to Jerry, he sends me a debit card so that I can draw on his account if I need more money. When I open the letter and it falls out, I think he's lost his mind, or maybe the war is doing something to his brain. Ex-husbands don't give ex-wives free access to their bank accounts. Not if they want to keep said bank account. But I'm fair and spend everything I take out only on the boys, sending the receipts to Jerry to prove it.

"You don't have to send me the receipts. I trust you," he writes after I've done some early Christmas shopping.

"I just want you to know, I'm not spending your money on me or Emma," I write back in my next letter.

A week later, I get a call from Jerry, and one of the first things he says is, "I want you to spend some on yourself and Emma. If I meant it for just the boys, I would have increased the support payment. Why must you make such a big deal about what you spend and on whom?"

"Because the boys are still your responsibility. Emma and I aren't," I say, and I hear the hurt in his next words.

"We're not talking responsibility, Freddy." I call the boys to come and talk to their father before we both say something we might be sorry for, and I'm not talking about being mean or arguing either. Because even if I tried to argue, I don't think Jerry would. He's just so good to me lately, and I could kill Angela for sleeping with him. Out of all the guys she could have, why him?

For Jimmy's birthday his father sends him a digital camera, and from that day on there is no peace in our house. We are forever posing or if we don't pose, he takes our picture anyway. After seeing some of the photos he's taken, I try to pose every time he says, "Smile." He sends his father pictures of us sleeping, eating, watching television, and on every outing, even to the grocery store. There is one picture of me he takes and sends to his father that, had I seen it first, I would have ripped it up. I still have on my nightshirt, bending over to pick up Emma, and all I can say is I'm sure glad I have underwear on. Jerry writes after getting that picture and wants to know when I started wearing panties under my nightshirt.

"You never used to when I slept with you," he writes.

"When I started having kids that sneak up on me, especially with a camera," I write back, then go out and buy myself a pair of pajamas, taking the money out of Jerry's account.

Sending daddy pictures of family and outings to the grocery store is boring, and one weekend, Jimmy begs to go someplace interesting. I can't take him to Disney World like his father promised to take them next summer, but I do promise to take him for a ride in the country.

"Right after church," I promise, like first you have to earn it by being good in church. Mrs. Davis is delighted when I tell her that we'll go to church with her, then for a ride after. She's been after me to return to the fold after rebelling against God for taking so much. Mrs. Davis promises to take us out for lunch after, as if first I have to earn it by repenting.

The day is unseasonably warm for November, and I wonder if maybe God is rewarding me for coming back. Jimmy and Ben sit next to each other until Jimmy takes Ben's hymn book, and Ben hits Jimmy on the head with mine. I take all the hymnals, put them back in their rack on the pew in front of me. I put Jimmy on one side of me and Ben on the other side, all faster than the congregation can sing one chorus of "A Mighty Fortress is Our God." And I thank God that I left Emma home with Mom.

At the restaurant, I'm a little smarter and separate the boys right away, putting Mrs. Davis in between on one side and me on the other. Of course, that doesn't stop them from arguing across the table. And before we finally get to dessert, I've heard more of "Have too," and "Have Not" than any one person should have to bear, especially on a day of rest like a Sunday.

On our way out of the restaurant, I make a suggestion. "Let's go see that new subdivision that Carl and Brian are landscaping."

"Do we have to?" Jimmy asks.

"It's only a bunch of houses and dirt," Ben says.

"I didn't like the last one you took us to see," Mrs. Davis says.

"I want to see some cows," Jimmy says.

"I want to see some horses," Ben says.

"I just want to see something different than houses, especially those houses," Mrs. Davis says as if I were suggesting we join ranks with the Devil. She doesn't like the new subdivision being built outside of town anymore than the last one built we visited where the developer cut down a bunch of trees. In fact, it was a whole forest, to make room for houses.

"It's progress," I say. Then when they all turn their noses up at progress, I add, "We'll take the long way and see cows and horses, Okay?"

We kick up clouds of dirt driving on country roads, with loose gravel hitting under the car, looking for cows and horses. When we finally come to a pasture of cows Jimmy has to get out to take a picture. Of course, we all have to pose in front of the fenced-in cows, just to prove to Daddy that we were there.

When we come to a white fence with horses corralled in it, we have to get out so Ben can reach through and pet the nose of one of the horses. We all stand in front of the fence to prove once again to Daddy that the horses are real, and that Ben actually petted one. Mrs. Davis doesn't have to prove anything and sits back against the car seat saying over and over, "This is God's country, Freddy. You don't have to go to church to feel the presence of God. You just have to come here." Now she tells me, after I suffered through one hour of keeping two 'hells-on-wheels' quiet.

When we get to the subdivision none of us gets

out. It's not the kind of place we want Jerry to see, and I wish to God I hadn't suggested it.

"Joey would hate this place," Jimmy says.

"Yeah, there's no flowers," Ben says.

"My God, they cut down all the trees, every last one of them," Mrs. Davis says, and I think that even progress is no excuse for this devastation. No matter how much money is involved, even the money we're making on the landscaping.

"They'll plant more trees," I say. "Just as soon as Carl and Brian get everything evened out and plant grass."

"There were trees, nice big ones. They didn't have to cut everything down," Mrs. Davis says, like it was all my idea.

"That's how developers work. It's easier to remove them than work around them," I say, heading the car back home.

After that, Jimmy is content to take pictures of us doing what we do best: working, eating, sleeping, and shopping. He sends Jerry pictures of our Thanksgiving dinner, all of us seated at the big table. There is even a picture of us cleaning up after. There are pictures of Christmas carolers that come one night to our house, and a photo of Santa standing on the street corner ringing his bell. Jerry gets a blow-by-blow account of the Christmas pageant Ben is in, first in a letter from Ben, and then with pictures from Jimmy. There's even a picture of Ben sprawled out on the floor after he tripped on his Wise Man's robe. Of course, the story wouldn't be complete without one of him crying after the teacher runs on stage to pick him up.

There are dozens of pictures of us trimming the tree and wrapping presents. On Christmas Eve, Jimmy takes pictures of us opening the presents, especially the ones from Jerry. And there's one picture of me in a red robe after the opening, surrounded by bright wrapping paper. I'm staring into the fireplace, a blazing fire casting shadows on my face when Jimmy says "Smile." I look up just in time as the flash goes off.

Either I'm getting better at posing or Jimmy is getting better at picture taking, but that picture is Christmas. In that one picture is captured the hope, the promise, and mostly wonder. My eyes sparkle with the love and peace that should be in every "Merry Christmas" that we wish someone.

I don't tell anyone that the wonder is actually me wondering how I'm going to get rid of all the paper, hoping I don't burn the house down if I throw it on the fire, and promising myself that next year I'm going to buy those gift bags you can use year after year. The peace and love come from the fact that all three of my kids are here with me and ready for bed.

Our holiday unfolds in a colorful story of words and pictures to Jerry, and I think Jerry misses us more than his letters say because he calls right after New Year's and tells me he's planning on coming home for Easter.

"Can I spend Easter with you and Emma and the boys?" he asks.

"We're invited to Mom's for Easter."

"You mean your mother will mind if I come along?"

"I mean Angela and Harry will be there," and I emphasize Angela's name. "Don't you think it will be a little awkward, considering?" I don't explain the considering. I figure Jerry can fill in the rest.

"I can live with that."

"Well, I can't," I say, wishing Jimmy or Ben were here. Now would be a good time to call them to come and talk to their father.

"Then come to New York to me. I promise you won't have to cook; I'll do it."

"Emma's teething. It would just be miserable for all of us."

"You always have an excuse, don't you, Freddy?"

"I'm a mother, Jerry, what else can I say?"

"You were always a mother, Freddy, even to Joey."

I don't say anything to that. It's hard talking with a lump in the throat.

"Do you mind if I carry your picture in my wallet?" he asks, and I hope to God it's not the one of me in my nightshirt.

"What picture?"

"The one of you by the fire at Christmas."

"Where do you keep your wallet?" I ask.

"In my breast pocket, like I always have."

"Okay, you can carry my picture in your wallet," I say, thinking it's one thing to have my nose rubbed in the dirt; it's another to have him sitting on my face.

After that we don't talk about Easter anymore, and the boys are okay with staying home with the promise that as soon as they're out of school, they get to go with their dad to Disney World.

"Come with us, Mommy," Ben pleads two weeks before school lets out, and I'm in the boys' bedroom pulling out clothes, making a mental note of what still fits, and what I have to buy.

"Daddy hasn't asked me," I say absent-mindedly, immediately forgetting what I just answered to. But Ben doesn't. A week before the boys are to leave, Jerry calls me.

"Ben said if I ask, that you'll come with us. Will you, Freddy? I can send you a ticket. I'll get you and Emma a room."

Jerry sounds excited, like it's a done deal, but the only thing done is one hell of a mistake.

"Jerry, I have no intention of going with you. Emma's too young to go away for a week."

"She's a year old. Parents take their kids like Emma to Disney World all the time."

"We're not her parents, Jerry. You're not," I say without thinking again, but it stops Jerry dead in his tracks, and I wish that just once I'd think before I speak, or at least keep my mouth shut. Jerry's real polite after that, and I know we're back to either polite or fight.

The night before the boys are to be picked up by

Jerry, Ben asks me again to go, but Jimmy doesn't ask. He just tells me what he thinks.

"You don't like Dad, do you, Mom?"

"I never said that, Jimmy."

"You don't have to, I can tell. How can you hate Dad so much and still love us?"

"Mom doesn't hate Dad, she loves him," Ben says in my defense. "She told me she does."

"Did not," Jimmy says.

"Did too," Ben argues, and I stand speechless. My kids are fighting over whether or not I love their father.

After about three rounds of "Did not," and "Did too," I finally regain control and say, "The reason I can't go with is because Emma is too little to walk and too heavy to carry. I can't expect Jerry to haul her around, can I?"

"We can put her in a stroller," Jimmy suggests.

"Emma gets fussy in a stroller."

"I'll carry her, Mom," Ben volunteers.

I think I might cry for the difficulty of it all. They don't understand about last summer. They only know that Aunt Angela made them breakfast every morning and she was fun during the day. They don't know about the nights after they were in bed.

"Let's skip the story and say our prayers," I say. "We have to be up early tomorrow."

We all kneel at the beds and do the "God Bless" prayer, putting emphasis on Mickey Mouse and all the inhabitants of the Magic Kingdom. It's a long prayer, and I'm grateful when we finally say, "Amen," so I can get up off my knees and quietly leave. I stand outside the door for a while, listening to make sure that they stay in bed when I hear two little voices pleading with God. Obviously "Amen" wasn't the end of their prayers.

"Please, God, make Mommy love Daddy again, and make her say yes and come with us."

I go into my bedroom and lie down on the bed, wondering why God's divine intervention seems more like a commandment. Then, after a half-hour of trying to make up my mind, I reach for the phone and call Jerry.

"Is it too late for me to change my mind and come with you and the boys?"

"No, it's not too late. But how come you changed your mind?"

"Divine intervention," I say. Before Jerry can ask me what the hell I mean by that, I say, "Instead of you coming here to pick us up, I'll meet you at the airport."

"I'm not going to make you handle three kids all by yourself. I'll come and get you."

"When I get to the airport, I'm going to dump two of them on you," I say, laughing like it's a joke, but it's not. I really mean to let him handle Ben and Jimmy. I'm going to have my hands full with Emma.

The next morning with three kids and more baggage than I thought we had clothes, I take a taxi to the airport. I'm already at the gate and waiting for Jerry, looking at the clock every couple of minutes, thinking that he'll never make it on time. I'll be stuck going to Disney World with three little kids, all by myself. Ben plays with Emma while Jimmy watches out the window as our plane is loaded. It's time to board, and I'm wondering if I should chance it, hoping that maybe when I get to Florida, Jerry will catch up, when he comes running to the gate.

"What happened?" I ask.

"The damn plane was late," he says, taking Emma out of my arms so that now he's juggling a baby, a car seat, and his own carry-on.

"Jerry, you don't have to do it all," I say, taking the car seat. The boys run ahead on the jetway, then wait for us to catch up at the door of the plane. It's a scramble stowing the gear, getting us all seated, and finally all buckled in. After that, it's a piece of cake for me. Jerry has his hands full, though. Emma has taken a liking to Jerry and wants him by her side while we take off. She wants him next to her while we're finally up, and he has to share with her when she has a snack.

"Mommy can feed you," I say, holding out the spoon to her.

She pushes my hand away, and when Jerry takes the spoon and holds it out to her, she eats.

"I'm sorry," I say to Jerry. "She usually doesn't take to strangers like this."

"Daddy's no stranger. Is he, Emma?" Ben says, leaning across the aisle to put in his two cents' worth. And I swear Emma understands every word Ben says, because she gives Jerry this great big laugh, an Erik kind of laugh. And I think my heart will break.

Once we're at Disney World, it's the same thing. Jerry's the one who has to hold her on the rides, or when the rides are too scary, he waits while I take the boys. People smile when they see us. We look so perfect, so much like a family, but they don't know that Mommy has one room and Daddy has another. I get used to it all. I even tell myself that I'm happy it's all working out so well, until Emma calls Jerry "Da-Da." Then I know that I have to leave. I can't go to the beach house with them like Jerry wants me to.

The night before we're suppose to leave, while I'm helping the boys get ready for bed in Jerry's room, Jerry is in my room rocking Emma to sleep, I tell them I'm not going. I go through the same questions that I did the night before I got myself into this mess, but this time when they accuse me of not liking Daddy, I'm ready.

"It's not a matter of liking. It's just that sometimes people do things to each other that make it hard for them to be together."

"It's because Dad took us to live with him. That's why Mom hates him," Jimmy tells Ben.

"Maybe Daddy can tell Mom he's sorry," Ben says, struggling with the tops of his pajamas; he has them inside out.

I turn them right-side out, all the while explaining, "Sometimes just saying you're sorry isn't enough."

"But when Jimmy and I argue, you tell us to say

we're sorry and we have to forgive each other. That's what Mrs. Davis says, that God forgives no matter what."

"Well, there are some things even God doesn't have to put up with," I say, thinking that I don't remember reading in the Bible that he had a sister. We are his children, so God has to love us.

"Let's pray," I say, and decide to sit on the bed while the boys kneel. After the prayer I get up to go to my room, but first I pause to think of what the boys just said about forgiveness.

"Please, God, let Mommy forgive Daddy, so she can like him again." Ben's voice comes to me out of the shadows.

"And let Mom like him enough to say yes and come to the beach house with us tomorrow." Jimmy's voice floats past me just like Ben's did a minute ago.

When I go through the door to our adjoining rooms, I touch Jerry's shoulder to wake him up, and then take a sleeping Emma out of his arms.

"What time did you say we have to leave for the airport tomorrow?" I whisper over my sleeping daughter's head.

"Ten o'clock," Jerry answers.

"I'll be ready."

CHAPTER 45

The afternoon sun shines on the water, creating a shimmering mirage of light blue. Only the sailboats, like white flags floating on the blue, tell me all this is real. We drive along the highway that runs parallel to the ocean in our rented van, passing houses that look like they might be swallowed up by the water. They're built on stilts just in case. There are houses that I think rich people must live in, because they're the only ones who could afford them. Right now, I don't care what kind of house we are headed to-I just want to get there.

"Hey, Dad?" Jimmy gets Jerry's attention. "Can we go sailing again this year?"

I look over at Jerry, like he's trying to ignore the question and I ask, "You took them sailing? You don't know how to sail. Or do you?"

"Angela took them; I didn't."

"You trusted Angela in a boat alone with my kids? She doesn't know how to swim, let alone sail a boat," I say, not at all pleased with this news.

"Some old guy who lives around here owns a sailboat, and he took them," Jerry says casually. Too casually, and it's making me anxious.

"How old?" I ask, thinking that not only did Jerry put their physical lives in danger, but also their innocence. Put Angela on a boat alone with a man and who knows what could happen? And right in front of my sons, no less.

"Freddy, he's too old, even for Angela."

"Are you sure?" I ask, kind of doubtful. I consider maybe he is telling the truth, but then, maybe not.

"I'm sure."

"But how can you be so sure?" I ask.

"I just am, okay?" I can tell he's beginning to get irritated, and I don't want to fight anymore. I'm so tired of fighting. So I let it go. After all, Jerry *was* sleeping with her, and he would know if she came back too tired.

Emma is fascinated with the word *Da Da* and repeats it over and over. I can't tell her to stop, not when I don't tell Ben and Jimmy to stop calling Jerry "Daddy."

I turn to look back and say to Ben sitting next to her, "Would you give her a cracker, honey?"

"She doesn't want one, Mom. I tried a little while ago, but she spit it out all over the car seat."

"Maybe she would like her teddy bear."

"She doesn't want that either. She threw it in back by Jimmy."

"She's okay, Mom," Jimmy pipes up way in back. "She's just practicing her talking. It doesn't bother us."

We make a quick stop to pick up some groceries. Jerry goes in while I stay in the car and wait with the kids. After about another half hour of listening to

"Da-Da" we pull up in front of a gray clapboard cottage with a deck-like porch running clear around, and I wonder how in the hell did Jerry ever find this place? There are no houses here, rich or otherwise. Just this weather-beaten, not very big cottage. Maybe he wanted to hide when he first came here, but I don't think it was from me. It's not like I was ever looking for him. I decide that maybe Angela was the one. Not to hide from, but with.

Once we are in the house, after dragging in suitcases and storing away groceries, Jerry shows me to my room; the boys already know where theirs is.

"This is the room Angela stayed in," Jerry explains, like I really care about this room. It's *his* room that bothers me.

"You mean one of them, right?"

"There are only three bedrooms in this house, Freddy," Jerry says, and I wonder if he really is that dense or have all the years of war affected his ability to take a hint.

After Jerry leaves, I search the room to make sure there's no trace of Angela left, and then check out the crib, which definitely wasn't here when Angela occupied this room. I know, because while I was putting away groceries, Jerry dragged it out of storage somewhere and set it up. I put on the sheets and supply the blanket. After putting Emma down for her nap, I go out onto the little balcony off my room. Leaning against the railing I look out across the loneliness of it all. I ask myself what am I doing here anyway, but I don't want to know. I can blame God for Divine Intervention, but these old feelings for Jerry, the ones that I once felt when he kissed me in the snow, keep slipping into my conscious and I don't like it. I'm supposed to hate him. I am the ex-wife betrayed twice. Well, maybe not twice, but his sleeping with Angela is all it takes.

I go back inside through the door in my room, taking a peek at Emma, now sound asleep, then go to check out the rest of the house, starting with the boys' room.

"Hey, guys, this is really nice," I say, noting the big-screen television, the CD player, and, of course, a video game hooked up to the television.

"I like home better," Ben says.

"This is better than home," Jimmy says.

"Is not," Ben says.

"Is too," Jimmy says.

I say "For now it is home, so let's enjoy ourselves, okay?"

On my way downstairs, I stand by the door to Jerry's room and wonder if I should knock. Just what does his room look like? Does his have a large-screen television, too? Mine doesn't, but then if Angela wanted to watch television she could just watch it in Jerry's room. I don't think they watched television, and I wonder again just what am I doing here anyway? Maybe God works in mysterious ways, but it's still a mystery what Jerry ever saw in Angela. I always thought he had better taste.

I head for the stairs, and when I get into the living room, Jerry is sprawled out on the couch watching television. It's one of those super-big screens and I say, "Doesn't anybody around here ever go fishing and swim, or just go for a walk on the beach?"

"I don't like fishing or swimming, but if you want to go for a walk with the boys, I'll watch Emma," he offers, but I decide he's not getting off that easy.

"We can all go when Emma wakes up," I say, and settle down next to Jerry to watch the big super-size screen.

We both nod off, and when I wake up I'm curled up against Jerry with his arms around me. Just like how we used to watch television in that little house of his a lifetime ago. I pull myself up, apologizing, while Jerry just lays back staring at me.

"You don't have to apologize, Freddy. I don't mind."

"But I do," I say, real huffy like as I get up to check on Emma. When I come downstairs again I'm carrying my daughter, dressed in a little sun suit and covered with sunscreen from head to toe for our walk on the beach. I have on shorts and a T-shirt, with my baseball cap pulled down over my forehead.

"You guys ready to go for a walk?" I call upstairs, and suddenly it sounds like a herd of cattle instead of two boys running down the steps.

While the boys run ahead, gathering seashells, Jerry and I walk, with Emma on Jerry's shoulders. We all stop for a while and play in the sand, until the sun starts going down. Leaving sandcastles and footprints behind, we shuffle through the sand in bare feet back to the house.

"I'm hungry enough to eat a horse," Jerry says.

That doesn't sit too well with Ben, so I say, "You mean a cow, don't you?"

Of course, that doesn't sit too well with Jimmy, so I say, "Let's have hot dogs." And I just hope to God the boys don't want to know what those're made of.

We eat hot dogs cooked on the grill. Emma eats cooked carrots and mashed potatoes. For dessert we all have ice cream. Emma's ice cream ends up in her hair, along with the carrots and mashed potatoes.

"Why does she always eat so messy?" Ben asks.

"Because she's a girl, and girls are messy," Jimmy explains.

"Are not," Ben says.

"Are too," Jimmy says. "Dad said Aunt Angela is messy, and she's a girl," my son adds, like it's a matter of fact.

"Dad said Aunt Angela is a pig," Ben says. "He didn't say she's messy."

"It's the same thing," Jimmy says.

"Is not." Ben says.

I ask Jerry, "Is that what you said?"

"Not exactly like that. I told her that when she gets through in a kitchen, it looks like a pigsty. I ended up cleaning up after her all the time."

"Now you know how I used to feel sharing a bathroom with her," I say, getting up to clear off the table. I make a show of just how neat I am by not just scraping off the dishes before putting them in the dishwasher, but rinsing them, too. Jerry helps me with the scraping and rinsing, loading the dishwasher like a pro. No wonder Angela liked it here. Not only is he good in bed, but he's really good at housework, too. We all sit and watch the big super-size screen in the living room until bedtime.

While I get Emma ready, Jerry gets the boys ready. Finally we have the house all picked up and the kids all tucked in, and we go out on the porch to watch the stars come out. It's so quiet, with only the sound of waves breaking on shore and I wonder again how Jerry ever found a place like this.

"It's so deserted around here. How did you find this place anyway, Jerry?"

"Don't you like it?" Jerry asks, like I've just said I don't like his favorite football team.

"It is wonderful. It's so peaceful. Now I know why you come here every summer. After covering a war, a person has to find peace someplace."

"Just the last couple of summers. Before that I could never get the time off. Now I threaten to quit and I get off."

"What would you do if they let you quit?"

"Then I'd have to look for another job."

"I thought it was your dream job. That's what you told me once."

"It's not anymore," Jerry says, and we both lapse into silence as we remember that time in our lives, a time when we still had dreams.

"What's the war like, Jerry? I mean, you talk about it on television like it's all a bunch of facts. You stand in front of a bombed-out building or in front of some dead bodies and use the words *carnage* and *destruction*, but what's it really like?"

"It's not just death and destruction, Freddy. It's insanity. There are kids who, instead of learning in school how to make the world better, are on a battlefield learning to use a gun to kill. There're mothers who, instead of raising their children, are burying them. Instead of weddings, they're going to funerals."

"Once Erik took me up in his plane. It was so quiet up there, so beautiful. It's hard to believe that killing can be beautiful. But that's what killed Erik-- flying in a plane."

"At least he was doing what he loved. War isn't about love. It's about hate."

"Jimmy thinks war is a game. He watches you on television talking about it and says he wants to be like you."

"I'll have to do something about that."

"How?" I ask. "If you're thinking of just telling him not to, it won't work. I've already tried."

"By taking him fishing and swimming."

"I thought you don't like those things."

"I'd rather set an example for being a lousy fisherman than somebody who talks about war like it's just a lot of facts and statistics."

"Why do you do it, Jerry? You said Erik died doing what he loved, but why do you cover a war when it's all about hate?"

"Because people have to know what hate can do. We can't sit on the other side of the world and pretend that hate doesn't exist."

I suddenly feel cold, and I take the blanket lying across one of the chairs and wrap myself in it.

"I don't want to lose you, Jerry," I say, surprised at the sound of the words, that I actually said what I am thinking.

Jerry comes and stands over me, then kneeling down, he cups my face in his hand and he says, "Then marry me, Freddy. Give me a reason to want to stay here."

"You have the boys."

"It's not enough. I need you, too."

I pull away, turning my face from his. "I can't. Don't ask me to."

"Because of Erik? I know I'll always be second-best, but I can live with that. It's you I can't live without."

"It's not because of Erik."

"Then why? Is it because I took the boys? I never wanted to hurt you. For those times I made you mad, I'm sorry, Freddy. I never wanted a divorce. I thought if I forced a decision, you would come to New York. All I ever wanted was to love you and you to love me back."

I turn to look at him. I have to see his face when I accuse him.

"Because you slept with my sister," I spit out the words like a person spits out poison. I have kept this poison inside me too long, eating away at my pride; now I'm finally rid of it. Jerry stands up and stares down at me in disbelief.

"My God, is that what all those remarks were

about? You think I fucked Angela?"

"She said you did."

"And you believe her? You actually believe that lying little bitch?"

"Don't call her that. She's still my sister."

"Yeah, well, she's not mine," Jerry says, starting to walk away but then turns back to me and says, "The only reason I let her stay was for the boys' sake, and because I knew you would be mad if I kept them away from her. I haven't been with a woman since I kicked Lisa out."

"I thought you said you didn't kick her out."

"I lied," Jerry says, then marching through the door into the house, goes up the stairs, slamming the door to his room.

I stay out on the porch and watch the stars light up the sky. I read once that by the time I see the light, some of the stars are already dead, and I wonder if now that I've finally seen the light, that I finally know the depth of Jerry's love, is it too late? He was so mad, even saying that *F* word that he detests. He looked so hurt when he went upstairs. I stare at the stars and wonder how I could have been so stupid. I wear myself out with wondering, so I go in the house and upstairs to my room.

I lie in bed and listen to the soft stirrings of my daughter sleeping. I toss and turn and pound my pillow into submission. Finally I get out of bed and march over to Jerry's room and knock on the door. When he tells me to come in, I march over to his bed, look down at him, without blinking even once, I say, "Yes."

"Yes what?" he asks, putting down the book he's reading, taking off his glasses.

I answer, "Yes, I'll marry you."

For a while we both stare at each other, like we've both lost our minds, then Jerry reaches up and pulls me into bed with him.

"It's been awhile since we've been with someone. Do you think we still remember what to do?" I say, wondering if my voice is as nervous as I am.

"Sex is like riding a bicycle. Once you learn, you never forget," Jerry says, lifting my nightshirt up and finding no underwear.

"I have a reputation for running people over with a bicycle," I say, reaching down to see if I still have that magic touch.

"I'll be careful," Jerry says.

I think, where have I heard that before? I've got three reasons to believe that being careful doesn't always work.

Just before falling asleep, I go to take one last check on Emma, leaving the doors to both bedrooms open so I can hear if she needs me.

I ask, "Did the boys say their prayers tonight?"

"Uh-huh," Jerry answers in a sleepy voice, adjusting his body to make room for mine.

"When they did their God Bless prayer, they didn't sneak in a 'Make Mommy say yes,' did they?"

"I don't think so; why?"

"Nothing," I say. "I was just wondering."

"Your feet are cold," Jerry says when I put mine next to his.

"Do you mind?" I ask, ready to move away.

He pulls me close and says, "I never did before. Did I?"

"No," I say, cuddling up to his warmth. "There were a lot of things I used to do when we were together in the beginning that you didn't mind."

"I don't now either." Then in a soft voice, like he always did in the beginning, just before we would fall asleep, he says, "I love you, Freddy." And it's like a sentence without a period after.

"I sure am tired. Emma gets me up so early." I say, trying to ignore that sentence without a period.

"I'll get up with her and you can sleep in tomorrow morning," Jerry offers.

"Jerry, you don't have to." I want to add that she's my responsibility, but I don't think now is a good time to remind him that Emma's not his.

"But I want to," Jerry argues.

"You don't have to." I argue back.

"But I want to," And I think we're beginning to sound like our boys.

It's quiet, so quiet that I think maybe he's fallen asleep, but I know he hasn't. He's just waiting, and I put the period after the sentence.

"I love you, too, Jerry." And for a minute the words sound strange. Then I remember how it used to be in the beginning, and they don't sound strange anymore. And I think Mrs. Davis is right about 'Forgiveness' and 'Divine Intervention.' I just don't know what comes first, the intervention or the forgiveness. I just know that 'Love' comes first and last.

"He's back, Daddy, and I think this time it's to

stay," I whisper into the dark. The only sound is Jerry's breathing softly in his sleep. I will let him sleep. After all, he has to get up early with Emma. I get to sleep in.

CHAPTER 46

One Year Later

The mail comes, and after sorting out the bills from the junk mail I take the letter I got from Mom and lay it on the table to take with me to read outside later. I put Jerry's and my newest addition to our family into her stroller and wheel her outside through the big French doors onto the patio. Before I settle down to read, I call to Emma, who's digging up worms with Jimmy and Ben. "Come here and I'll give you a push."

I walk over to the swing hanging from the big tree next to the patio and wait while Emma comes running as fast as her little legs can go. She loves being pushed on the swing even more than digging in dirt. I strap her in and give her a couple of good pushes saying, "Whee! Emma's flying!" with just about every push, then go to check on my sleeping baby.

I've put off reading Mom's letter for as long as I could, but now I've run out of excuses, and I pick up the envelope. When I open it, a check comes fluttering out. I examine the card the check fell out of. It says, "Happy Anniversary," and inside where Mom and Carl signed their names, she's added a few

words of her own. "Maybe you can use some of this
to buy a dog." The thought of buying Jerry a dog for
our anniversary makes me want to laugh.

Jerry doesn't like dogs. He doesn't like walking
them, feeding them, and especially cleaning up after
them, but I can't get Mom to understand this. Ever
since the gun episode Mom is on a crusade for
people to throw out their guns and get dogs. Jerry
and I don't blame Mom for having the gun. She
didn't even know it was still in the house. She
thought Daddy got rid of it before he died. It was
Jimmy who told me it was left loaded in plain view
on the closet shelf, but the truth is, Jimmy knew
about that gun being in one of Daddy's old tackle
boxes for a long time. It just took him a while to
find the bullets and figure out how to put them in
the gun. I lay the check on the patio table with the
card, then and give Emma a couple of more pushes.
After I've got her squealing with happiness, I go
back to read the letter.

"Dear Felicia," Mom writes. She always starts out
real formal-like.

"I hope this letter finds you and your family in
good health, and that you and Jerry have a Happy
Anniversary." Mom is still into formalities, and I sort
of skip over all that until I get to what Jerry calls "the
meat and potatoes part", where Mom scolds me.

"I thought by now you would have the dog that
you promised you'd get as soon as you moved out of
Jerry's apartment, but it's almost six months now

and you still haven't gotten one. If you can't afford it after all the expense of buying the house, you should have told me. That's why I'm sending you a check instead of a present. Go buy that dog. You can't afford not to."

I think of that present she talked about sending, glad that it's a check and not the dog. I take the letter along with me when I go to give Emma another push. Reading and pushing can sure take a lot out of you, especially when it's a letter from your mother bawling you out, and before long I go back to the table and sit down.

"We finally sold the store, and have decided to sell the house, too, but I think you should come home and help," her letter continues. "I have no idea what to do with all your things that are still left here. Besides, I haven't seen my grandchildren since I came out there when Katey was born. She is already three months old, so she should be able to travel. At least that's what I told Carl, and he thinks so, too."

After this bit of news, I have to put the letter down again. Mom is selling our house. The house that we kids grew up in. Where Joey and I used to play together in the yard. I go to the stroller where Katey is sleeping and take a tissue from my pocket to wipe my eyes. Boy, Mom sure knows how to wish a person a Happy Anniversary. I take my time going back to reading, then decide that maybe there's some good news. She's already scolded me and told me the bad; what's left?

"By the way, Angela has finally made it big. She has a starring role in a movie. I always said she was the one with talent in our family. I can't wait to see it."

I should have known there was more. It's time to brag about Angela, that's what comes next, and I just hope for Mom's sake that the starring role has nothing to do with taking her clothes off. You don't need talent to screw on a super-size screen. You just have to look good, say stupid things, and have a big mouth. All are attributes of Angela.

"I hope you don't mind, but I helped Harold out with some of the money from the sale of the store. He's having financial trouble again, and on top of that, his wife is filing for a divorce."

By now, I'm wishing that I had read the formalities and skipped the rest, until Mom adds on the bottom of the last page:

"I wish Angela and Harold had the common sense you have, Felicia. You're married to a good man, have a beautiful home and four beautiful children. What more could any woman want?"

"Nothing, Mom," I say, folding the letter in half. "I've got everything I want."

Then, noting on the half still showing, the formal ending, "Love always, your mother, Margaret".

I always get a kick out of the way Mom always signs her letters, like she has to identify herself. Like maybe I have more than one mother.

Because of my habit of skipping over formalities, I almost miss it. At the very end, like a postscript Mom adds,

"They finally recovered Erik's body and his father

buried him next to his mother."

I put my head on the table, cradling it in my arms and soak my sleeves with tears, little puddles forming on the table.

It's a hot summer day, but I'm so cold that I start to shiver. "I *don't* have everything I want, Mom." I sob, "I don't have Erik, and I wanted him the most of all."

I sit for a long time remembering Erik. Amazed that after all this time, I can still remember how I felt every time he touched me. I keep my head on the table and I don't hear the boys arguing in the yard. I don't even hear my baby start to cry. I finally come to when Emma calls, "Mommy, push me!"

I take more tissue to wipe my eyes, then go to push her. Before I push, I bend down and kiss the top of her head. Her soft blonde hair, so much like Erik's, and I know that Jerry was right that night he told me he knows he's second-best. I love Jerry, but not like I love Erik. Just like Mom loves Carl, but not like she still loves Daddy.

I give Emma a couple of pushes, then take Katey out of the stroller to nurse her. Katey is three months old, and I'm not sure, but I suspect that Jerry wasn't as careful that night as he promised. But then Angela never accused me of being pregnant at the wedding, so maybe I wasn't. Of course, Angela might be wrong, and that makes me feel good.

While Katey nurses, I run my hand over her head. The fuzz of new hair soft on my fingertips, thinking that, of all my children, Katey looks the most like me, with red hair and all. When Katey was born, it was the first time the father was with me, and not my mother. I think my mother was happy about that, and so was I. I got to scream at the father for a change, but when the doctor handed Jerry our baby he forgot all about the screaming, and I think he cried. When he kissed me, his cheeks were wet. Jerry finally got his Katey O'Hara. I think Mom would have preferred something more impressive. I'm not into impressive so just plain Katey, no middle name, is fine with me. But I think if Jerry's mom were still alive, she'd work a Scarlett in somewhere. Emma calls for another push. I call to Jimmy, but not so loud that it startles the child sleeping close to my heart. When Jimmy doesn't pay attention, Emma calls again and maybe Jimmy doesn't come, but Ben does.

I'm done nursing and ready to burp her when Jerry walks out onto the patio. His tall frame steps through the open patio doors, and then he closes it behind. Jerry is tall, good-looking and still slim, and I think there are some women out in television-land that envy me. Especially my sister, but Jerry says, he would rather stand in front of a firing squad without a blindfold than take her into his bed. Jerry is good-looking, but not as good-looking as Erik. Nobody is as handsome as Erik, except my Dad.

"You're home early," I say, looking up, and Jerry comes and leans over, first to kiss me, then kissing the fuzz on Katey's head.

"I figured you might need some help with the

packing," Jerry says, straightening up.

"I'm all through," I say, "but these kids got me all pooped out."

Jerry starts to laugh. Then he takes Katey from me saying, "It's usually the other way around; it's the kids that are all pooped out. Do you want me to change Katey?"

"Not this time, but she does need to be burped," and while Jerry goes about the task of burping Katey, I go about the task of telling Jerry about the letter. There are some parts I decide to leave out, but I'm not sure what. I can't just tell him about the formal part. Jerry knows my mother better than that.

"Mom still wants us to get a dog," I say, showing him the check. "She even sent us some money, thinking we can't afford one."

"We can't," Jerry says. "We can barely afford the kids."

"Oh come on, Jerry. How much can a dog cost anyway?"

"When you figure in the feeding, the walking, and the cleaning up, a dog can be expensive. Not to mention fixing it and other vet expenses. I don't mind changing a dirty diaper now and then, but I'm not cleaning up after a dog."

"I will," I say, but I already know the argument to that.

"You already have enough to do. I'll end up doing it"

"The boys will"

"No they won't, and you'll end up doing it. You won't have time, so we're back to my doing it."

"But Mom says a dog is safer than having a gun."

"Honey, we don't have a gun either, so what are you so worried about?"

I decide to drop the dog subject. Besides, I've heard all these arguments before. I'll never change Jerry's mind, and so instead, I change the subject, saying, "Mom and Carl sold the store and are thinking of selling the house. She wants me to come and sort out all the stuff I left behind when I moved in with you."

"Tell her to throw it away. All that's left is clothes that don't fit the boys anymore, and some other junk."

"Not all junk," I say, thinking of the locket and ring that are still in a drawer in my room. The other ring from Erik, the expensive one along with a diamond necklace and earrings are in a safety deposit box, waiting for Emma to get old enough for me to give it to her. A gift from her Daddy, for when she is old enough to understand how it really was between her parents and not what the newspapers wrote.

"Angela is starring in a movie," I say real fast, like I will get that part over before Jerry even realizes I've mentioned her name. We don't mention her very often in this house, not since Jerry found out all the lies she told me about him.

"So she finally screwed her way to the top," Jerry says with a laugh, and I go over to him and hit him playfully.

"Jesus, Jerry, she's still my sister."

"Yeah, but she's not mine."

"You told me once you always wanted a brother or sister."

"After meeting yours, I've changed my mind. So, what did Mom say about Harry? Anything good this time?"

"He's broke and getting a divorce," I say, and decide to forget about the letter. There is no way I'm going to mention Erik's name now.

"What time do you want to start out tomorrow for the beach house?" I ask, changing the subject again.

"Whenever you're ready."

"Our vacation might be over by then. Or were you able to get more time off than three weeks?"

"Not exactly," Jerry says, shifting Katey to his other shoulder.

"What do you mean, not exactly? Either your threat worked or it didn't."

"They made me another offer," he says, like if he doesn't elaborate, the whole thing will just pass.

"What kind of offer? You didn't actually quit, did you? Jerry, we can't afford that."

"They want me to go back overseas. They said they'd double my salary."

For a minute I think I heard Jerry wrong, then it dawns on me that nothing has really changed, except now I've got more kids to raise by myself.

"I guess it was too good to last, wasn't it?"

"Does this mean you're kicking me out of your bed again?"

I get up from the table like I have this weight holding me down. I believed and I trusted, but in the end it turns out the same. I look out across the green grass at the flowerbeds that I've taken care of by myself, weeding and planting alone, remembering when I wasn't always alone. When I still had Joey. I wonder if this is the silent death I once told Jerry about, and I say, "No, it just means that while you're gone, I'll be sleeping alone."

My voice must sound like I'm crying. I'm sure there must be some tears in it somewhere, because Jerry says, "Sweetheart, I didn't take the job."

I hear the words, but at first I don't believe them until I look at Jerry and see that he's grinning.

"So you quit instead. Well, I'd rather have an unemployed husband than an absent one."

"Nope! Actually, they gave me a better job. I get to anchor my own news show, prime time at that, and double the salary. We can even afford more kids."

"Damn you, Jerry, you were testing me, weren't you? Just to see what I'd say. Why didn't you tell me the good news first?" I ask, going over to hit him, and it won't be playfully. He deserves it, even with a baby in his arms. Our baby.

"You sure know how to give a woman an anniversary present. You couldn't just send me flowers or something normal, could you?" Now I think I'll hit him. But before I get the chance, he reaches into his pocket and pulls out a box and hands it to me.

"Speaking of presents--here's yours." And I wonder if all that sitting at a desk in front of a camera, broadcasting facts has affected Jerry's romantic tendencies. I guess after a couple of kids, romance doesn't fit in anymore. I take the box and see the ring sparkle inside. I stare at it for what seems like forever. It's not just any ring, but the one I picked out, kind of.

We were in a jewelry store picking out a Mother's Day present for Mom, all of us, including Jerry, when Jimmy pointed to a ring and said, "That's just like the one you gave Lisa."

Jerry never did give me an engagement ring. The first time around we kind of dispensed with that formality, once we knew I was pregnant. The second time, there was no place to buy one until we got to New York, and then we didn't have time. Mom and Carl were already there, visiting Angela, and it was almost like going from the airport to the ceremony. Maybe he bought Lisa a ring, but I picked out a more expensive one for me, really expensive. Of course, we couldn't afford it, but I did make my point. And maybe Jerry's not all romance anymore, but he does get the point. Instead of hitting Jerry, now I hug him. Twice married, and three kids later, Jerry and I are finally engaged.

Slipping it on my finger he says, "I love you, Freddy. I will never leave you. You know that."

"I know," I say, "I know," and before I sound completely like my mother, I add, "But a girl likes to be told once in a while."

"But we always have an audience around."

"Not in bed," I say, going back to the table, picking up my baseball cap and putting it on.

"Thanks for not kicking me out of it," he says, and I run my hand across the visor, pulling it down over my forehead.

"It's my pleasure," I say, and then go to give Emma one more push. I hear a plane overhead, and looking up I see that it's the same kind that Erik once took me up in. I hesitate between pushes, listening to the sound. The world pauses, and the galaxies form a circle around this one moment in time. I experience again the beauty of endless space, the silent peace of floating among clouds. I remember the joy when Erik gave me a ring and asked me to marry him.

The plane circles once, dips its wings, then disappears into the clouds, like it always does in my dreams. I imagine myself still in that plane as it disappears. Erik will always carry a part of me with him through all eternity.

"I don't want to swing anymore," Emma announces, and I take her down. She runs over to Jerry and crawls on the part of his lap that isn't occupied by Katey. Emma is a little jealous of Katey and when Jerry holds the baby, he has to hold her, too.

Jerry doesn't mind, but sometimes I do, though I don't let him see that I mind. Just like when Jerry said that to get Emma under his insurance plan, he had to adopt her. God, that hurt, but I let him adopt her. Emma deserves to be treated like the rest of the family. It's not her fault her daddy isn't here now to take care of her. But he would want to. If he were still alive he would.

I go over to where the boys are digging for worms to take along on our vacation. Jerry doesn't know a thing about fishing yet, but I have a feeling that by the end of the summer he will. Jimmy is a natural-born fisherman like his grandpa. My dad loved fishing, and there were many afternoons when, after a couple of hours of digging in the dirt and finding a few choice worms he'd say to Joey and me, "How about it, guys? Let's go fishing," and we'd go down to the creek and fish.

"Look at all the worms we got, Mom," Ben says, holding out the tin can I gave the boys to put them in.

"You have to put some dirt in there with them," I say, noting that the can is full of worms, but no dirt.

"There's not enough room," Jimmy protests.

"Is too," Ben argues.

Jimmy says, "I should know. Mom says I'm as good at fishing as Grandpa, and Grandpa knew *all* about fishing."

"Yes, he did," I agree, smiling at my son's obvious pride. "He loved to go fishing."

"Well, I know all about worms. Joey knew all about bugs and worms and stuff, and Mom says I take after Joey," Ben says.

"Joey was stupid," Jimmy mutters, and I look at this firstborn of mine like he never came out of me. Then I remember how hard Jimmy cried when Joey died, and I know he loved him.

When we moved in with Jerry, Jimmy had to bring with all the pictures that Joey and he once colored together. In his room he has a shrine dedicated to Joey, made up of snapshots, old decks of cards, and pictures torn out of coloring books. I think Jimmy is testing me like Jerry just did. Jimmy wants to make sure he has a place in my heart.

Before the boys go into their "Is not" and "Is too" argument, I pick up a caterpillar crawling on a leaf.

"Did you ever feel a caterpillar crawl up your arm?" I ask Jimmy.

"No," Jimmy says, and I take the small creature and put it on Jimmy's bare arm.

"It tickles," Jimmy giggles. Then I take it and put it on Ben's arm.

"Does it tickle you, too?" I ask, and Ben nods, smiling.

"That's what Joey taught me," I say. "That it tickles when a caterpillar crawls up your arm. He taught me to be kind and gentle, even with caterpillars, because some day they will be beautiful butterflies."

"How?" Ben asks.

"All summer long, they crawl on leaves and eat, then in fall they make a cocoon for themselves and sleep through the cold winter. In spring, they wake up and they're beautiful butterflies."

"Last winter you said Joey was still sleeping. Is Joey a butterfly now, Mom?" Ben asks, and before I can answer Jimmy does.

"Of course he is. You don't think Joey would

sleep all summer long, do you? He's in Heaven now, with wings like a butterfly."

"Let's put the caterpillar back on the leaf, Mom," Ben says, removing it gently off his arm and putting it back where we plucked it off.

"Let's go show Dad the worms," Jimmy says, and without any more said about caterpillars or butterflies, the boys take off with the tin can of worms to show their father. Jerry can't take cleaning up after a dog, and I wonder how he's going to handle putting a worm on a hook.

I pick up the caterpillar and put it on my arm, watching it crawl all the way up to my shoulder before taking it off and putting it back on its leaf.

"Are you okay, Freddy?" I hear Joey ask.

I answer, "Yeah, Joey--I'm okay. This time I really am okay."

CHILD OF THE HEART

ABOUT THE AUTHOR

I am a wife, mother and grandmother, and consider my writing time as my sanity time. Of course there are some after reading my books think it a bit odd that I call it sanity since there is mystery, conflict, drama and romance in my work, but at least in my writing I do have some control. Anyone who has experienced being a wife or a parent, or has been in a romantic relationship, a mystery or drama, knows there is sometimes very little we can control.

In all honesty though there are times that even I as the writer do not know exactly how the story is going to end, and there are times I write a character out of the story when in fact I do not want to. But so goes life, even if it is only a story.

82333957R00345

Made in the USA
Columbia, SC
09 December 2017